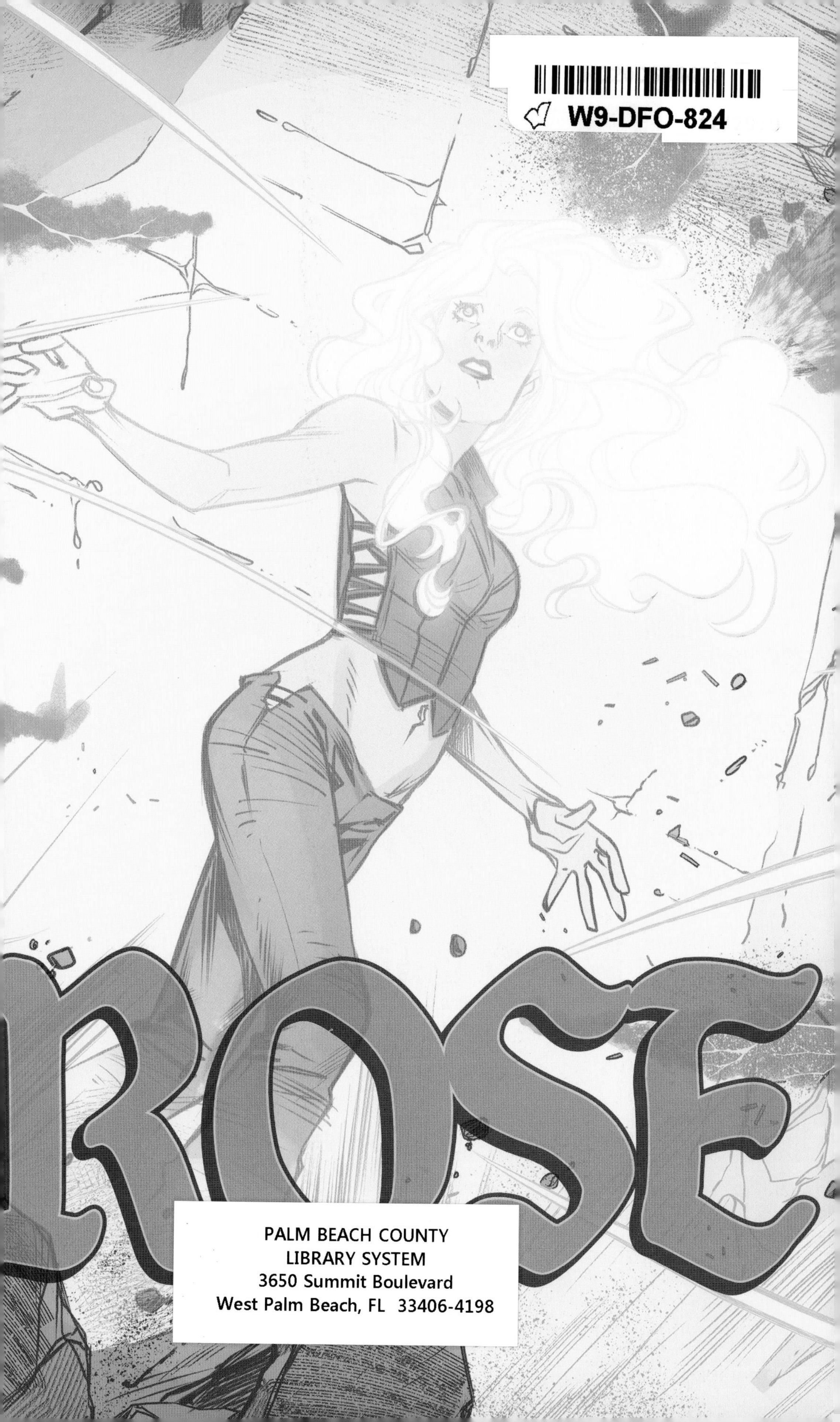
ROSE

SE, VOL. 3: THE LAST LIGHT.
First printing. April 2019.
ed by Image Comics, Inc. Office of
cation: 2701 NW Vaughn St., Suite
Portland, OR 97210. Copyright ©
Meredith Finch. All rights reserved.
ins material originally published in
magazine form as ROSE #13–17.
," its logos, and the likenesses of all
herein are trademarks of Meredith
h, unless otherwise noted. "Image"
Image Comics logos are registered
arks of Image Comics, Inc. No part
s publication may be reproduced or
itted, in any form or by any means
for short excerpts for journalistic or
rposes), without the express written
ission of Meredith Finch, or Image
Inc. All names, characters, events,
cales in this publication are entirely
Any resemblance to actual persons
g or dead), events, or places, without
ntent, is coincidental. Printed in the
r information regarding the CPSIA
on this printed material call:
-595-3636. For international rights,
reignlicensing@imagecomics.com.
ISBN: 978-1-5343-1203-6.

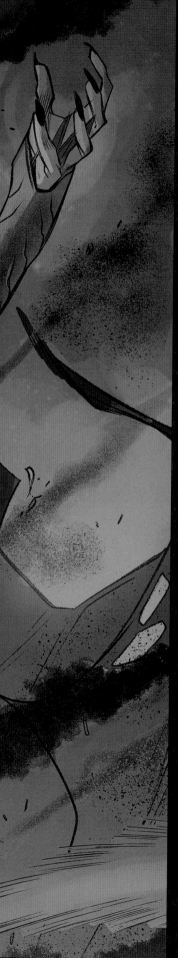

written by
MEREDITH FINCH

pencils & inks by
IG GUARA

colors by
TRIONA FARRELL

letters by
CARDINAL RAE

collection cover by
IG GUARA &
TRIONA FARRELL

collection design by
CAREY HALL

ROSE created by
MEREDITH FINCH

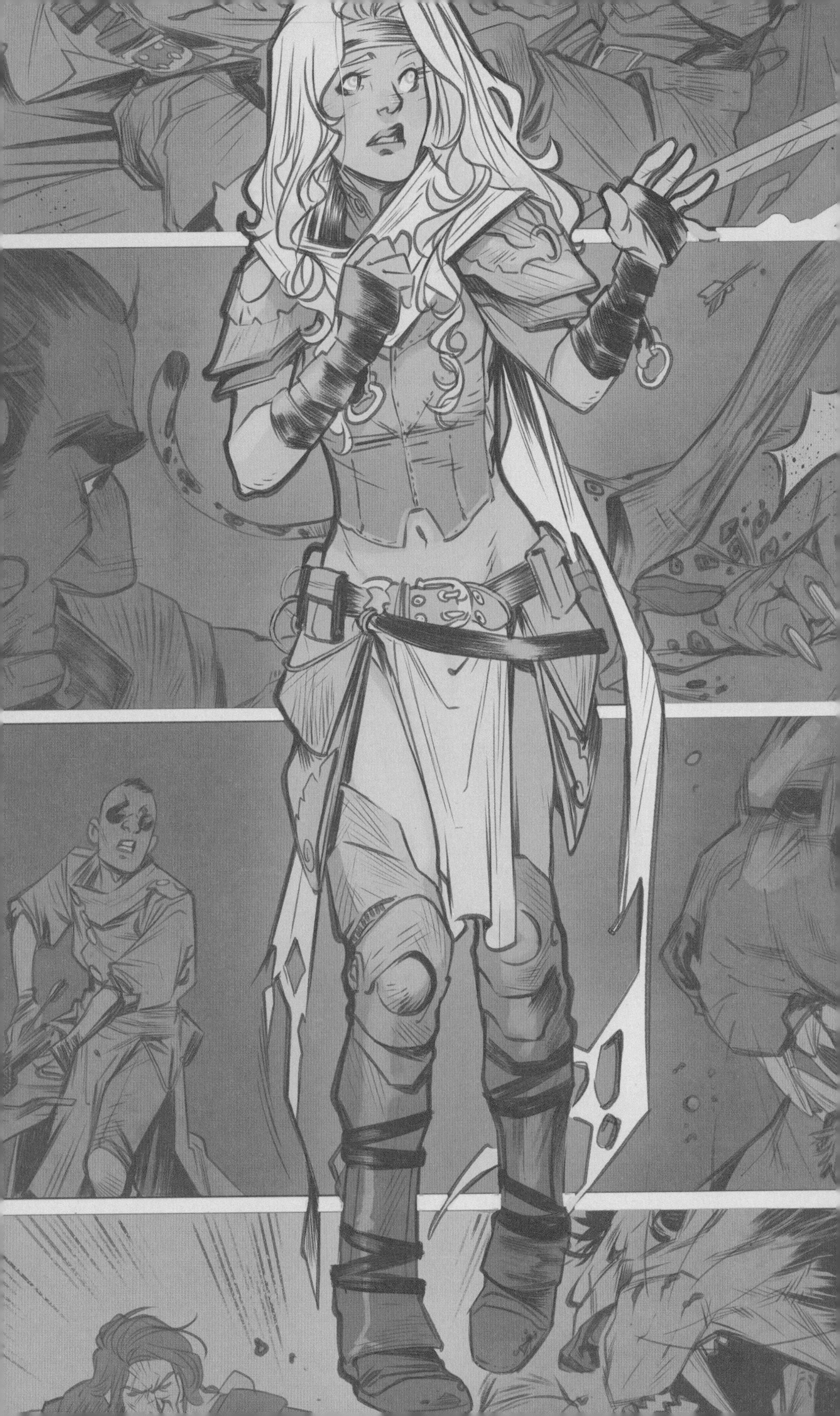

THIRTEEN

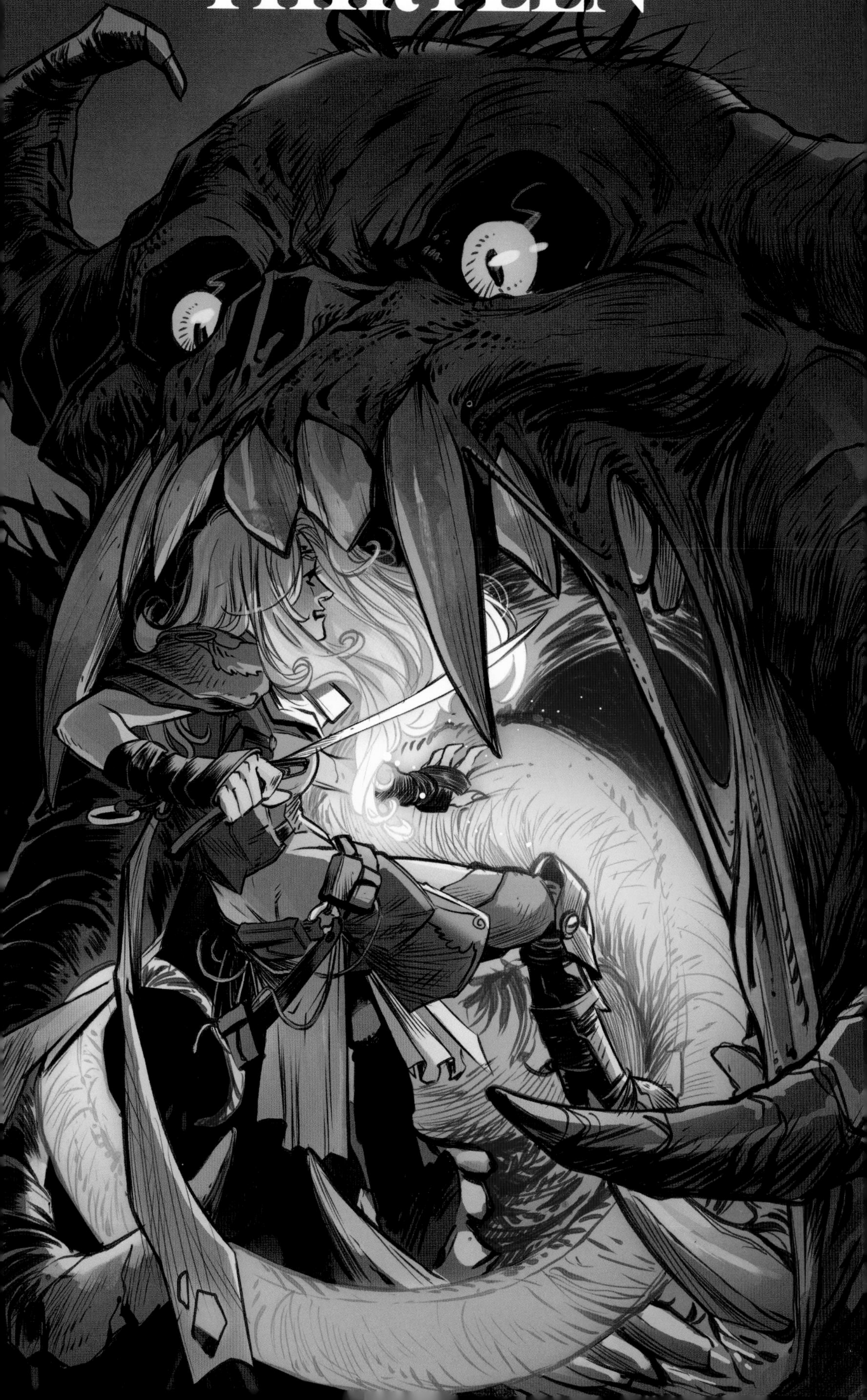

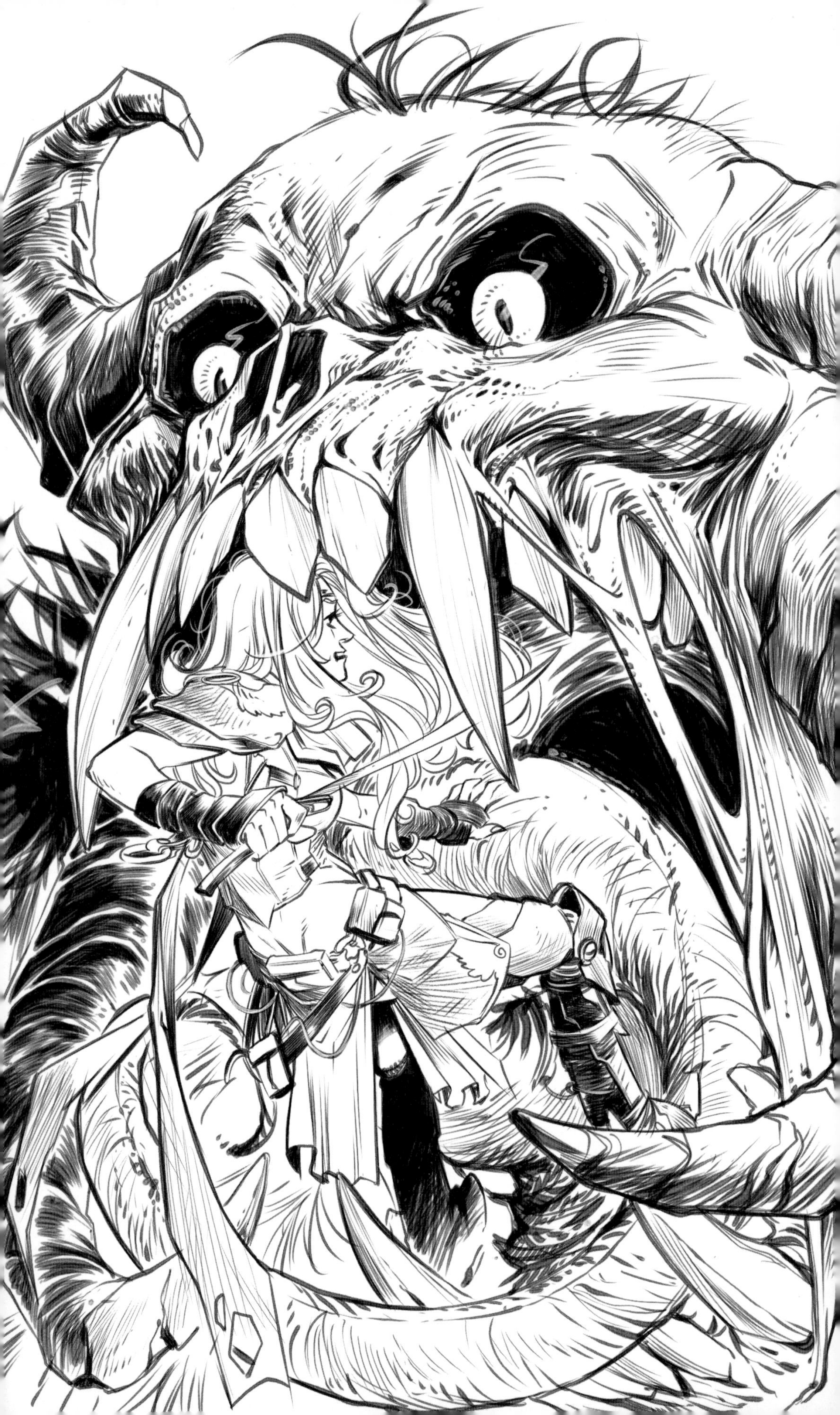

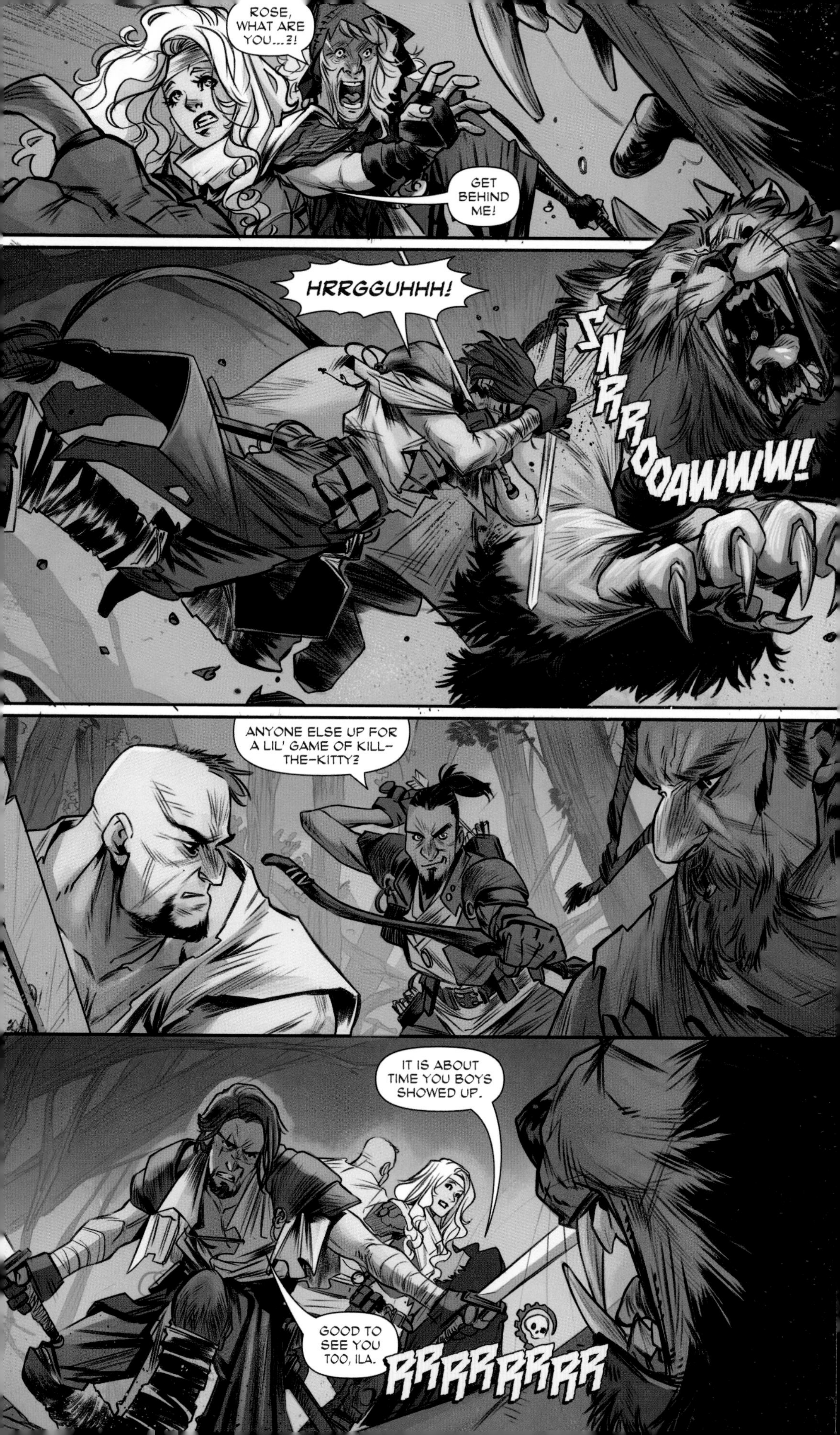
ROSE, WHAT ARE YOU...?!
GET BEHIND ME!
HRRGGUHHH!
SNRROOAWWW!
ANYONE ELSE UP FOR A LIL' GAME OF KILL-THE-KITTY?
IT IS ABOUT TIME YOU BOYS SHOWED UP.
GOOD TO SEE YOU TOO, ILA.
RRRRRRRR

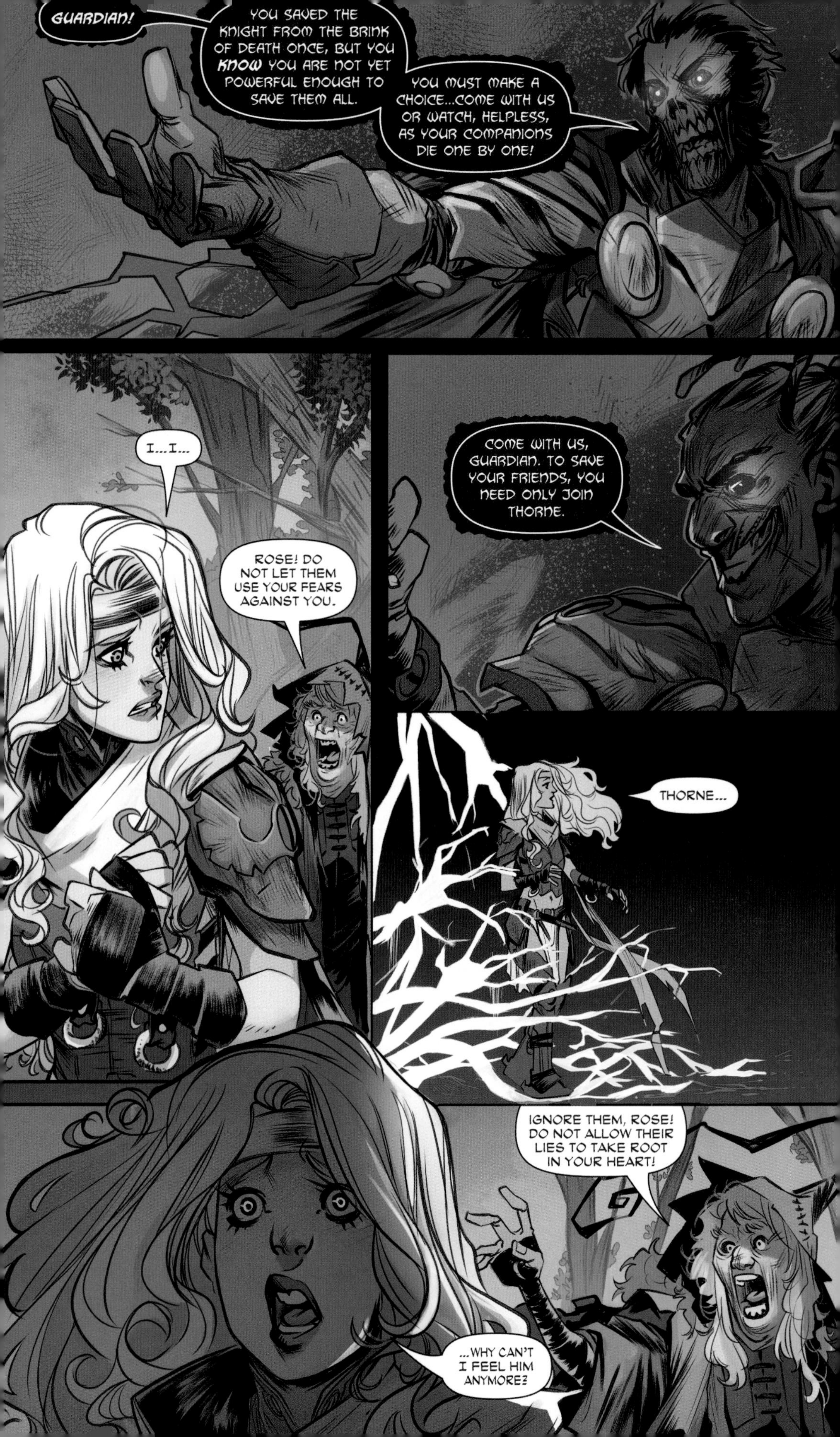
GUARDIAN!
YOU SAVED THE KNIGHT FROM THE BRINK OF DEATH ONCE, BUT YOU KNOW YOU ARE NOT YET POWERFUL ENOUGH TO SAVE THEM ALL.
YOU MUST MAKE A CHOICE...COME WITH US OR WATCH, HELPLESS, AS YOUR COMPANIONS DIE ONE BY ONE!
I...I...
ROSE! DO NOT LET THEM USE YOUR FEARS AGAINST YOU.
COME WITH US, GUARDIAN. TO SAVE YOUR FRIENDS, YOU NEED ONLY JOIN THORNE.
THORNE...
IGNORE THEM, ROSE! DO NOT ALLOW THEIR LIES TO TAKE ROOT IN YOUR HEART!
...WHY CAN'T I FEEL HIM ANYMORE?

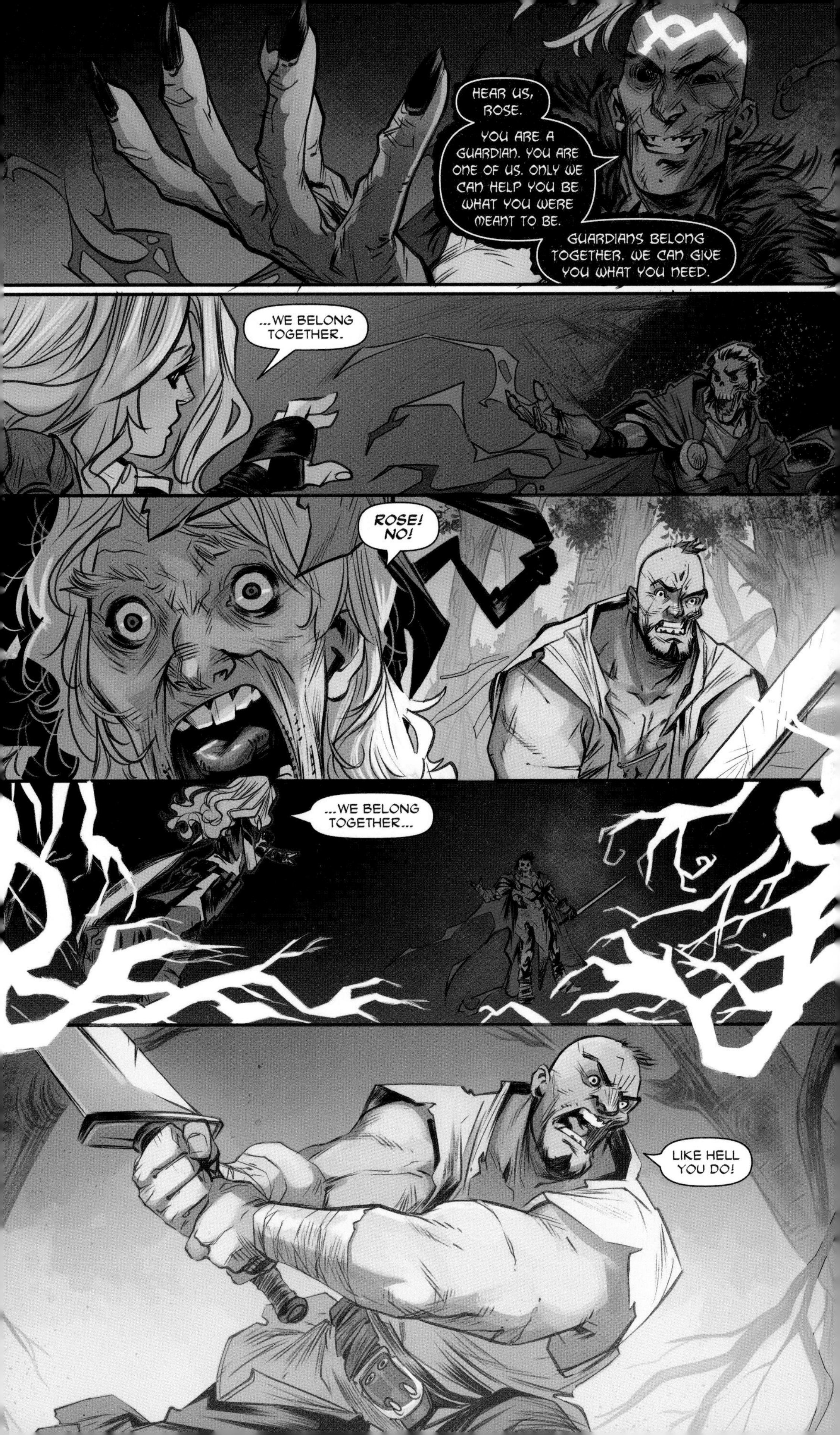
HEAR US, ROSE.
YOU ARE A GUARDIAN. YOU ARE ONE OF US. ONLY WE CAN HELP YOU BE WHAT YOU WERE MEANT TO BE.
GUARDIANS BELONG TOGETHER. WE CAN GIVE YOU WHAT YOU NEED.
...WE BELONG TOGETHER.
ROSE! NO!
...WE BELONG TOGETHER...
LIKE HELL YOU DO!

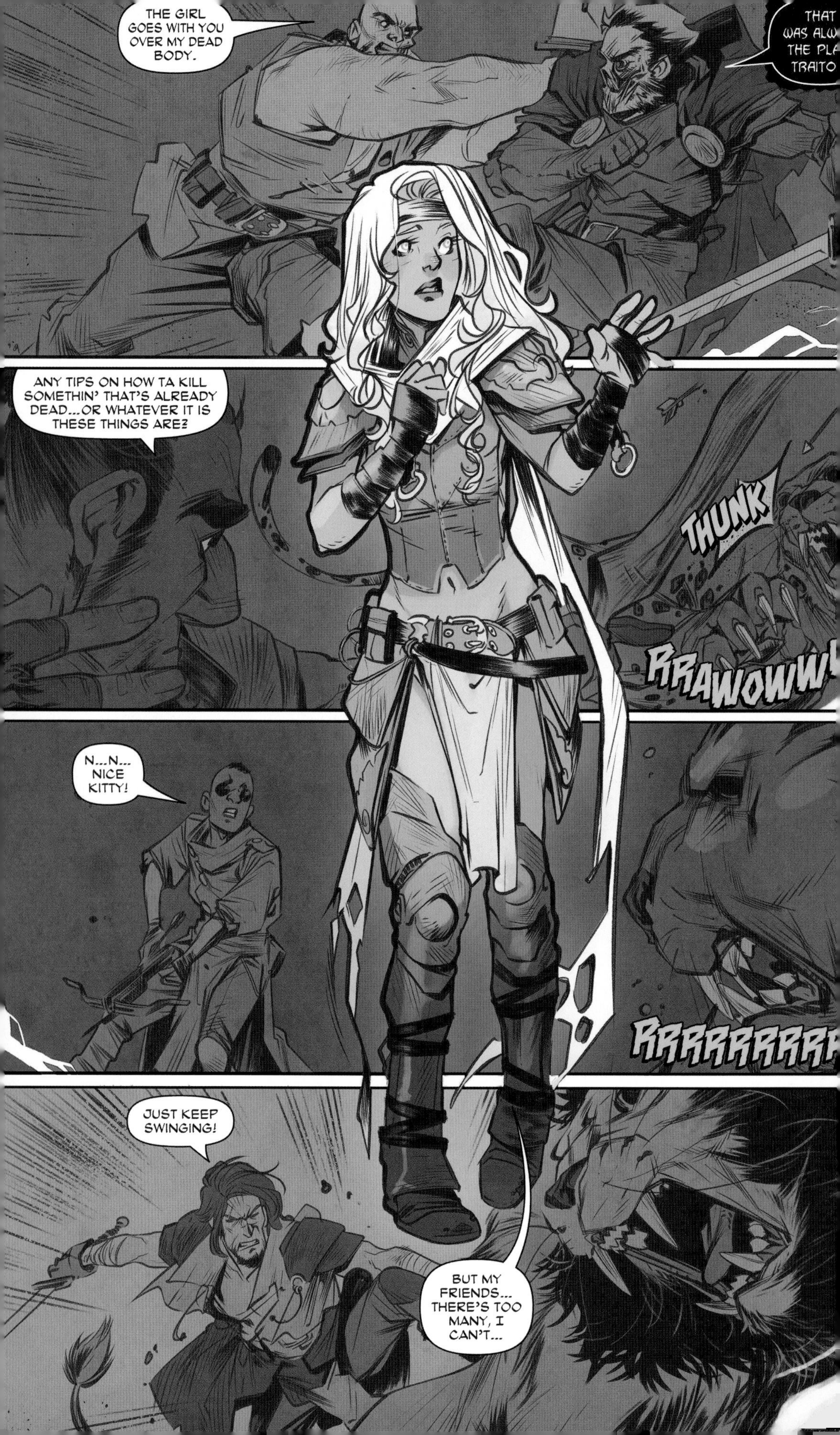
THE GIRL GOES WITH YOU OVER MY DEAD BODY.
THAT
ANY TIPS ON HOW TA KILL SOMETHIN' THAT'S ALREADY DEAD...OR WHATEVER IT IS THESE THINGS ARE?
THUNK
N...N... NICE KITTY!
JUST KEEP SWINGING!
BUT MY FRIENDS... THERE'S TOO MANY, I CAN'T...

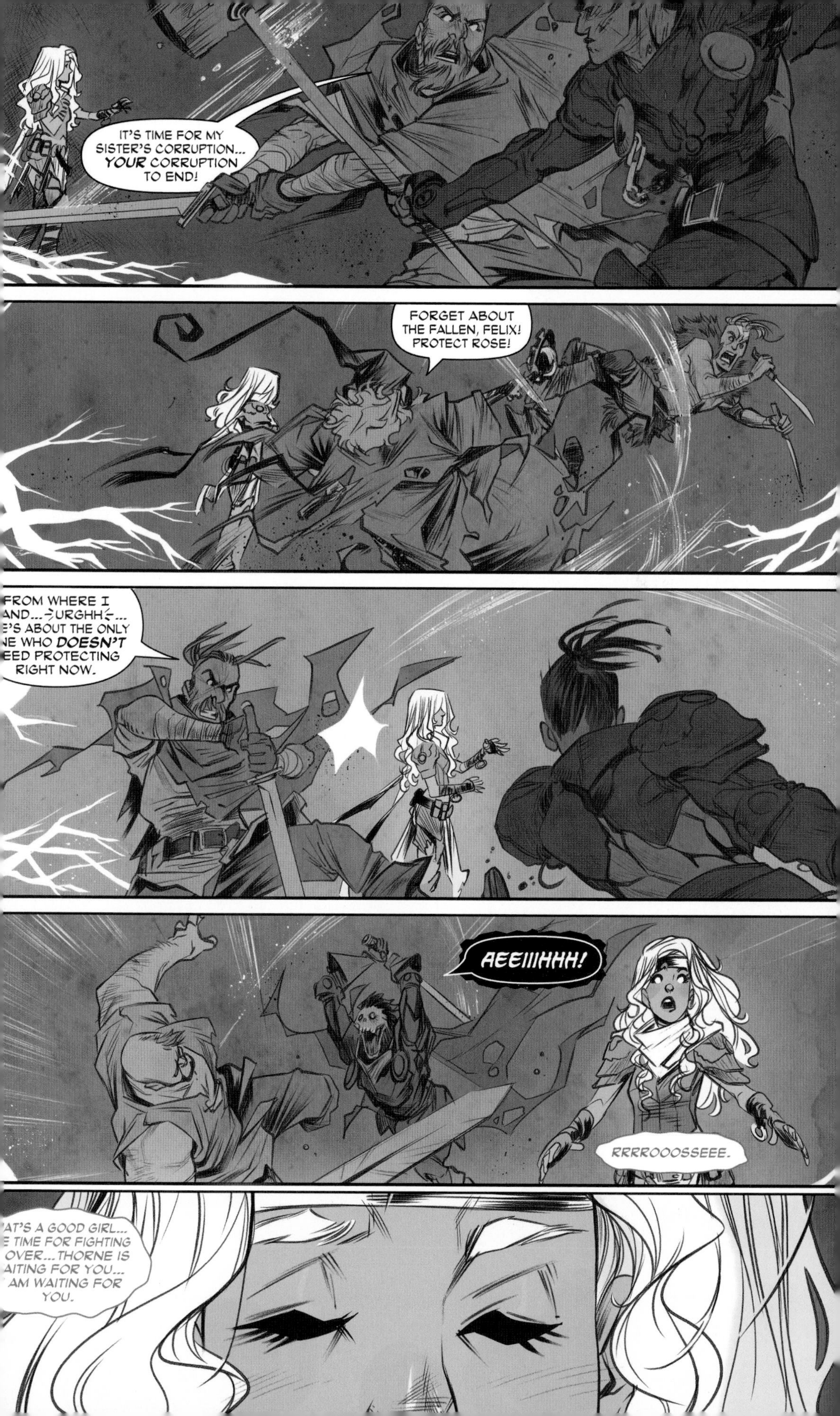
IT'S TIME FOR MY SISTER'S CORRUPTION... YOUR CORRUPTION TO END!
FORGET ABOUT THE FALLEN, FELIX! PROTECT ROSE!
FROM WHERE I AND...URGHH... E'S ABOUT THE ONLY NE WHO DOESN'T EED PROTECTING RIGHT NOW.
AEEIIIHHH!
RRRROOOSSEEE.
AT'S A GOOD GIRL... E TIME FOR FIGHTING OVER...THORNE IS AITING FOR YOU... AM WAITING FOR YOU.

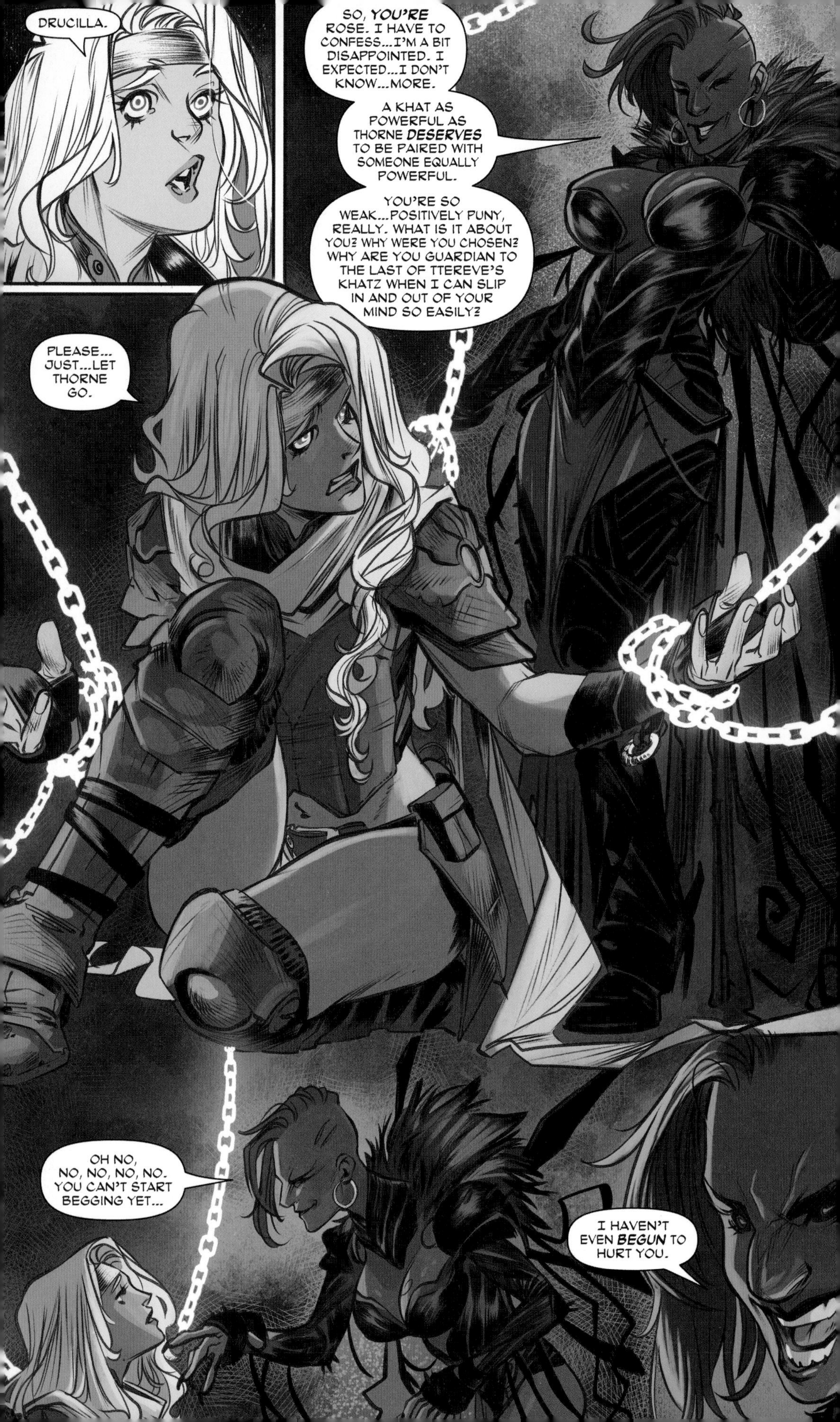
DRUCILLA.
SO, YOU'RE ROSE. I HAVE TO CONFESS...I'M A BIT DISAPPOINTED. I EXPECTED...I DON'T KNOW...MORE.
A KHAT AS POWERFUL AS THORNE DESERVES TO BE PAIRED WITH SOMEONE EQUALLY POWERFUL.
YOU'RE SO WEAK...POSITIVELY PUNY, REALLY. WHAT IS IT ABOUT YOU? WHY WERE YOU CHOSEN? WHY ARE YOU GUARDIAN TO THE LAST OF TTEREVE'S KHATZ WHEN I CAN SLIP IN AND OUT OF YOUR MIND SO EASILY?
PLEASE... JUST...LET THORNE GO.
OH NO, NO, NO, NO, NO. YOU CAN'T START BEGGING YET...
I HAVEN'T EVEN BEGUN TO HURT YOU.

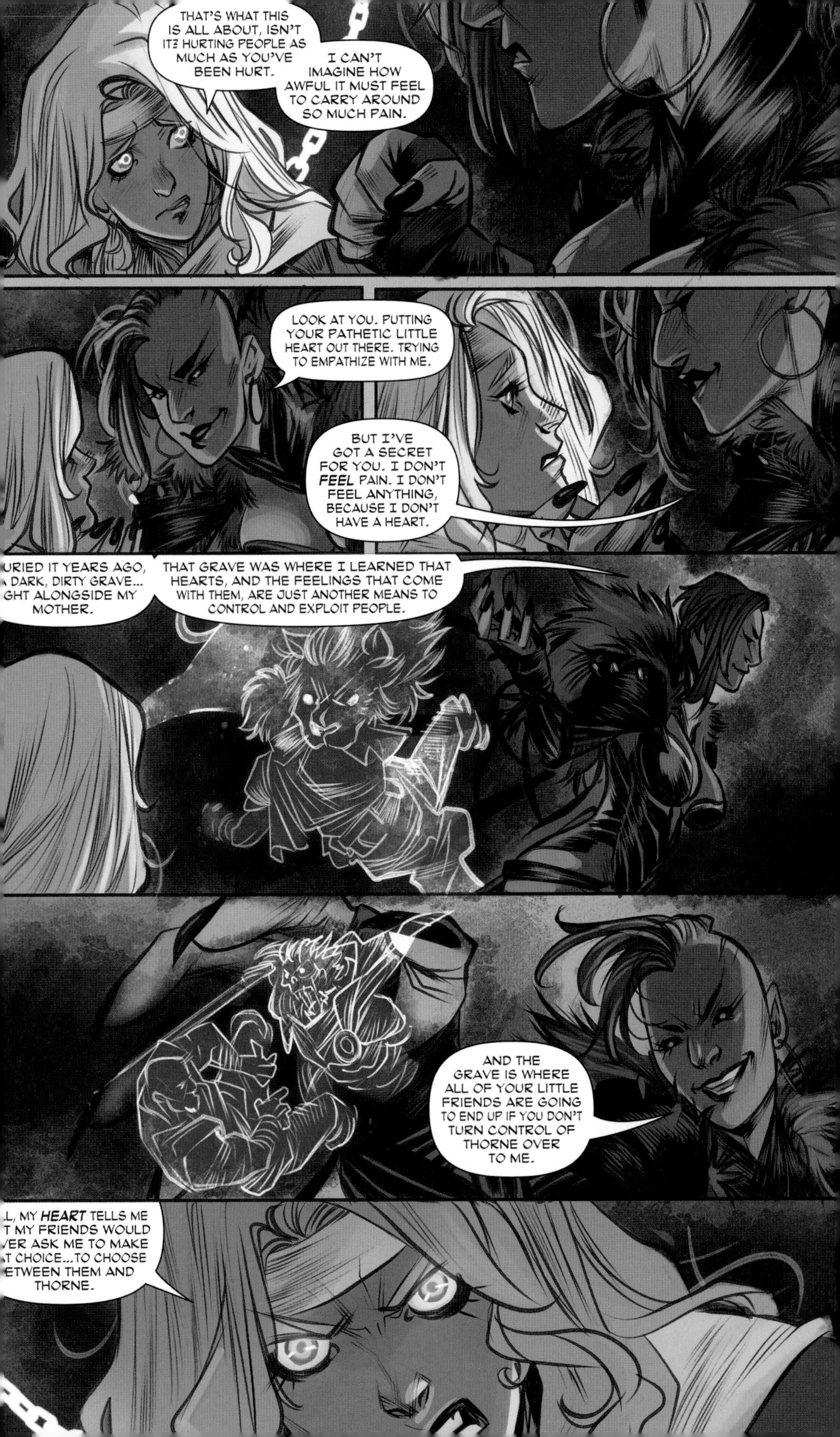
THAT'S WHAT THIS IS ALL ABOUT, ISN'T IT? HURTING PEOPLE AS MUCH AS YOU'VE BEEN HURT.
I CAN'T IMAGINE HOW AWFUL IT MUST FEEL TO CARRY AROUND SO MUCH PAIN.
LOOK AT YOU. PUTTING YOUR PATHETIC LITTLE HEART OUT THERE. TRYING TO EMPATHIZE WITH ME.
BUT I'VE GOT A SECRET FOR YOU. I DON'T *FEEL* PAIN. I DON'T FEEL ANYTHING, BECAUSE I DON'T HAVE A HEART.
URIED IT YEARS AGO, DARK, DIRTY GRAVE... GHT ALONGSIDE MY MOTHER.
THAT GRAVE WAS WHERE I LEARNED THAT HEARTS, AND THE FEELINGS THAT COME WITH THEM, ARE JUST ANOTHER MEANS TO CONTROL AND EXPLOIT PEOPLE.
AND THE GRAVE IS WHERE ALL OF YOUR LITTLE FRIENDS ARE GOING TO END UP IF YOU DON'T TURN CONTROL OF THORNE OVER TO ME.
L, MY ***HEART*** TELLS ME T MY FRIENDS WOULD VER ASK ME TO MAKE T CHOICE...TO CHOOSE ETWEEN THEM AND THORNE.

"YOU'RE PROBABLY RIGHT. NOBLE FOOLS TEND TO STICK TOGETHER.

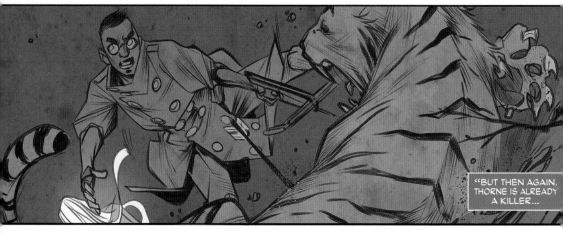

"IT'S WHAT MAKES YOU ALL SUCH EASY TARGETS.

"BUT THEN AGAIN, THORNE IS ALREADY A KILLER...

"...PERHAPS IT'S ONL RIGHT THAT HIS GUARD BECOMES ONE, TOO.

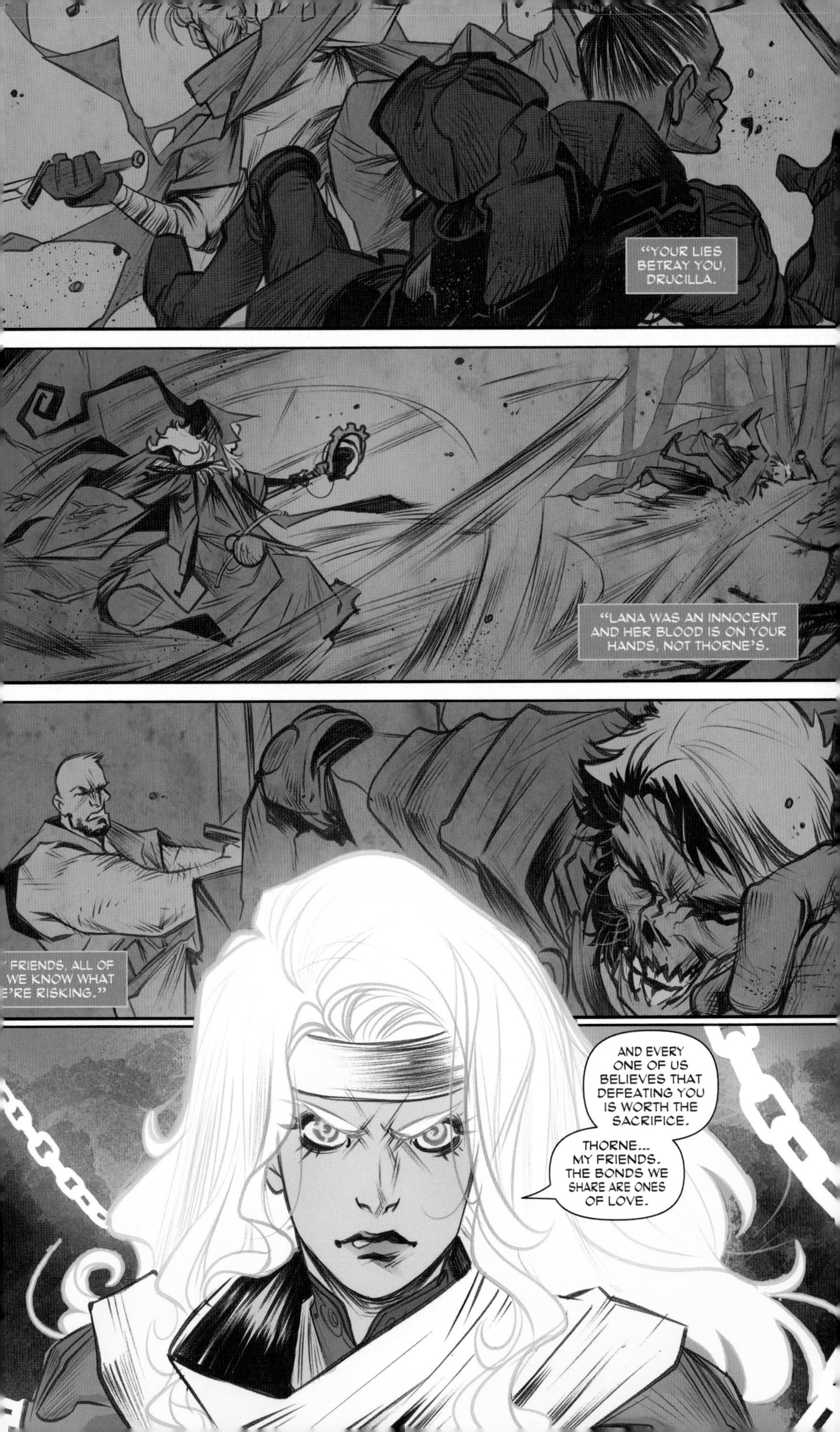
"YOUR LIES BETRAY YOU, DRUCILLA.
"LANA WAS AN INNOCENT AND HER BLOOD IS ON YOUR HANDS, NOT THORNE'S.
FRIENDS, ALL OF WE KNOW WHAT 'RE RISKING."
AND EVERY ONE OF US BELIEVES THAT DEFEATING YOU IS WORTH THE SACRIFICE.
THORNE... MY FRIENDS. THE BONDS WE SHARE ARE ONES OF LOVE.

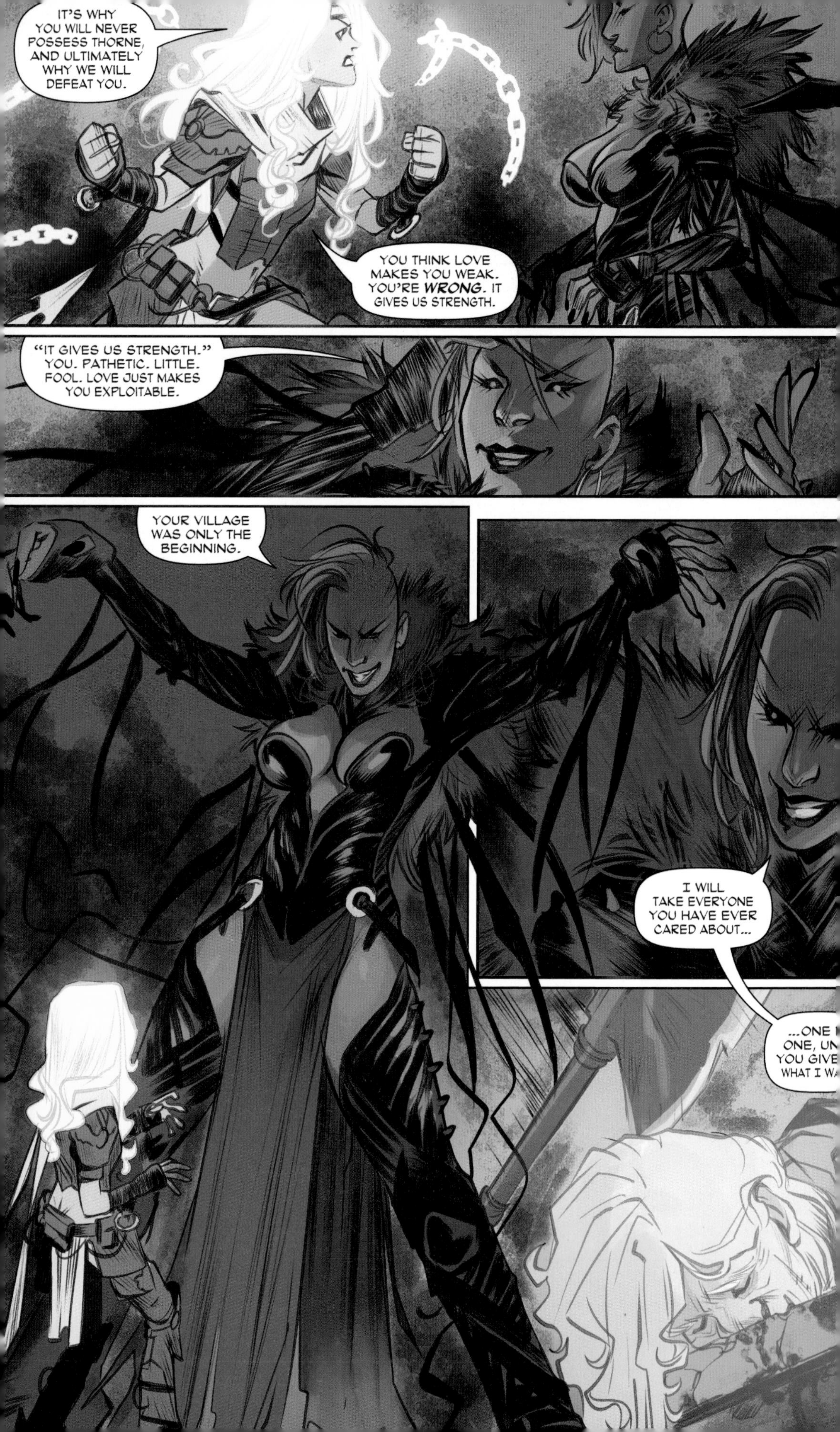
IT'S WHY YOU WILL NEVER POSSESS THORNE, AND ULTIMATELY WHY WE WILL DEFEAT YOU.
YOU THINK LOVE MAKES YOU WEAK. YOU'RE *WRONG*. IT GIVES US STRENGTH.
"IT GIVES US STRENGTH." YOU. PATHETIC. LITTLE. FOOL. LOVE JUST MAKES YOU EXPLOITABLE.
YOUR VILLAGE WAS ONLY THE BEGINNING.
I WILL TAKE EVERYONE YOU HAVE EVER CARED ABOUT...
...ONE
ONE, UN
YOU GIVE
WHAT I WA

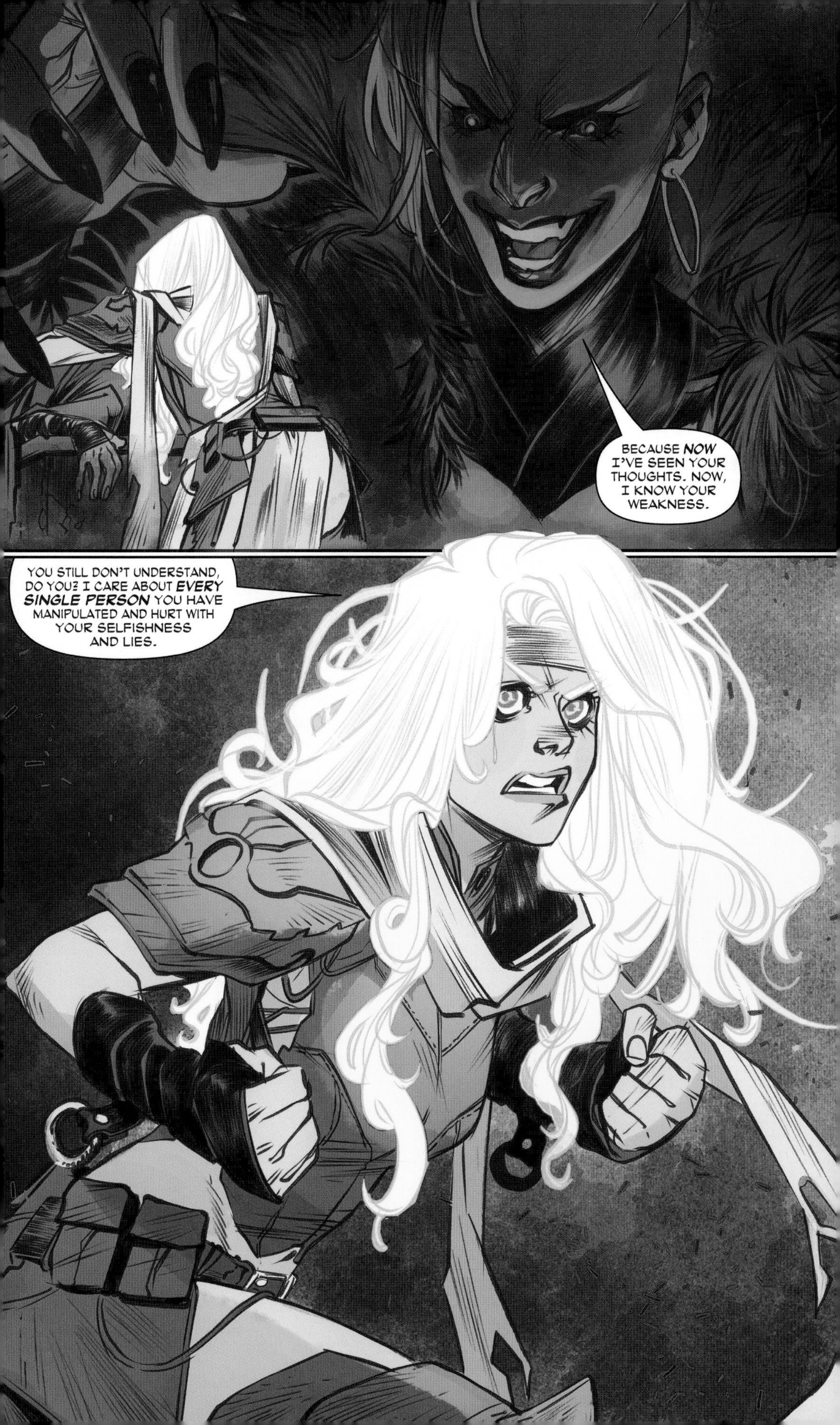
BECAUSE NOW I'VE SEEN YOUR THOUGHTS. NOW, I KNOW YOUR WEAKNESS.
YOU STILL DON'T UNDERSTAND, DO YOU? I CARE ABOUT EVERY SINGLE PERSON YOU HAVE MANIPULATED AND HURT WITH YOUR SELFISHNESS AND LIES.

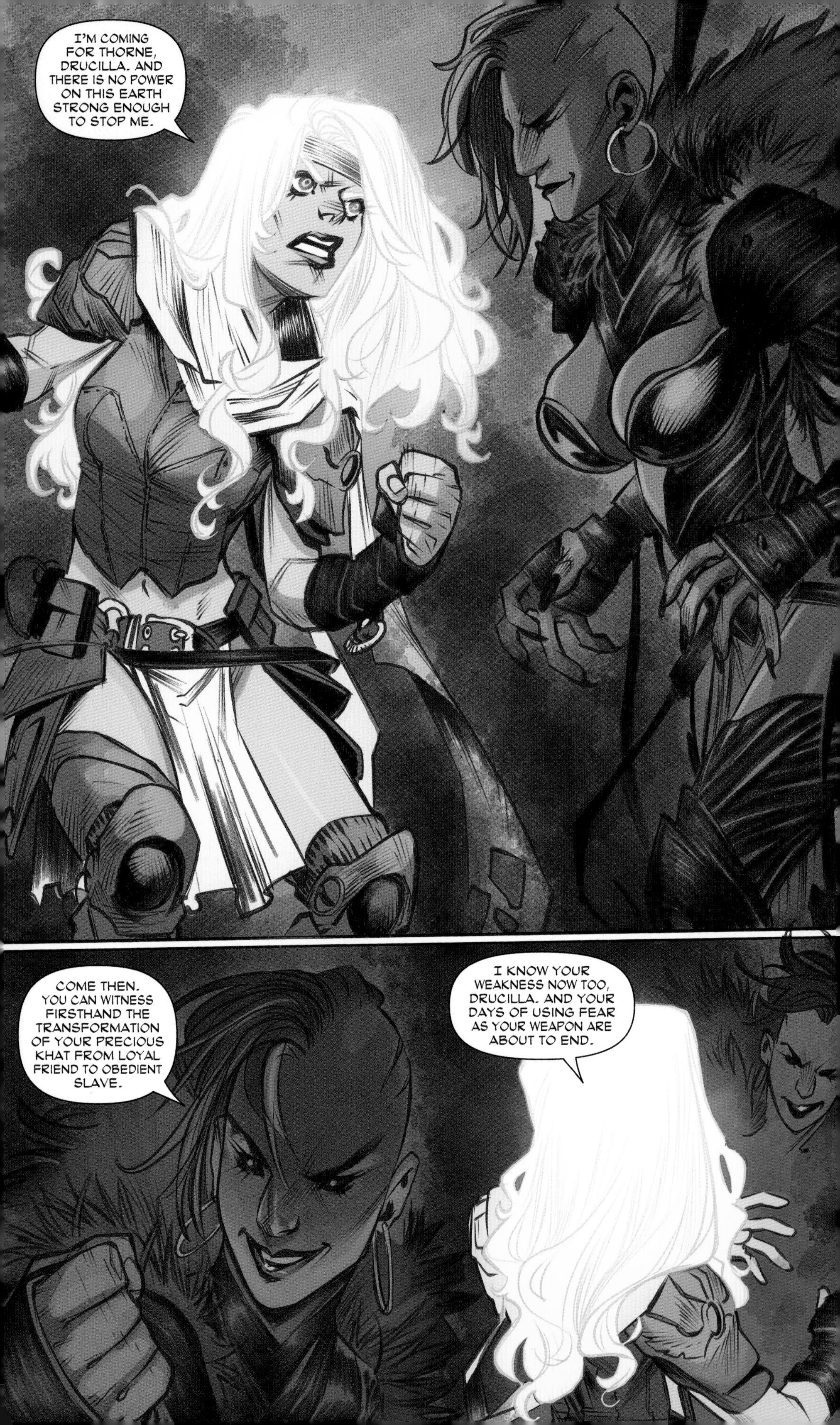
I'M COMING FOR THORNE, DRUCILLA. AND THERE IS NO POWER ON THIS EARTH STRONG ENOUGH TO STOP ME.
COME THEN. YOU CAN WITNESS FIRSTHAND THE TRANSFORMATION OF YOUR PRECIOUS KHAT FROM LOYAL FRIEND TO OBEDIENT SLAVE.
I KNOW YOUR WEAKNESS NOW TOO, DRUCILLA. AND YOUR DAYS OF USING FEAR AS YOUR WEAPON ARE ABOUT TO END.

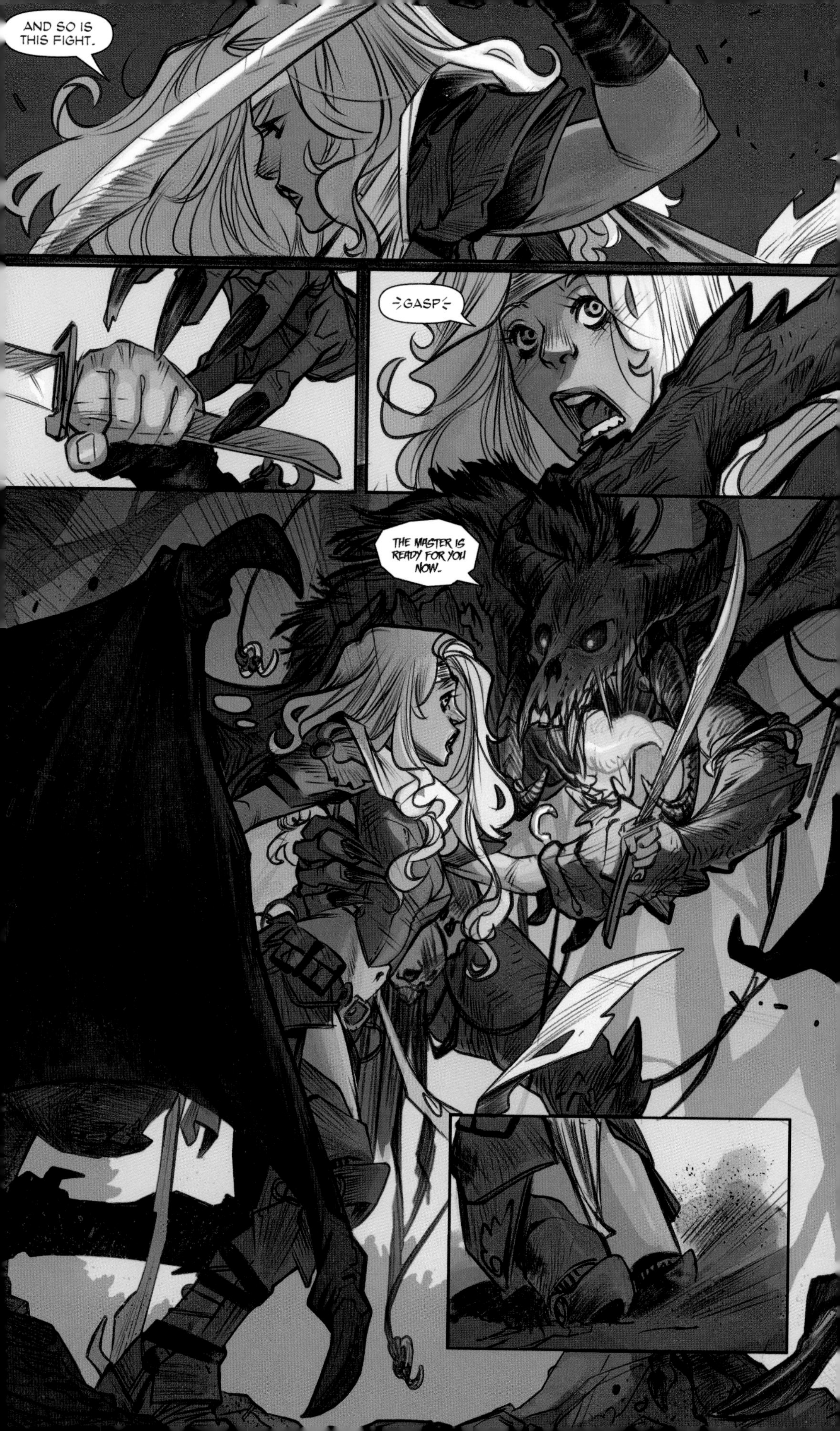
AND SO IS THIS FIGHT.
GASP
THE MASTER IS READY FOR YOU NOW.

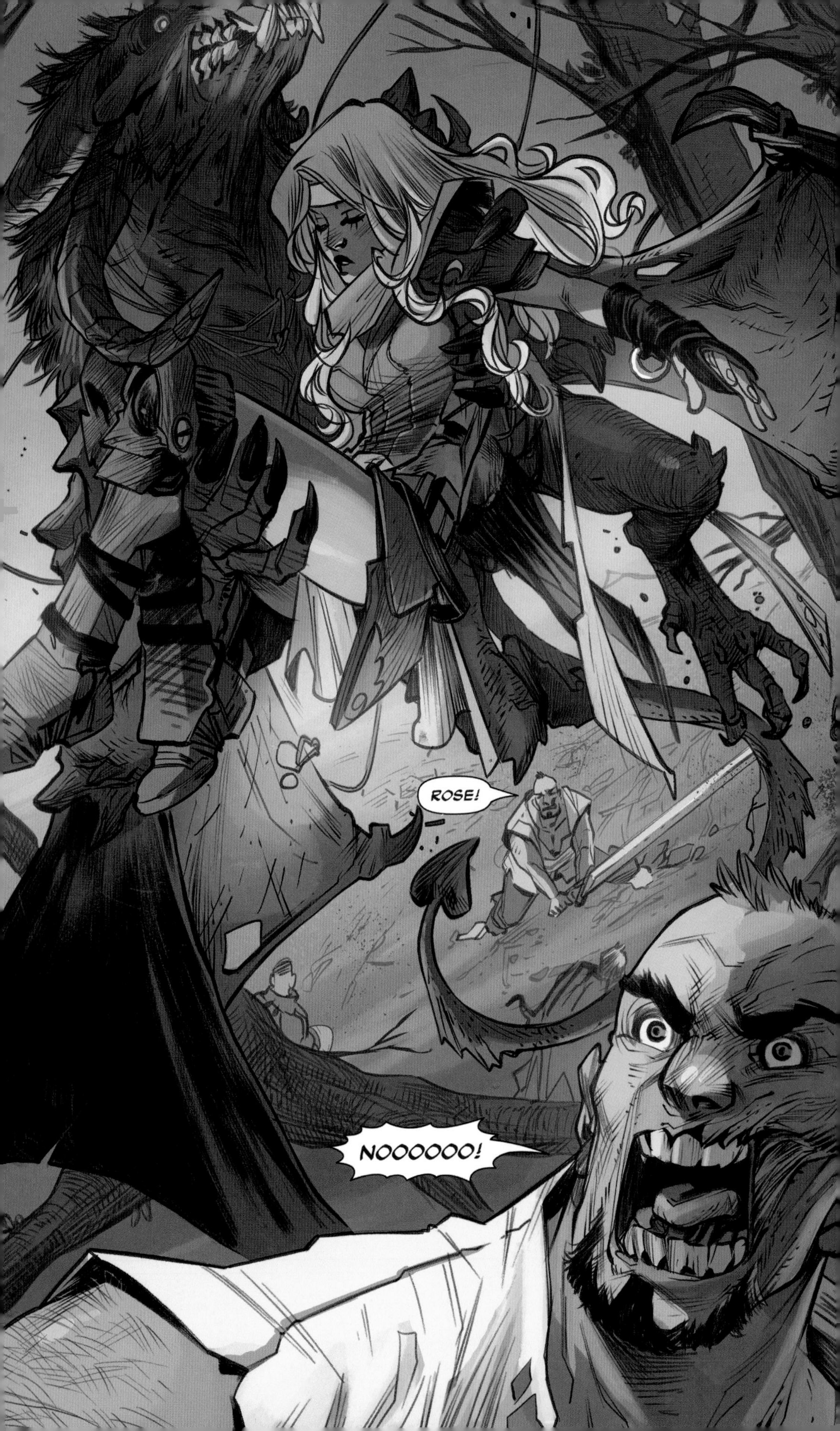
ROSE!
NOOOOOO!

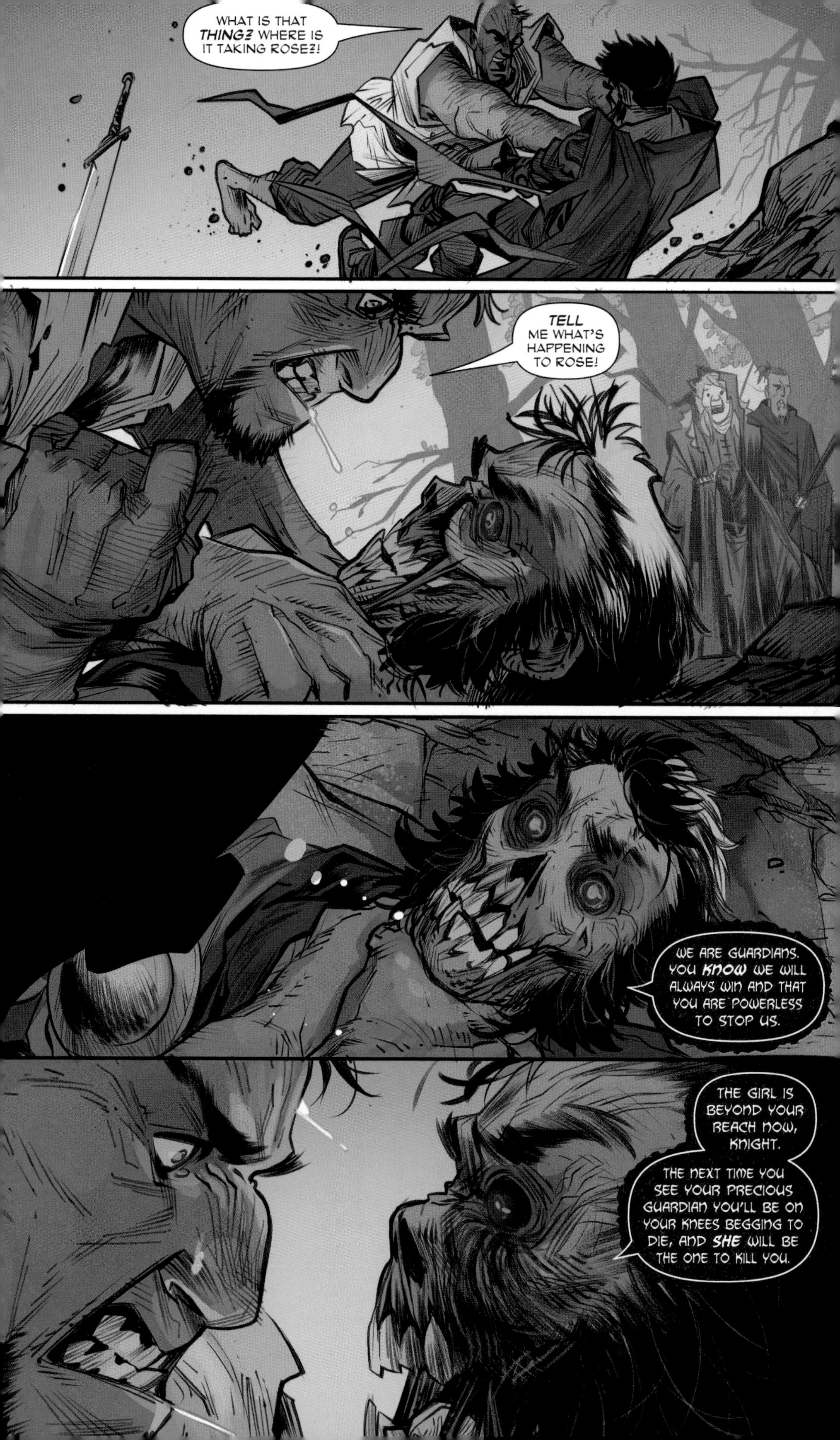
WHAT IS THAT THING? WHERE IS IT TAKING ROSE?!
TELL ME WHAT'S HAPPENING TO ROSE!
WE ARE GUARDIANS. YOU KNOW WE WILL ALWAYS WIN AND THAT YOU ARE POWERLESS TO STOP US.
THE GIRL IS BEYOND YOUR REACH NOW, KNIGHT.
THE NEXT TIME YOU SEE YOUR PRECIOUS GUARDIAN YOU'LL BE ON YOUR KNEES BEGGING TO DIE, AND SHE WILL BE THE ONE TO KILL YOU.

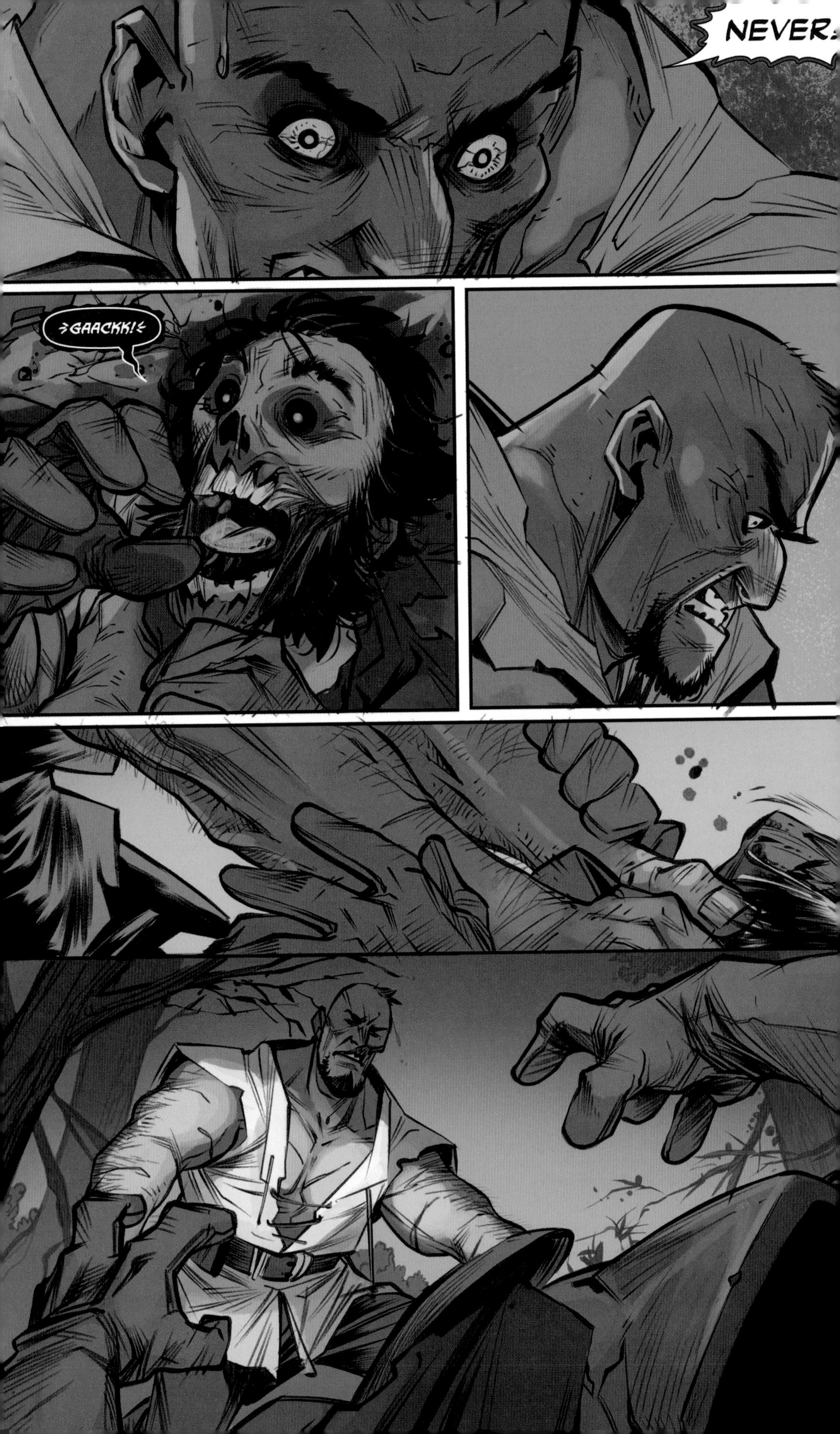
NEVER.
GAACKK!

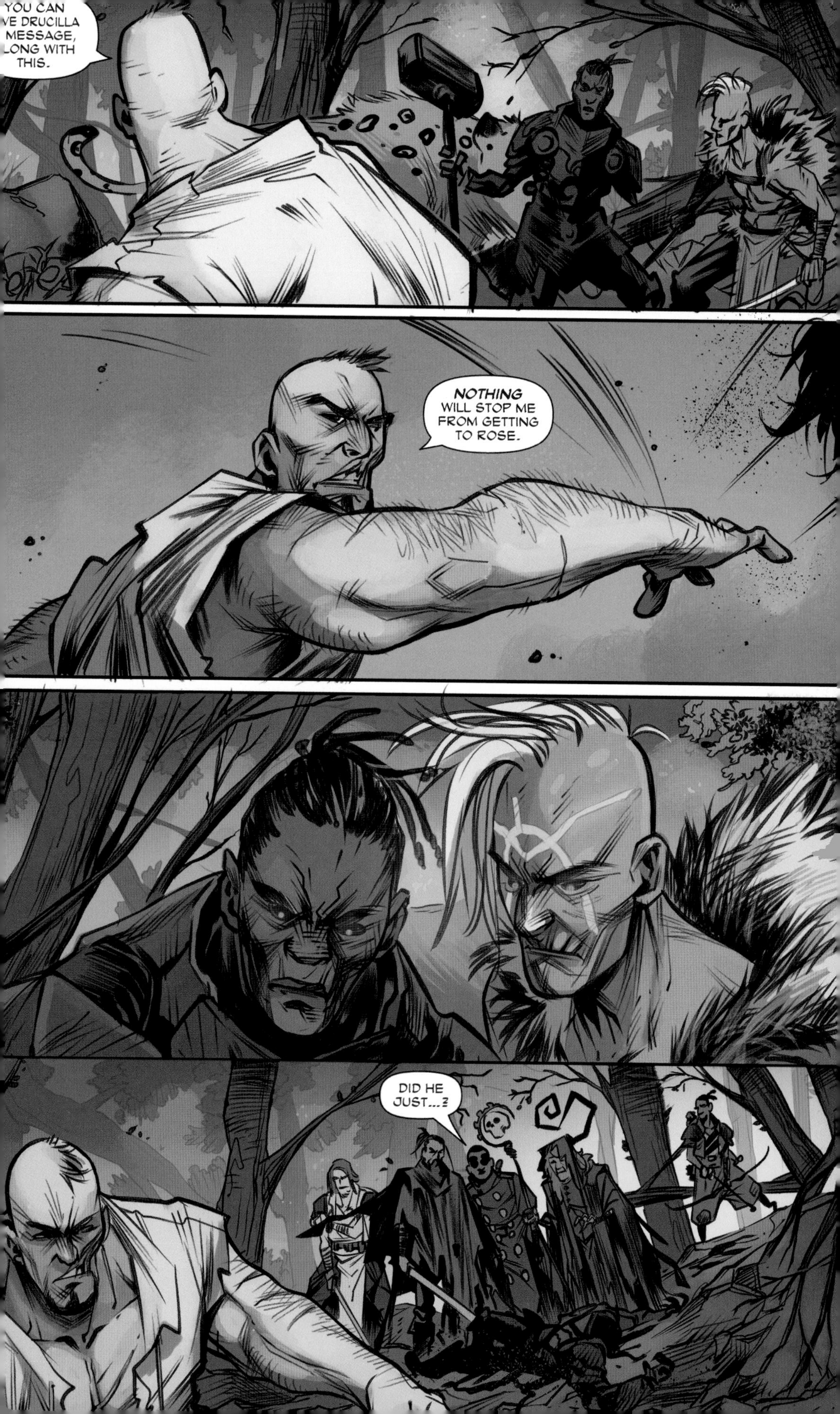
YOU CAN
VE DRUCILLA
MESSAGE,
LONG WITH
THIS.
NOTHING WILL STOP ME FROM GETTING TO ROSE.
DID HE JUST...?

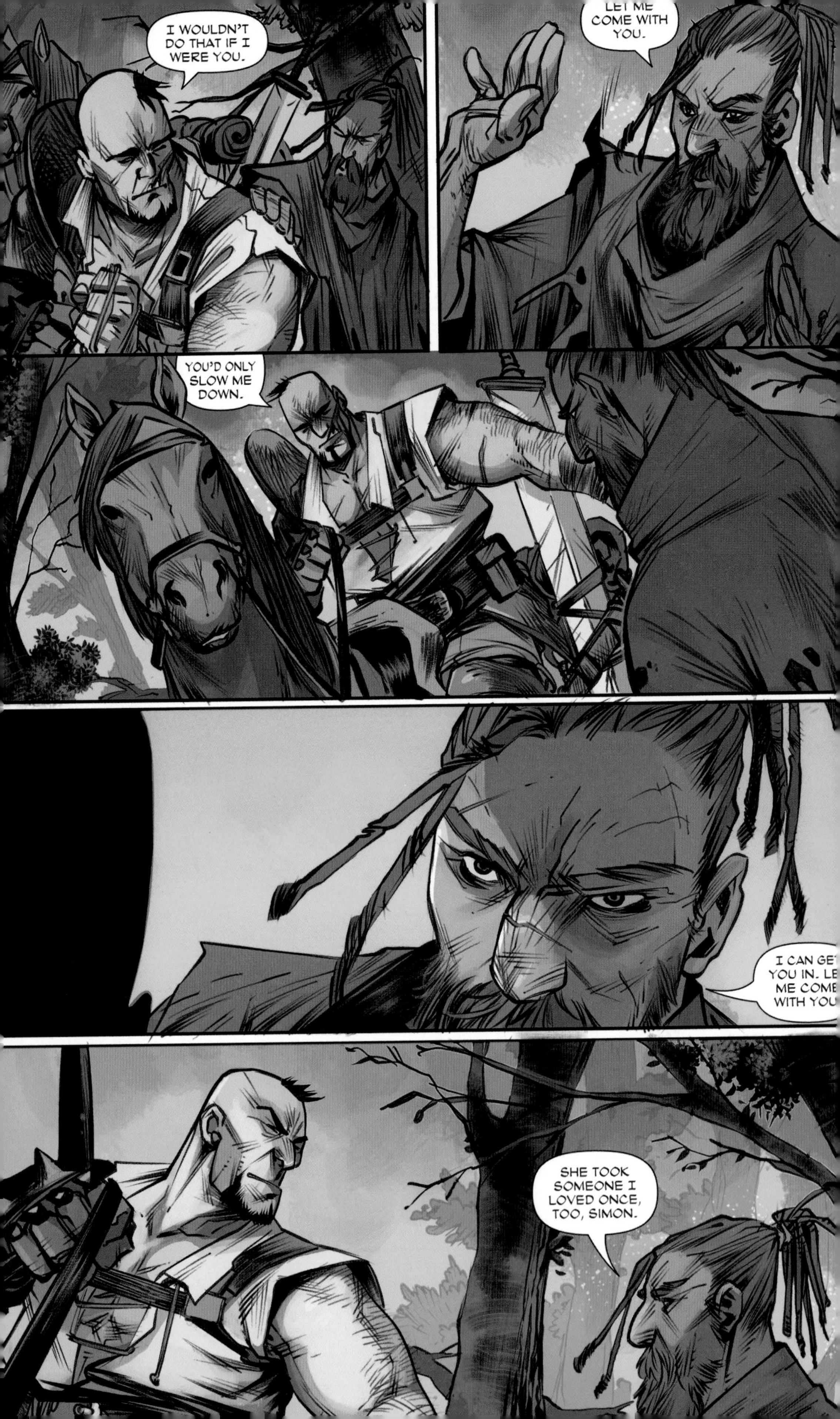

I WOULDN'T DO THAT IF I WERE YOU.
LET ME COME WITH YOU.
YOU'D ONLY SLOW ME DOWN.
I CAN GET YOU IN. LET ME COME WITH YOU
SHE TOOK SOMEONE I LOVED ONCE, TOO, SIMON.

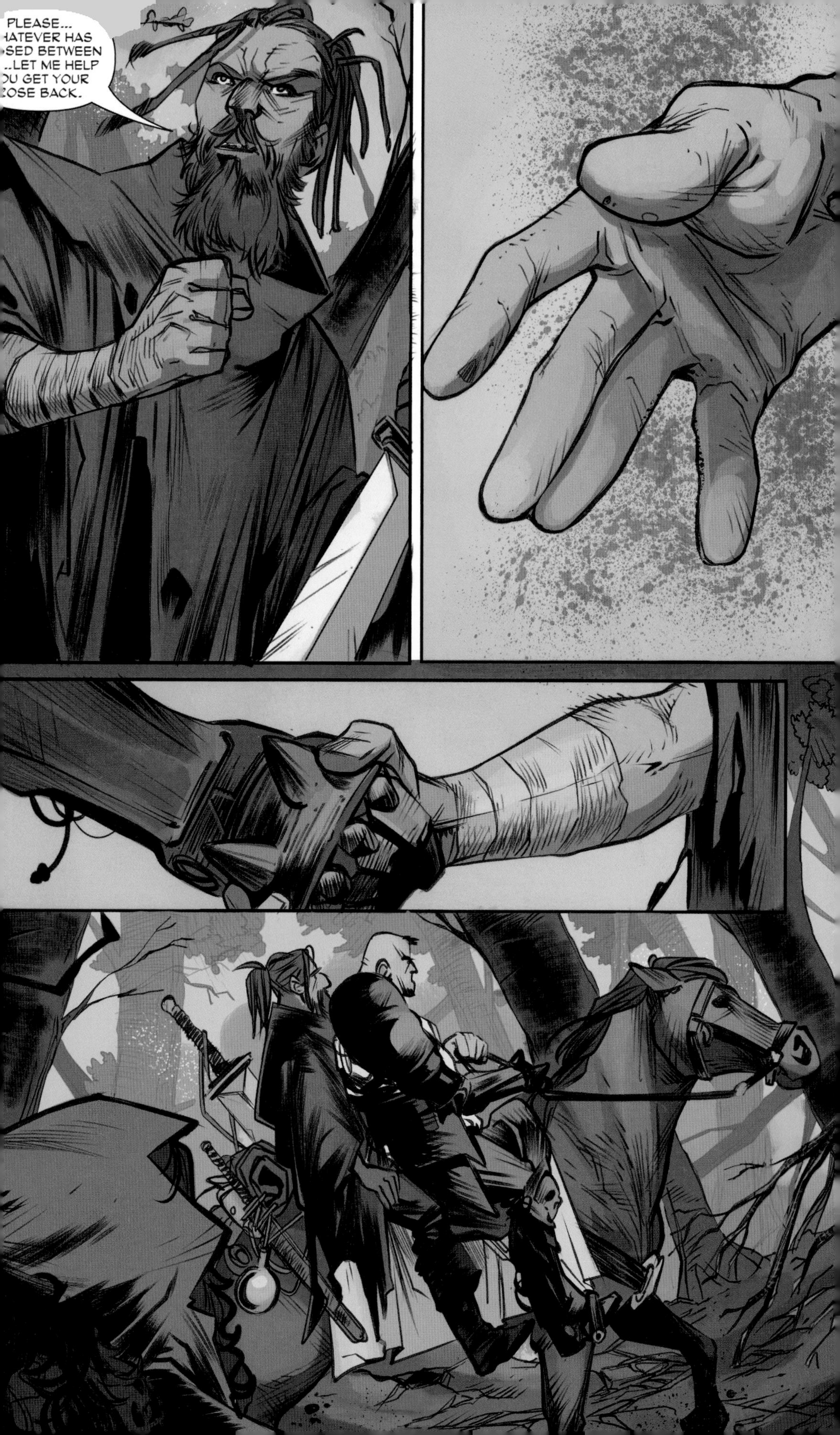
PLEASE... HATEVER HAS SED BETWEEN ...LET ME HELP OU GET YOUR OSE BACK.

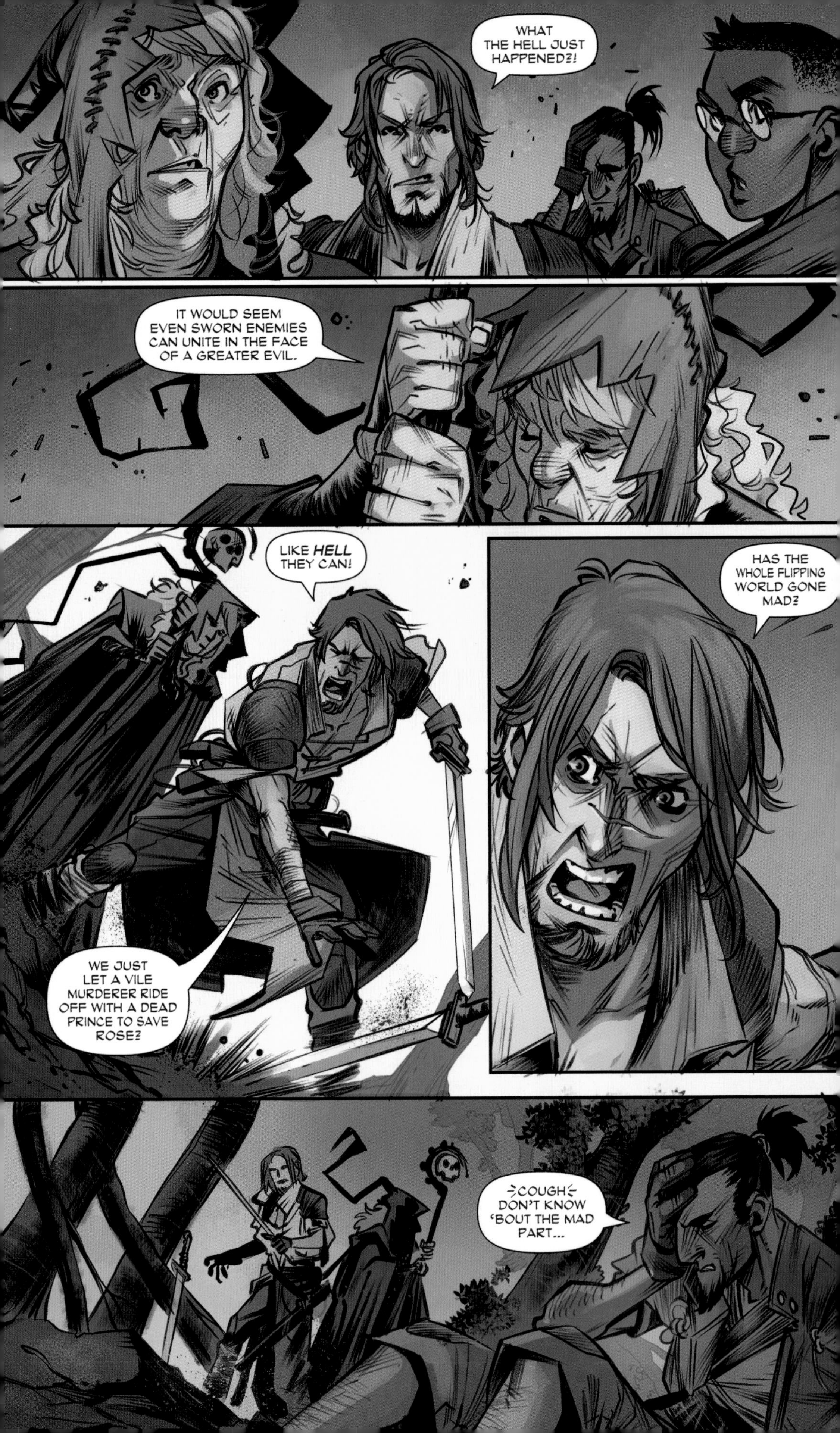
WHAT THE HELL JUST HAPPENED?!
IT WOULD SEEM EVEN SWORN ENEMIES CAN UNITE IN THE FACE OF A GREATER EVIL.
LIKE *HELL* THEY CAN!
WE JUST LET A VILE MURDERER RIDE OFF WITH A DEAD PRINCE TO SAVE ROSE?
HAS THE WHOLE FLIPPING WORLD GONE MAD?
COUGH DON'T KNOW 'BOUT THE MAD PART...

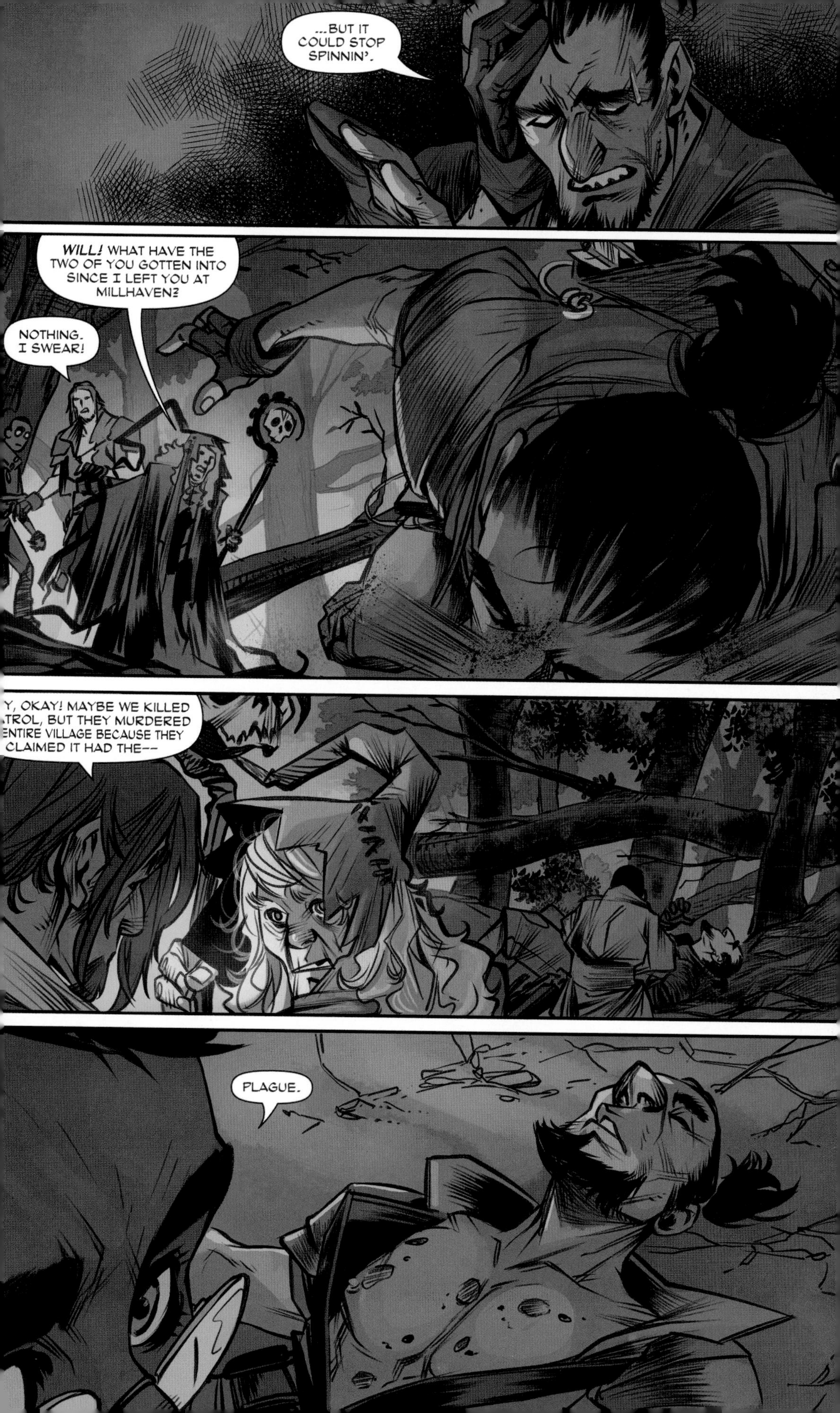
...BUT IT COULD STOP SPINNIN'.
WILL! WHAT HAVE THE TWO OF YOU GOTTEN INTO SINCE I LEFT YOU AT MILLHAVEN?
NOTHING. I SWEAR!
Y, OKAY! MAYBE WE KILLED TROL, BUT THEY MURDERED ENTIRE VILLAGE BECAUSE THEY CLAIMED IT HAD THE--
PLAGUE.

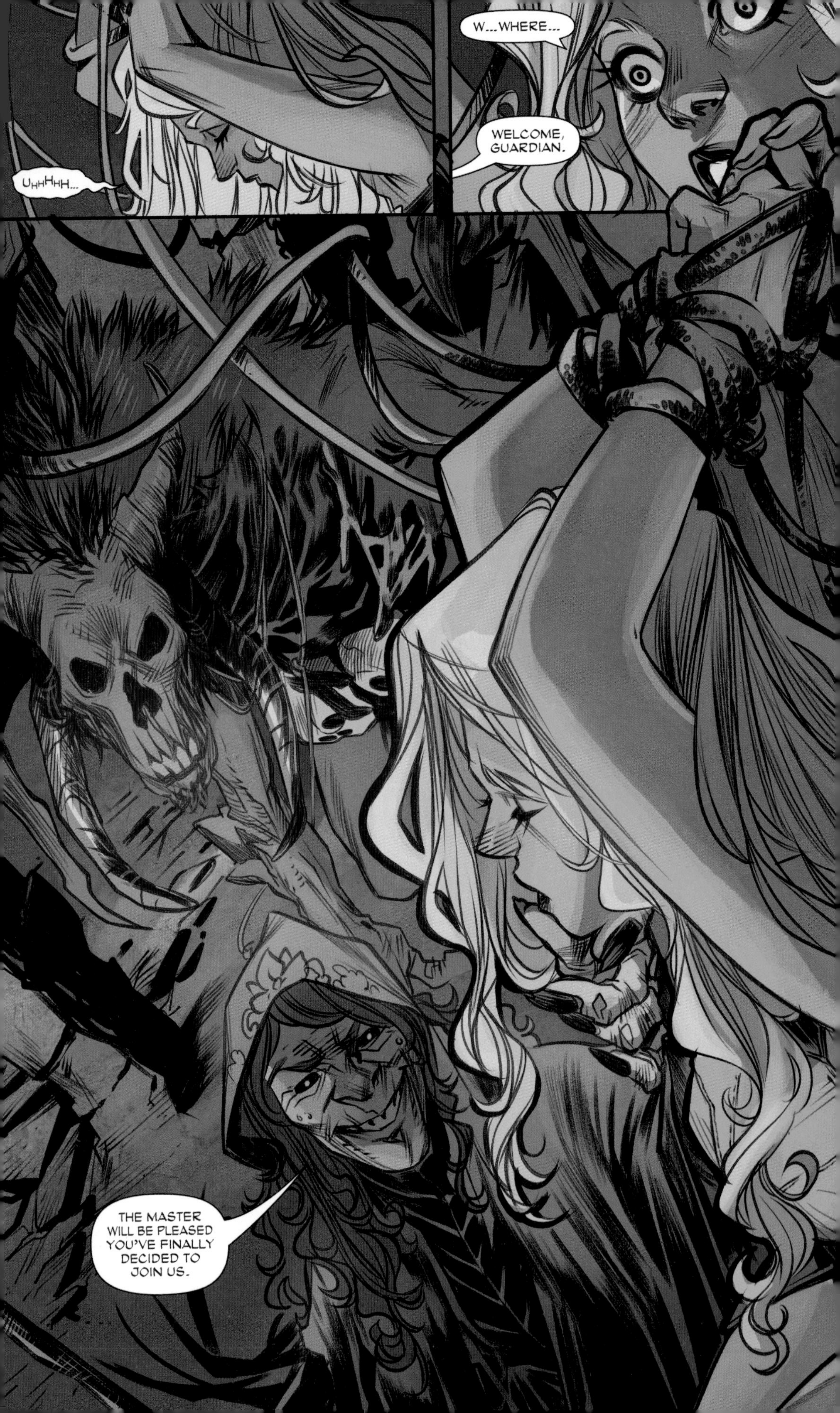
UHHHHH...
W...WHERE...
WELCOME, GUARDIAN.
THE MASTER WILL BE PLEASED YOU'VE FINALLY DECIDED TO JOIN US.

FOURTEEN

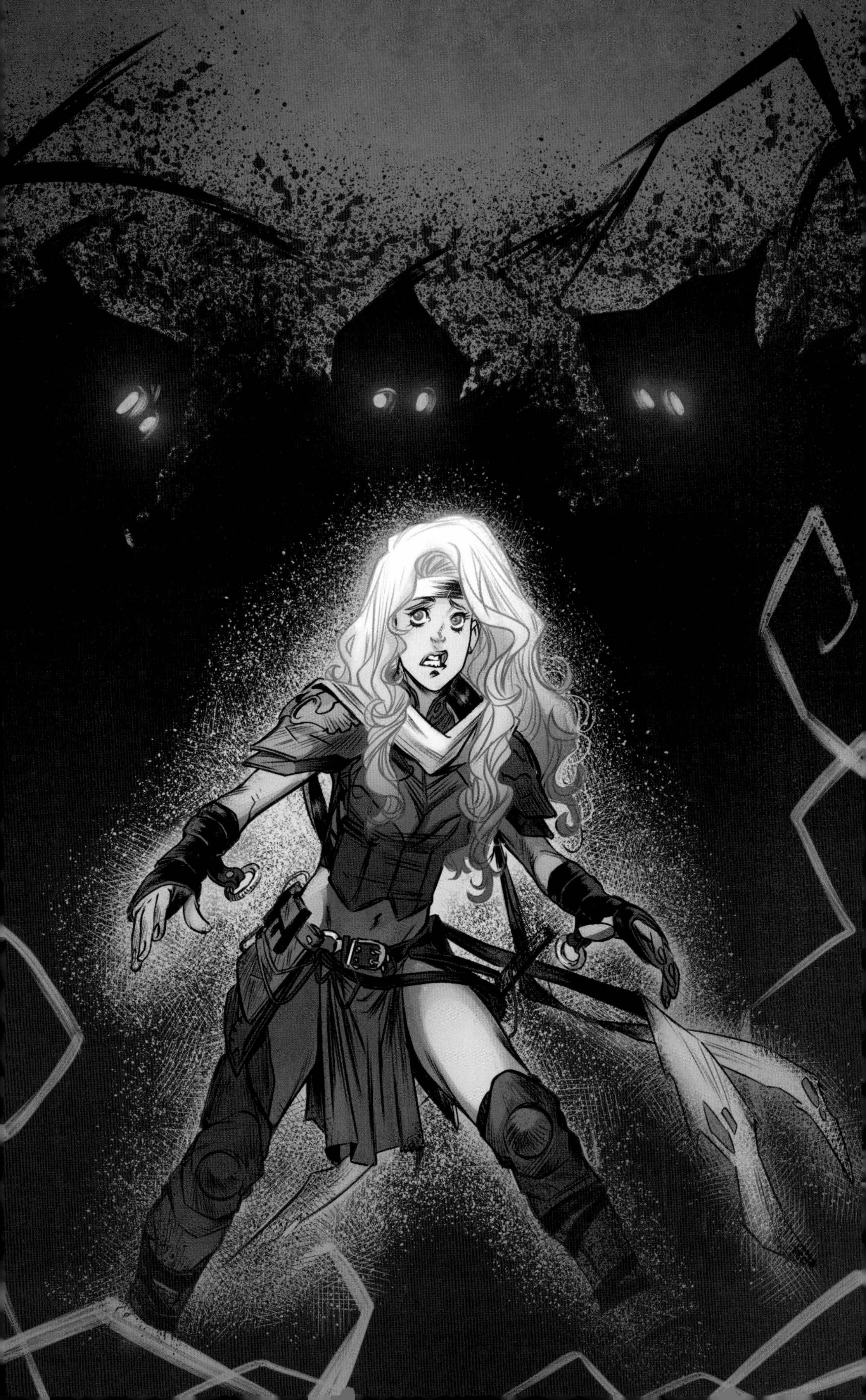

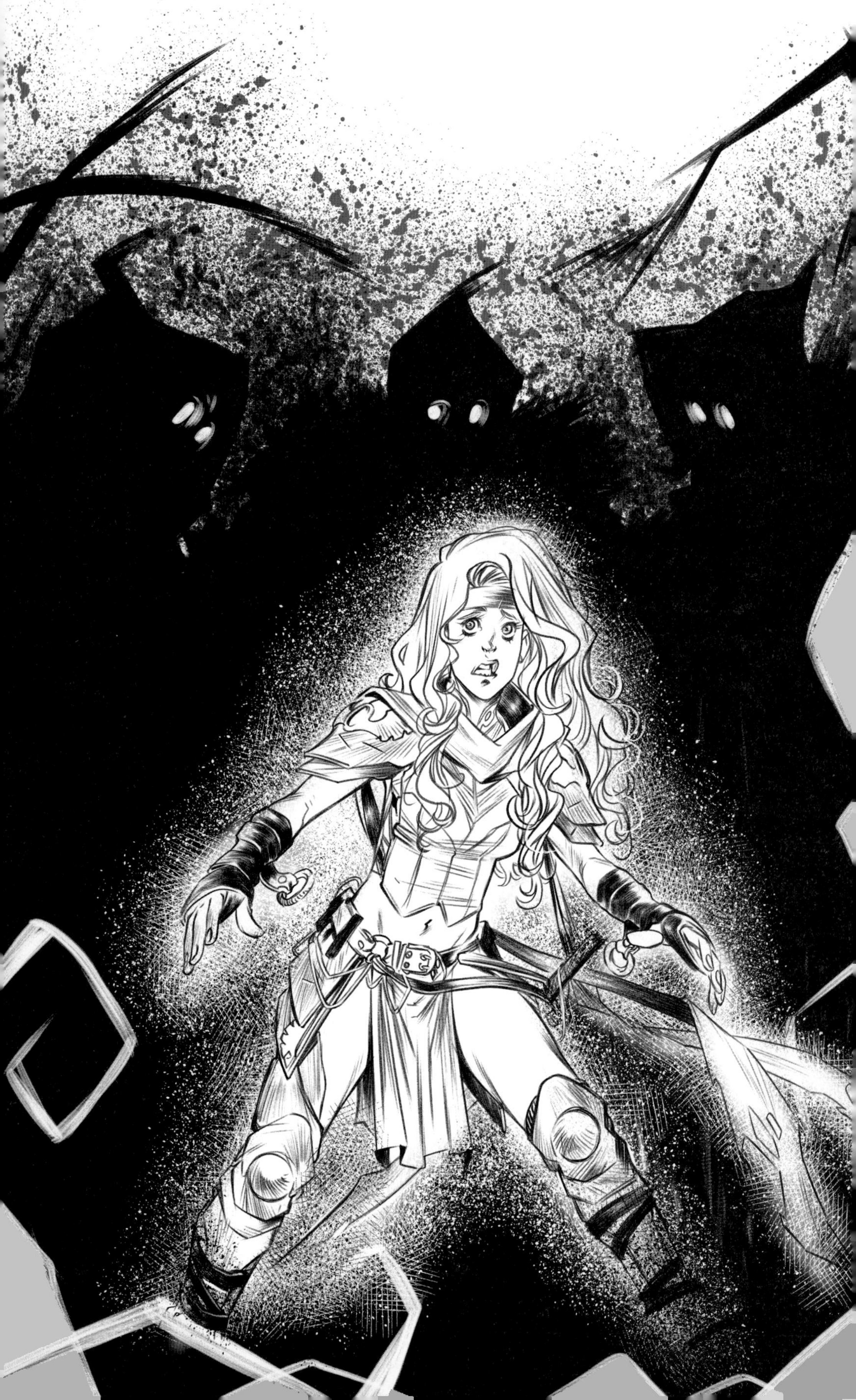

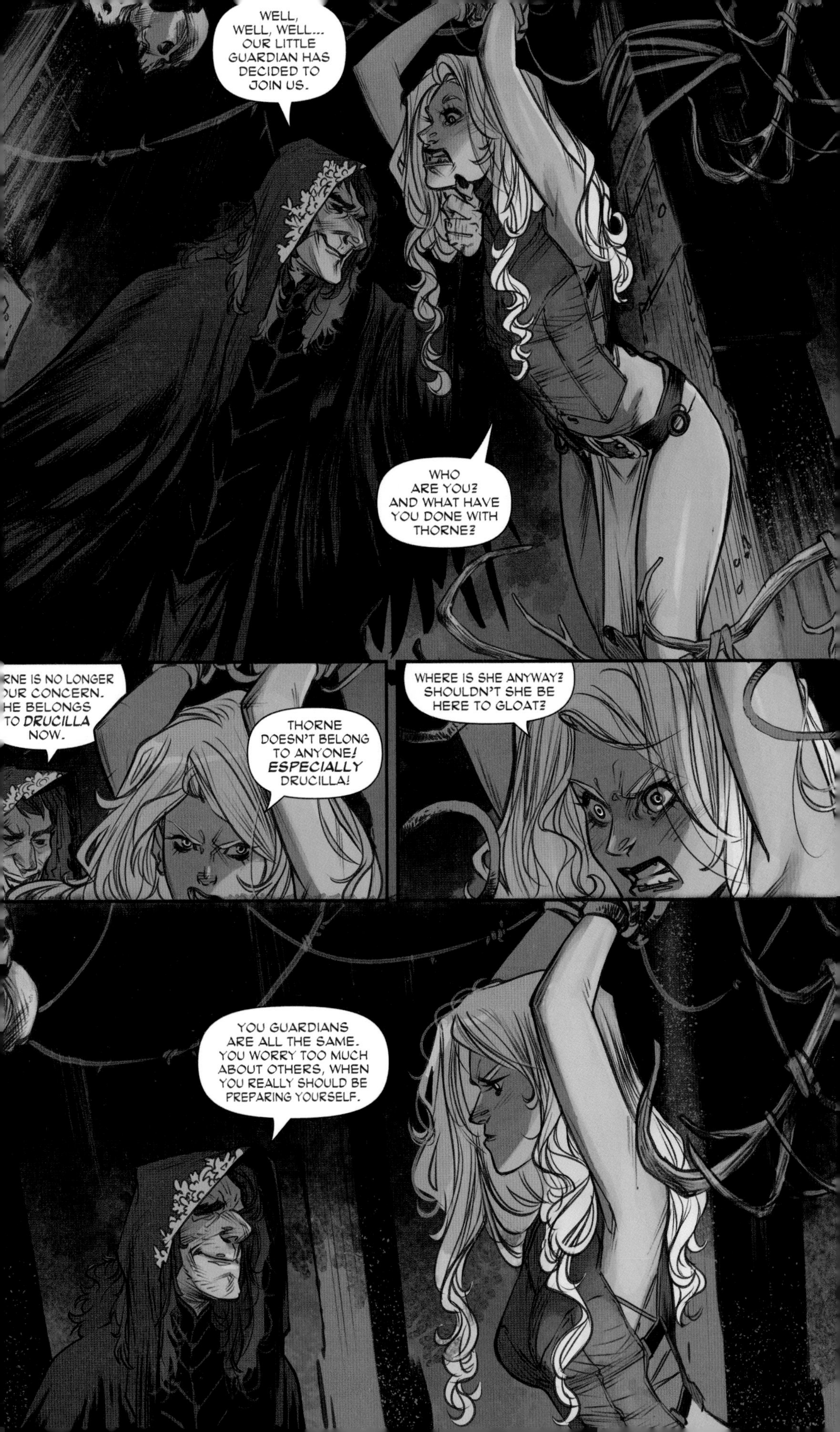
WELL, WELL, WELL... OUR LITTLE GUARDIAN HAS DECIDED TO JOIN US.
WHO ARE YOU? AND WHAT HAVE YOU DONE WITH THORNE?
RNE IS NO LONGER UR CONCERN. HE BELONGS TO DRUCILLA NOW.
THORNE DOESN'T BELONG TO ANYONE! ESPECIALLY DRUCILLA!
WHERE IS SHE ANYWAY? SHOULDN'T SHE BE HERE TO GLOAT?
YOU GUARDIANS ARE ALL THE SAME. YOU WORRY TOO MUCH ABOUT OTHERS, WHEN YOU REALLY SHOULD BE PREPARING YOURSELF.

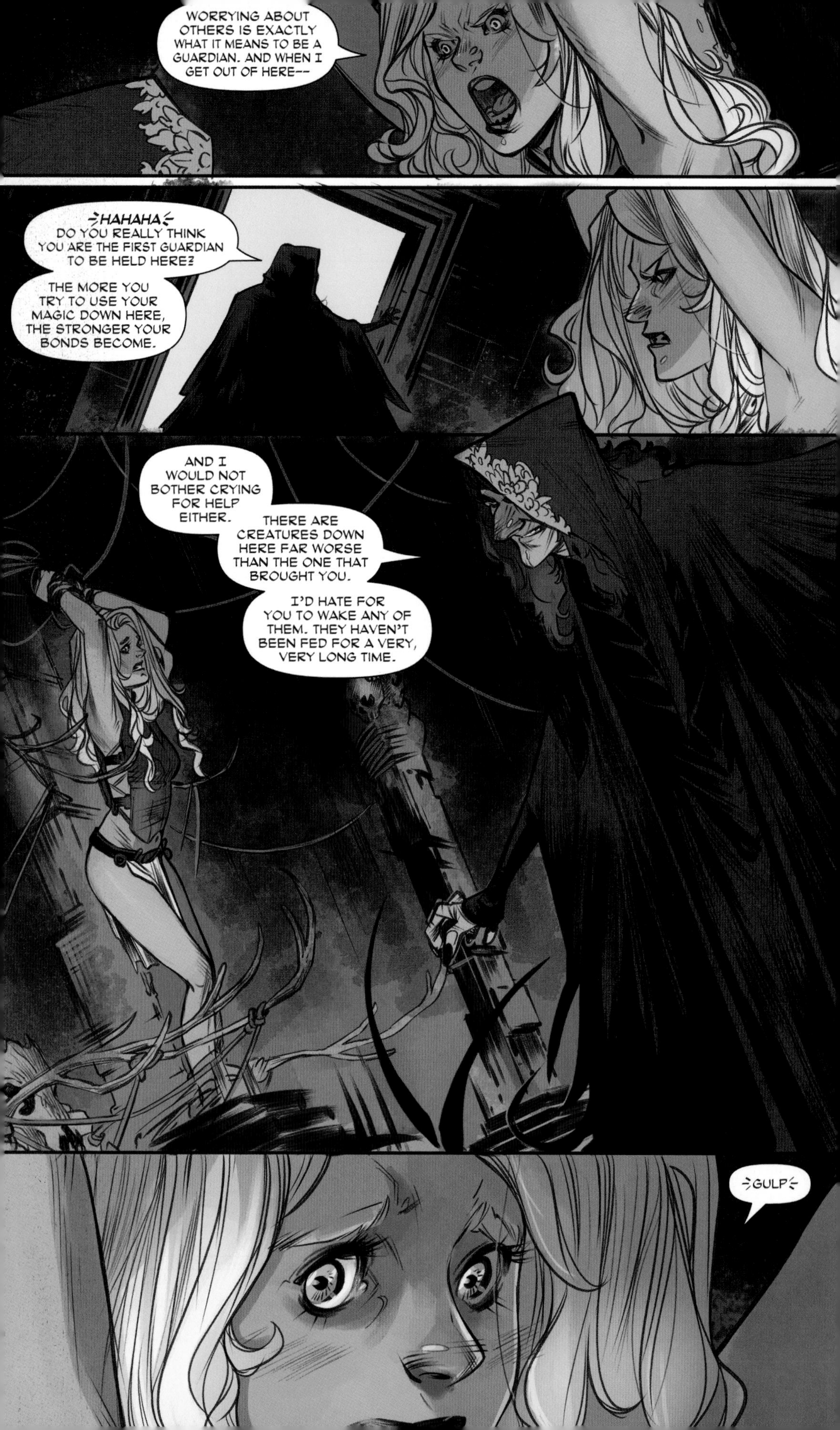
WORRYING ABOUT OTHERS IS EXACTLY WHAT IT MEANS TO BE A GUARDIAN. AND WHEN I GET OUT OF HERE--
HAHAHA
DO YOU REALLY THINK YOU ARE THE FIRST GUARDIAN TO BE HELD HERE?
THE MORE YOU TRY TO USE YOUR MAGIC DOWN HERE, THE STRONGER YOUR BONDS BECOME.
AND I WOULD NOT BOTHER CRYING FOR HELP EITHER.
THERE ARE CREATURES DOWN HERE FAR WORSE THAN THE ONE THAT BROUGHT YOU.
I'D HATE FOR YOU TO WAKE ANY OF THEM. THEY HAVEN'T BEEN FED FOR A VERY, VERY LONG TIME.
GULP

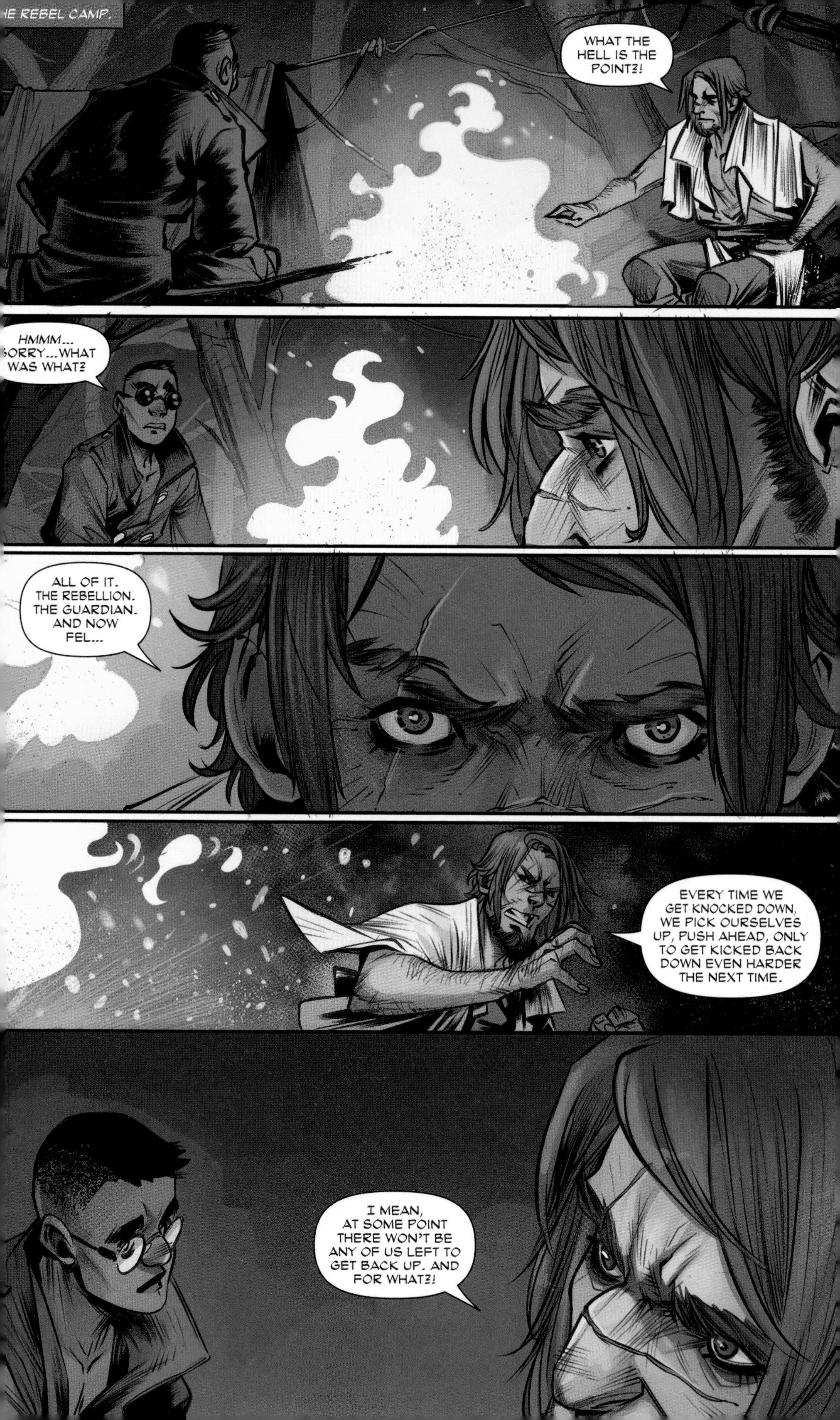
E REBEL CAMP.
WHAT THE HELL IS THE POINT?!
HMMM... ORRY...WHAT WAS WHAT?
ALL OF IT. THE REBELLION. THE GUARDIAN. AND NOW FEL...
EVERY TIME WE GET KNOCKED DOWN, WE PICK OURSELVES UP, PUSH AHEAD, ONLY TO GET KICKED BACK DOWN EVEN HARDER THE NEXT TIME.
I MEAN, AT SOME POINT THERE WON'T BE ANY OF US LEFT TO GET BACK UP. AND FOR WHAT?!

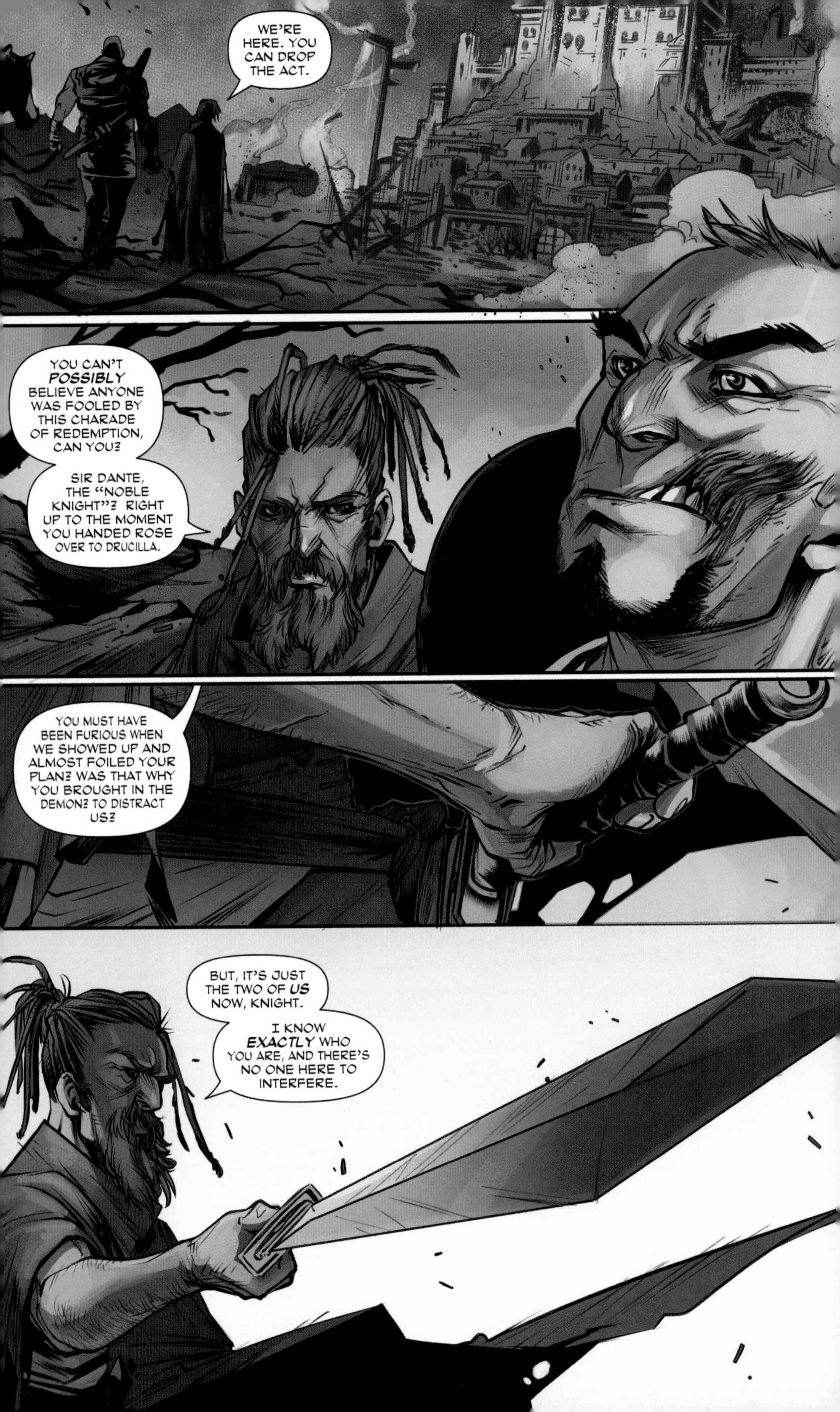
WE'RE HERE. YOU CAN DROP THE ACT.
YOU CAN'T *POSSIBLY* BELIEVE ANYONE WAS FOOLED BY THIS CHARADE OF REDEMPTION, CAN YOU?
SIR DANTE, THE "NOBLE KNIGHT"? RIGHT UP TO THE MOMENT YOU HANDED ROSE OVER TO DRUCILLA.
YOU MUST HAVE BEEN FURIOUS WHEN WE SHOWED UP AND ALMOST FOILED YOUR PLAN? WAS THAT WHY YOU BROUGHT IN THE DEMON? TO DISTRACT US?
BUT, IT'S JUST THE TWO OF *US* NOW, KNIGHT.
I KNOW *EXACTLY* WHO YOU ARE, AND THERE'S NO ONE HERE TO INTERFERE.

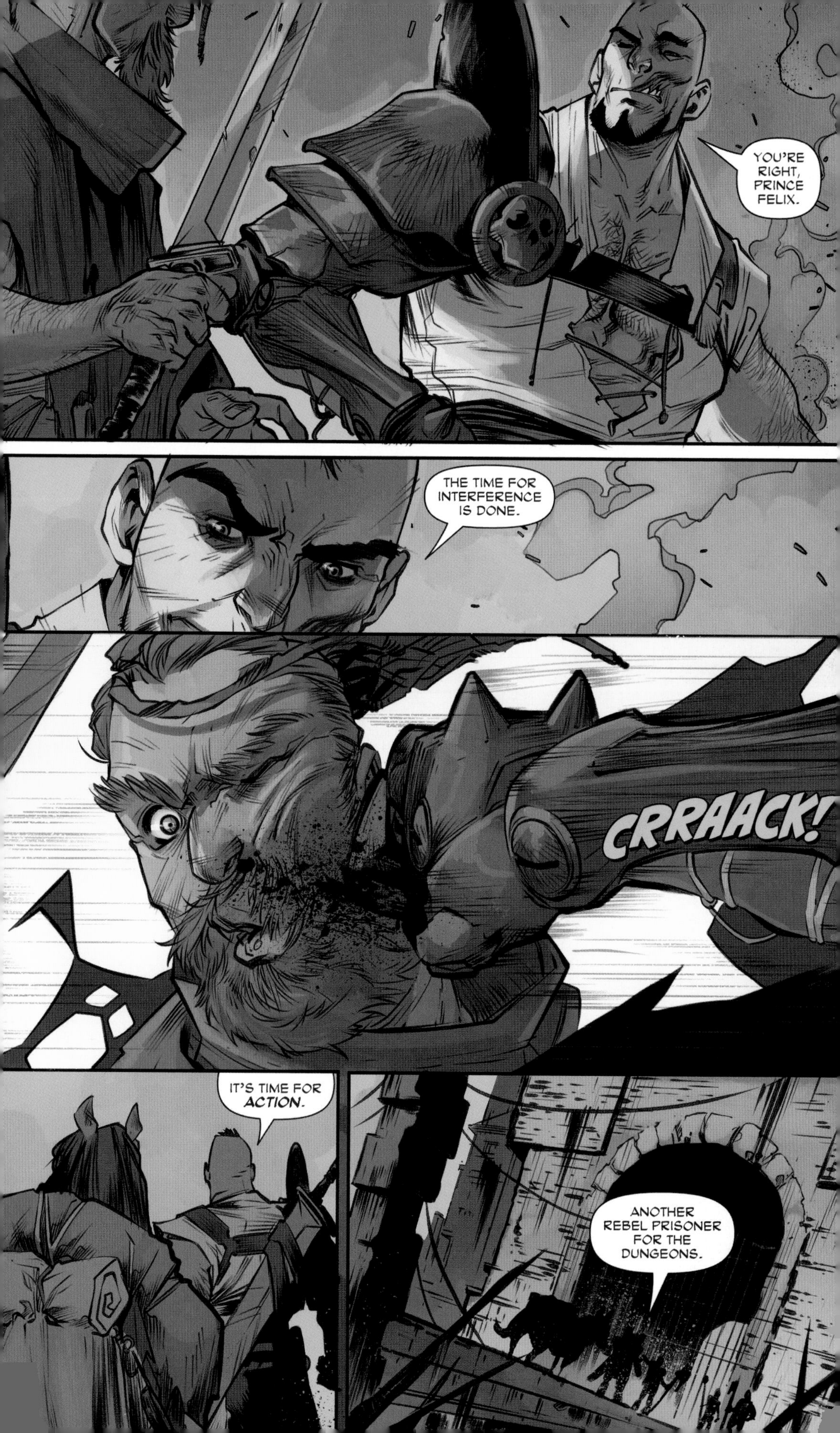
YOU'RE RIGHT, PRINCE FELIX.
THE TIME FOR INTERFERENCE IS DONE.
CRRAACK!
IT'S TIME FOR ACTION.
ANOTHER REBEL PRISONER FOR THE DUNGEONS.

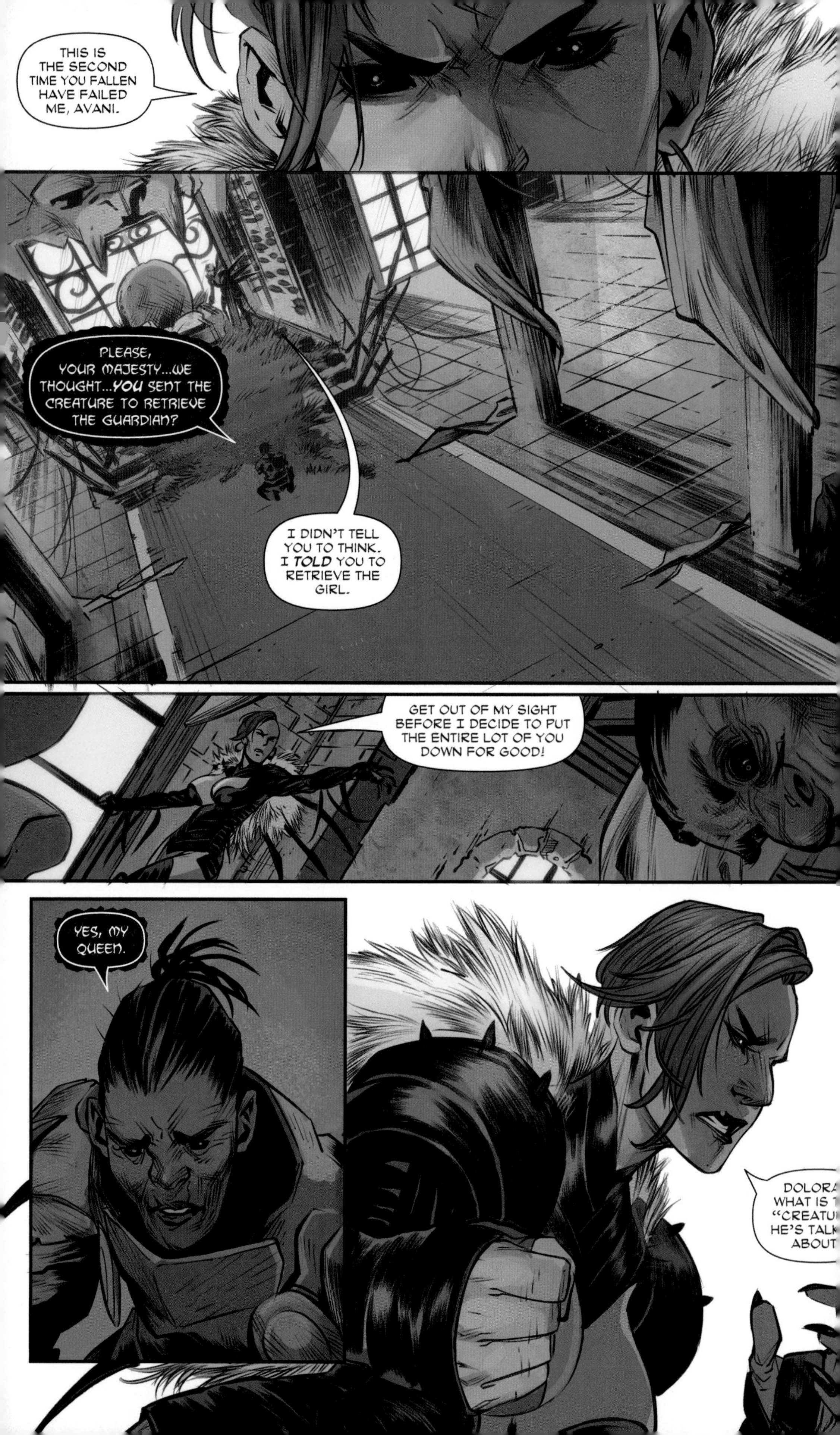
THIS IS THE SECOND TIME YOU FALLEN HAVE FAILED ME, AVANI.
PLEASE, YOUR MAJESTY...WE THOUGHT...YOU SENT THE CREATURE TO RETRIEVE THE GUARDIAN?
I DIDN'T TELL YOU TO THINK. I TOLD YOU TO RETRIEVE THE GIRL.
GET OUT OF MY SIGHT BEFORE I DECIDE TO PUT THE ENTIRE LOT OF YOU DOWN FOR GOOD!
YES, MY QUEEN.

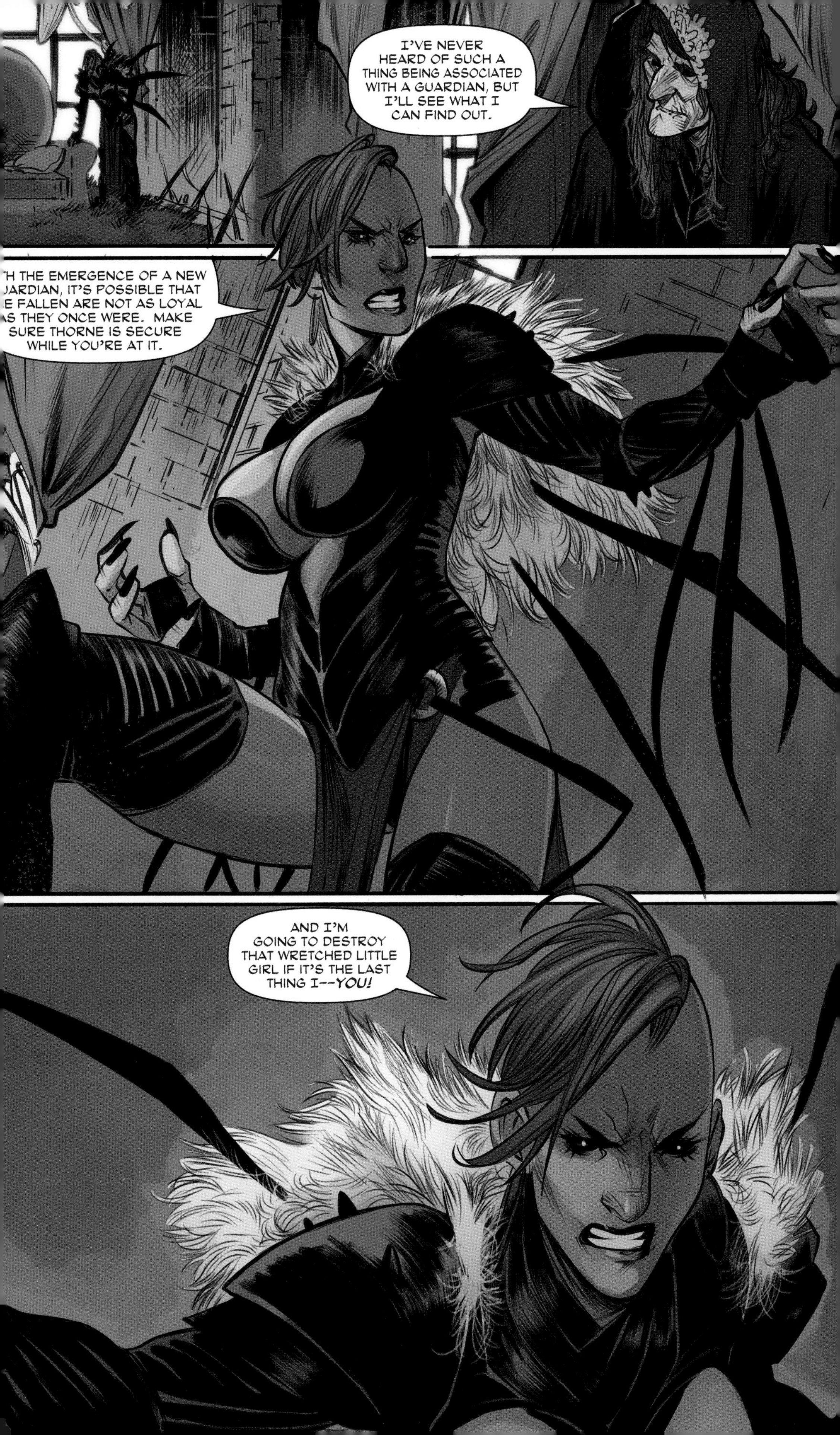
I'VE NEVER HEARD OF SUCH A THING BEING ASSOCIATED WITH A GUARDIAN, BUT I'LL SEE WHAT I CAN FIND OUT.
H THE EMERGENCE OF A NEW UARDIAN, IT'S POSSIBLE THAT E FALLEN ARE NOT AS LOYAL S THEY ONCE WERE. MAKE SURE THORNE IS SECURE WHILE YOU'RE AT IT.
AND I'M GOING TO DESTROY THAT WRETCHED LITTLE GIRL IF IT'S THE LAST THING I--*YOU!*

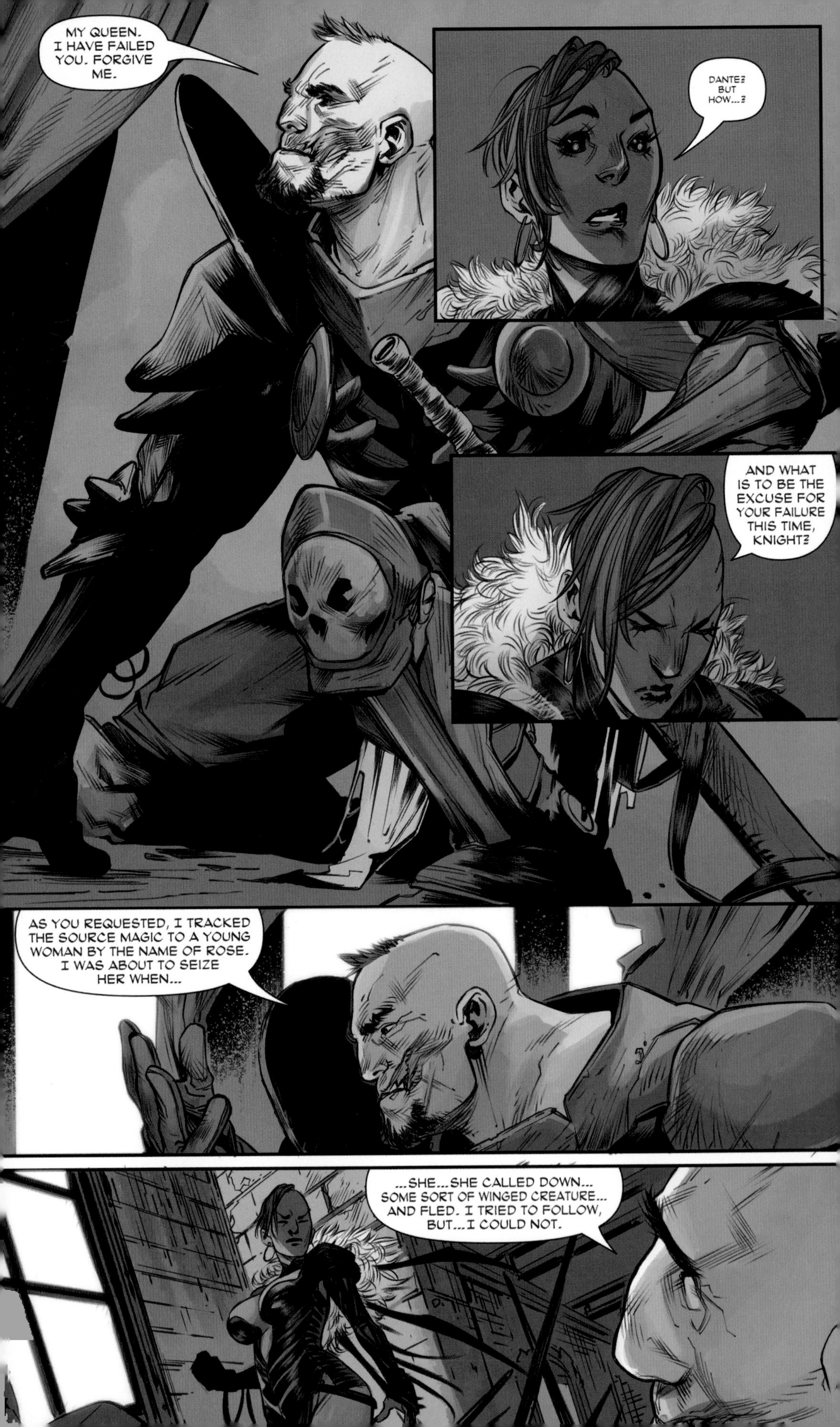
MY QUEEN. I HAVE FAILED YOU. FORGIVE ME.
DANTE? BUT HOW...?
AND WHAT IS TO BE THE EXCUSE FOR YOUR FAILURE THIS TIME, KNIGHT?
AS YOU REQUESTED, I TRACKED THE SOURCE MAGIC TO A YOUNG WOMAN BY THE NAME OF ROSE. I WAS ABOUT TO SEIZE HER WHEN...
...SHE...SHE CALLED DOWN... SOME SORT OF WINGED CREATURE... AND FLED. I TRIED TO FOLLOW, BUT...I COULD NOT.

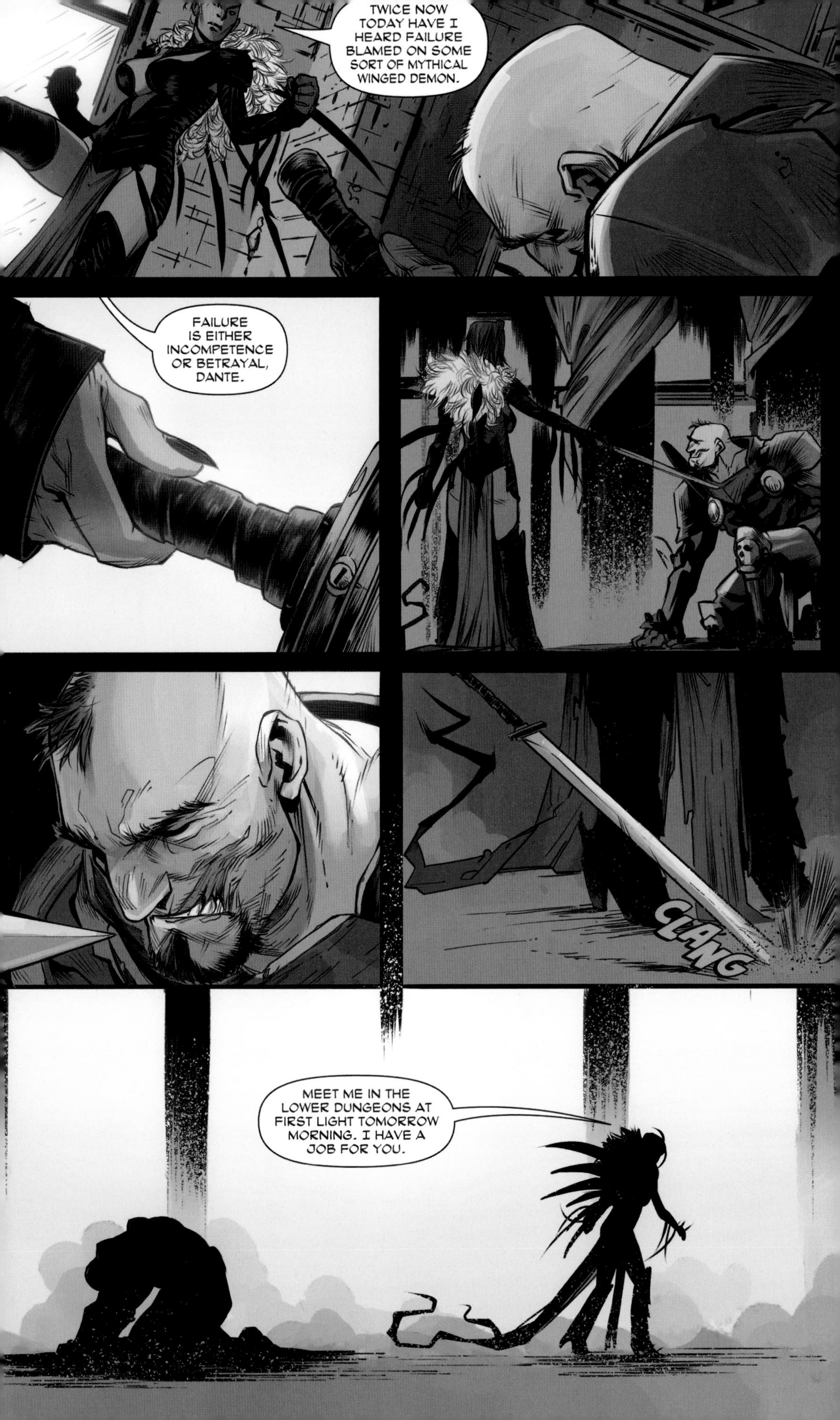
TWICE NOW TODAY HAVE I HEARD FAILURE BLAMED ON SOME SORT OF MYTHICAL WINGED DEMON.
FAILURE IS EITHER INCOMPETENCE OR BETRAYAL, DANTE.
CLANG
MEET ME IN THE LOWER DUNGEONS AT FIRST LIGHT TOMORROW MORNING. I HAVE A JOB FOR YOU.

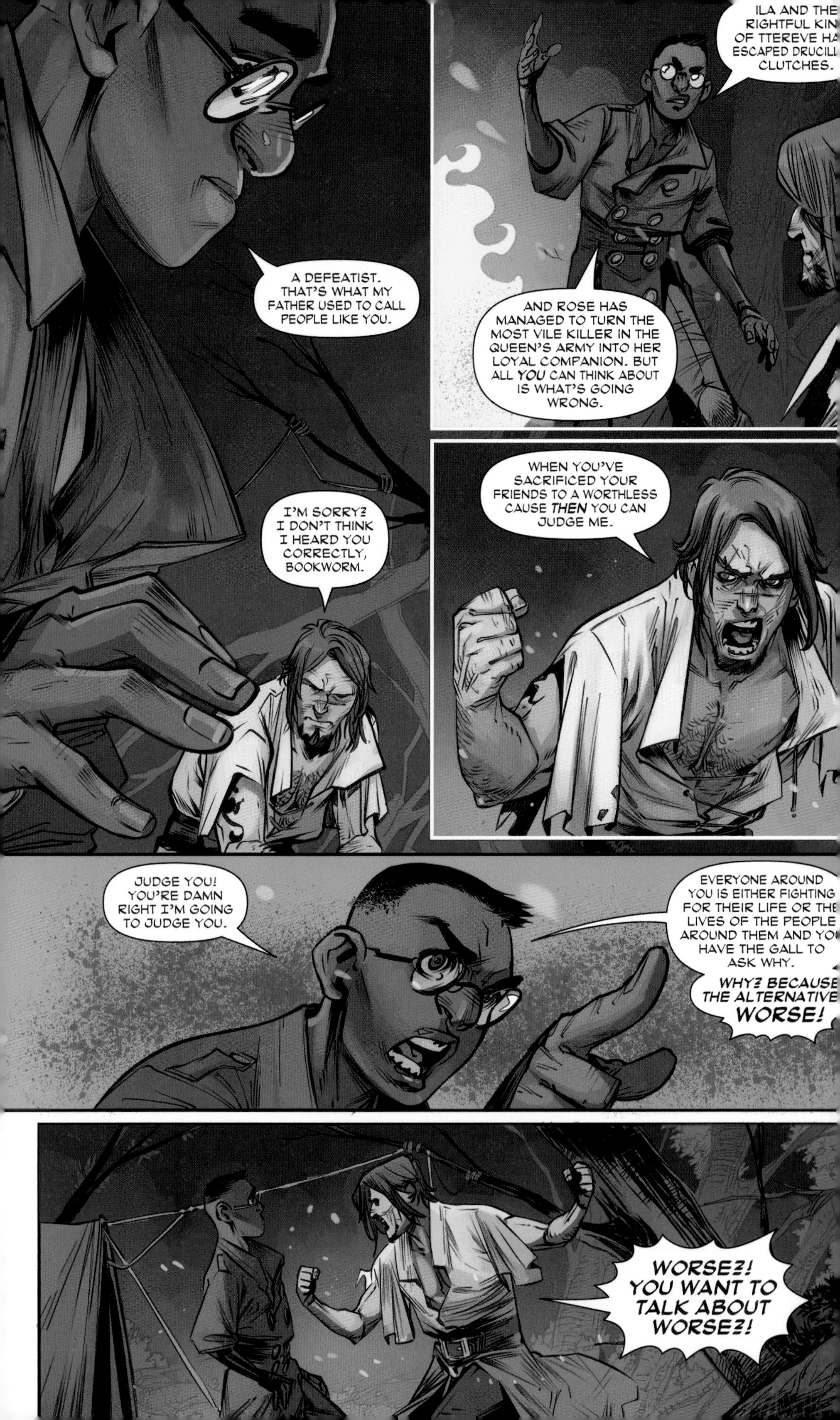
A DEFEATIST. THAT'S WHAT MY FATHER USED TO CALL PEOPLE LIKE YOU.
I'M SORRY? I DON'T THINK I HEARD YOU CORRECTLY, BOOKWORM.
ILA AND THE RIGHTFUL KIN OF TTEREVE HA ESCAPED DRUCILI CLUTCHES.
AND ROSE HAS MANAGED TO TURN THE MOST VILE KILLER IN THE QUEEN'S ARMY INTO HER LOYAL COMPANION. BUT ALL *YOU* CAN THINK ABOUT IS WHAT'S GOING WRONG.
WHEN YOU'VE SACRIFICED YOUR FRIENDS TO A WORTHLESS CAUSE *THEN* YOU CAN JUDGE ME.
JUDGE YOU! YOU'RE DAMN RIGHT I'M GOING TO JUDGE YOU.
EVERYONE AROUND YOU IS EITHER FIGHTING FOR THEIR LIFE OR THE LIVES OF THE PEOPLE AROUND THEM AND YO HAVE THE GALL TO ASK WHY.
WHY? BECAUSE THE ALTERNATIVE WORSE!
WORSE?! YOU WANT TO TALK ABOUT WORSE?!

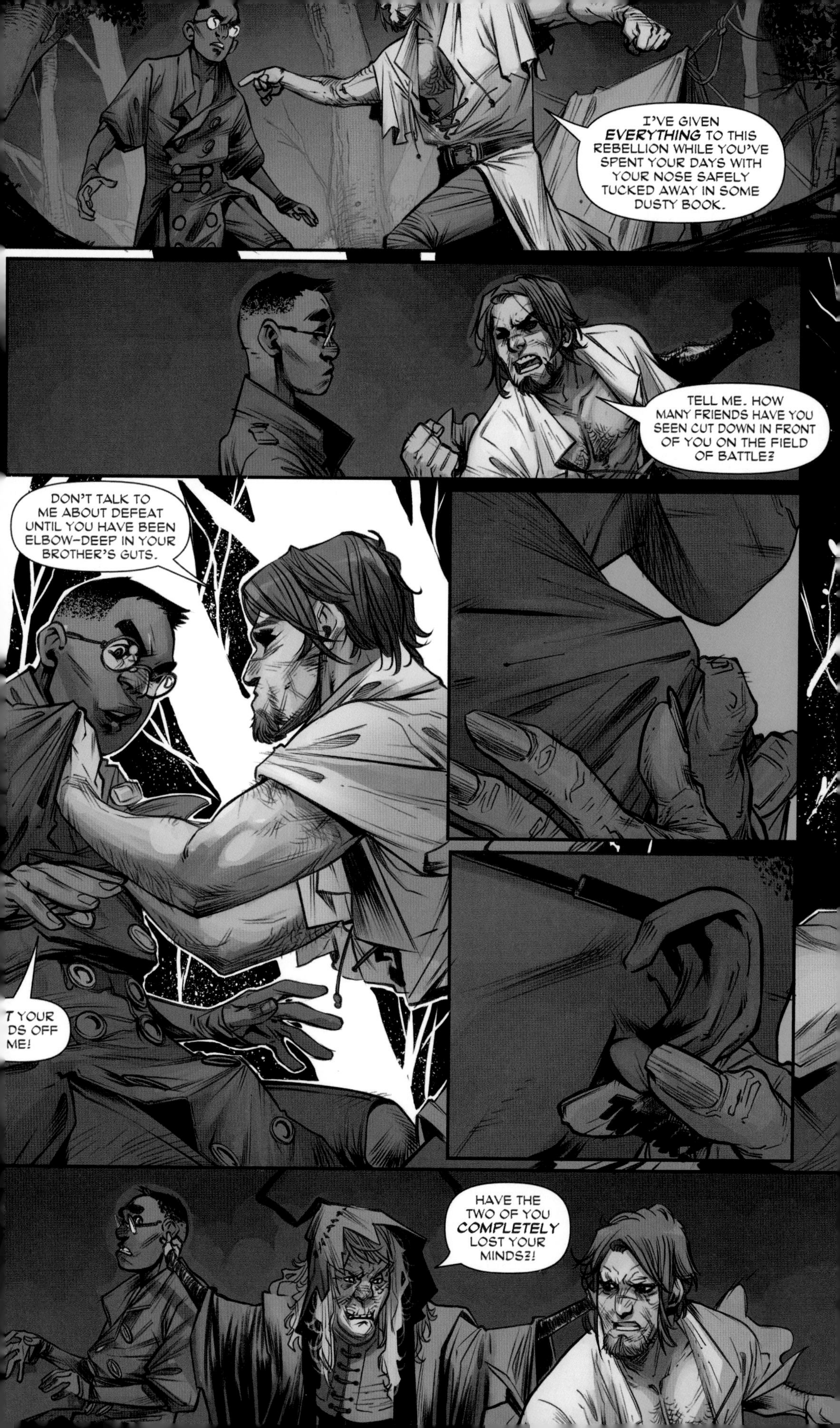
I'VE GIVEN EVERYTHING TO THIS REBELLION WHILE YOU'VE SPENT YOUR DAYS WITH YOUR NOSE SAFELY TUCKED AWAY IN SOME DUSTY BOOK.
TELL ME. HOW MANY FRIENDS HAVE YOU SEEN CUT DOWN IN FRONT OF YOU ON THE FIELD OF BATTLE?
DON'T TALK TO ME ABOUT DEFEAT UNTIL YOU HAVE BEEN ELBOW-DEEP IN YOUR BROTHER'S GUTS.
T YOUR DS OFF ME!
HAVE THE TWO OF YOU COMPLETELY LOST YOUR MINDS?!

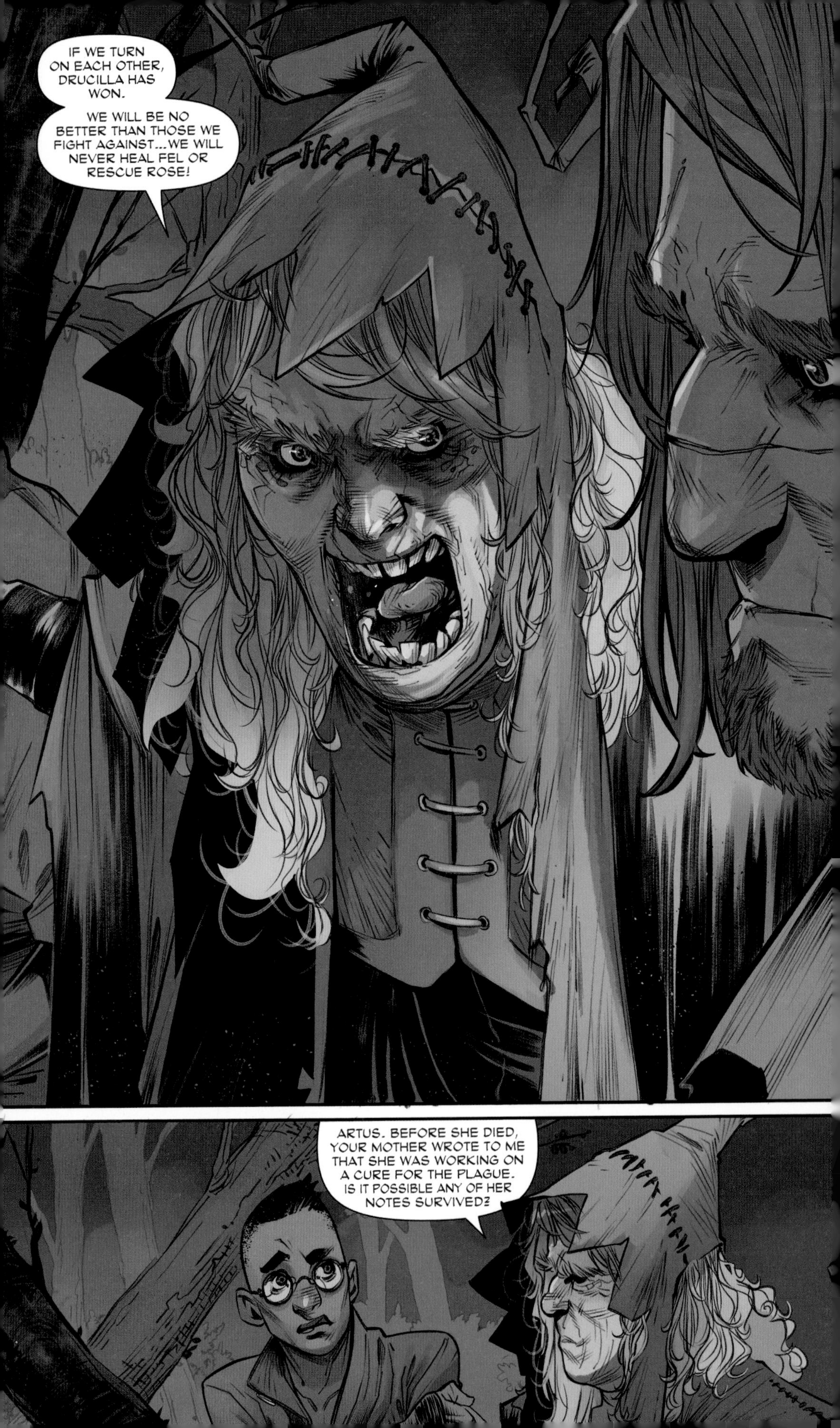
IF WE TURN ON EACH OTHER, DRUCILLA HAS WON.
WE WILL BE NO BETTER THAN THOSE WE FIGHT AGAINST...WE WILL NEVER HEAL FEL OR RESCUE ROSE!
ARTUS. BEFORE SHE DIED, YOUR MOTHER WROTE TO ME THAT SHE WAS WORKING ON A CURE FOR THE PLAGUE. IS IT POSSIBLE ANY OF HER NOTES SURVIVED?

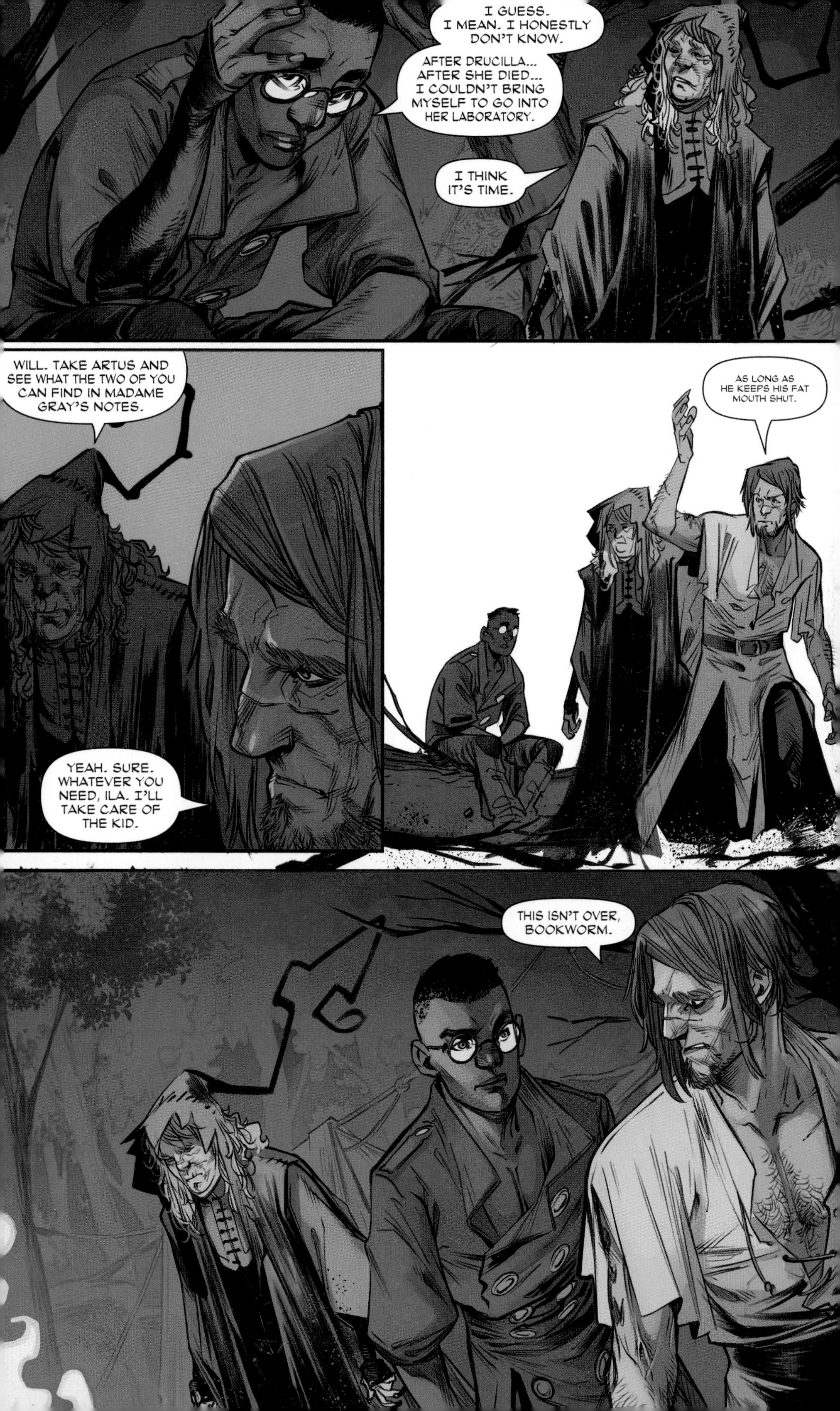
I GUESS.
I MEAN. I HONESTLY DON'T KNOW.
AFTER DRUCILLA... AFTER SHE DIED... I COULDN'T BRING MYSELF TO GO INTO HER LABORATORY.
I THINK IT'S TIME.
WILL. TAKE ARTUS AND SEE WHAT THE TWO OF YOU CAN FIND IN MADAME GRAY'S NOTES.
YEAH. SURE. WHATEVER YOU NEED, ILA. I'LL TAKE CARE OF THE KID.
AS LONG AS HE KEEPS HIS FAT MOUTH SHUT.
THIS ISN'T OVER, BOOKWORM.

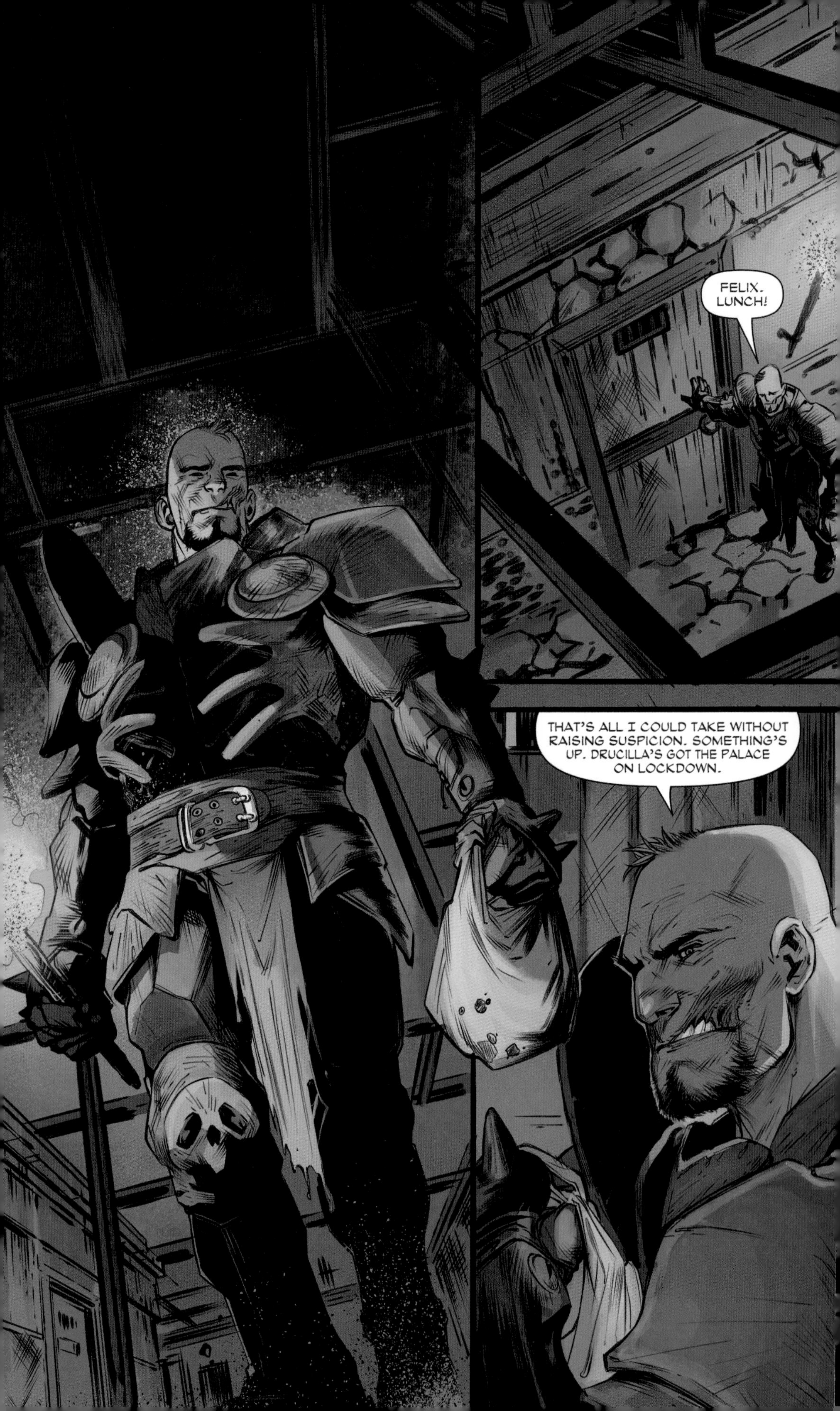
FELIX. LUNCH!
THAT'S ALL I COULD TAKE WITHOUT RAISING SUSPICION. SOMETHING'S UP. DRUCILLA'S GOT THE PALACE ON LOCKDOWN.

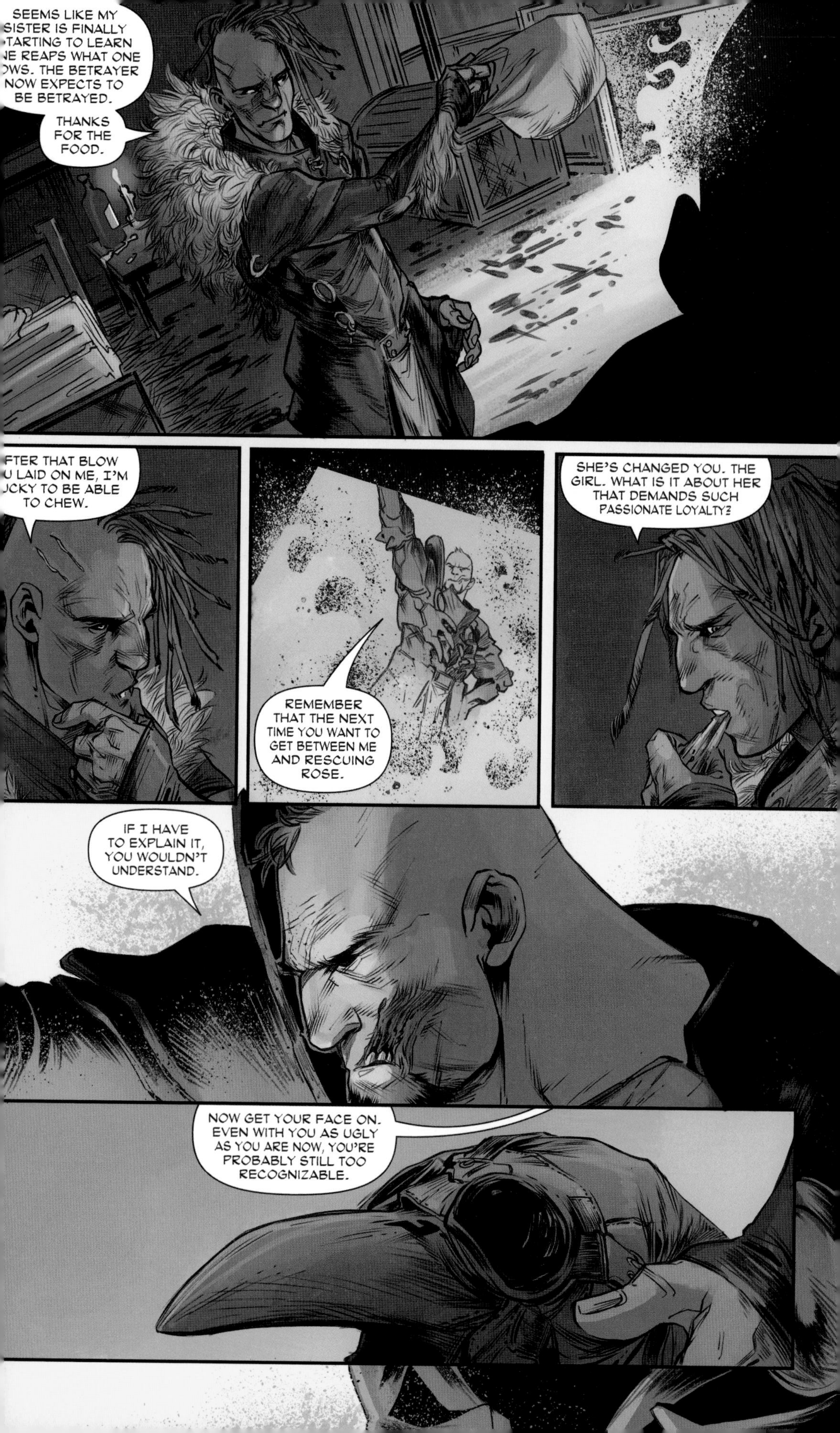
SEEMS LIKE MY SISTER IS FINALLY TARTING TO LEARN NE REAPS WHAT ONE OWS. THE BETRAYER NOW EXPECTS TO BE BETRAYED.
THANKS FOR THE FOOD.
FTER THAT BLOW U LAID ON ME, I'M UCKY TO BE ABLE TO CHEW.
REMEMBER THAT THE NEXT TIME YOU WANT TO GET BETWEEN ME AND RESCUING ROSE.
SHE'S CHANGED YOU. THE GIRL. WHAT IS IT ABOUT HER THAT DEMANDS SUCH PASSIONATE LOYALTY?
IF I HAVE TO EXPLAIN IT, YOU WOULDN'T UNDERSTAND.
NOW GET YOUR FACE ON. EVEN WITH YOU AS UGLY AS YOU ARE NOW, YOU'RE PROBABLY STILL TOO RECOGNIZABLE.

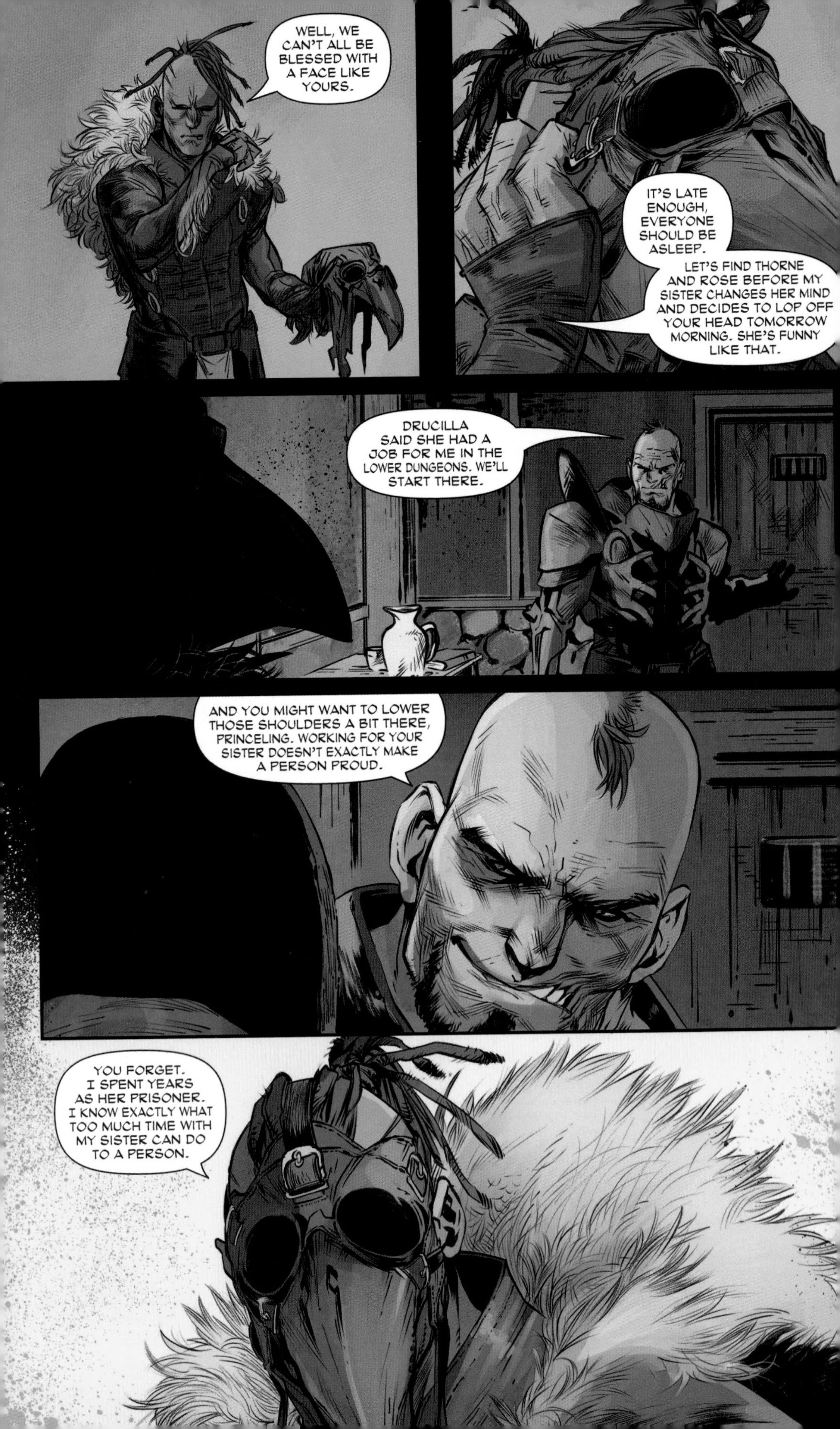
WELL, WE CAN'T ALL BE BLESSED WITH A FACE LIKE YOURS.
IT'S LATE ENOUGH, EVERYONE SHOULD BE ASLEEP.
LET'S FIND THORNE AND ROSE BEFORE MY SISTER CHANGES HER MIND AND DECIDES TO LOP OFF YOUR HEAD TOMORROW MORNING. SHE'S FUNNY LIKE THAT.
DRUCILLA SAID SHE HAD A JOB FOR ME IN THE LOWER DUNGEONS. WE'LL START THERE.
AND YOU MIGHT WANT TO LOWER THOSE SHOULDERS A BIT THERE, PRINCELING. WORKING FOR YOUR SISTER DOESN'T EXACTLY MAKE A PERSON PROUD.
YOU FORGET. I SPENT YEARS AS HER PRISONER. I KNOW EXACTLY WHAT TOO MUCH TIME WITH MY SISTER CAN DO TO A PERSON.

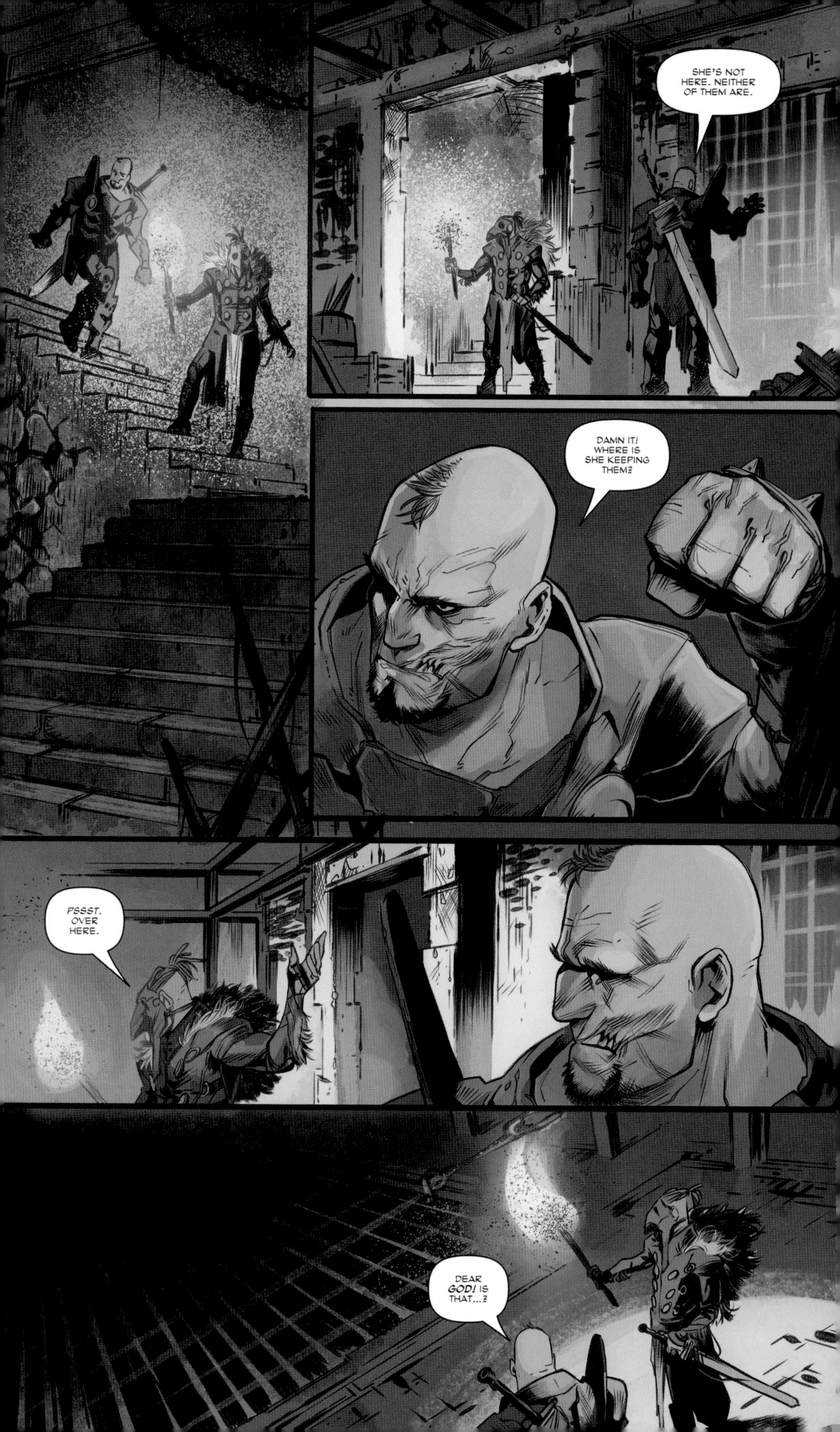
SHE'S NOT HERE. NEITHER OF THEM ARE.
DAMN IT! WHERE IS SHE KEEPING THEM?
PSSST. OVER HERE.
DEAR *GOD!* IS THAT...?

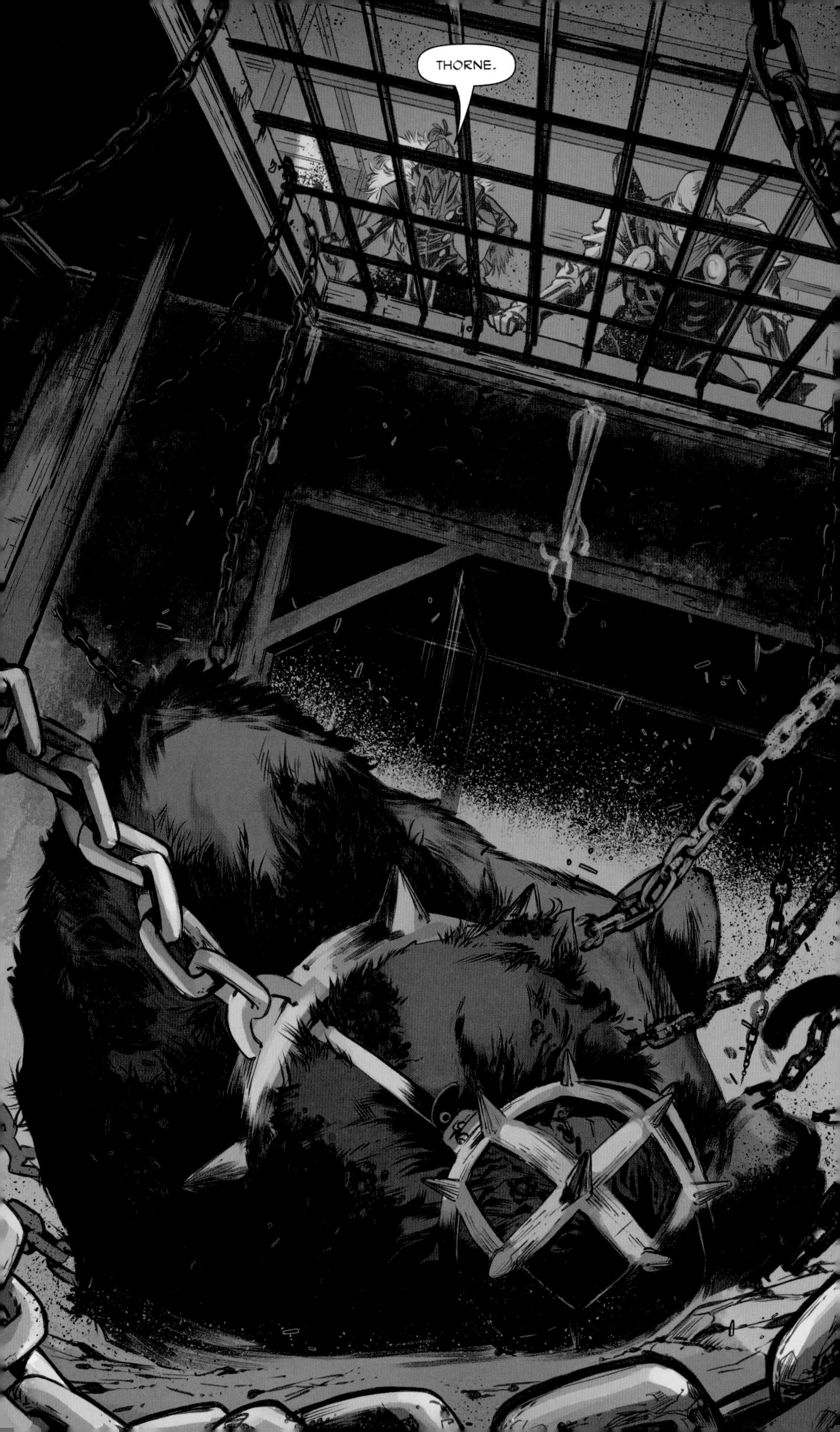
THORNE.

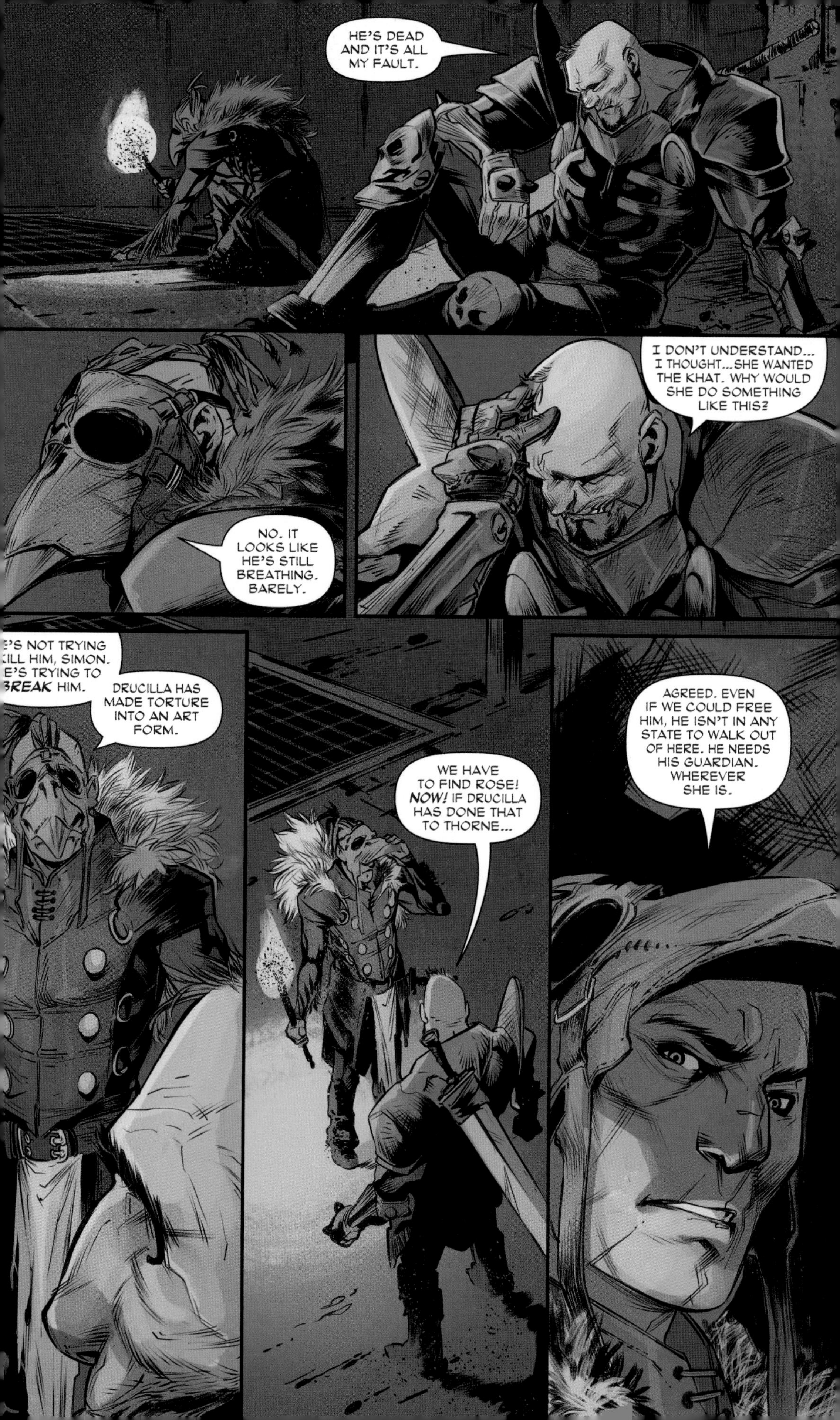

HE'S DEAD AND IT'S ALL MY FAULT.
NO. IT LOOKS LIKE HE'S STILL BREATHING. BARELY.
I DON'T UNDERSTAND... I THOUGHT...SHE WANTED THE KHAT. WHY WOULD SHE DO SOMETHING LIKE THIS?
'S NOT TRYING ILL HIM, SIMON. 'S TRYING TO REAK HIM.
DRUCILLA HAS MADE TORTURE INTO AN ART FORM.
WE HAVE TO FIND ROSE! *NOW!* IF DRUCILLA HAS DONE THAT TO THORNE...
AGREED. EVEN IF WE COULD FREE HIM, HE ISN'T IN ANY STATE TO WALK OUT OF HERE. HE NEEDS HIS GUARDIAN. WHEREVER SHE IS.

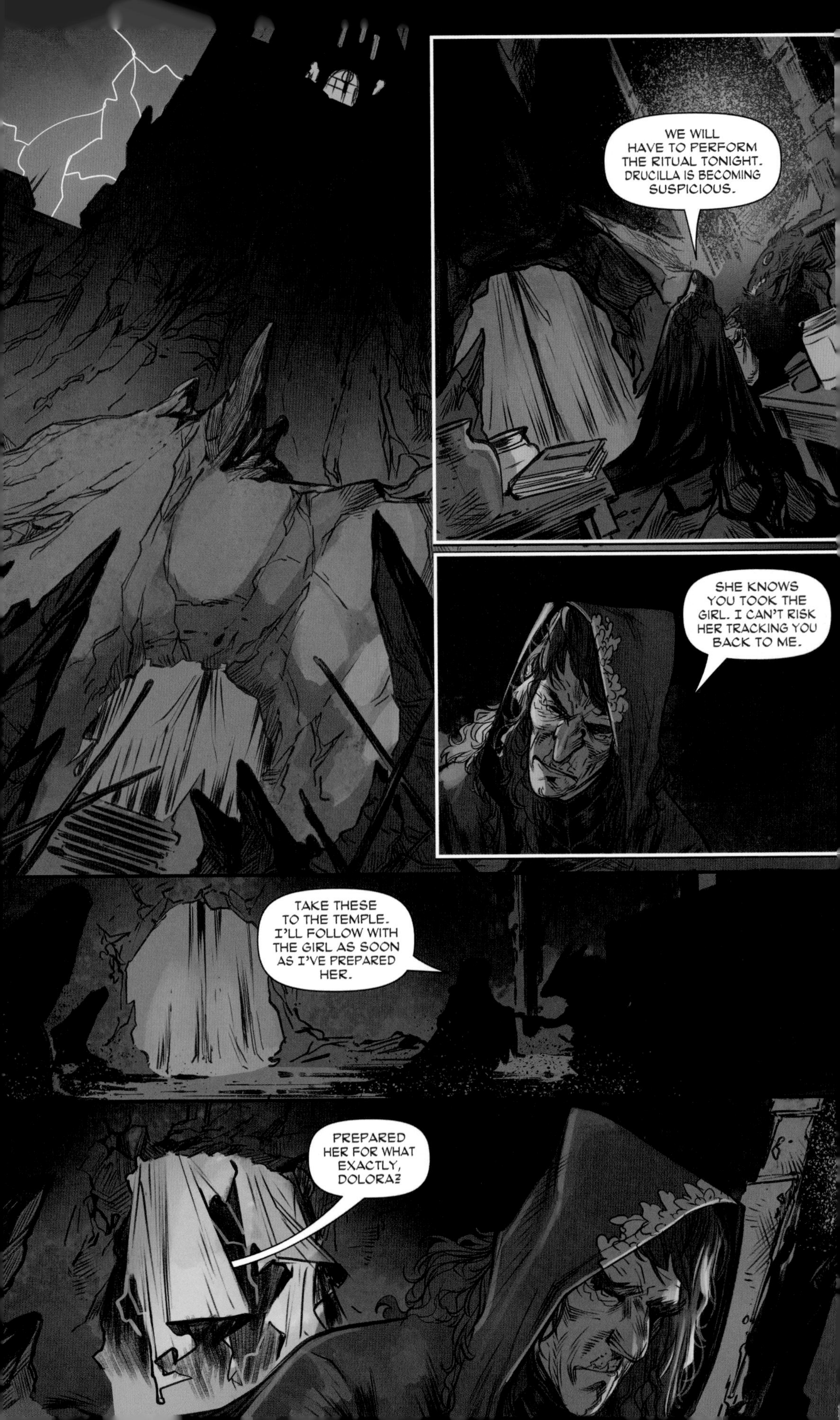
WE WILL HAVE TO PERFORM THE RITUAL TONIGHT. DRUCILLA IS BECOMING SUSPICIOUS.
SHE KNOWS YOU TOOK THE GIRL. I CAN'T RISK HER TRACKING YOU BACK TO ME.
TAKE THESE TO THE TEMPLE. I'LL FOLLOW WITH THE GIRL AS SOON AS I'VE PREPARED HER.
PREPARED HER FOR WHAT EXACTLY, DOLORA?

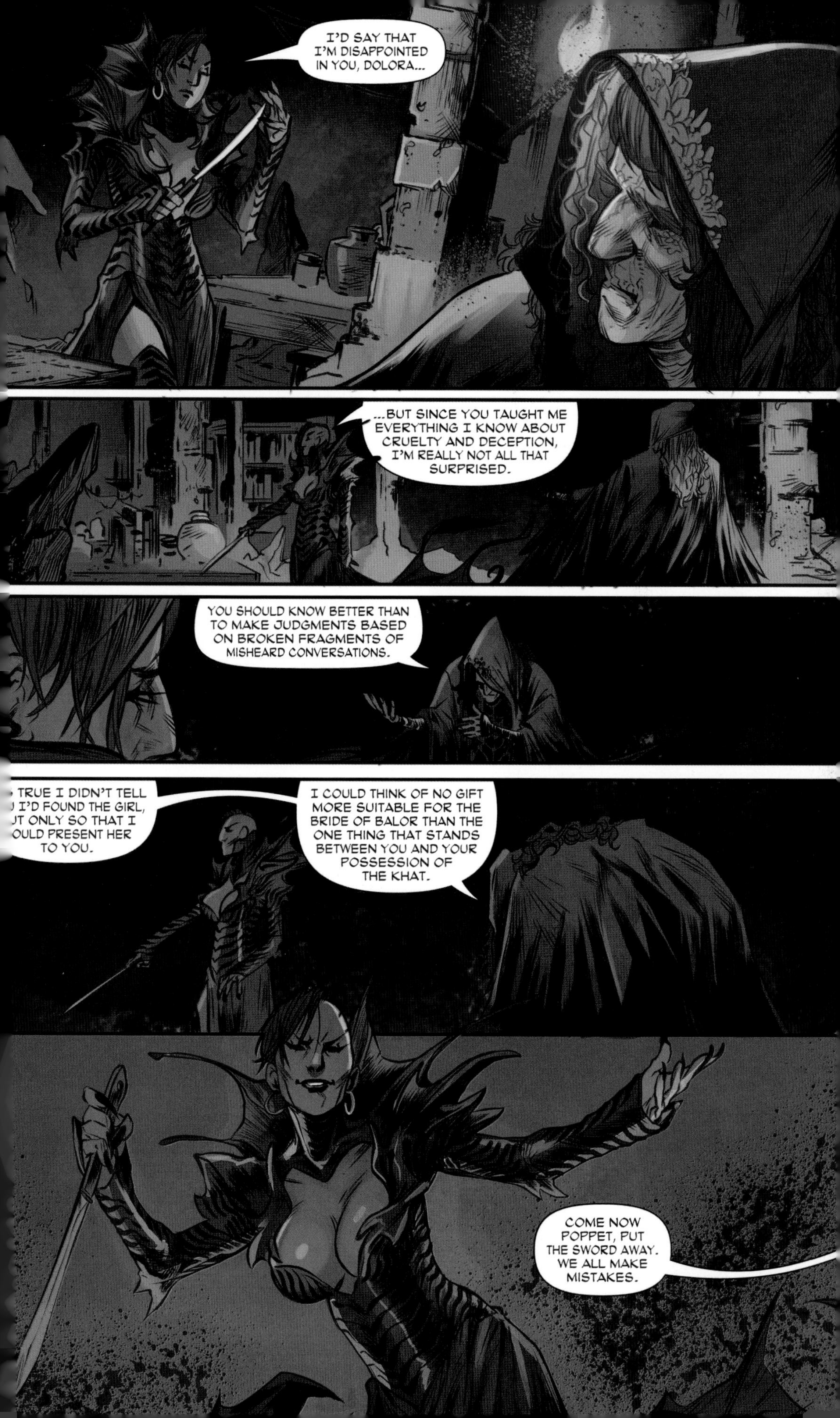
I'D SAY THAT I'M DISAPPOINTED IN YOU, DOLORA...
...BUT SINCE YOU TAUGHT ME EVERYTHING I KNOW ABOUT CRUELTY AND DECEPTION, I'M REALLY NOT ALL THAT SURPRISED.
YOU SHOULD KNOW BETTER THAN TO MAKE JUDGMENTS BASED ON BROKEN FRAGMENTS OF MISHEARD CONVERSATIONS.
TRUE I DIDN'T TELL I'D FOUND THE GIRL, UT ONLY SO THAT I OULD PRESENT HER TO YOU.
I COULD THINK OF NO GIFT MORE SUITABLE FOR THE BRIDE OF BALOR THAN THE ONE THING THAT STANDS BETWEEN YOU AND YOUR POSSESSION OF THE KHAT.
COME NOW POPPET, PUT THE SWORD AWAY. WE ALL MAKE MISTAKES.

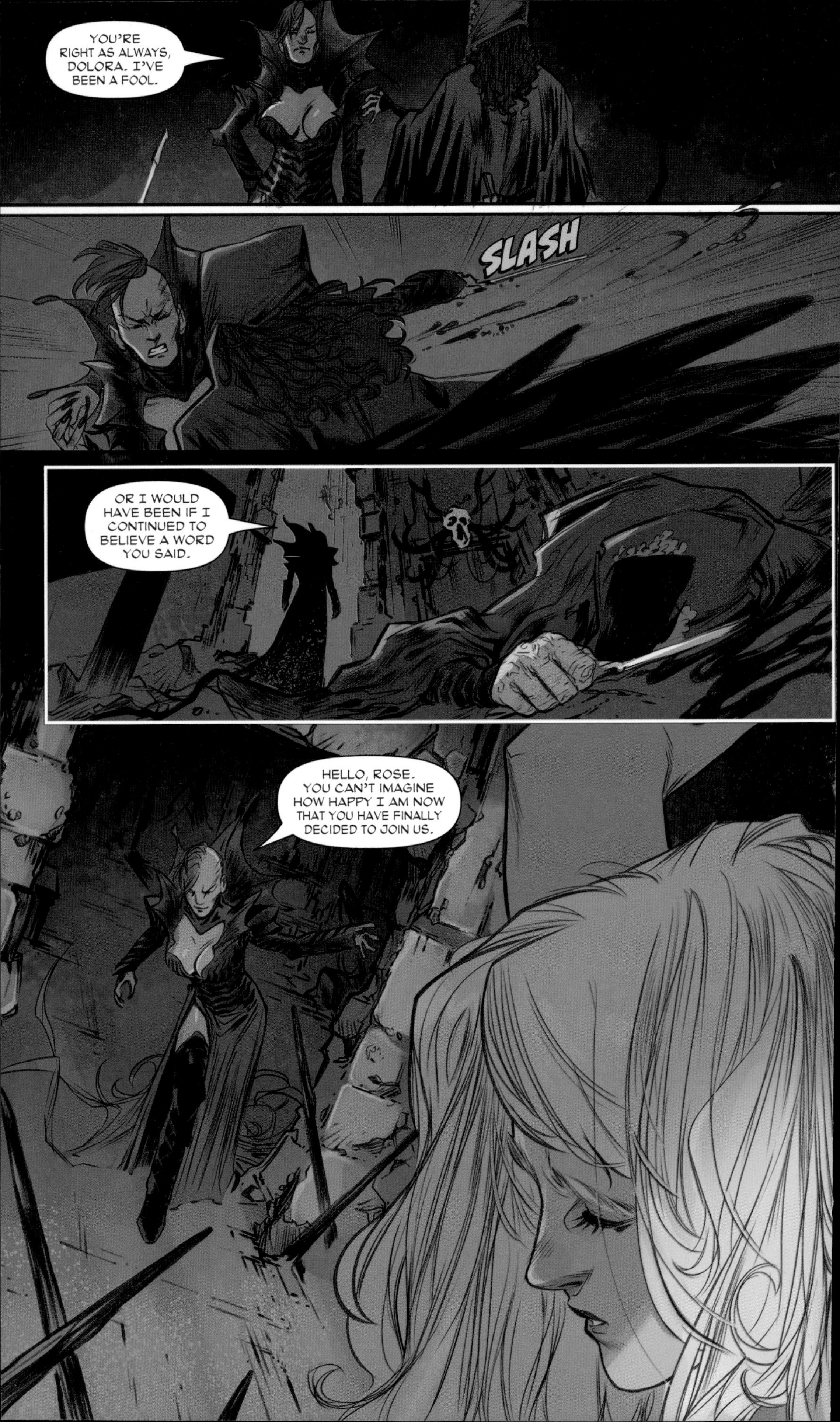
YOU'RE RIGHT AS ALWAYS, DOLORA. I'VE BEEN A FOOL.
SLASH
OR I WOULD HAVE BEEN IF I CONTINUED TO BELIEVE A WORD YOU SAID.
HELLO, ROSE. YOU CAN'T IMAGINE HOW HAPPY I AM NOW THAT YOU HAVE FINALLY DECIDED TO JOIN US.

FIFTEEN

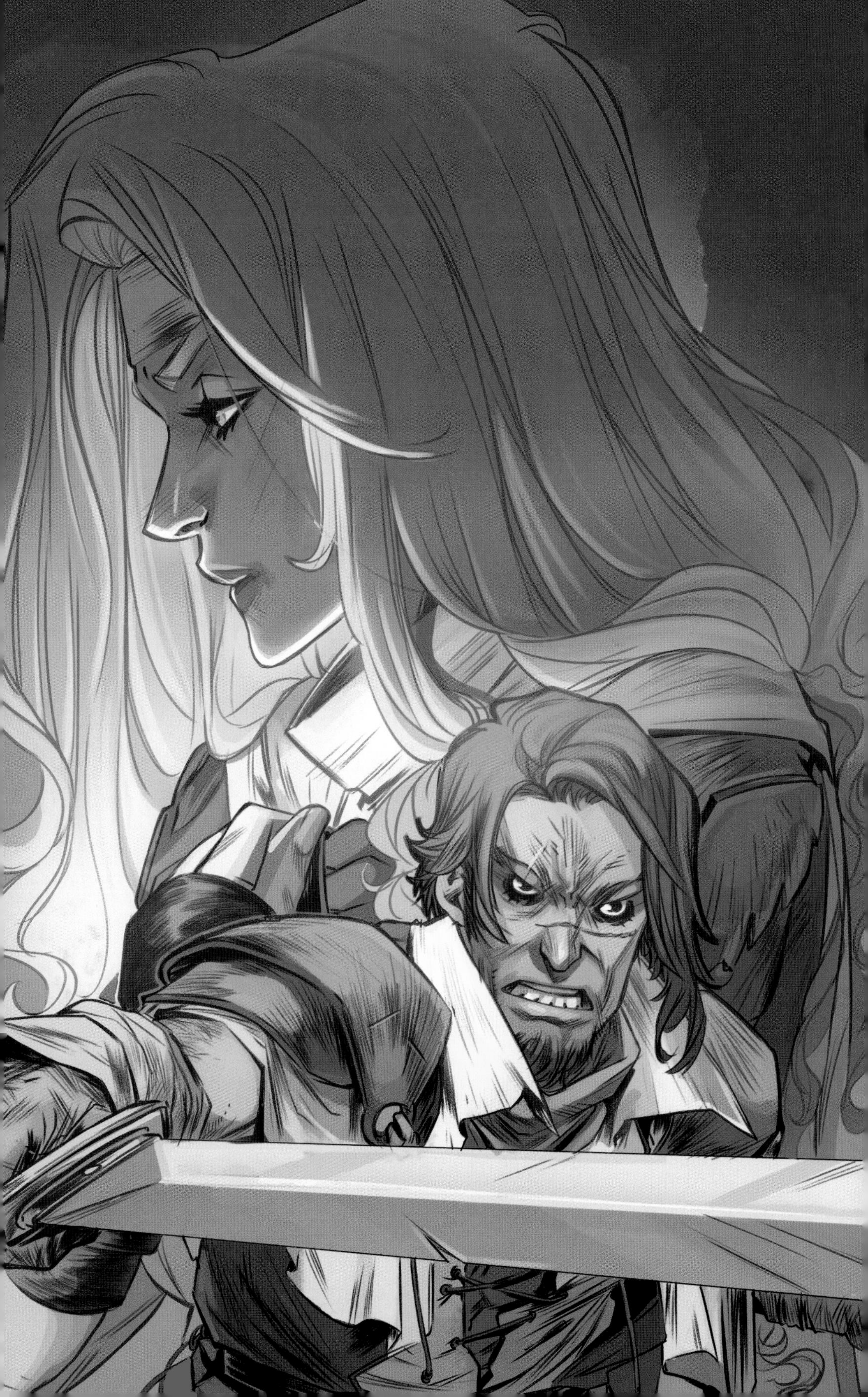

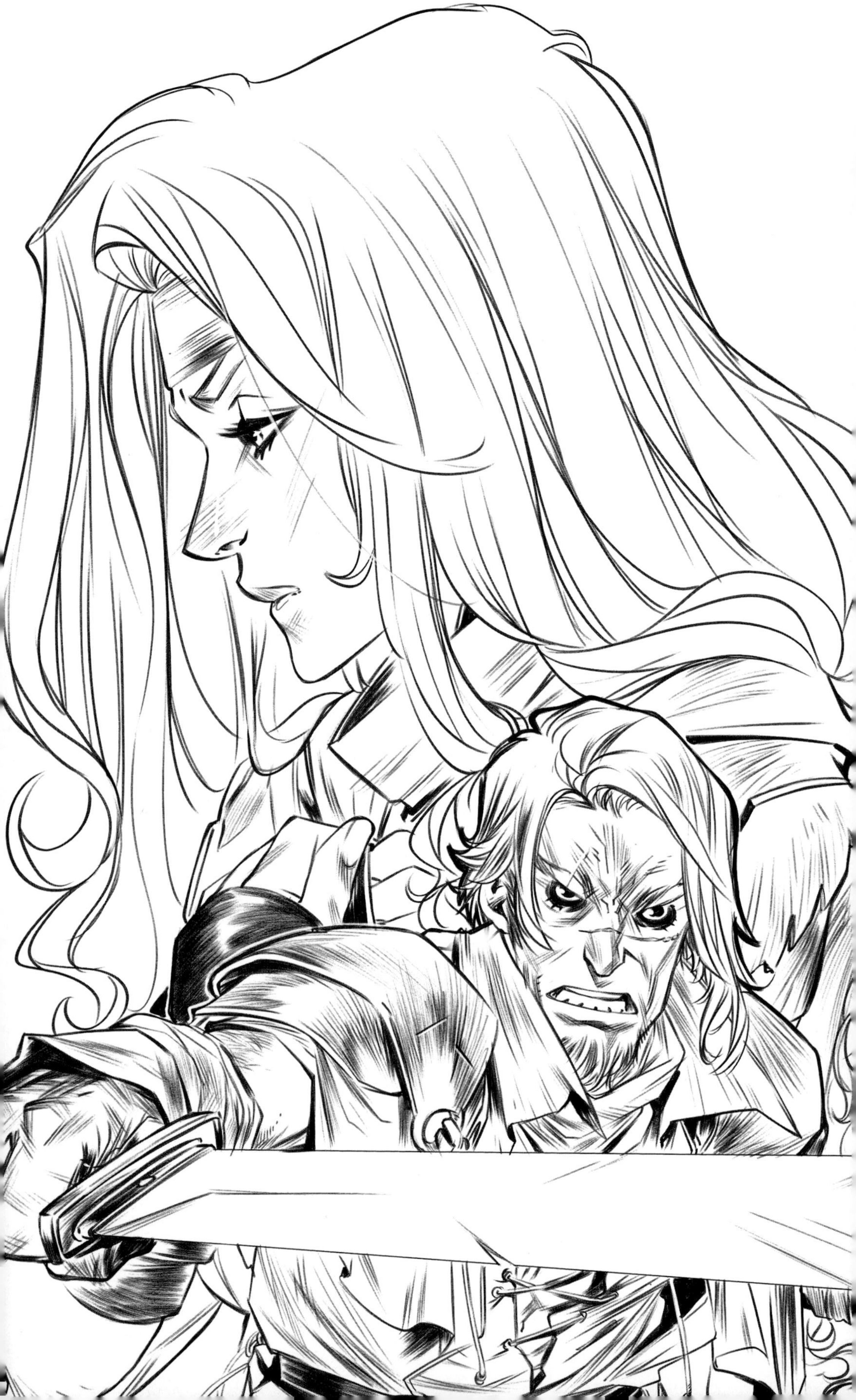

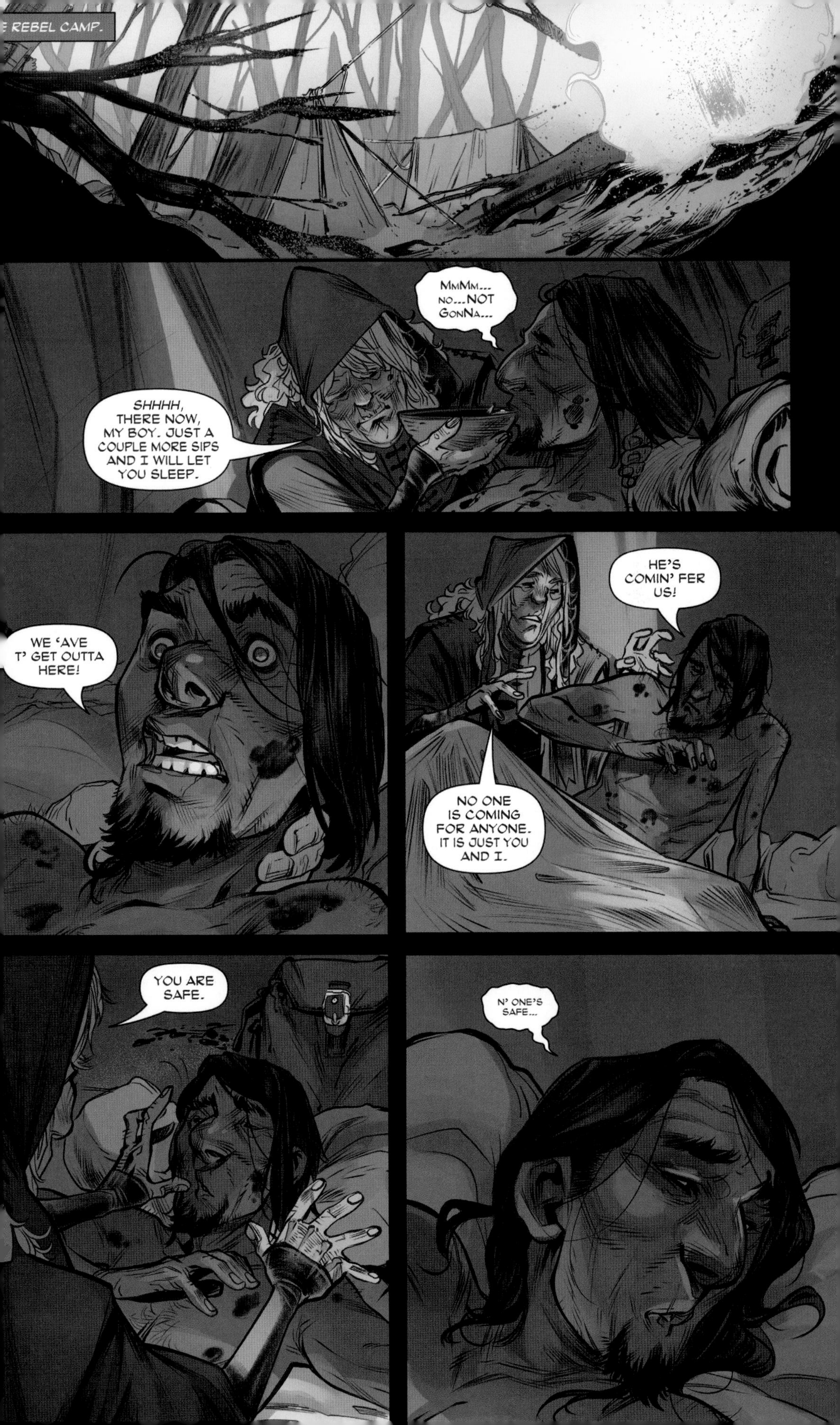

REBEL CAMP.
MMMM... NO...NOT GONNA...
SHHHH, THERE NOW, MY BOY. JUST A COUPLE MORE SIPS AND I WILL LET YOU SLEEP.
WE 'AVE T' GET OUTTA HERE!
HE'S COMIN' FER US!
NO ONE IS COMING FOR ANYONE. IT IS JUST YOU AND I.
YOU ARE SAFE.
N' ONE'S SAFE...

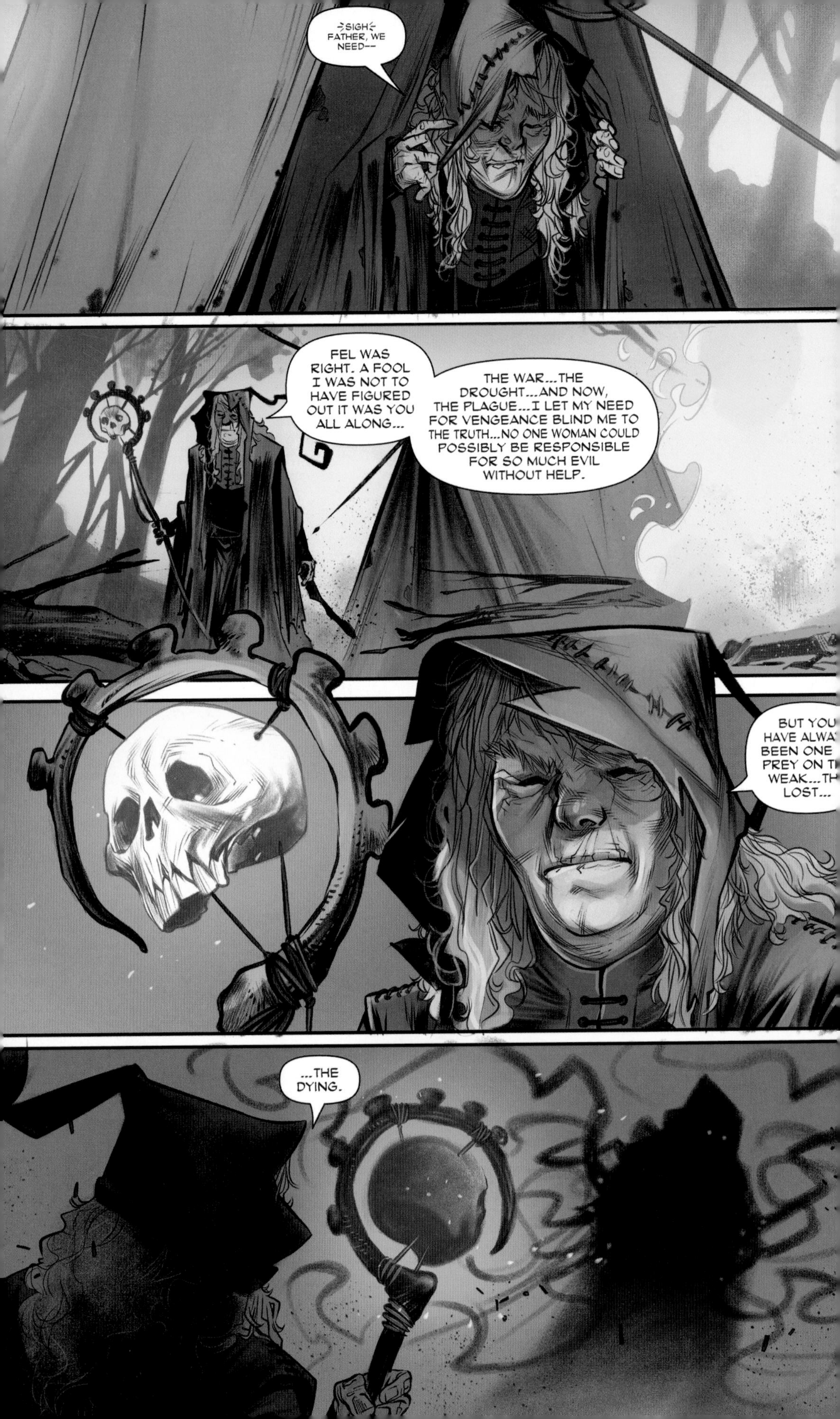

⊰SIGH⊱ FATHER, WE NEED--
FEL WAS RIGHT. A FOOL I WAS NOT TO HAVE FIGURED OUT IT WAS YOU ALL ALONG...
THE WAR...THE DROUGHT...AND NOW, THE PLAGUE...I LET MY NEED FOR VENGEANCE BLIND ME TO THE TRUTH...NO ONE WOMAN COULD POSSIBLY BE RESPONSIBLE FOR SO MUCH EVIL WITHOUT HELP.
BUT YOU HAVE ALWA BEEN ONE PREY ON T WEAK...TH LOST...
...THE DYING.

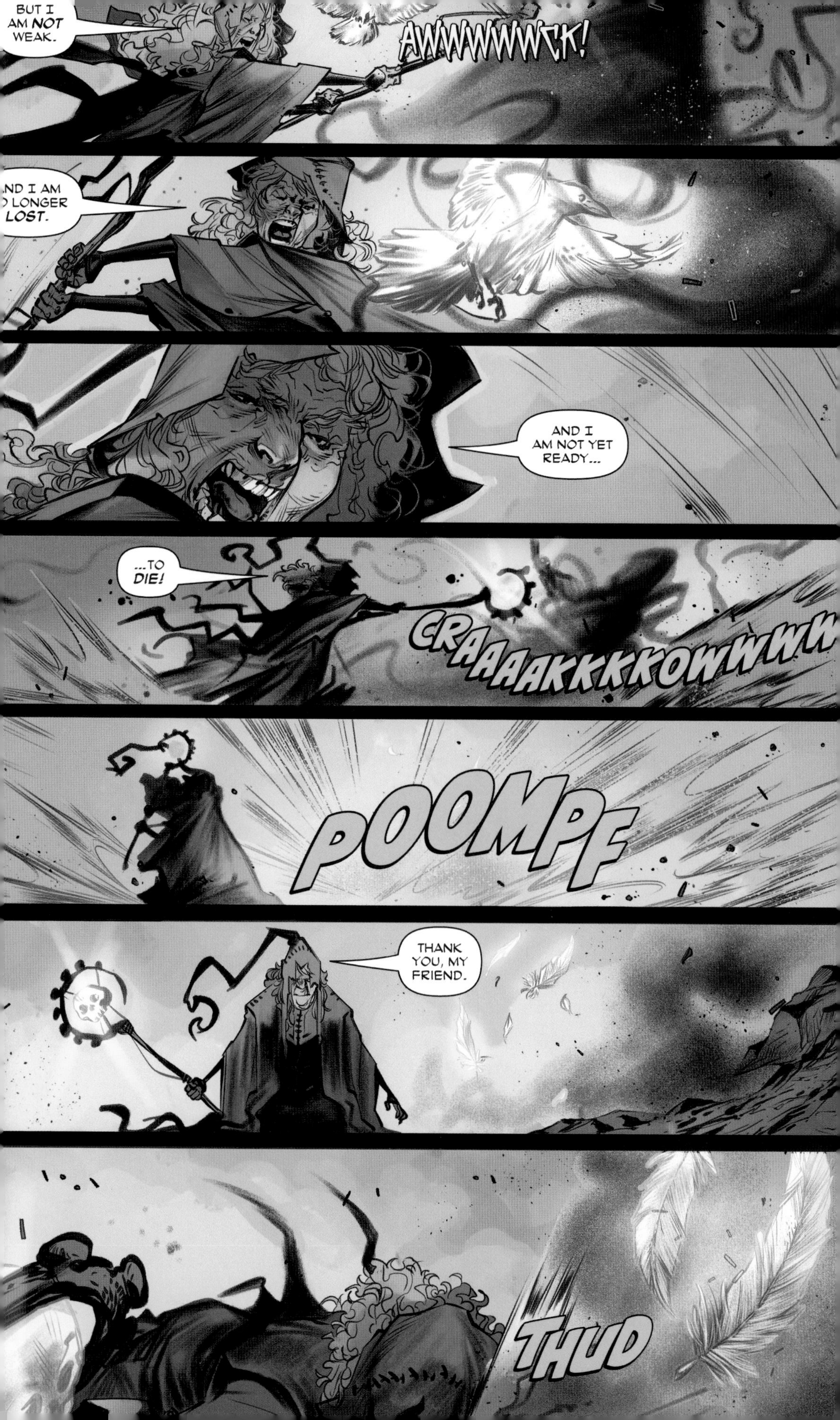
BUT I AM NOT WEAK.
AWWWWWCK!
ND I AM
O LONGER
LOST.
AND I AM NOT YET READY...
...TO DIE!
CRAAAAKKKKKOWWWWW
POOMPF
THANK YOU, MY FRIEND.
THUD

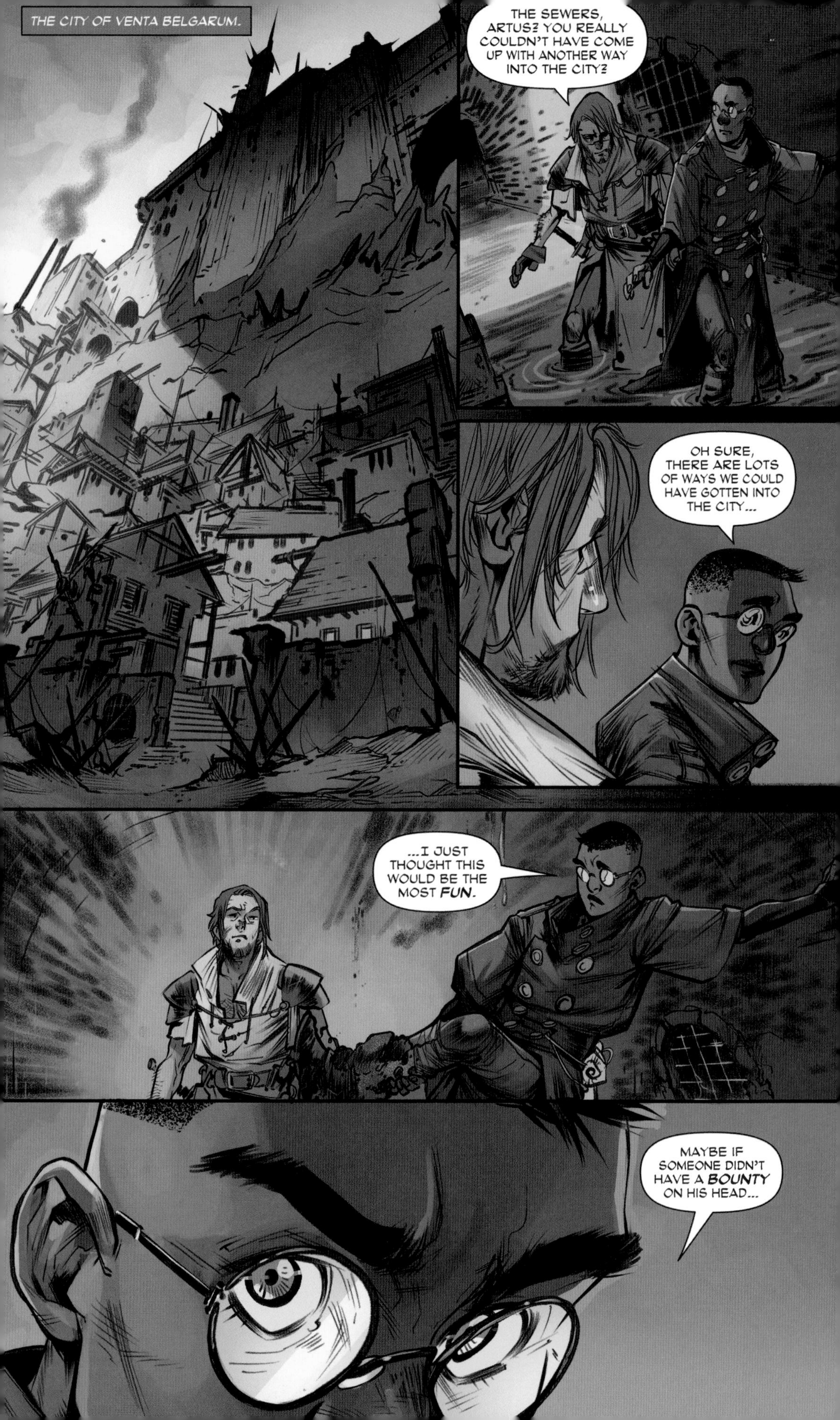
THE CITY OF VENTA BELGARUM.
THE SEWERS, ARTUS? YOU REALLY COULDN'T HAVE COME UP WITH ANOTHER WAY INTO THE CITY?
OH SURE, THERE ARE LOTS OF WAYS WE COULD HAVE GOTTEN INTO THE CITY...
...I JUST THOUGHT THIS WOULD BE THE MOST FUN.
MAYBE IF SOMEONE DIDN'T HAVE A BOUNTY ON HIS HEAD...

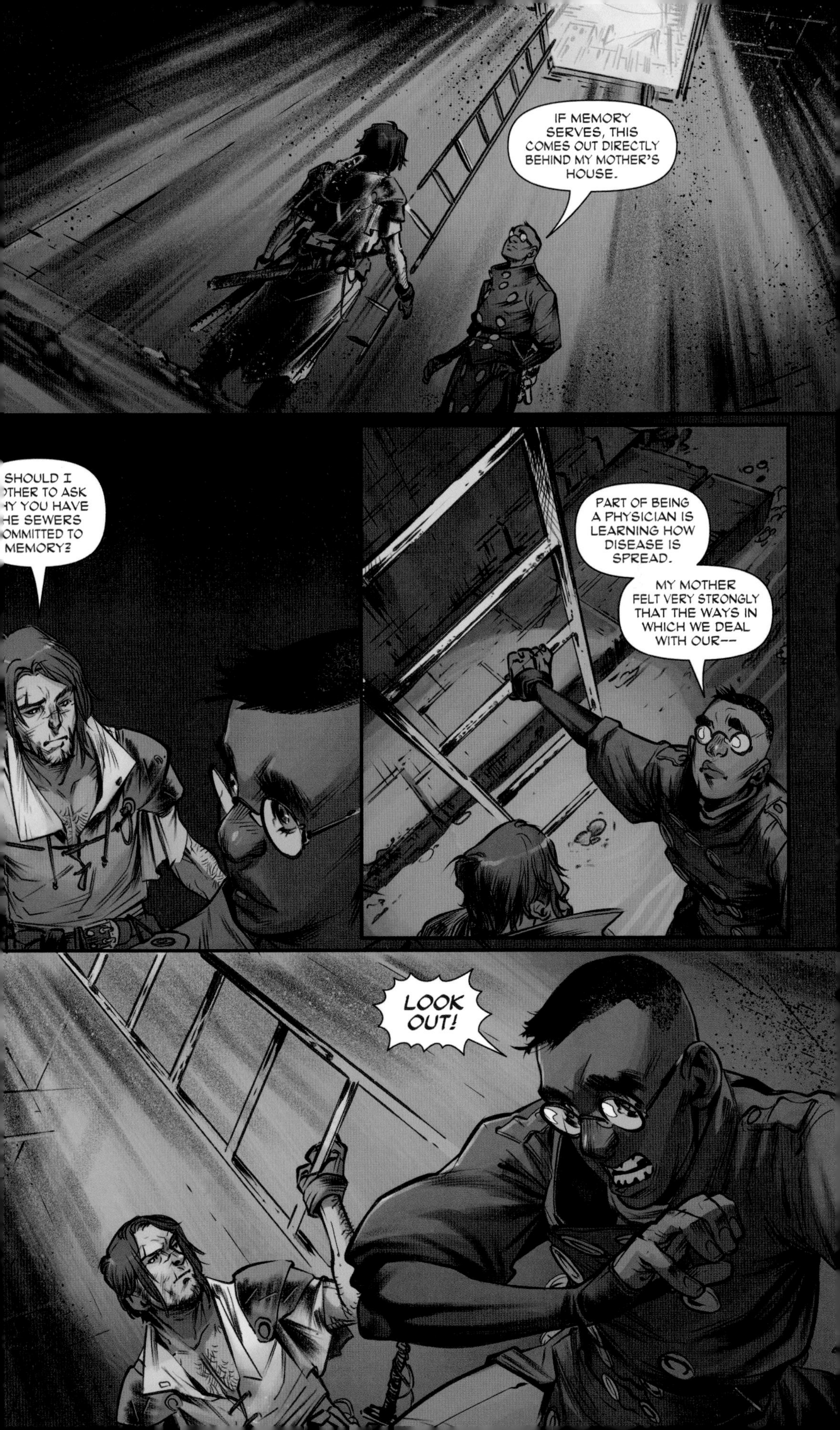
IF MEMORY SERVES, THIS COMES OUT DIRECTLY BEHIND MY MOTHER'S HOUSE.
SHOULD I OTHER TO ASK HY YOU HAVE HE SEWERS OMMITTED TO MEMORY?
PART OF BEING A PHYSICIAN IS LEARNING HOW DISEASE IS SPREAD.
MY MOTHER FELT VERY STRONGLY THAT THE WAYS IN WHICH WE DEAL WITH OUR--
LOOK OUT!

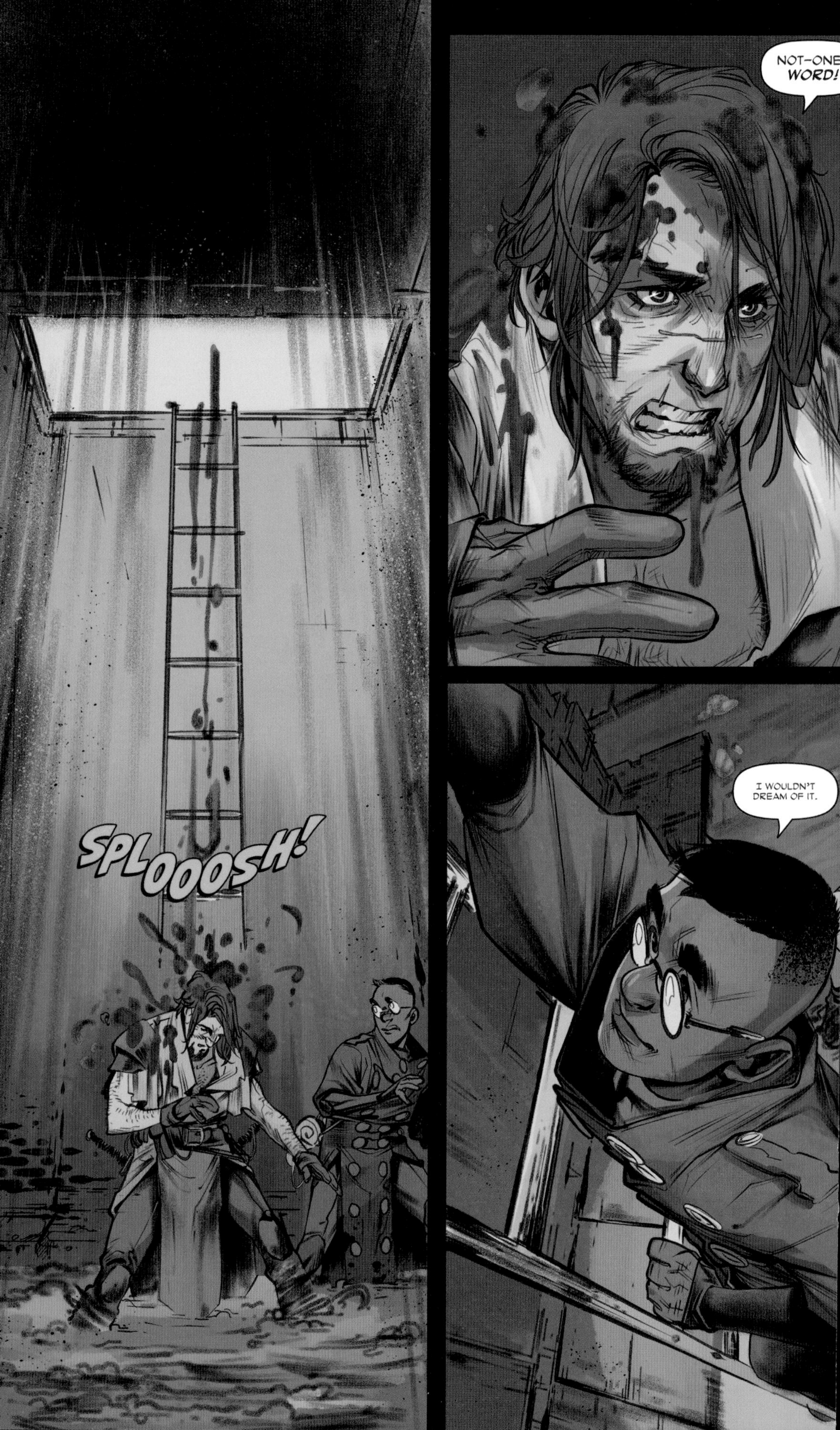
SPLOOOSH!
NOT-ONE WORD!
I WOULDN'T DREAM OF IT.

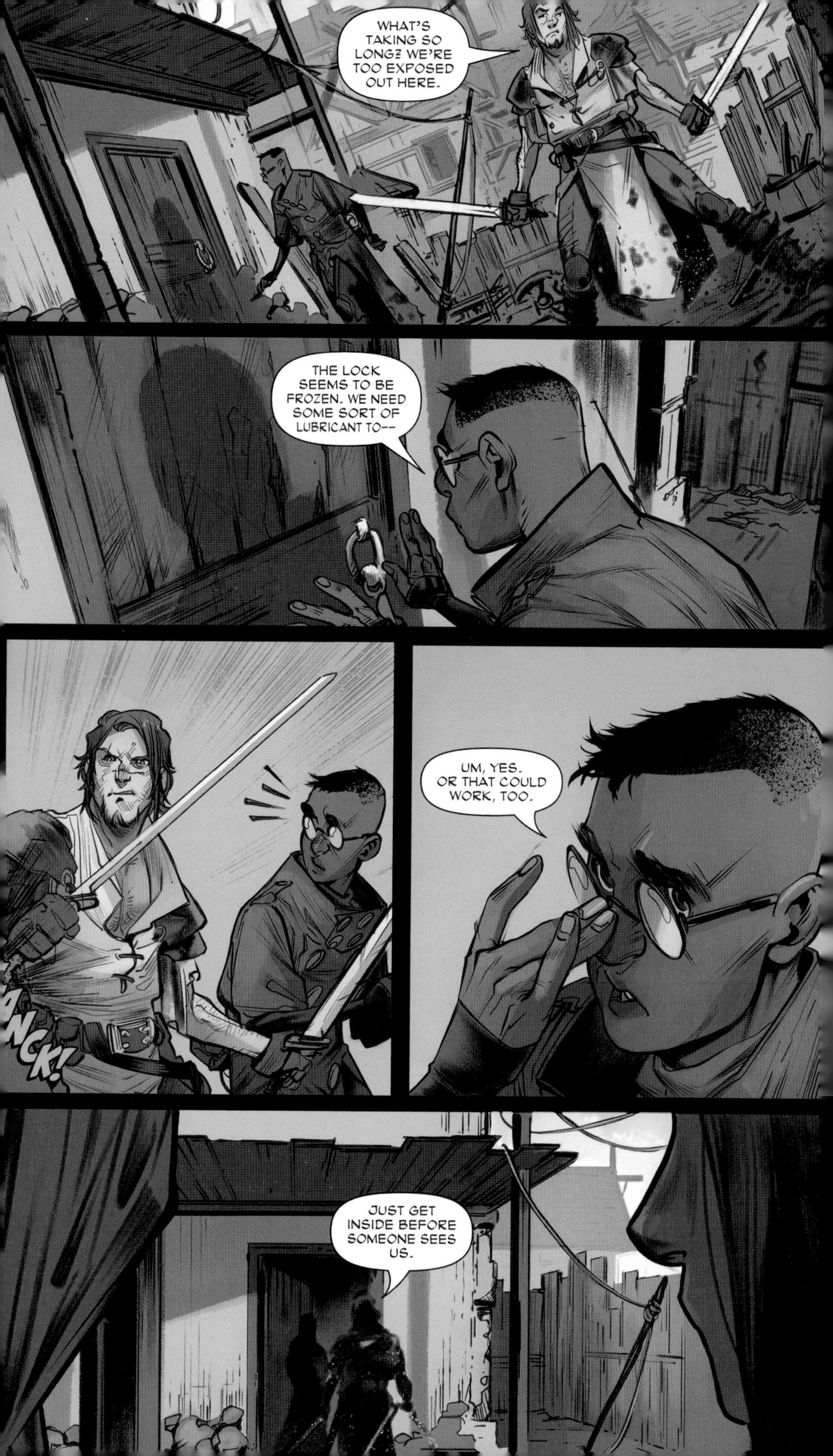
WHAT'S TAKING SO LONG? WE'RE TOO EXPOSED OUT HERE.
THE LOCK SEEMS TO BE FROZEN. WE NEED SOME SORT OF LUBRICANT TO--
ANCK!
UM, YES. OR THAT COULD WORK, TOO.
JUST GET INSIDE BEFORE SOMEONE SEES US.

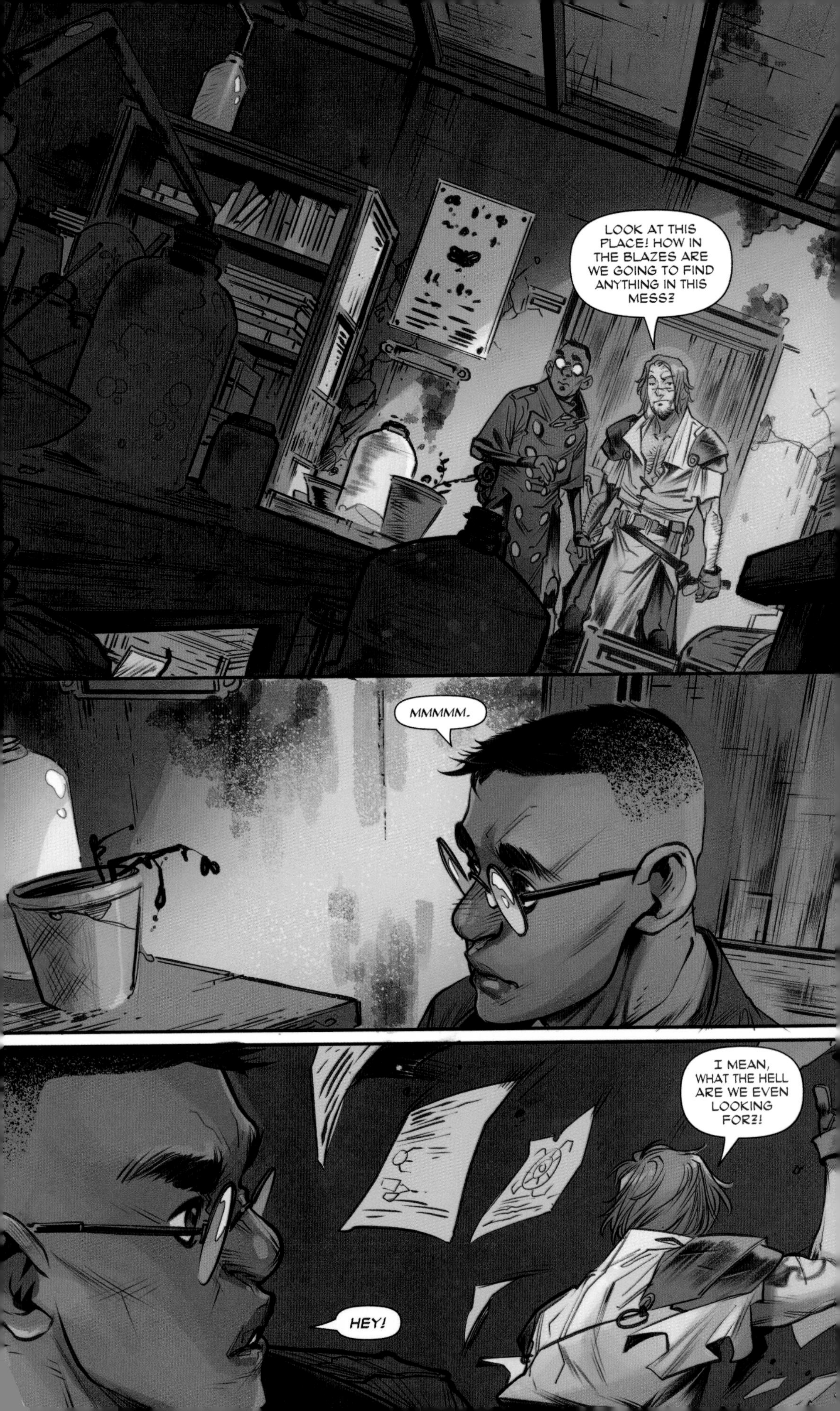
LOOK AT THIS PLACE! HOW IN THE BLAZES ARE WE GOING TO FIND ANYTHING IN THIS MESS?
MMMMM.
I MEAN, WHAT THE HELL ARE WE EVEN LOOKING FOR?!
HEY!

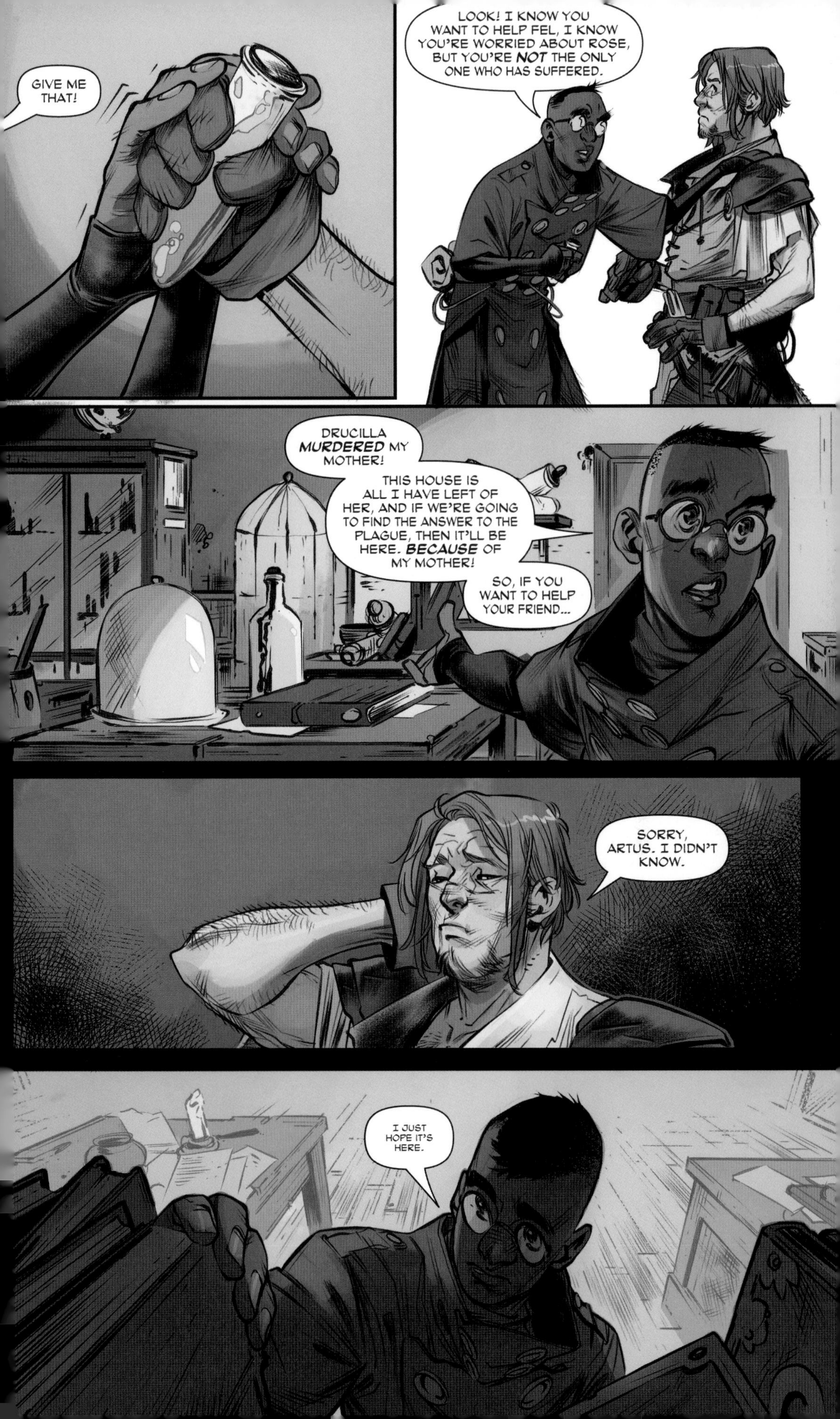
GIVE ME THAT!
LOOK! I KNOW YOU WANT TO HELP FEL, I KNOW YOU'RE WORRIED ABOUT ROSE, BUT YOU'RE NOT THE ONLY ONE WHO HAS SUFFERED.
DRUCILLA MURDERED MY MOTHER!
THIS HOUSE IS ALL I HAVE LEFT OF HER, AND IF WE'RE GOING TO FIND THE ANSWER TO THE PLAGUE, THEN IT'LL BE HERE. BECAUSE OF MY MOTHER!
SO, IF YOU WANT TO HELP YOUR FRIEND...
SORRY, ARTUS. I DIDN'T KNOW.
I JUST HOPE IT'S HERE.

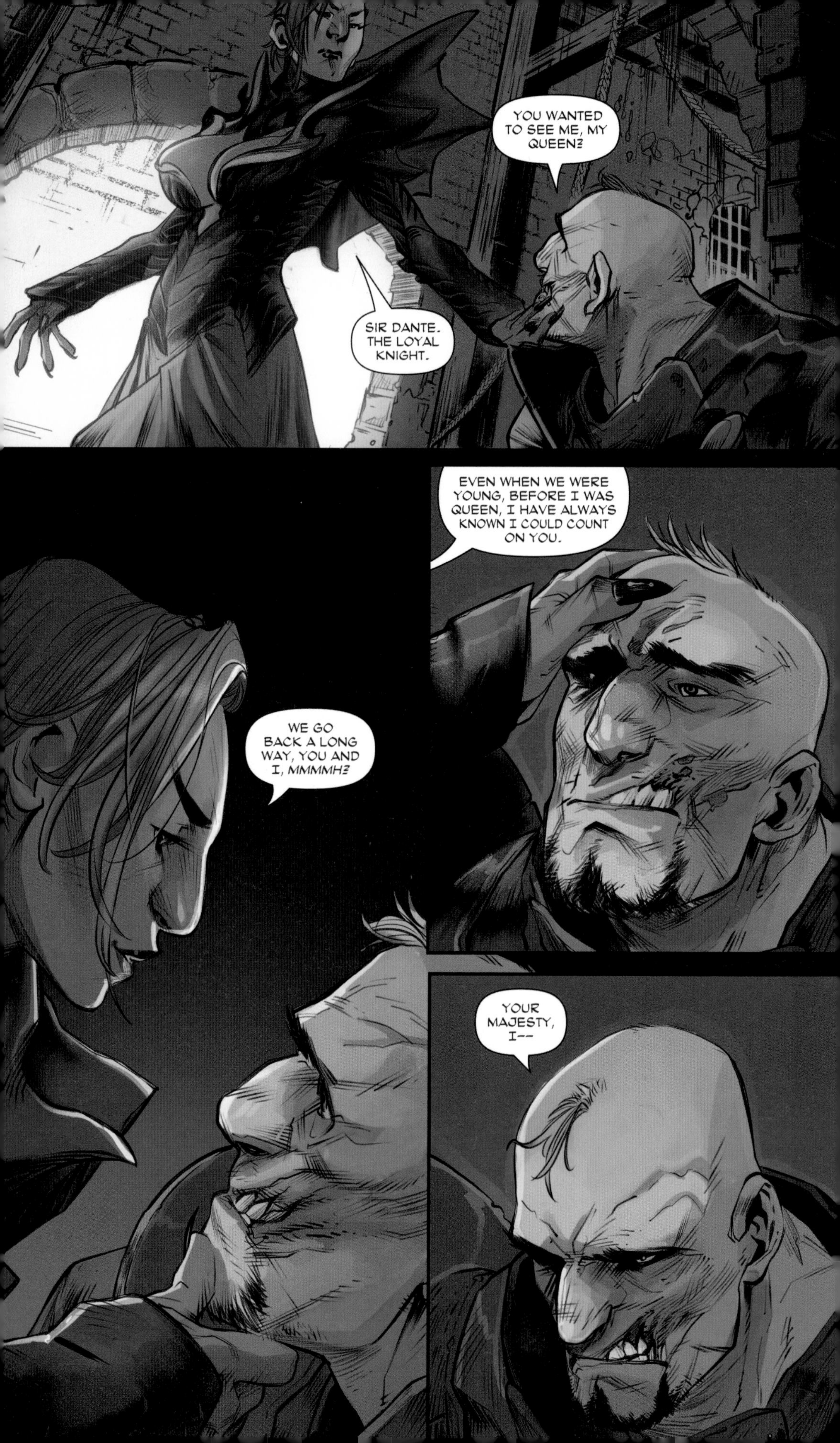
YOU WANTED TO SEE ME, MY QUEEN?
SIR DANTE. THE LOYAL KNIGHT.
EVEN WHEN WE WERE YOUNG, BEFORE I WAS QUEEN, I HAVE ALWAYS KNOWN I COULD COUNT ON YOU.
WE GO BACK A LONG WAY, YOU AND I, MMMMH?
YOUR MAJESTY, I--

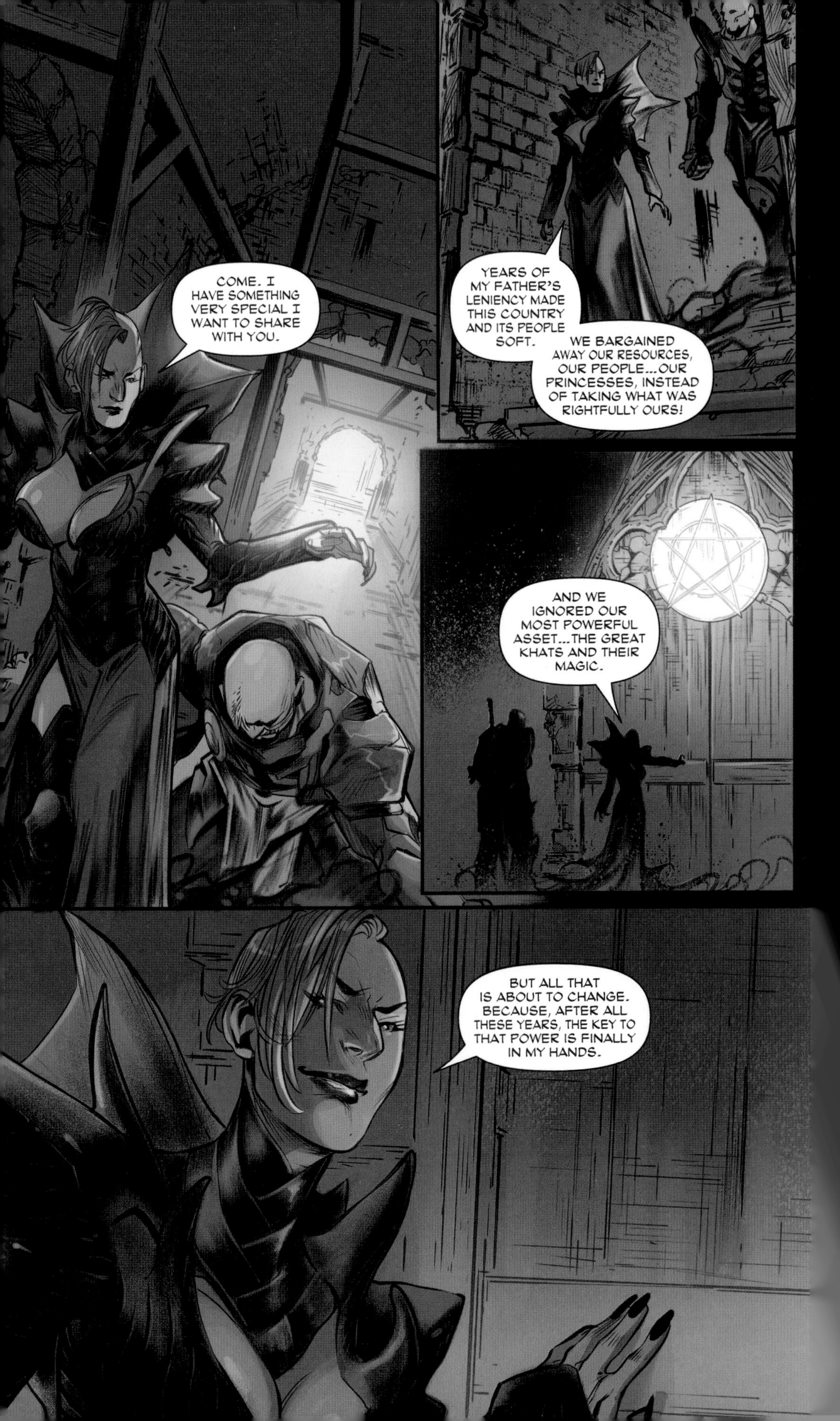
COME. I HAVE SOMETHING VERY SPECIAL I WANT TO SHARE WITH YOU.
YEARS OF MY FATHER'S LENIENCY MADE THIS COUNTRY AND ITS PEOPLE SOFT.
WE BARGAINED AWAY OUR RESOURCES, OUR PEOPLE...OUR PRINCESSES, INSTEAD OF TAKING WHAT WAS RIGHTFULLY OURS!
AND WE IGNORED OUR MOST POWERFUL ASSET...THE GREAT KHATS AND THEIR MAGIC.
BUT ALL THAT IS ABOUT TO CHANGE. BECAUSE, AFTER ALL THESE YEARS, THE KEY TO THAT POWER IS FINALLY IN MY HANDS.

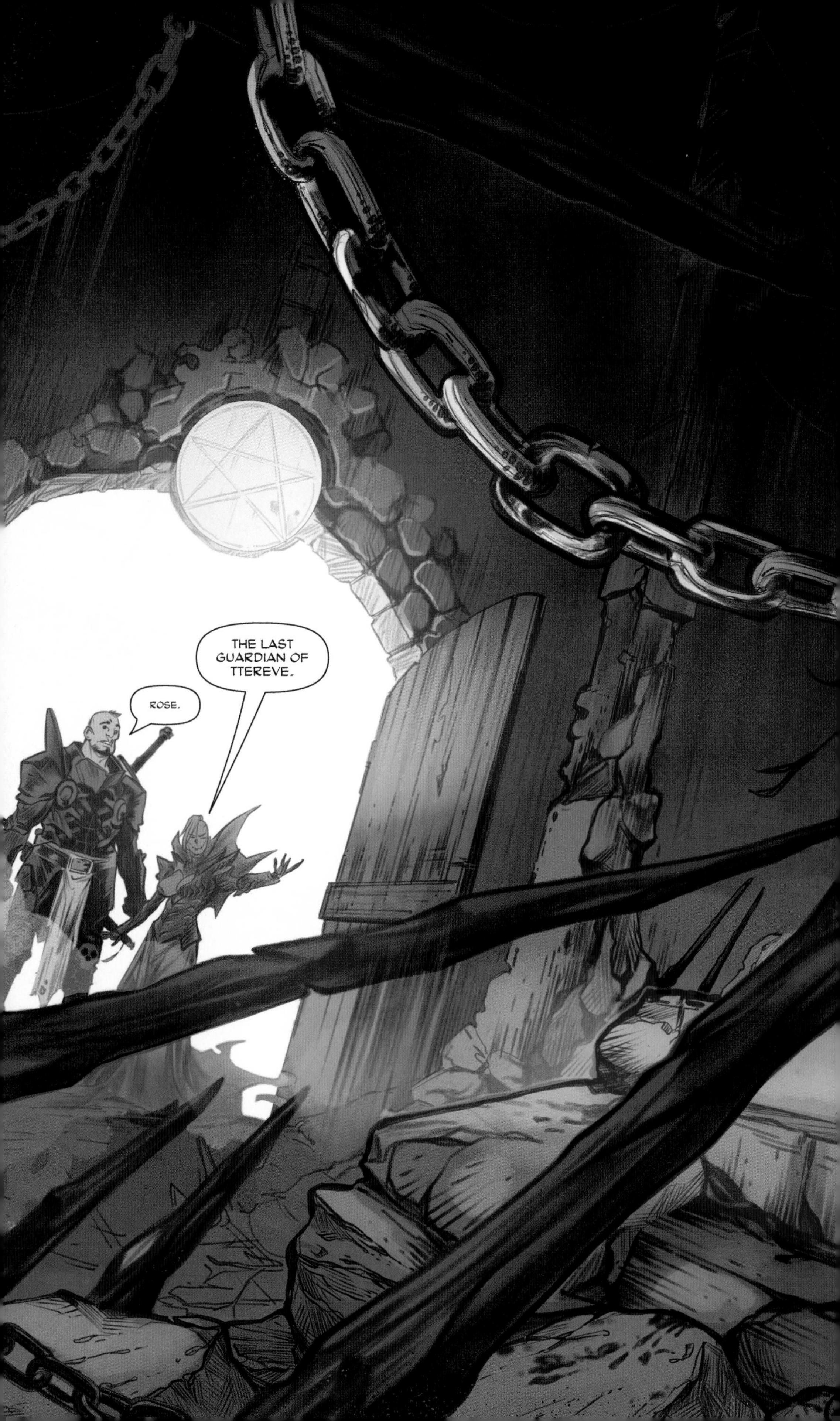
ROSE.
THE LAST GUARDIAN OF TTEREVE.

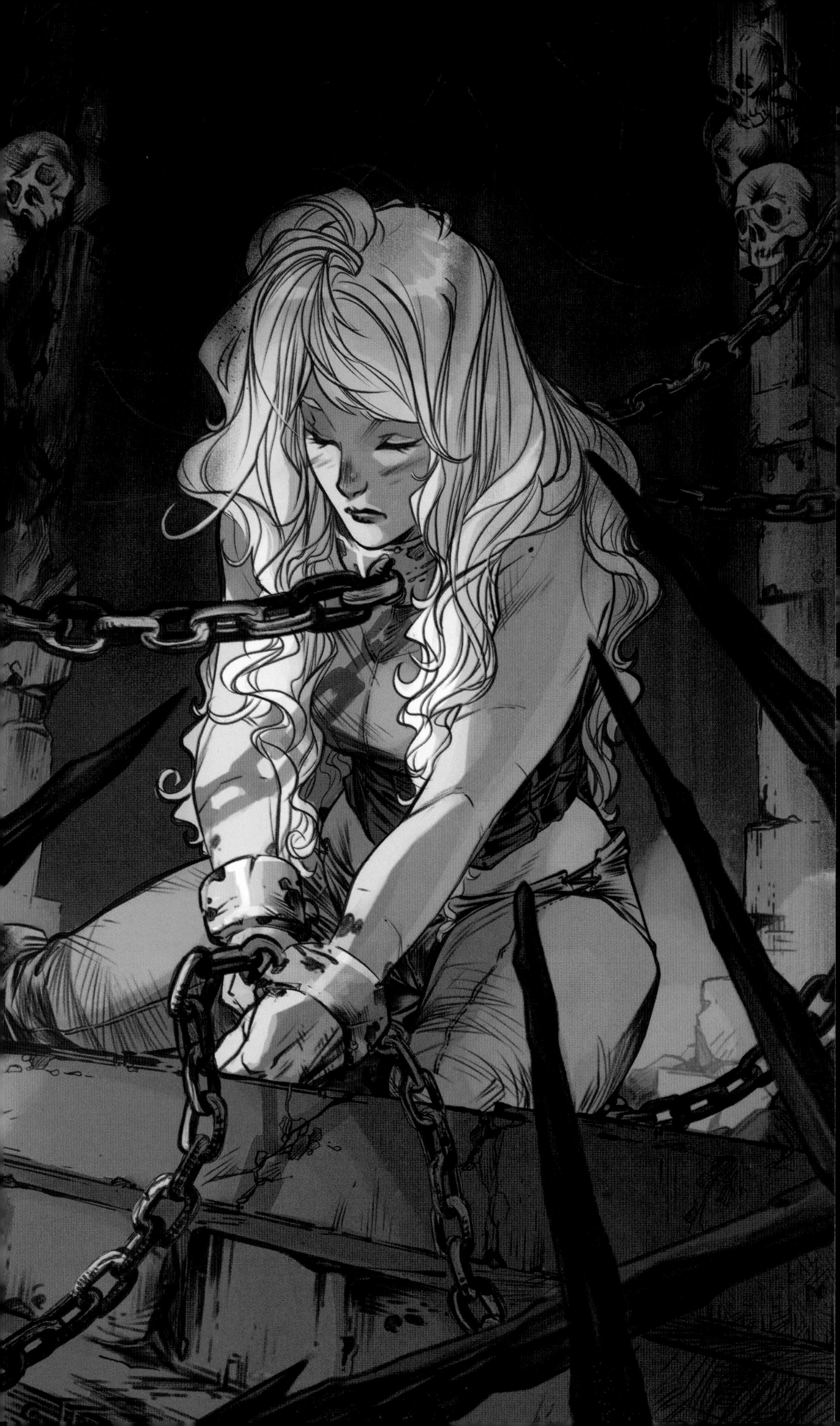

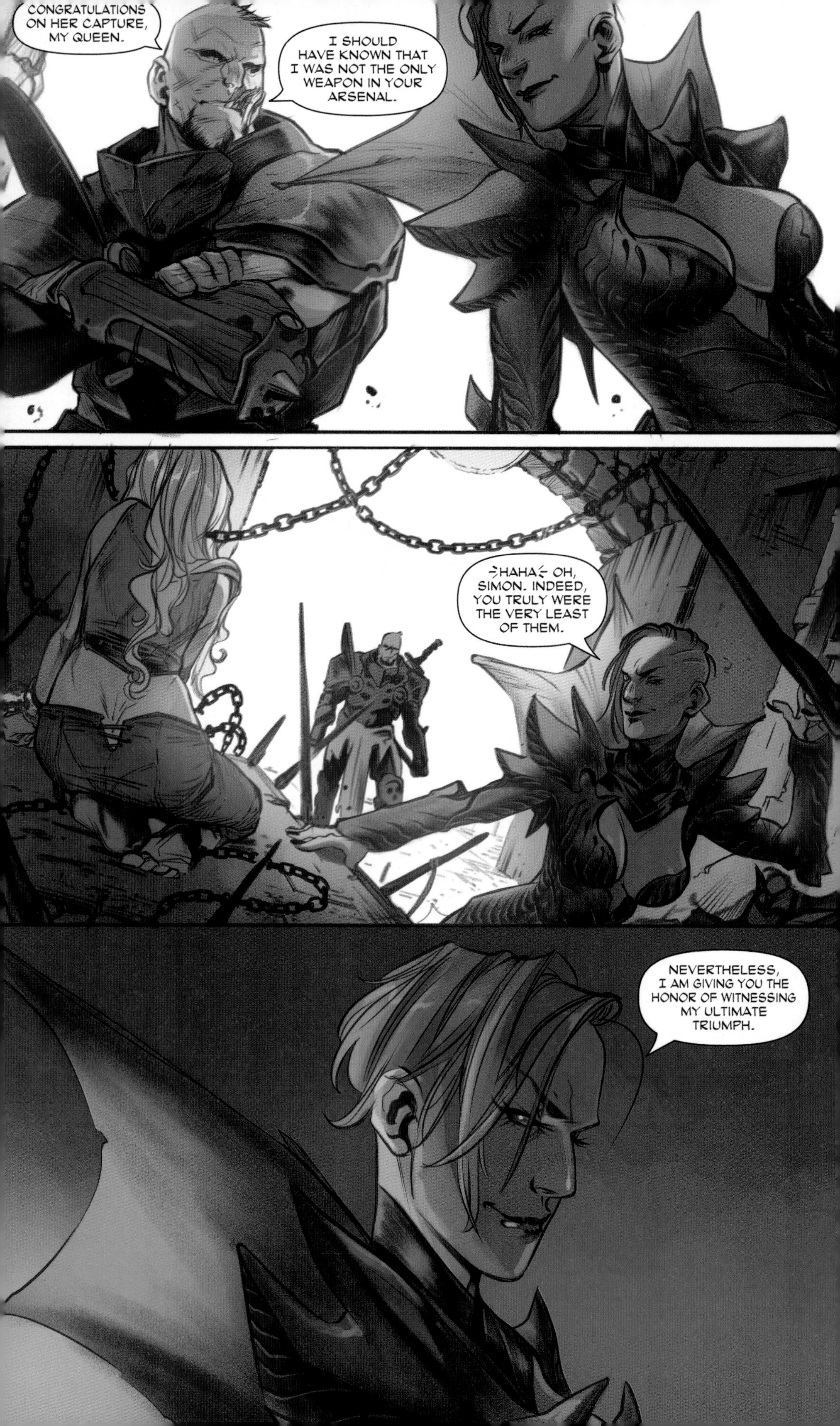
CONGRATULATIONS ON HER CAPTURE, MY QUEEN.
I SHOULD HAVE KNOWN THAT I WAS NOT THE ONLY WEAPON IN YOUR ARSENAL.
HAHA OH, SIMON. INDEED, YOU TRULY WERE THE VERY LEAST OF THEM.
NEVERTHELESS, I AM GIVING YOU THE HONOR OF WITNESSING MY ULTIMATE TRIUMPH.

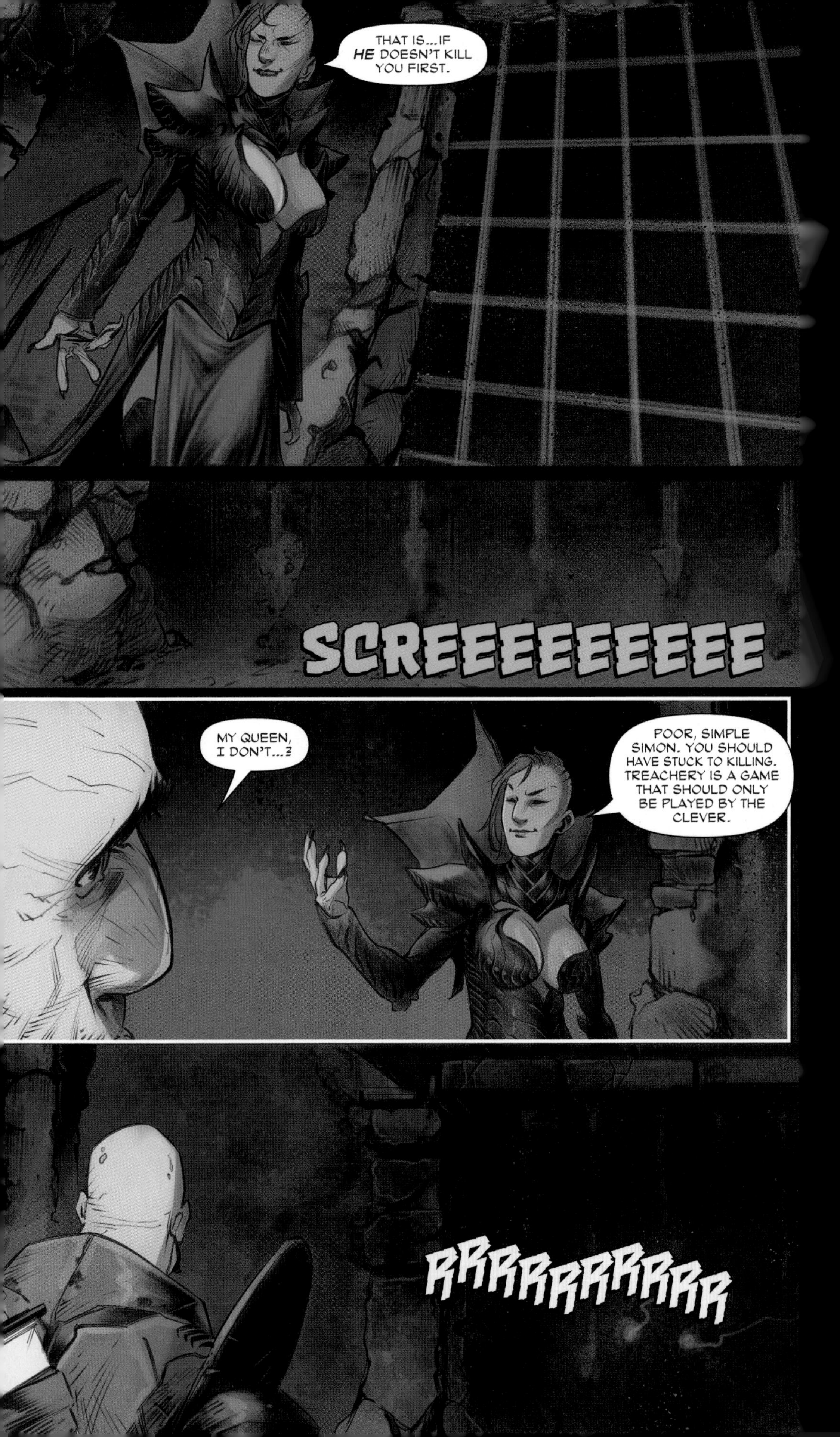
THAT IS...IF HE DOESN'T KILL YOU FIRST.
SCREEEEEEEEEE
MY QUEEN, I DON'T...?
POOR, SIMPLE SIMON. YOU SHOULD HAVE STUCK TO KILLING. TREACHERY IS A GAME THAT SHOULD ONLY BE PLAYED BY THE CLEVER.
RRRRRRRRRR

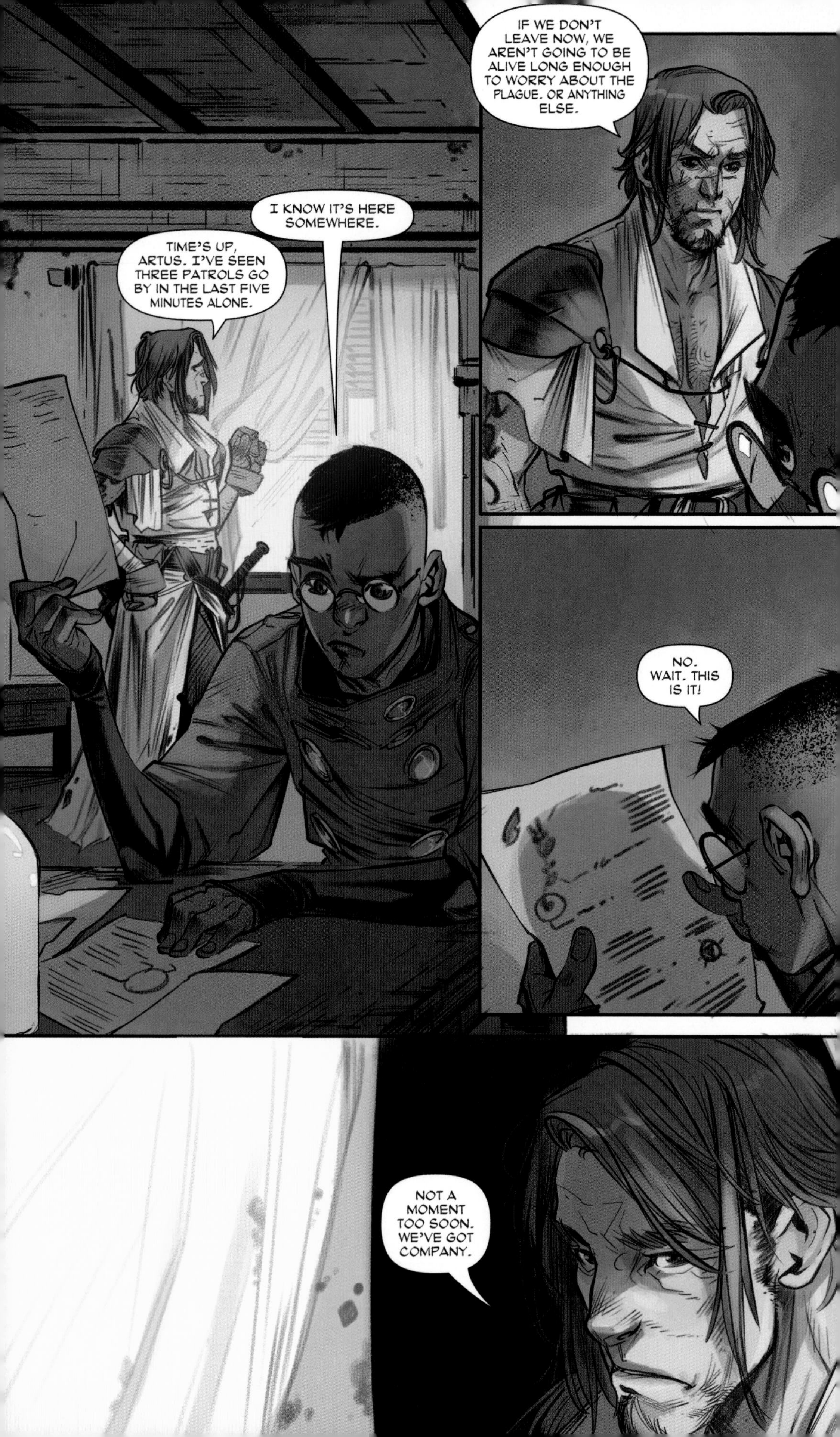
TIME'S UP, ARTUS. I'VE SEEN THREE PATROLS GO BY IN THE LAST FIVE MINUTES ALONE.
I KNOW IT'S HERE SOMEWHERE.
IF WE DON'T LEAVE NOW, WE AREN'T GOING TO BE ALIVE LONG ENOUGH TO WORRY ABOUT THE PLAGUE. OR ANYTHING ELSE.
NO. WAIT. THIS IS IT!
NOT A MOMENT TOO SOON. WE'VE GOT COMPANY.

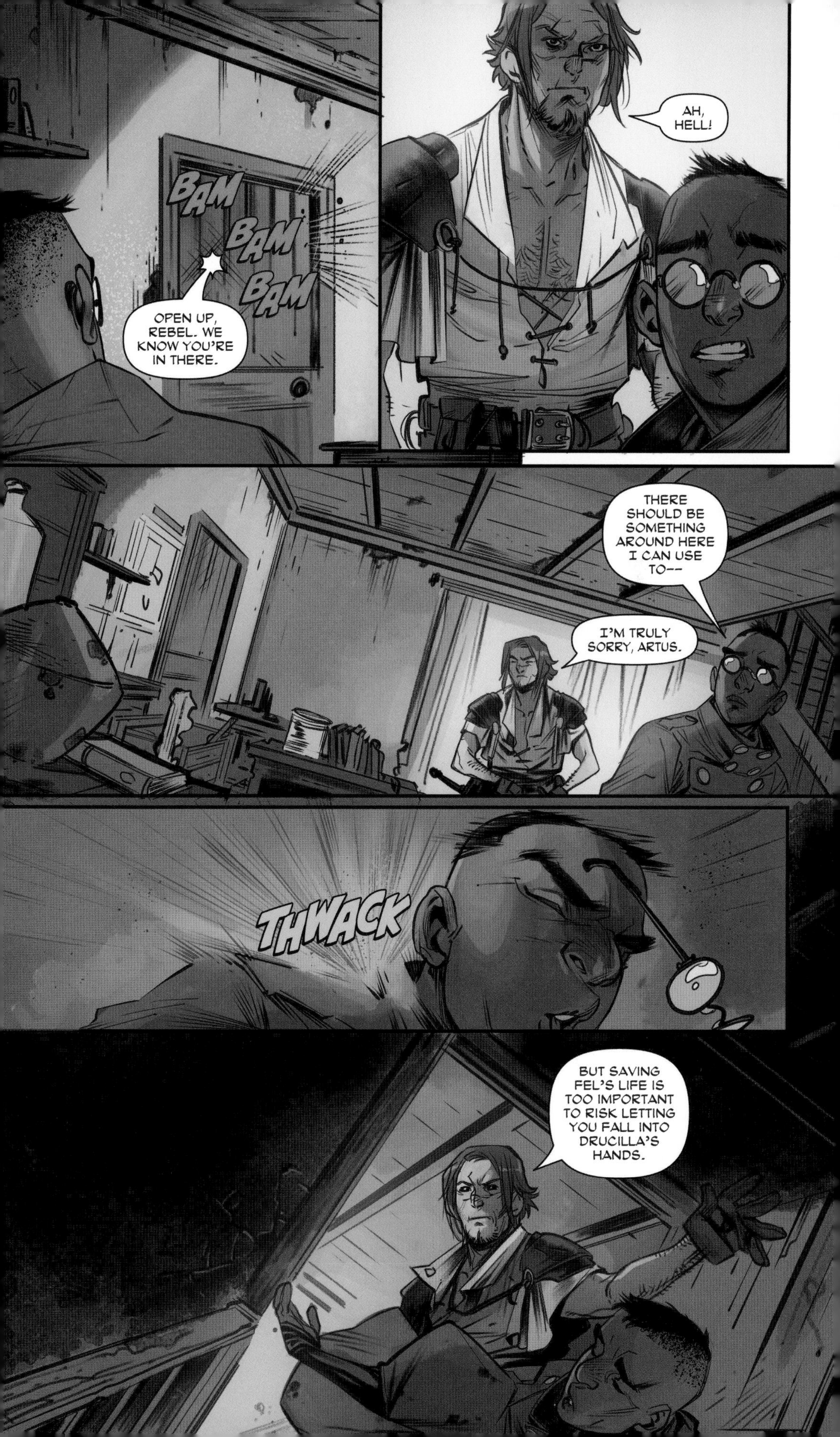
BAM
BAM
BAM
OPEN UP, REBEL. WE KNOW YOU'RE IN THERE.
AH, HELL!
THERE SHOULD BE SOMETHING AROUND HERE I CAN USE TO--
I'M TRULY SORRY, ARTUS.
THWACK
BUT SAVING FEL'S LIFE IS TOO IMPORTANT TO RISK LETTING YOU FALL INTO DRUCILLA'S HANDS.

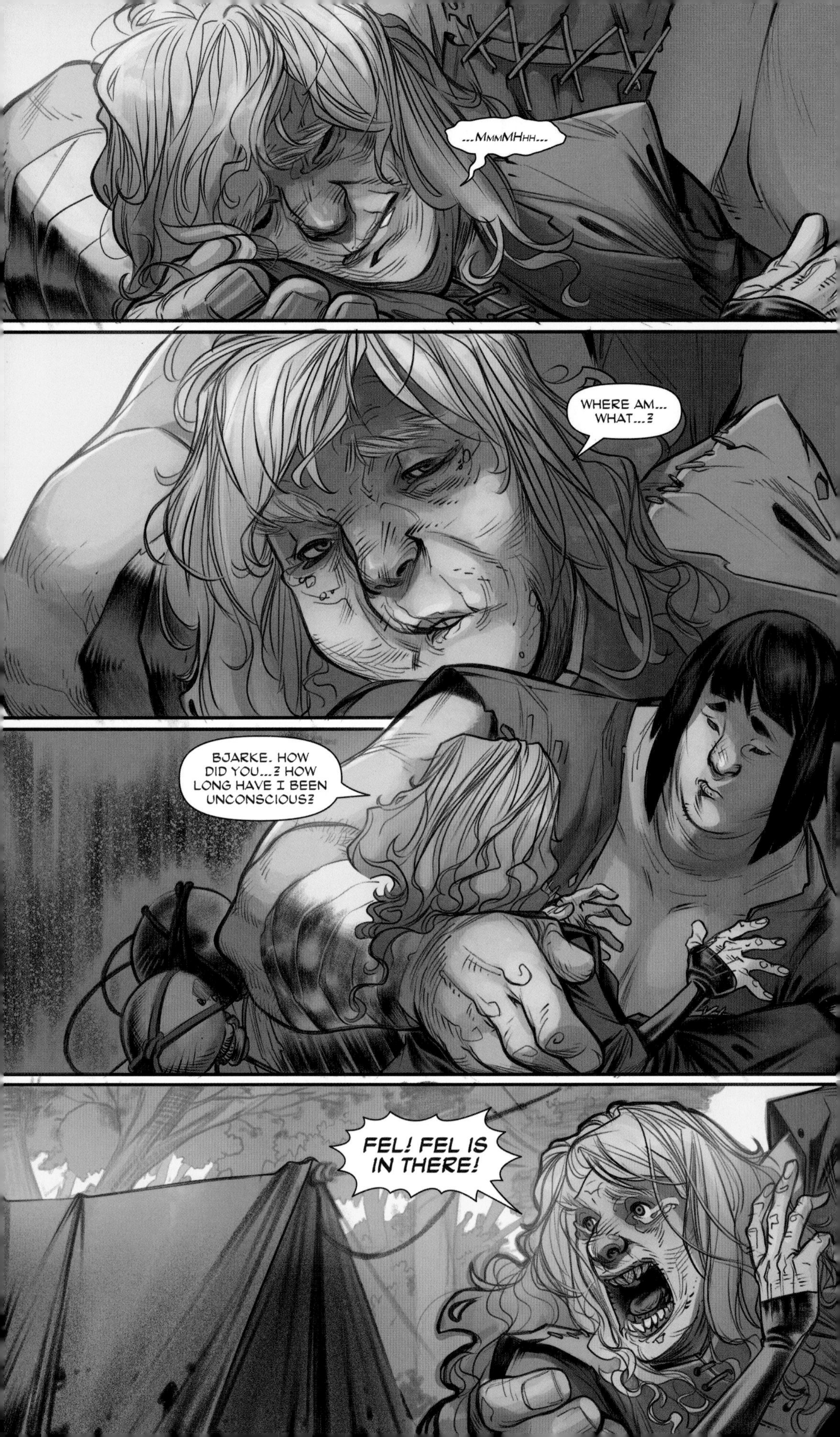
...MMMMHHH...
WHERE AM... WHAT...?
BJARKE. HOW DID YOU...? HOW LONG HAVE I BEEN UNCONSCIOUS?
FEL! FEL IS IN THERE!

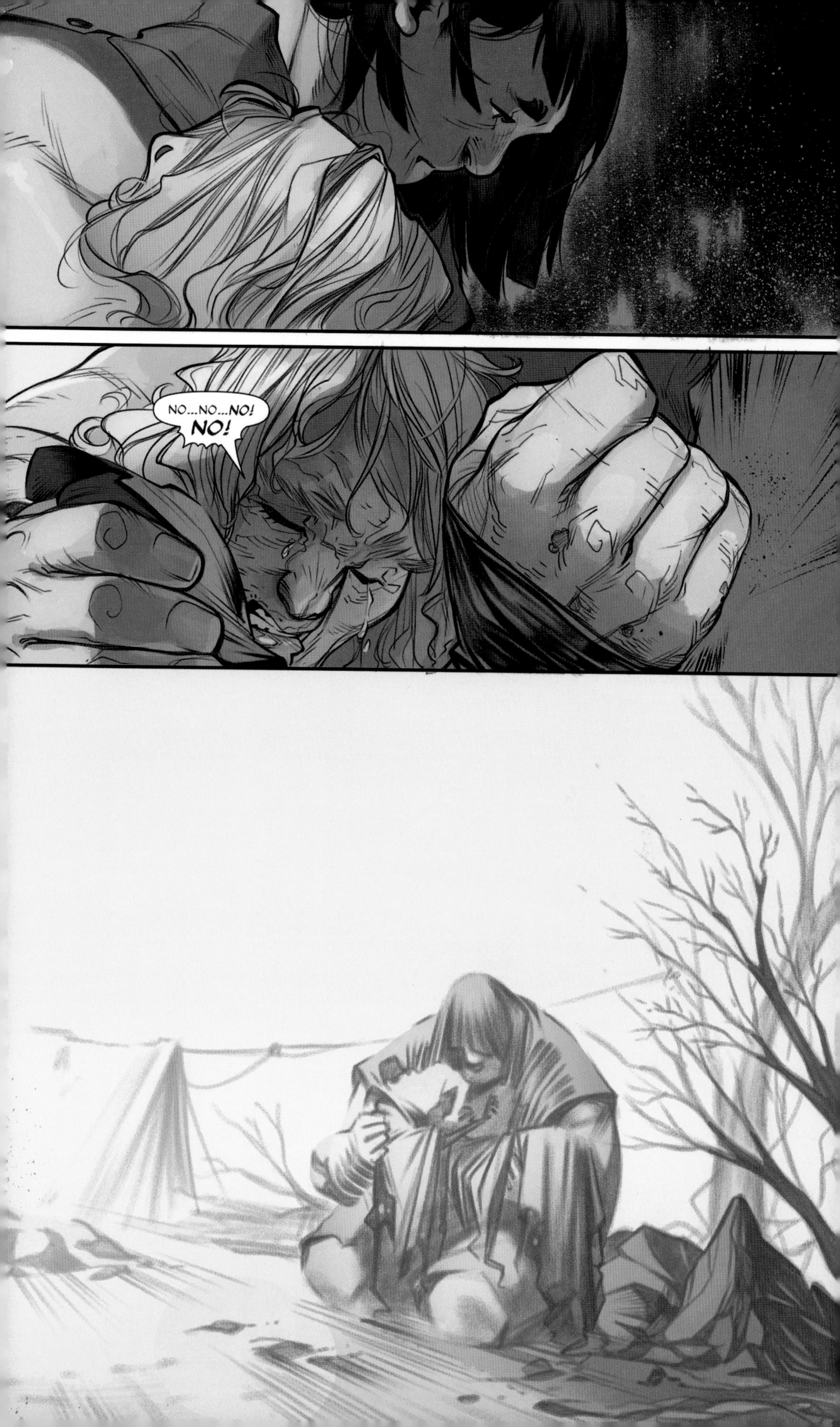
NO...NO...NO!
NO!

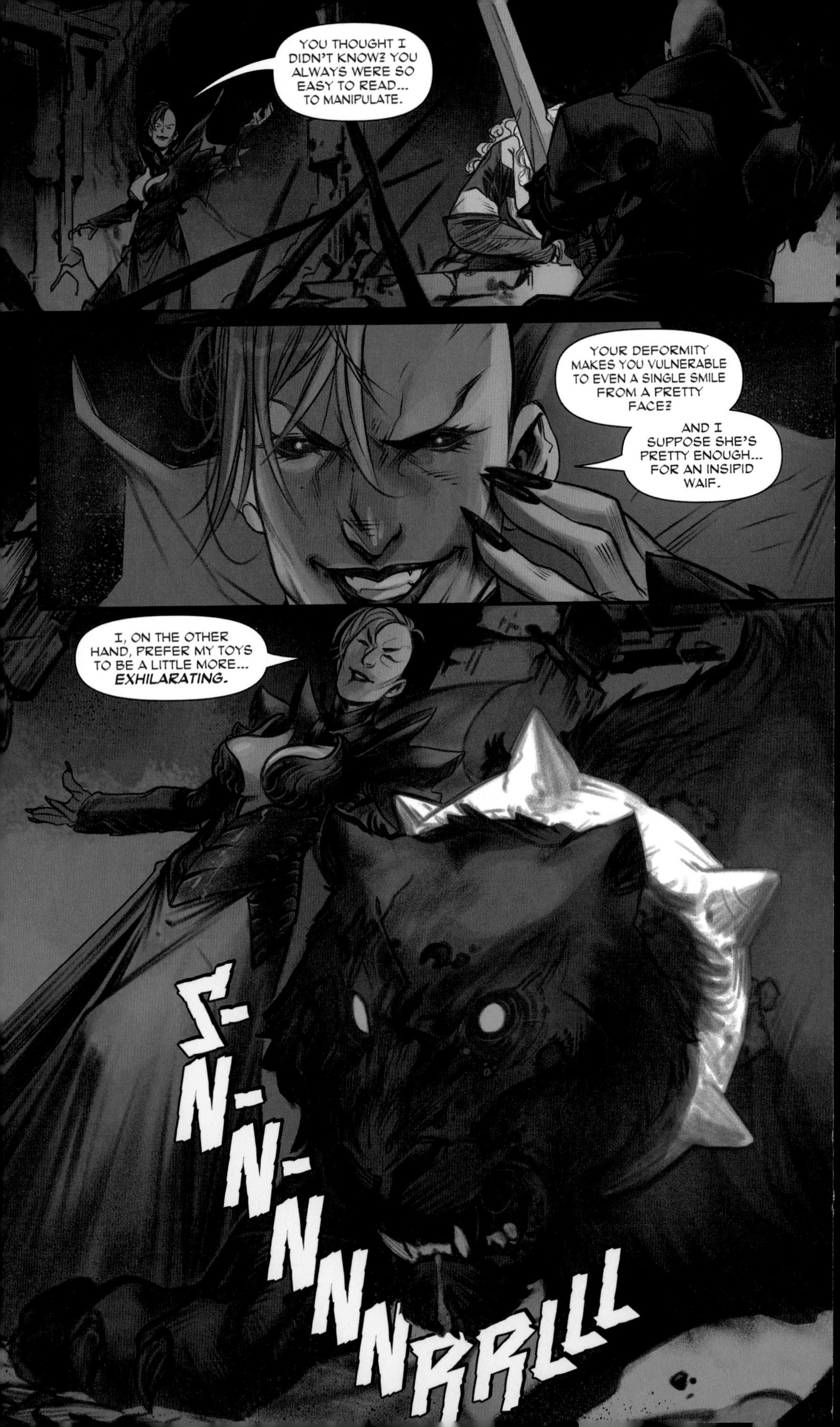
YOU THOUGHT I DIDN'T KNOW? YOU ALWAYS WERE SO EASY TO READ... TO MANIPULATE.
YOUR DEFORMITY MAKES YOU VULNERABLE TO EVEN A SINGLE SMILE FROM A PRETTY FACE?
AND I SUPPOSE SHE'S PRETTY ENOUGH... FOR AN INSIPID WAIF.
I, ON THE OTHER HAND, PREFER MY TOYS TO BE A LITTLE MORE... *EXHILARATING.*
S-N-N-NNNRRLLL

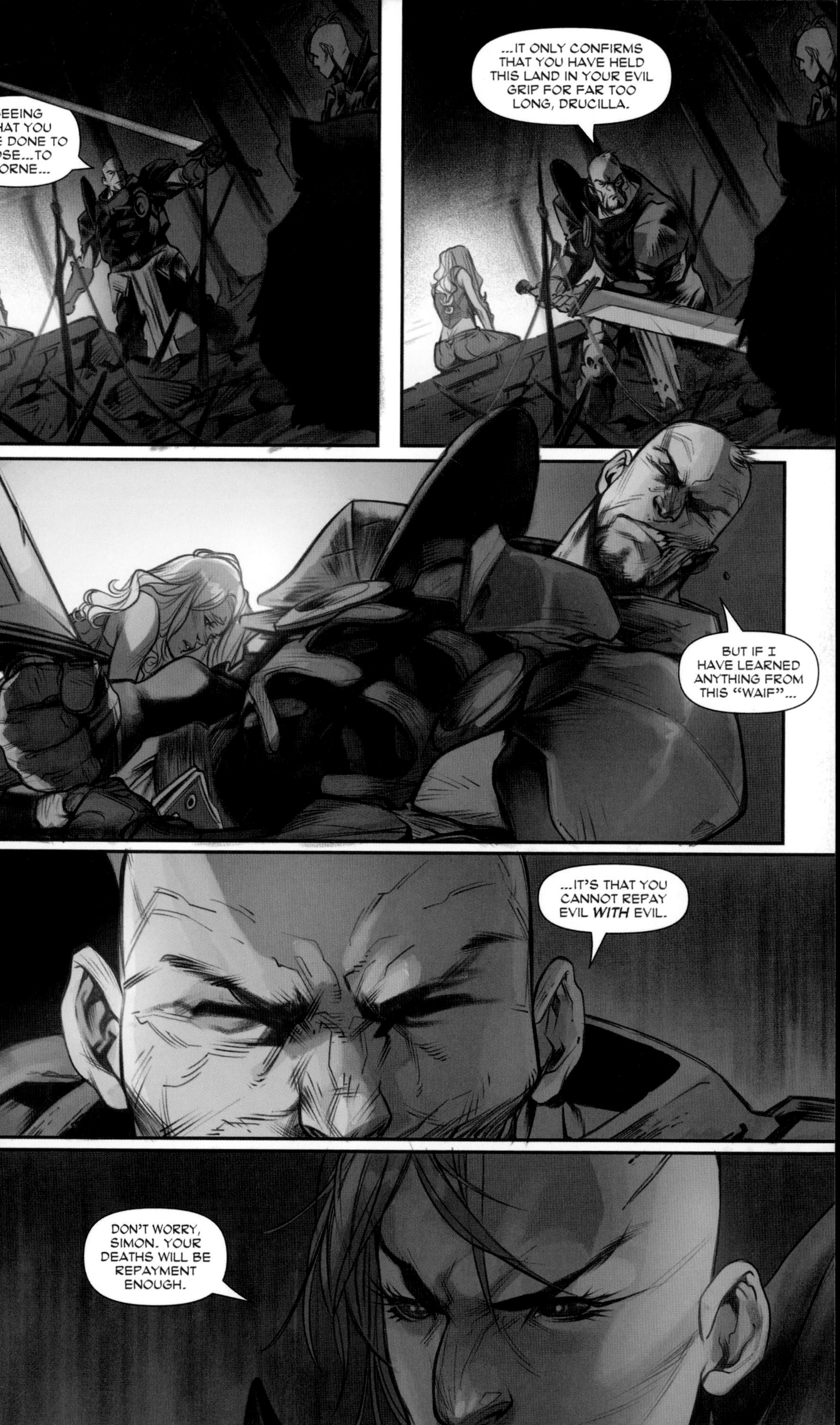
...EEING
HAT YOU
E DONE TO
OSE...TO
ORNE...
...IT ONLY CONFIRMS THAT YOU HAVE HELD THIS LAND IN YOUR EVIL GRIP FOR FAR TOO LONG, DRUCILLA.
BUT IF I HAVE LEARNED ANYTHING FROM THIS "WAIF"...
...IT'S THAT YOU CANNOT REPAY EVIL *WITH* EVIL.
DON'T WORRY, SIMON. YOUR DEATHS WILL BE REPAYMENT ENOUGH.

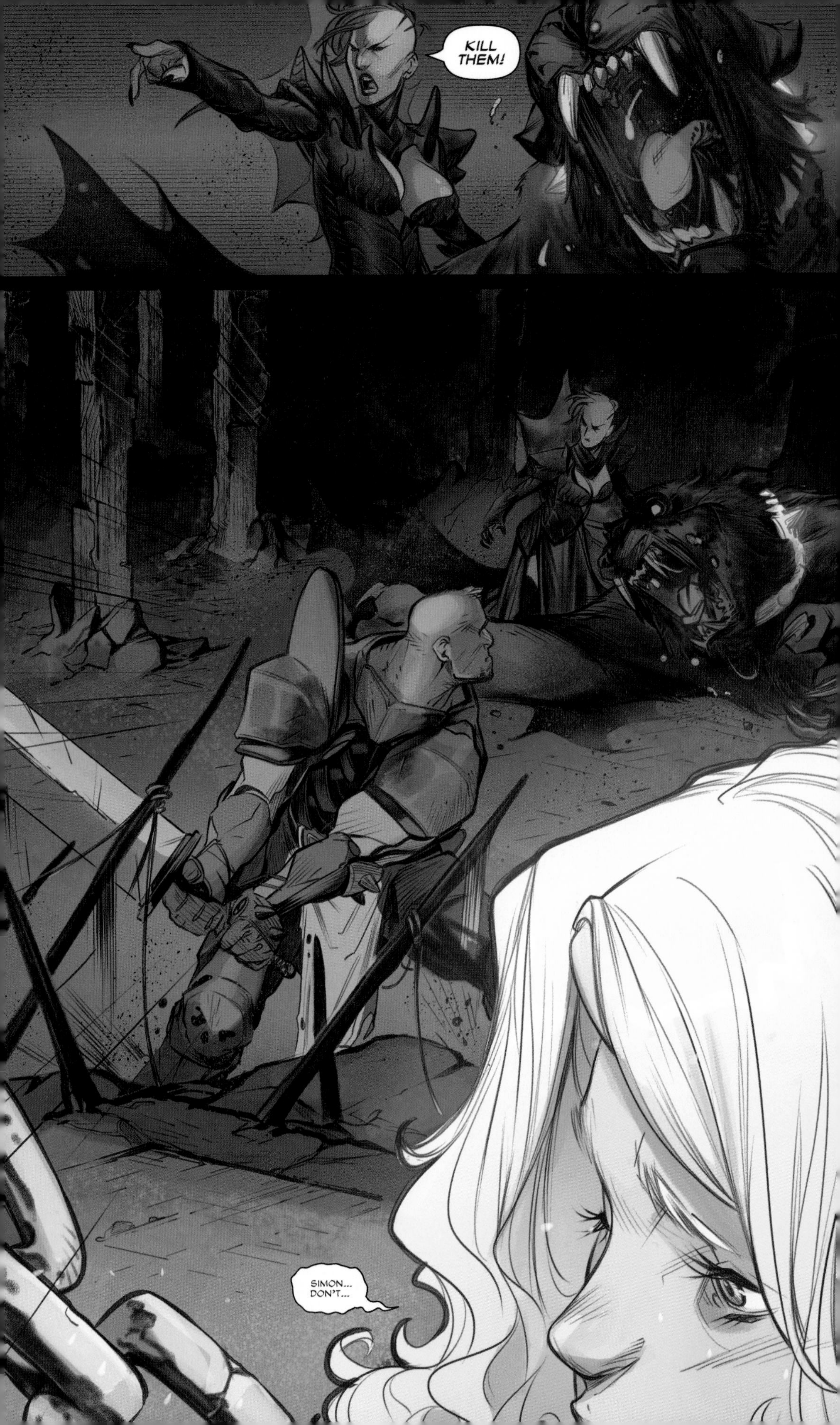
KILL THEM!
SIMON... DON'T...

SIXTEEN

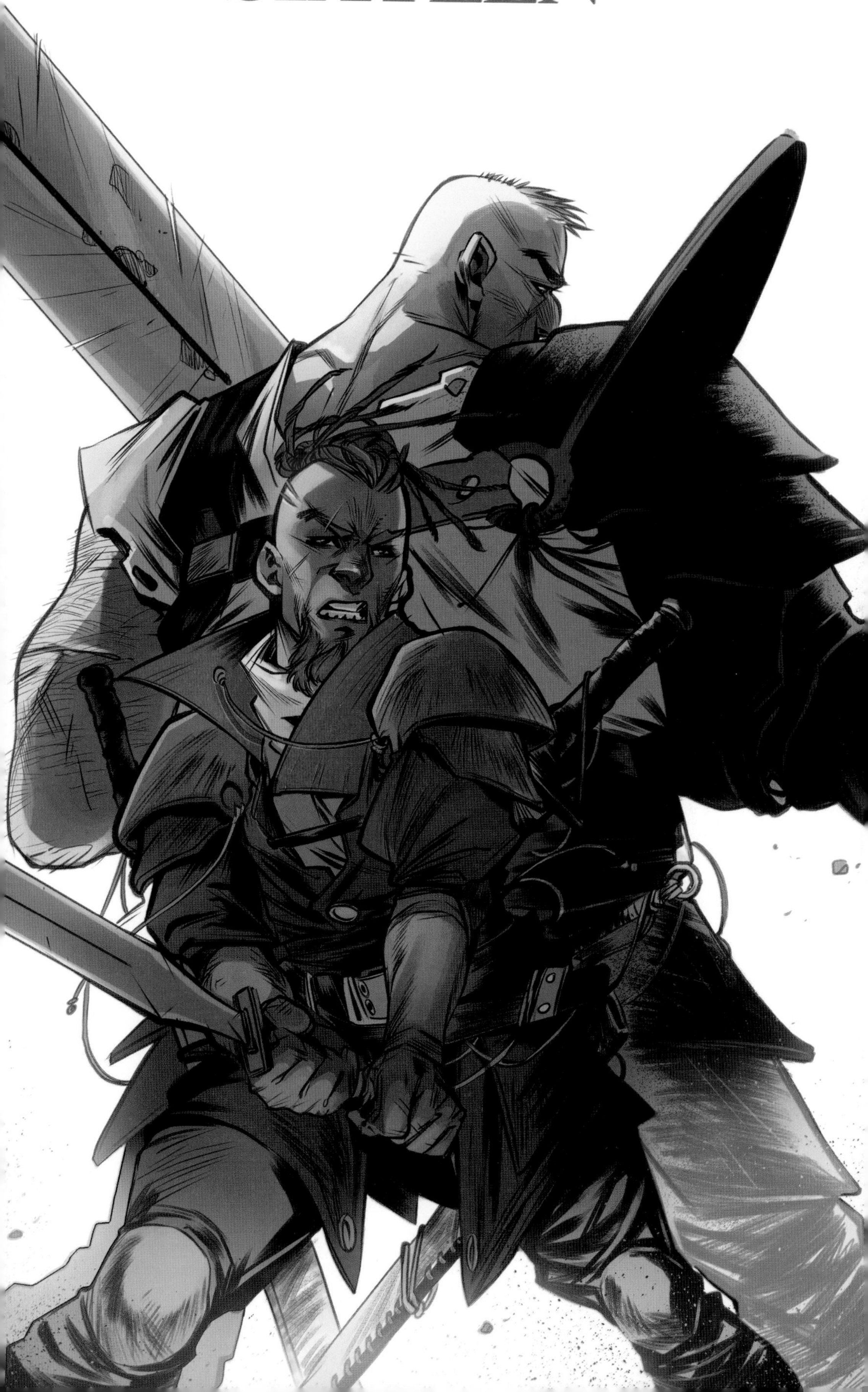

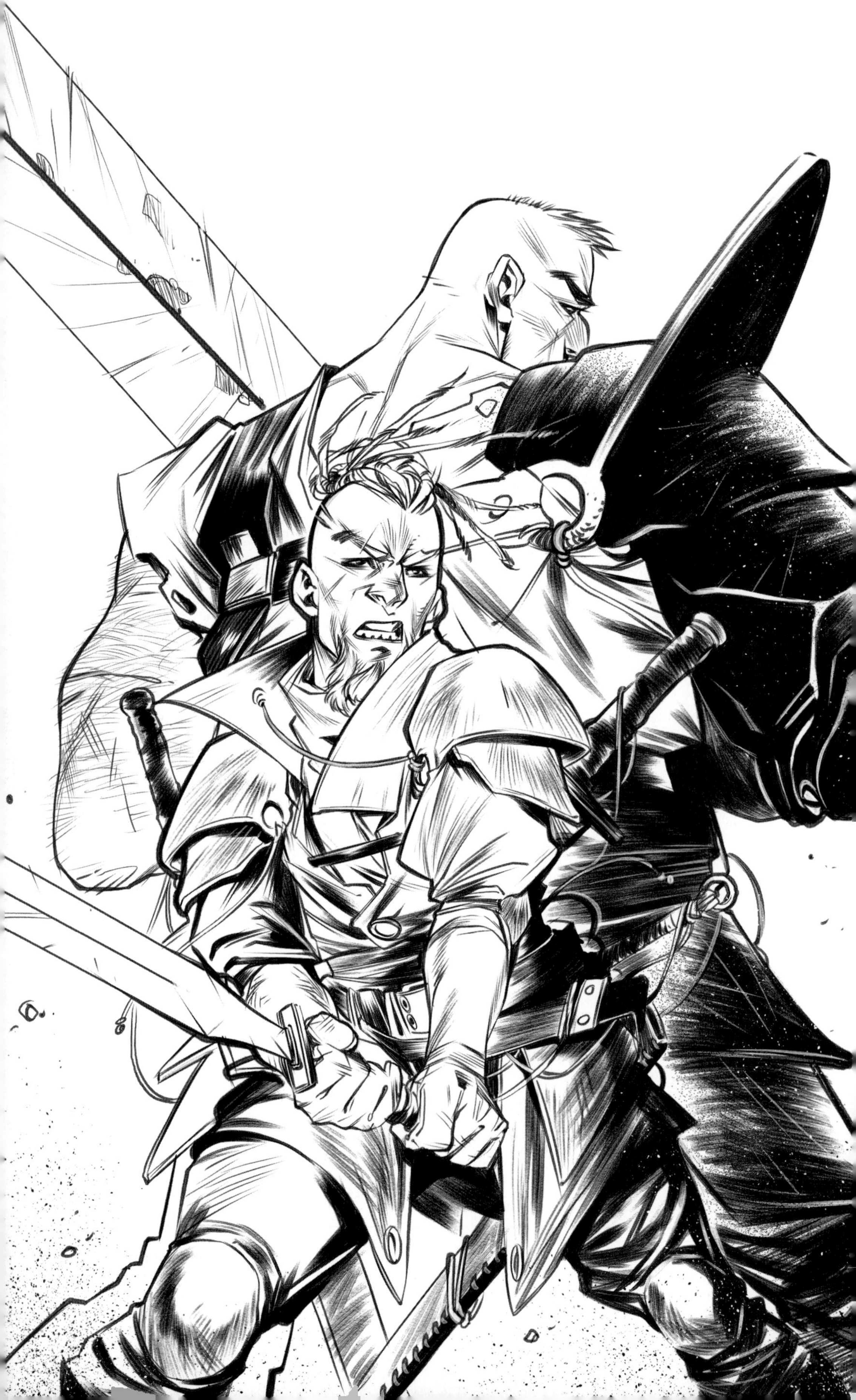

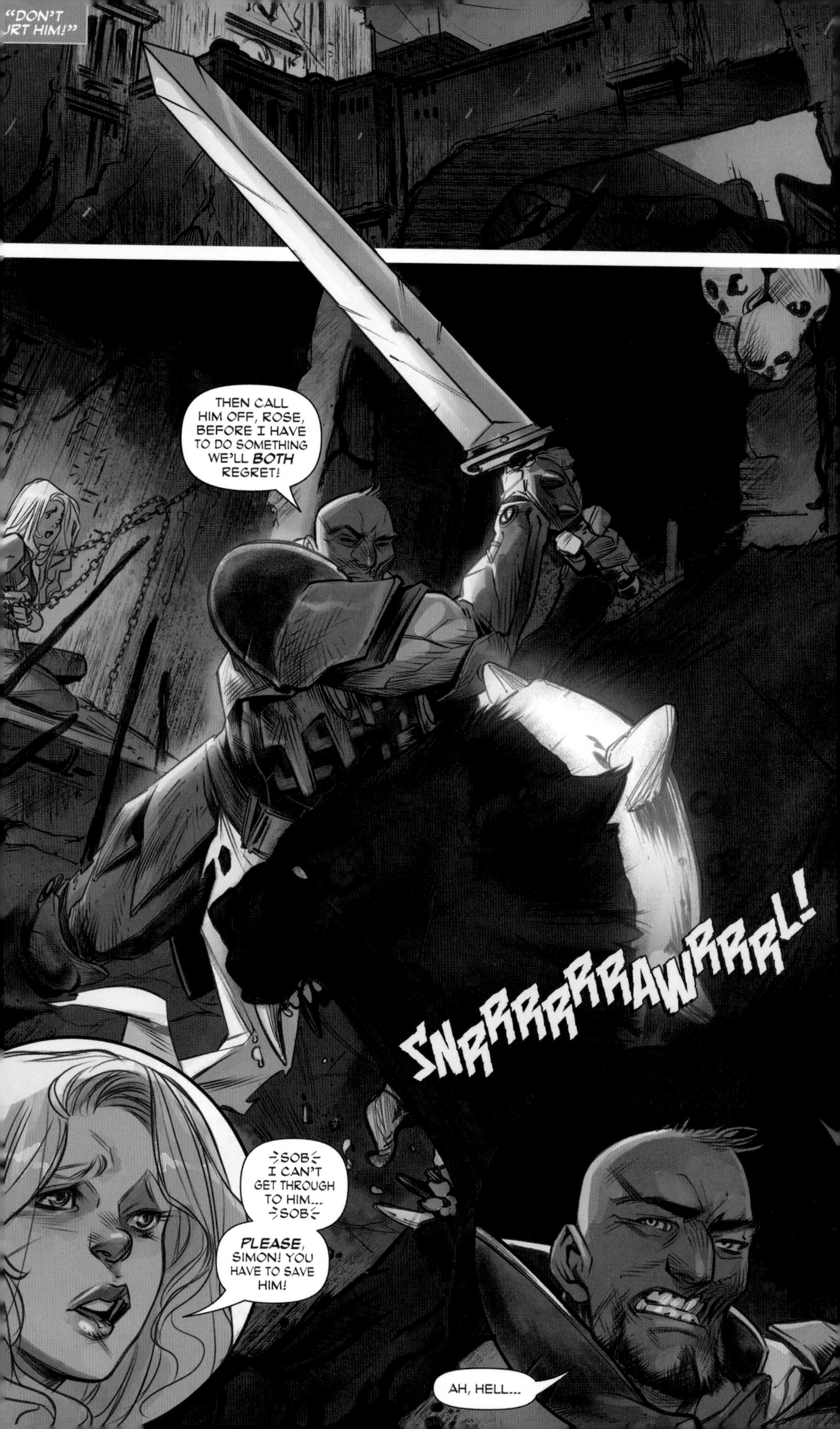
"DON'T
...RT HIM!"
THEN CALL HIM OFF, ROSE, BEFORE I HAVE TO DO SOMETHING WE'LL *BOTH* REGRET!
SNRRRRRRAWRRRL!
⊰SOB⊱ I CAN'T GET THROUGH TO HIM... ⊰SOB⊱
PLEASE, SIMON! YOU HAVE TO SAVE HIM!
AH, HELL...

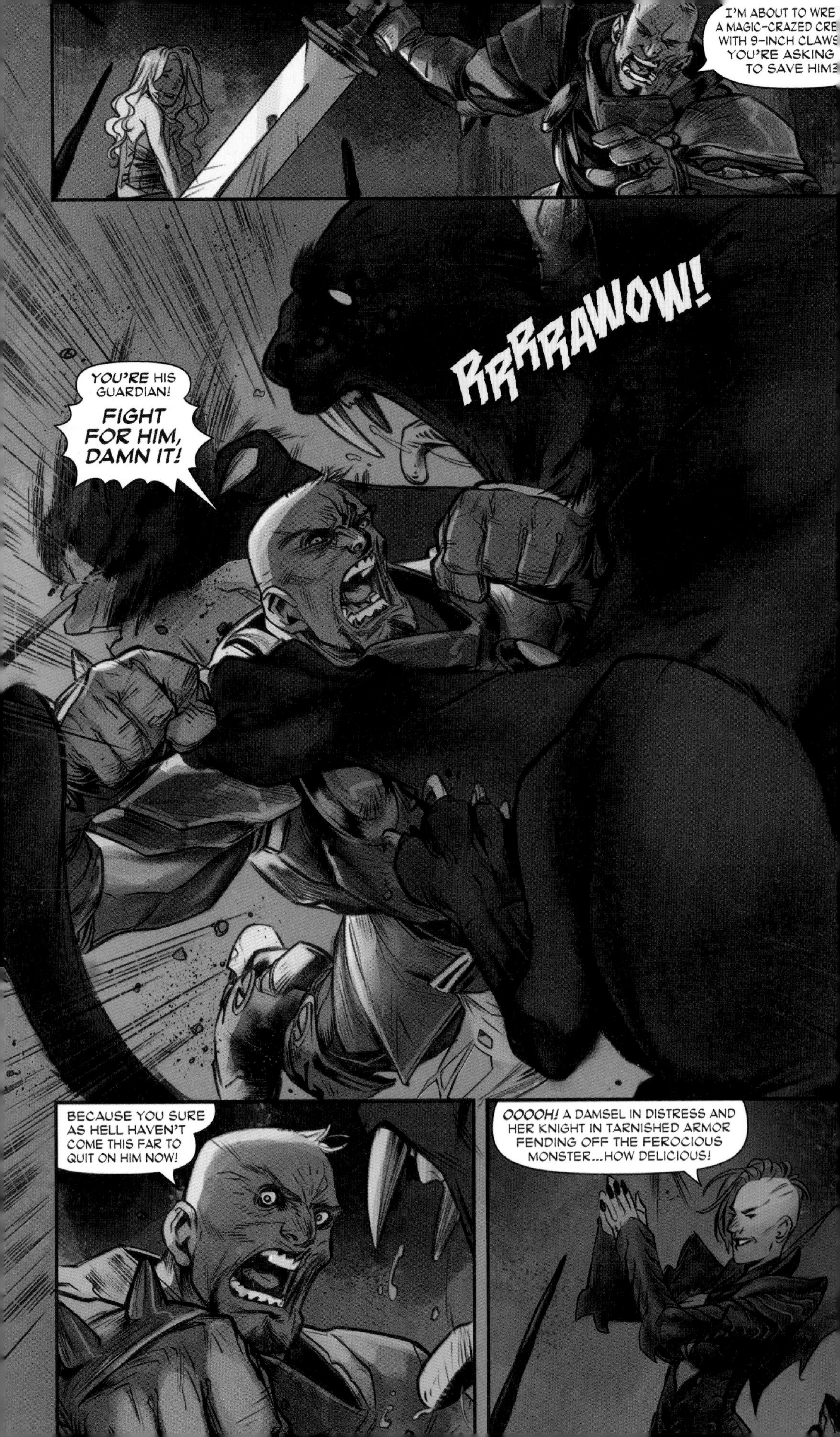
I'M ABOUT TO WRE
A MAGIC-CRAZED CRE
WITH 9-INCH CLAWS
YOU'RE ASKING
TO SAVE HIM?
YOU'RE HIS GUARDIAN! FIGHT FOR HIM, DAMN IT!
RRRRAWOW!
BECAUSE YOU SURE AS HELL HAVEN'T COME THIS FAR TO QUIT ON HIM NOW!
OOOOH! A DAMSEL IN DISTRESS AND HER KNIGHT IN TARNISHED ARMOR FENDING OFF THE FEROCIOUS MONSTER...HOW DELICIOUS!

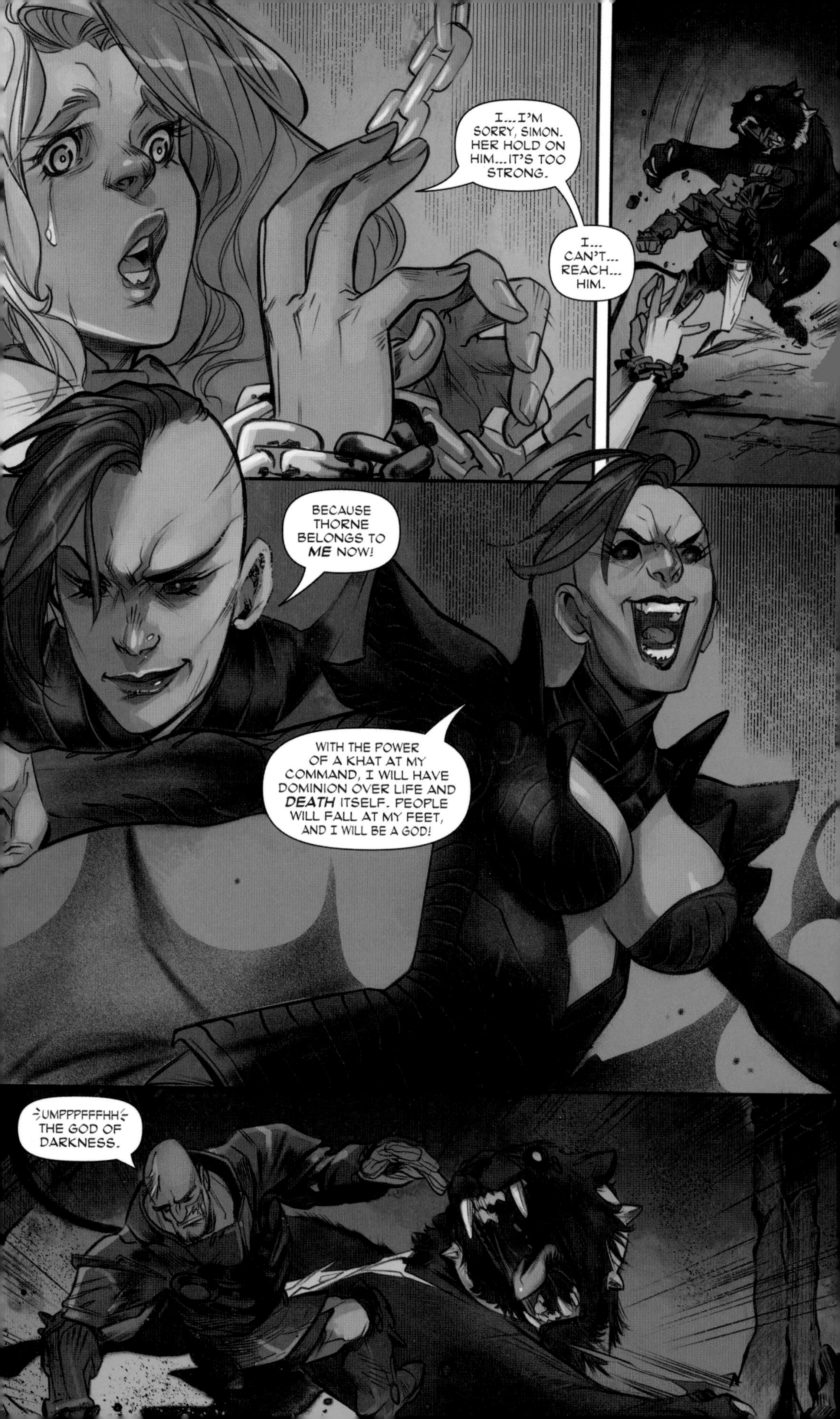
I...I'M SORRY, SIMON. HER HOLD ON HIM...IT'S TOO STRONG.
I... CAN'T... REACH... HIM.
BECAUSE THORNE BELONGS TO ME NOW!
WITH THE POWER OF A KHAT AT MY COMMAND, I WILL HAVE DOMINION OVER LIFE AND DEATH ITSELF. PEOPLE WILL FALL AT MY FEET, AND I WILL BE A GOD!
UMPPPFFFHH THE GOD OF DARKNESS.

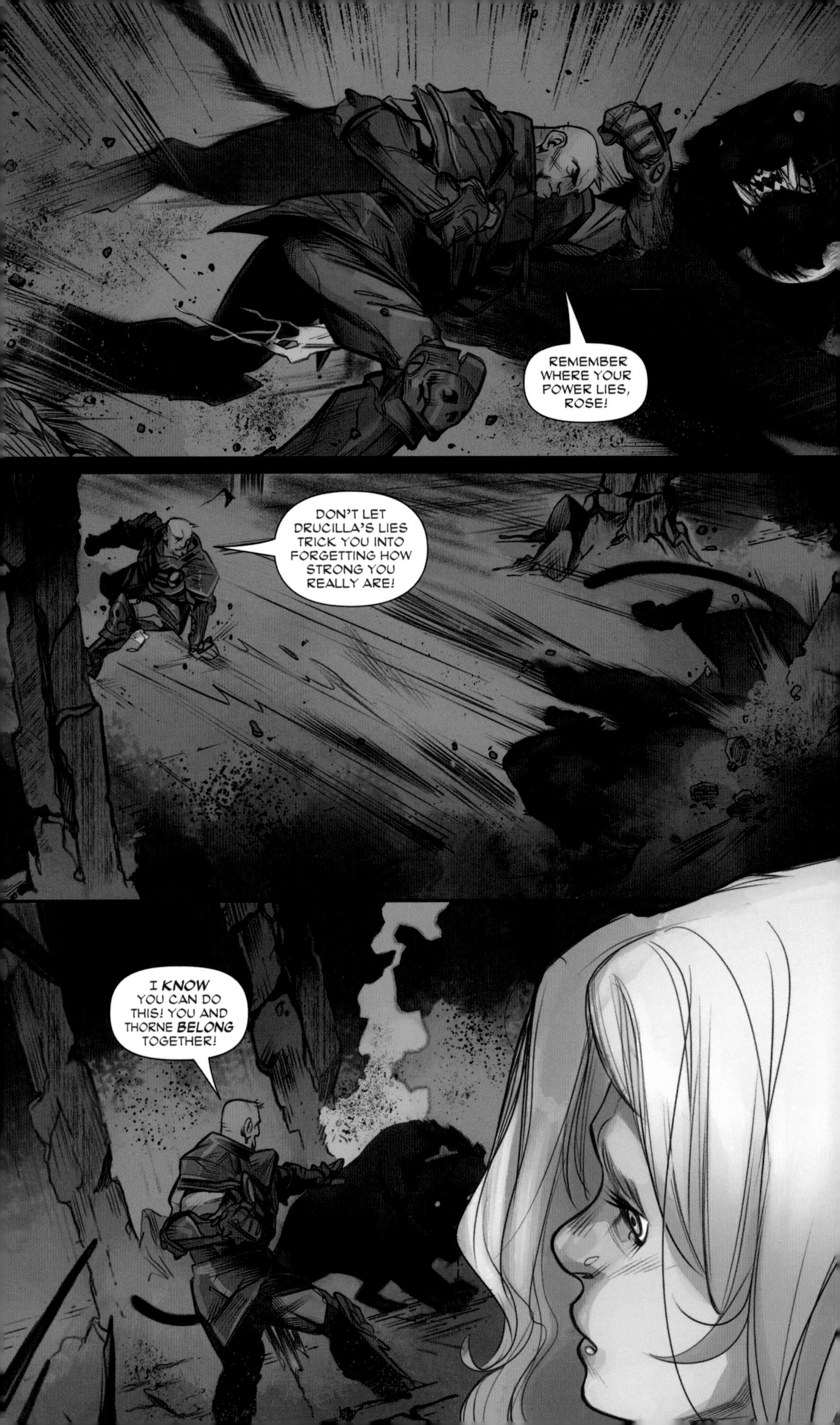
REMEMBER WHERE YOUR POWER LIES, ROSE!
DON'T LET DRUCILLA'S LIES TRICK YOU INTO FORGETTING HOW STRONG YOU REALLY ARE!
I *KNOW* YOU CAN DO THIS! YOU AND THORNE *BELONG* TOGETHER!

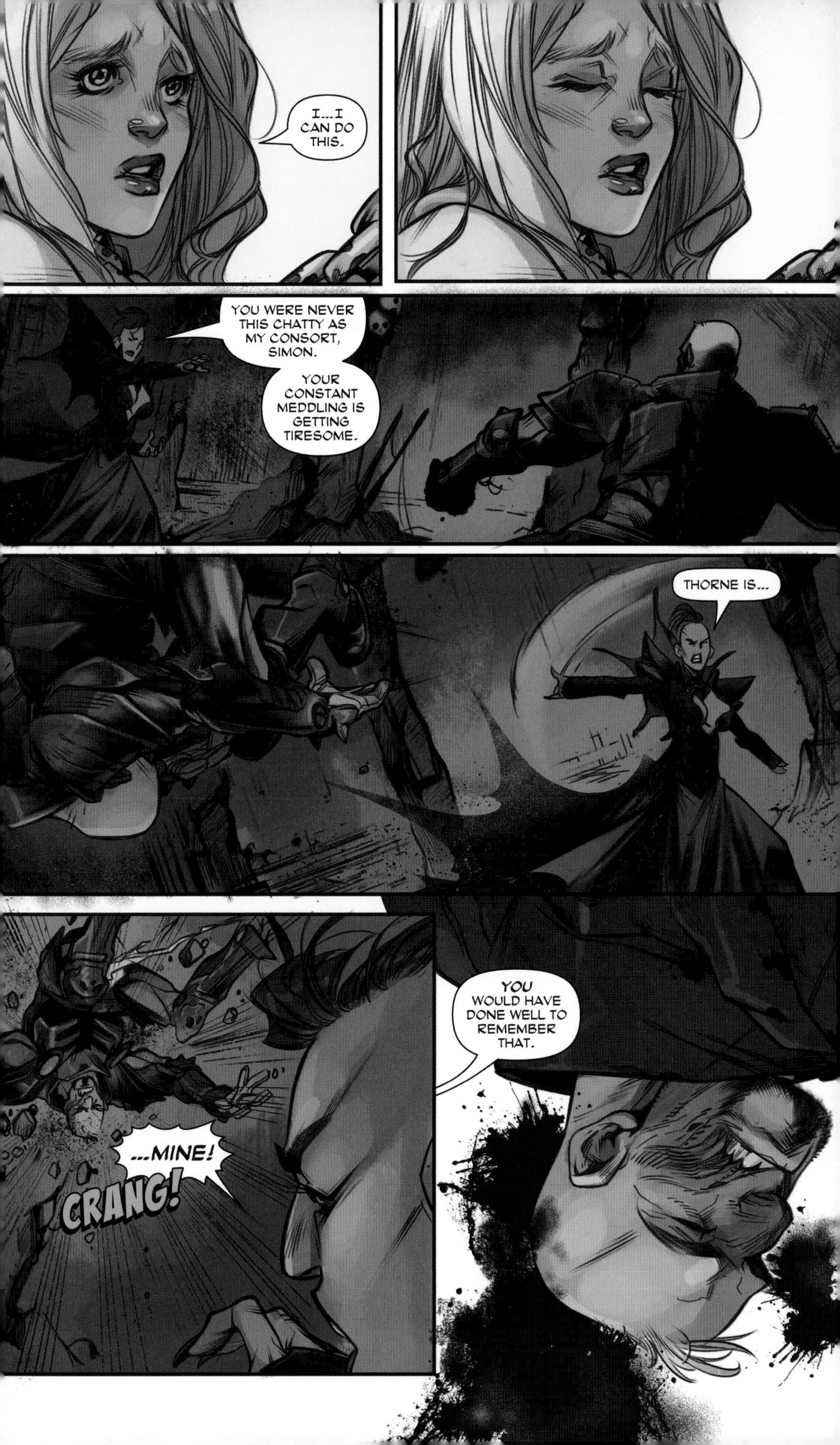
I...I CAN DO THIS.
YOU WERE NEVER THIS CHATTY AS MY CONSORT, SIMON.
YOUR CONSTANT MEDDLING IS GETTING TIRESOME.
THORNE IS...
...MINE!
CRANG!
YOU WOULD HAVE DONE WELL TO REMEMBER THAT.

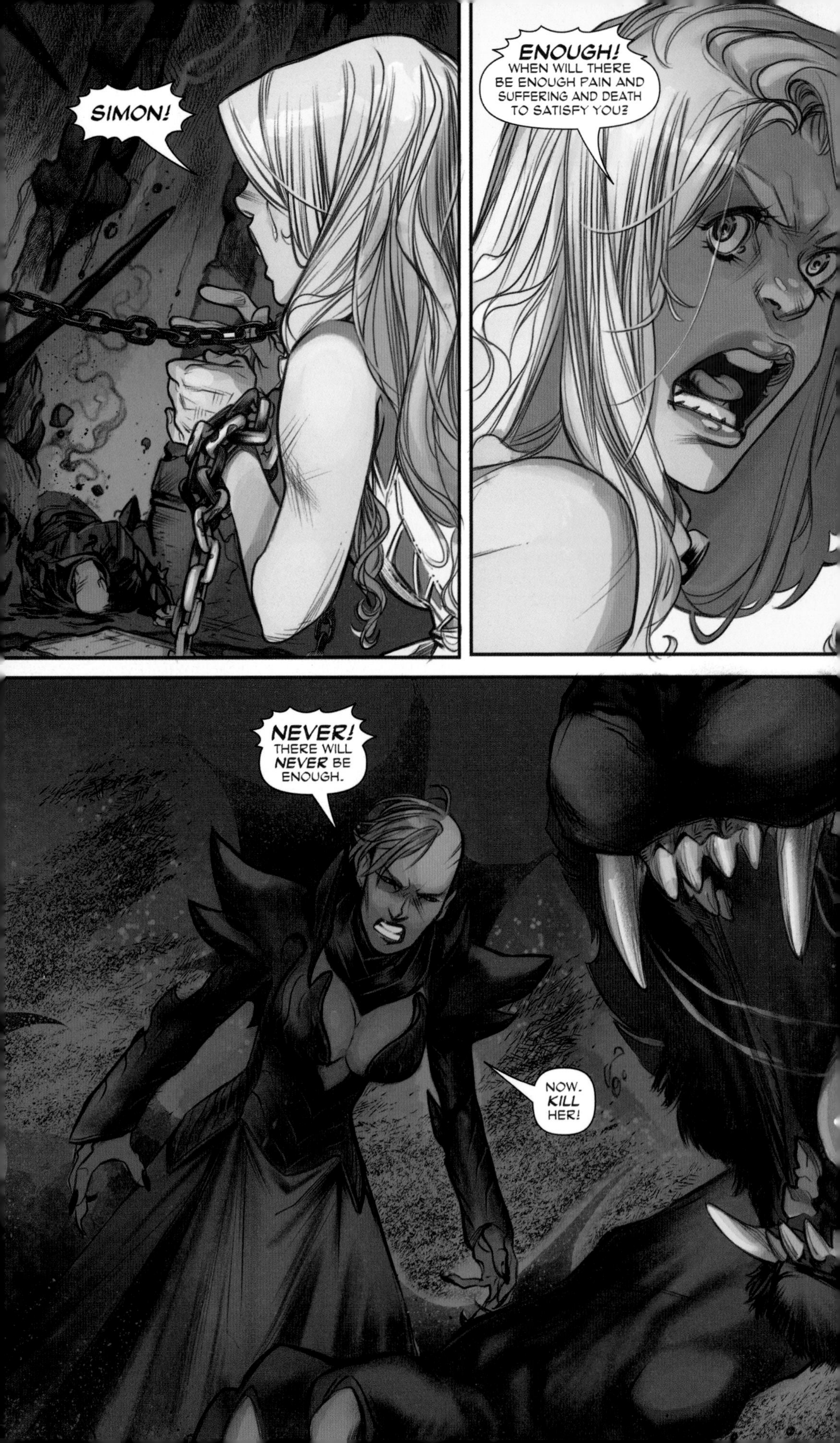
SIMON!
ENOUGH! WHEN WILL THERE BE ENOUGH PAIN AND SUFFERING AND DEATH TO SATISFY YOU?
NEVER! THERE WILL NEVER BE ENOUGH.
NOW. KILL HER!

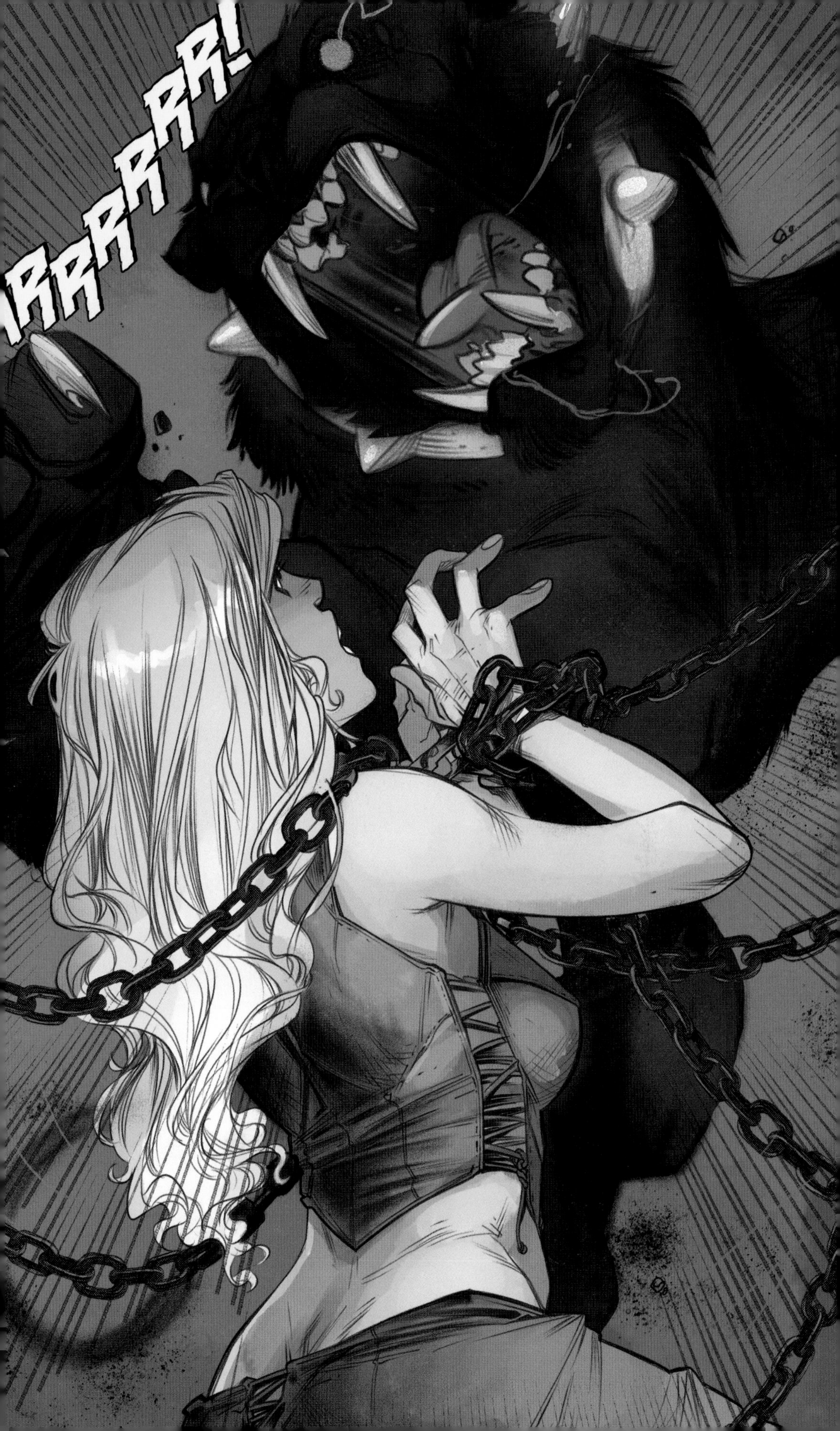
RRRRRRR!

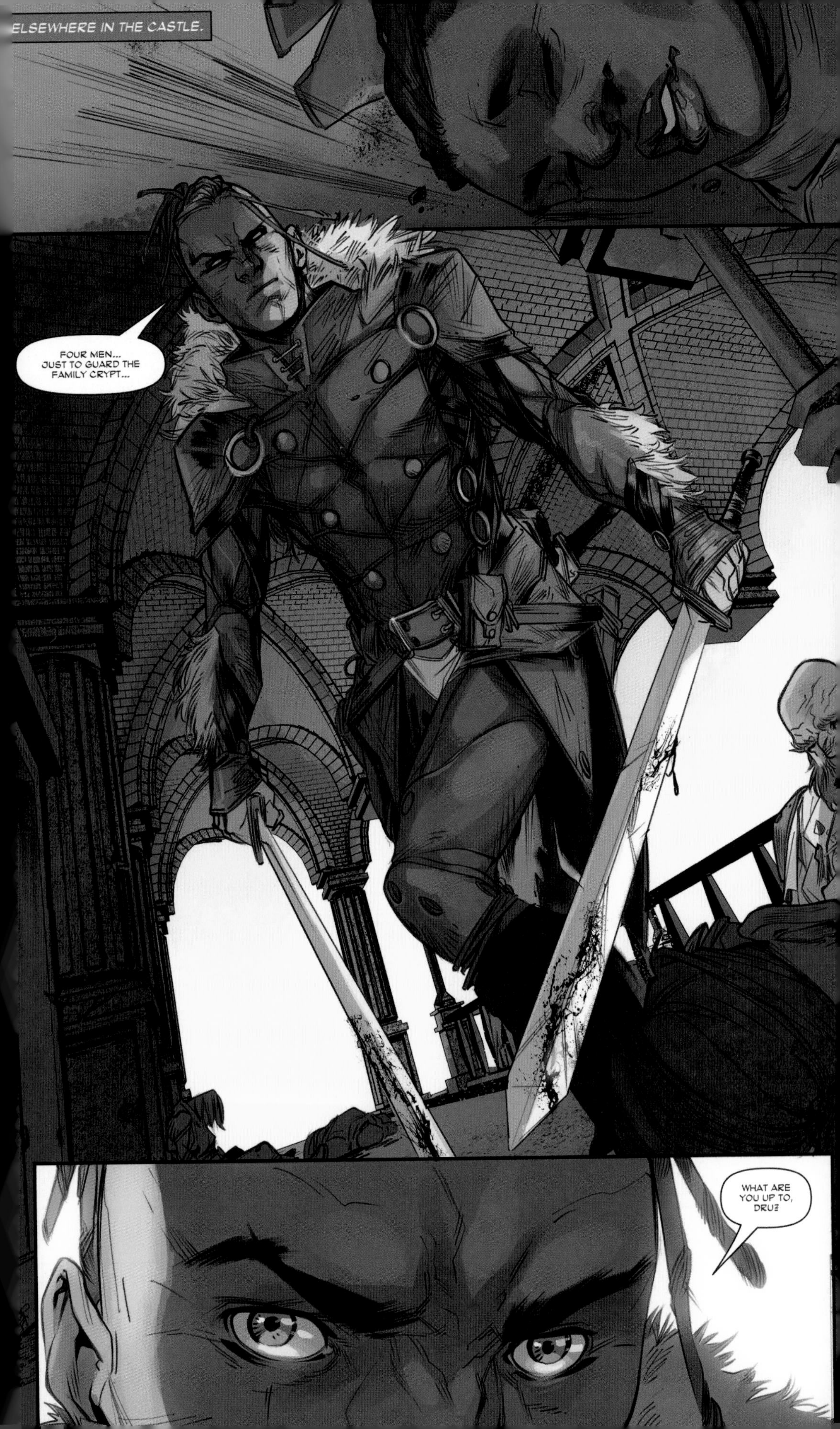
ELSEWHERE IN THE CASTLE.
FOUR MEN... JUST TO GUARD THE FAMILY CRYPT...
WHAT ARE YOU UP TO, DRU?

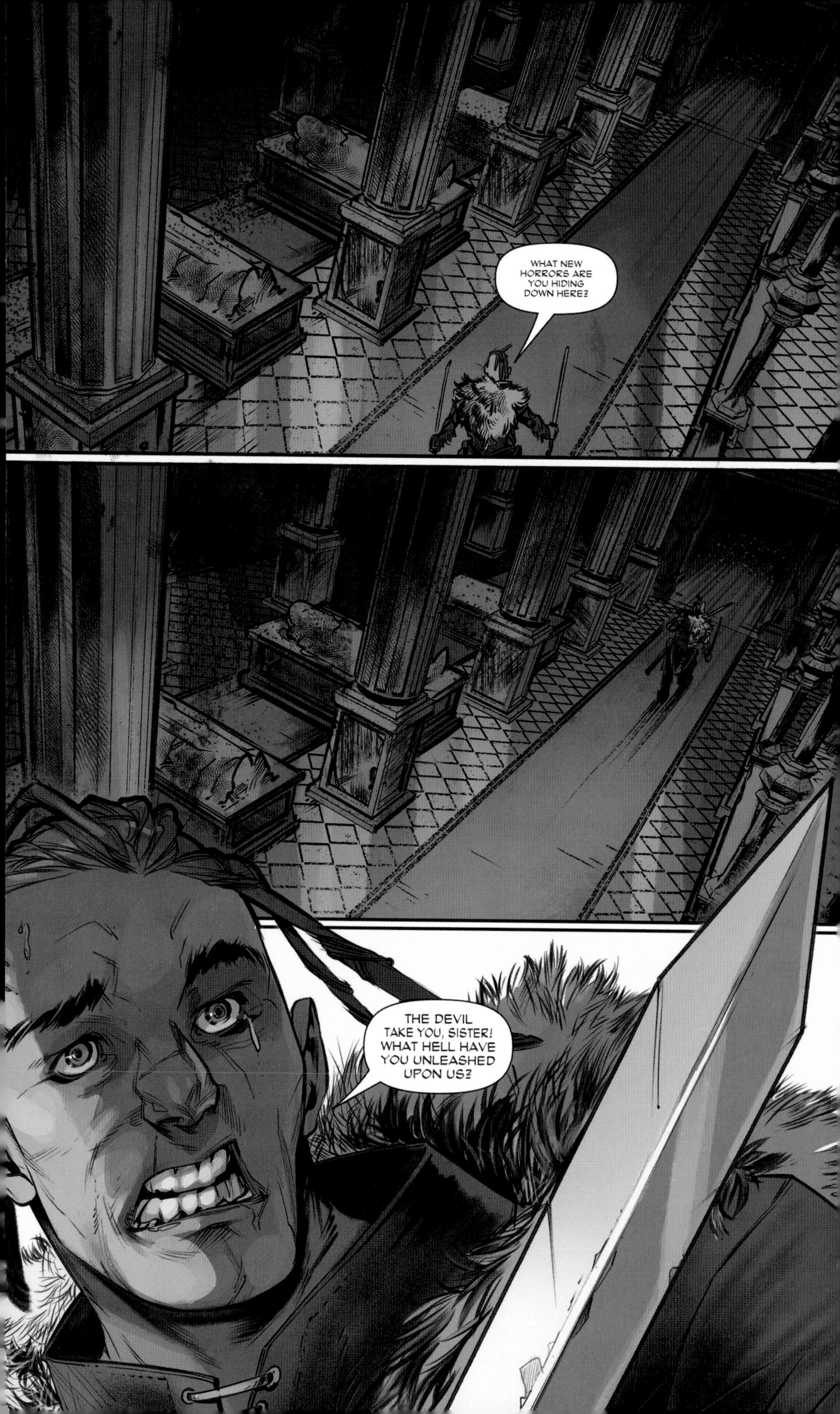
WHAT NEW HORRORS ARE YOU HIDING DOWN HERE?
THE DEVIL TAKE YOU, SISTER! WHAT HELL HAVE YOU UNLEASHED UPON US?

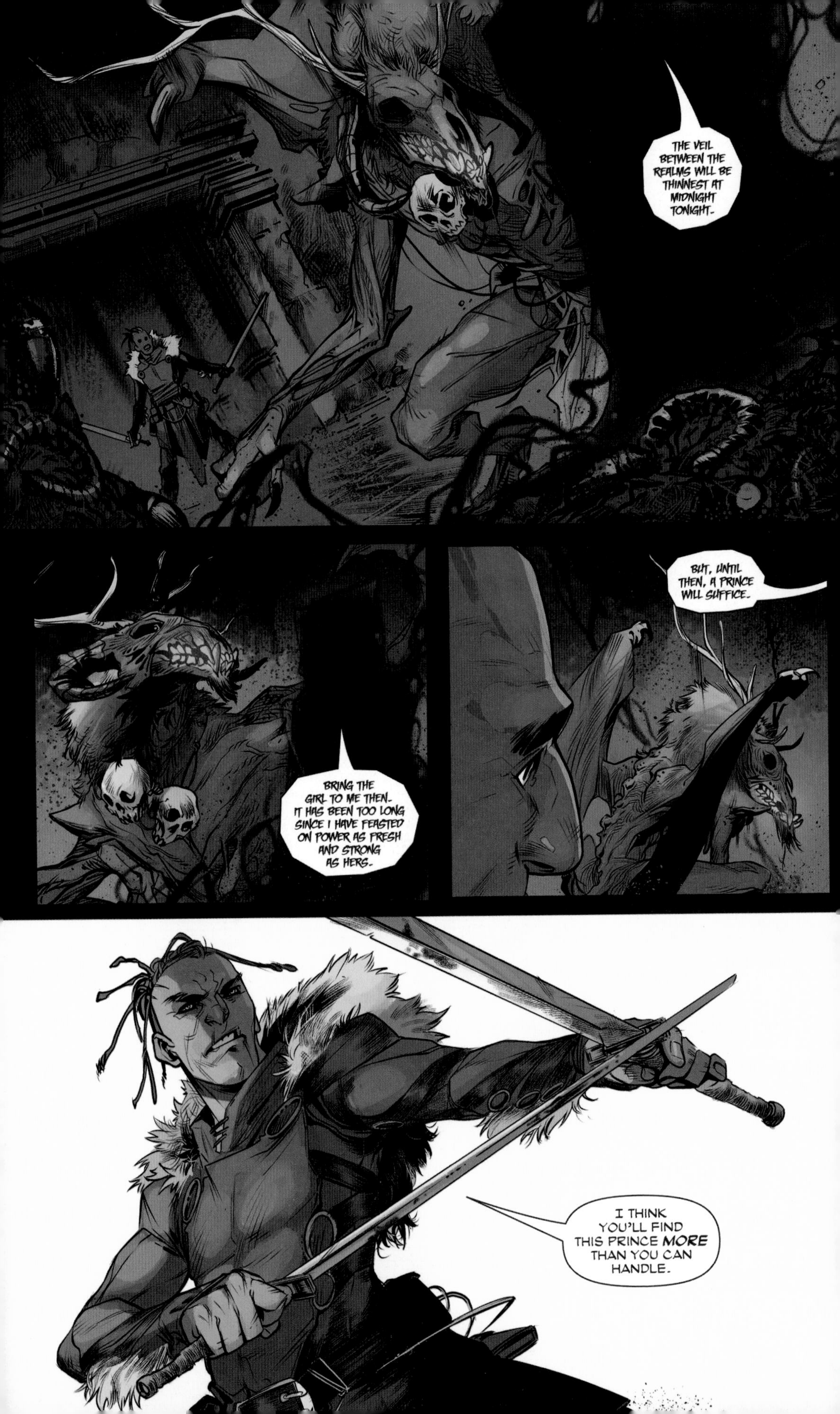
THE VEIL BETWEEN THE REALMS WILL BE THINNEST AT MIDNIGHT TONIGHT.
BRING THE GIRL TO ME THEN. IT HAS BEEN TOO LONG SINCE I HAVE FEASTED ON POWER AS FRESH AND STRONG AS HERS.
BUT, UNTIL THEN, A PRINCE WILL SUFFICE.
I THINK YOU'LL FIND THIS PRINCE MORE THAN YOU CAN HANDLE.

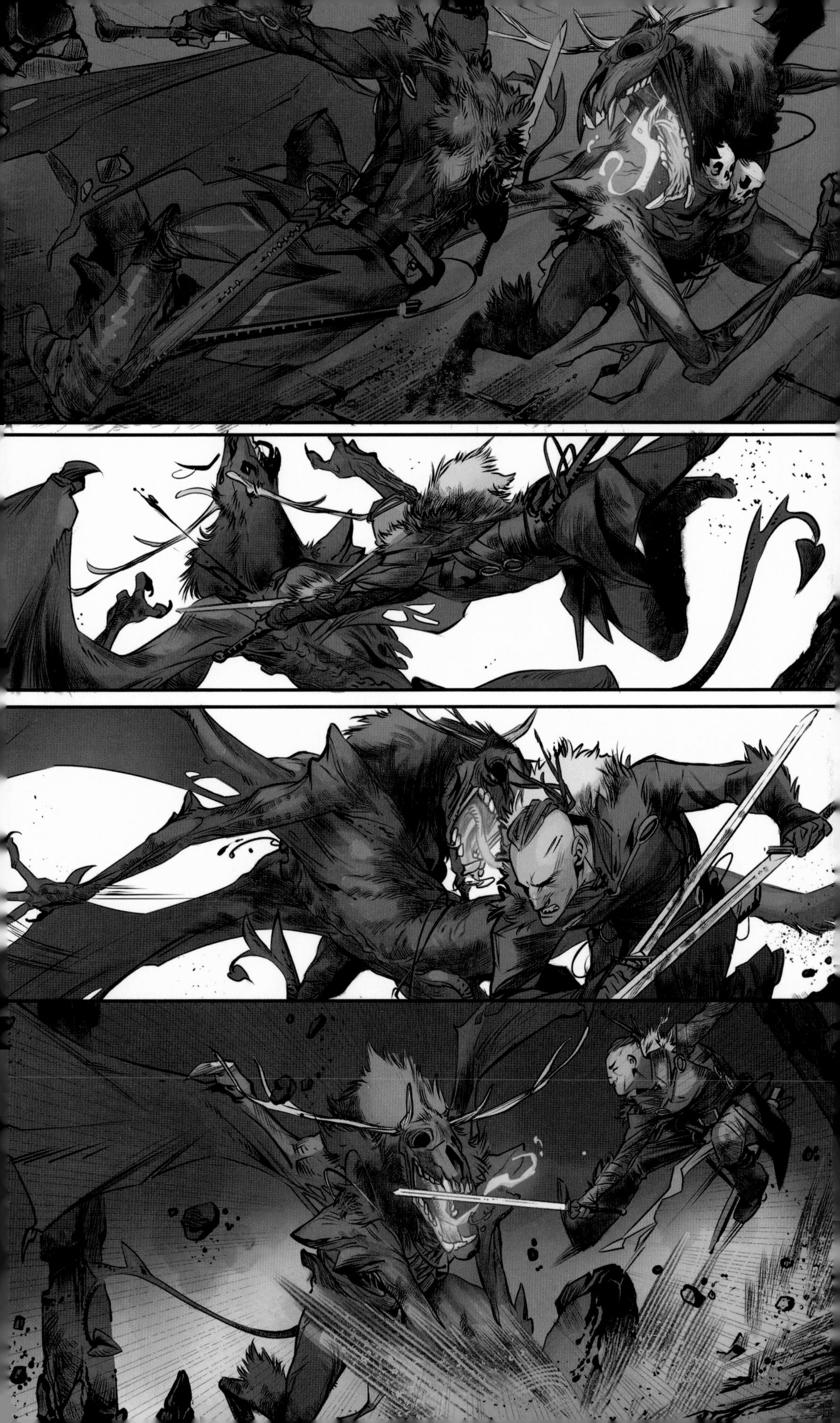

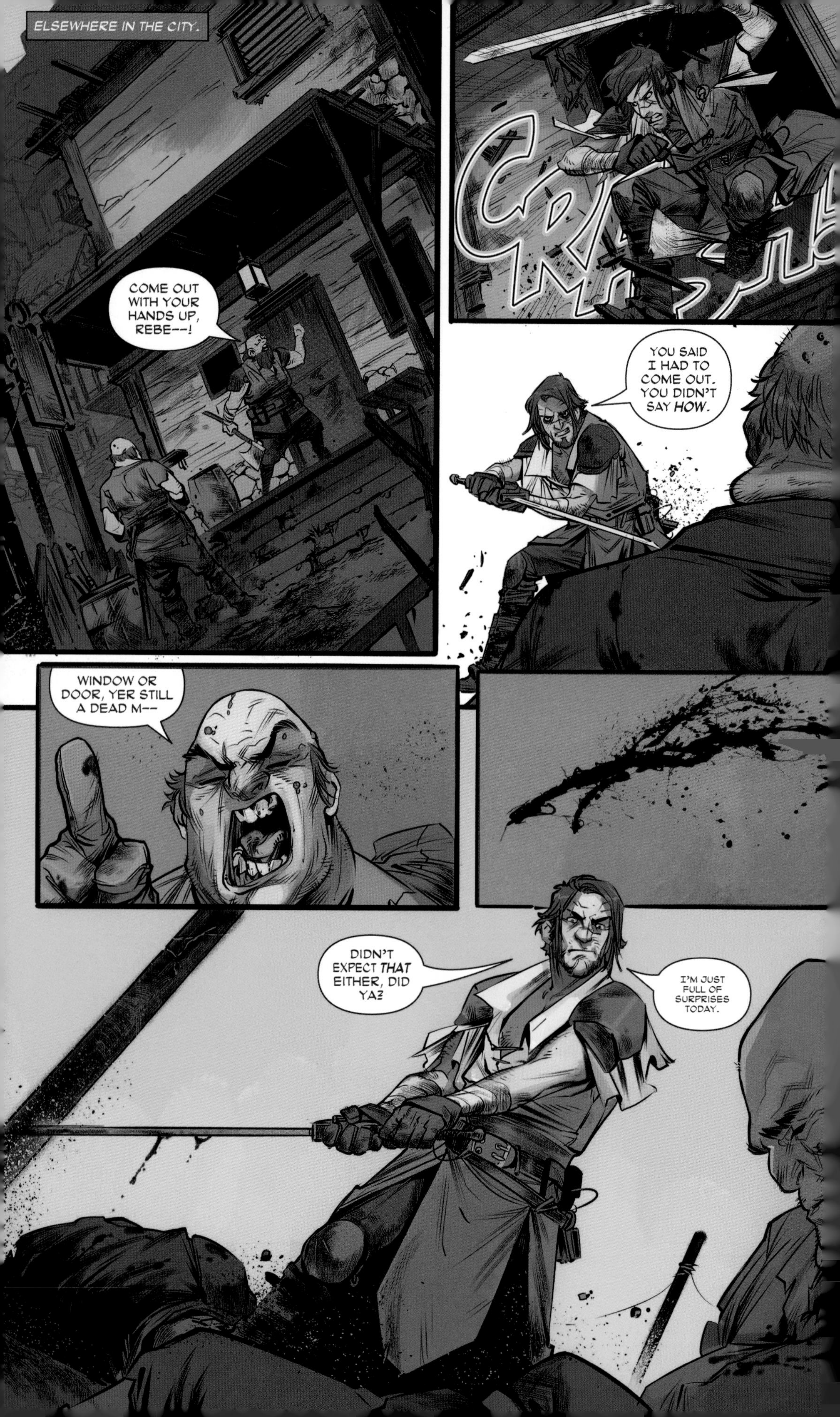
ELSEWHERE IN THE CITY.
COME OUT WITH YOUR HANDS UP, REBE--!
YOU SAID I HAD TO COME OUT. YOU DIDN'T SAY *HOW*.
WINDOW OR DOOR, YER STILL A DEAD M--
DIDN'T EXPECT *THAT* EITHER, DID YA?
I'M JUST FULL OF SURPRISES TODAY.

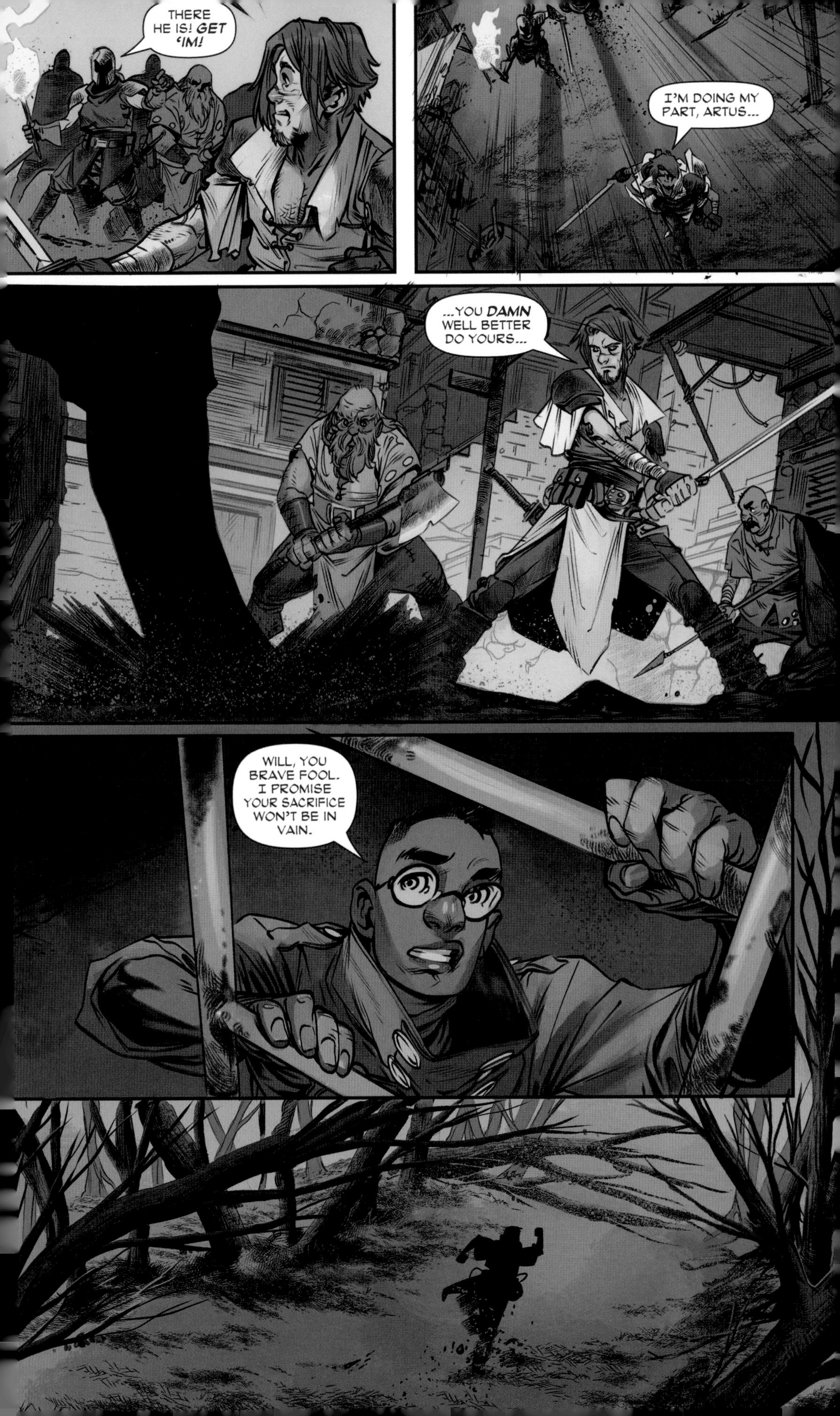
THERE HE IS! GET 'IM!
I'M DOING MY PART, ARTUS...
...YOU DAMN WELL BETTER DO YOURS...
WILL, YOU BRAVE FOOL. I PROMISE YOUR SACRIFICE WON'T BE IN VAIN.

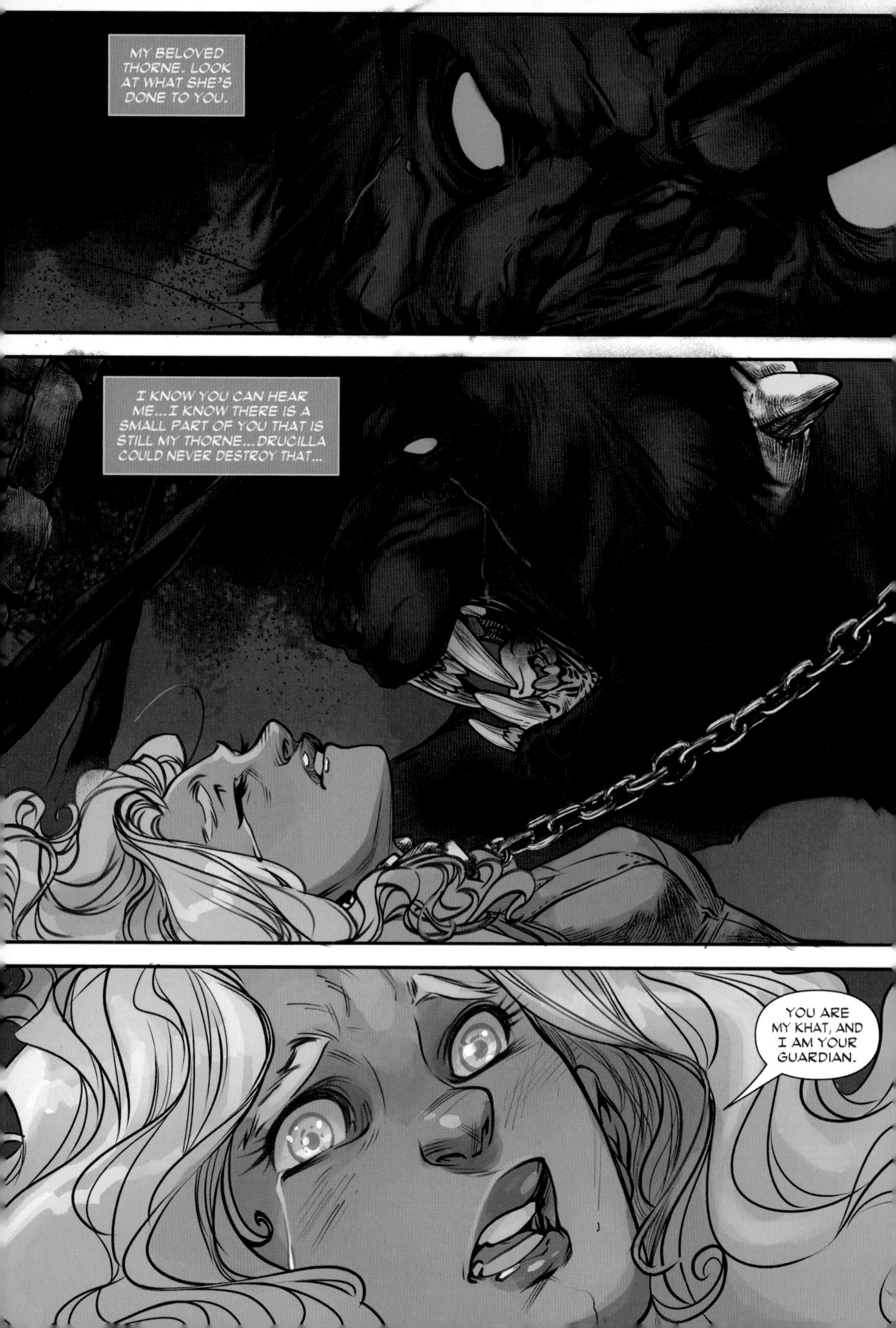
MY BELOVED THORNE. LOOK AT WHAT SHE'S DONE TO YOU.
I KNOW YOU CAN HEAR ME...I KNOW THERE IS A SMALL PART OF YOU THAT IS STILL MY THORNE...DRUCILLA COULD NEVER DESTROY THAT...
YOU ARE MY KHAT, AND I AM YOUR GUARDIAN.

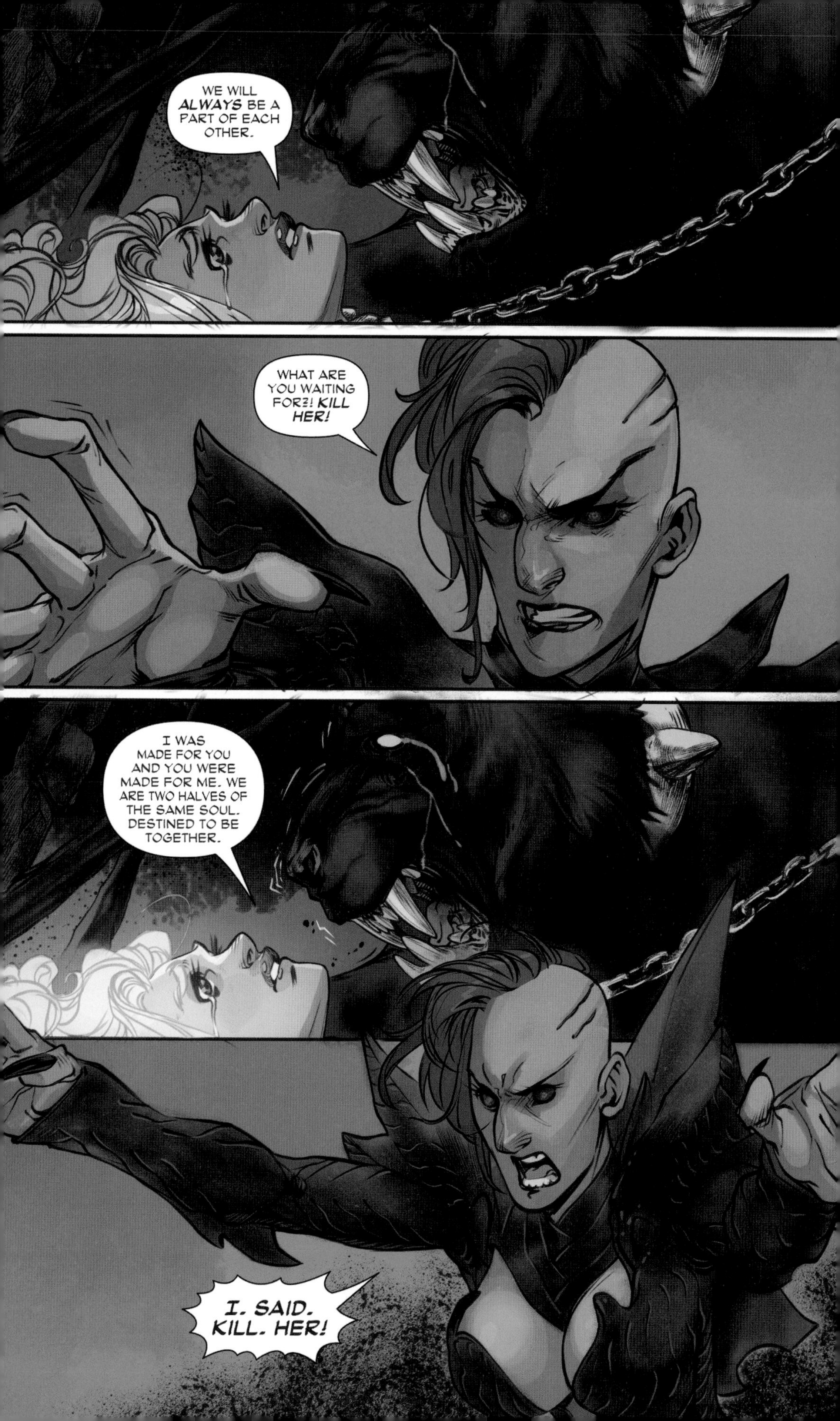
WE WILL ALWAYS BE A PART OF EACH OTHER.
WHAT ARE YOU WAITING FOR?! KILL HER!
I WAS MADE FOR YOU AND YOU WERE MADE FOR ME. WE ARE TWO HALVES OF THE SAME SOUL. DESTINED TO BE TOGETHER.
I. SAID. KILL. HER!

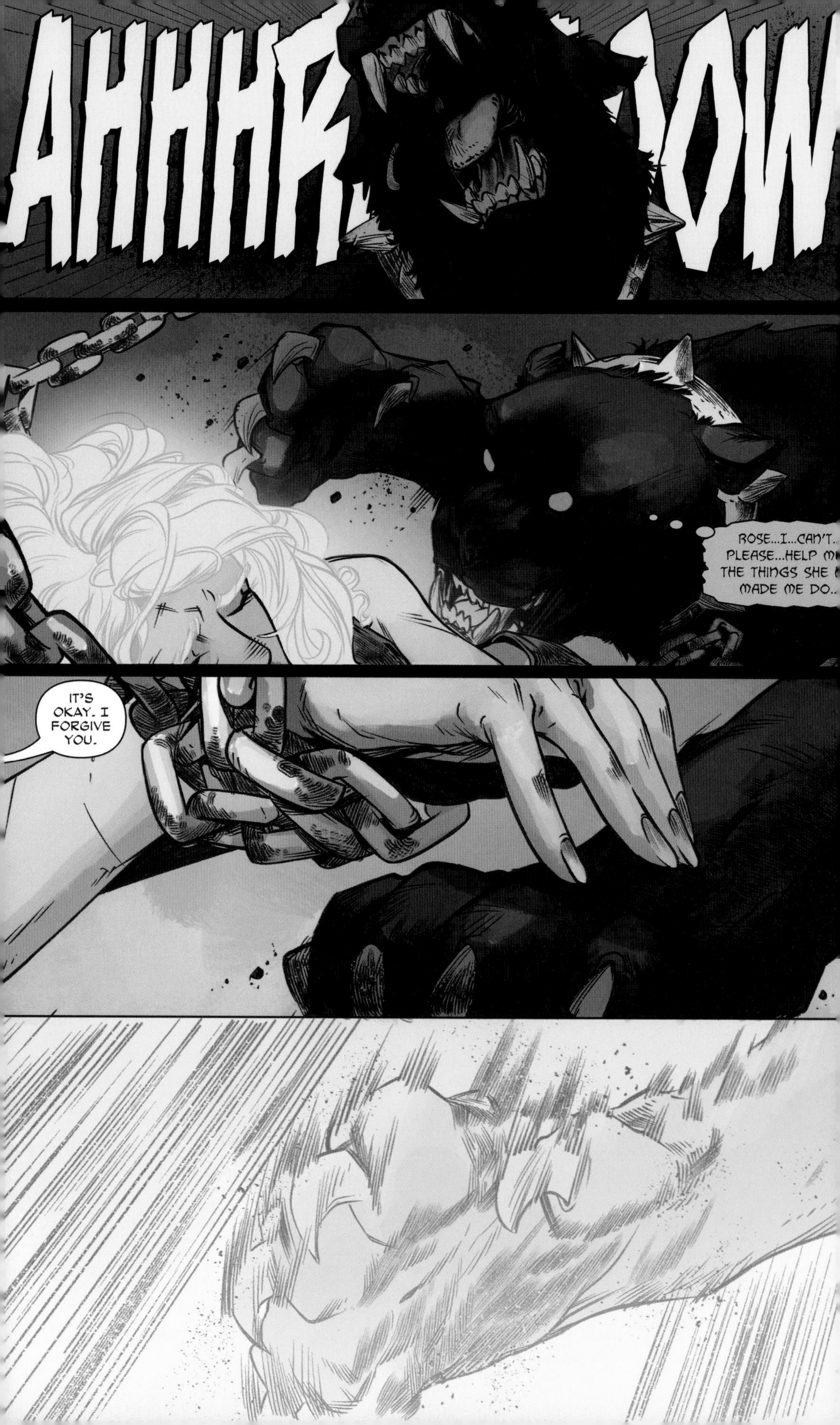
AHHHR OOW
ROSE...I...CAN'T... PLEASE...HELP M THE THINGS SHE MADE ME DO...
IT'S OKAY. I FORGIVE YOU.

LOVE YOU.

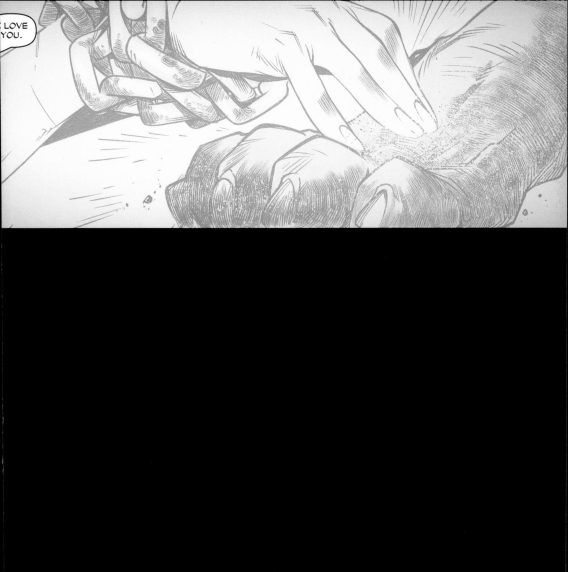

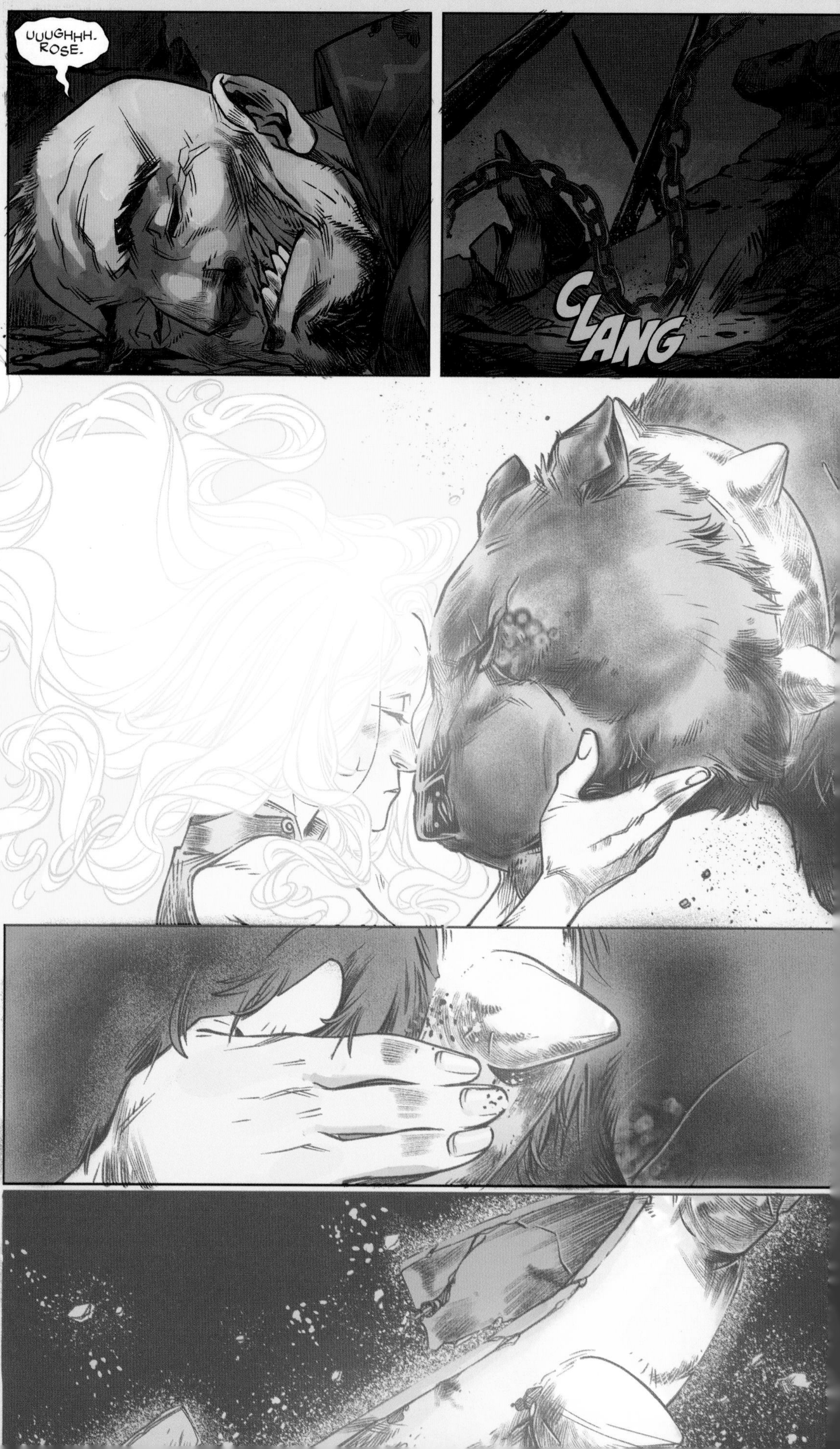
UUUGHHH. ROSE.
CLANG

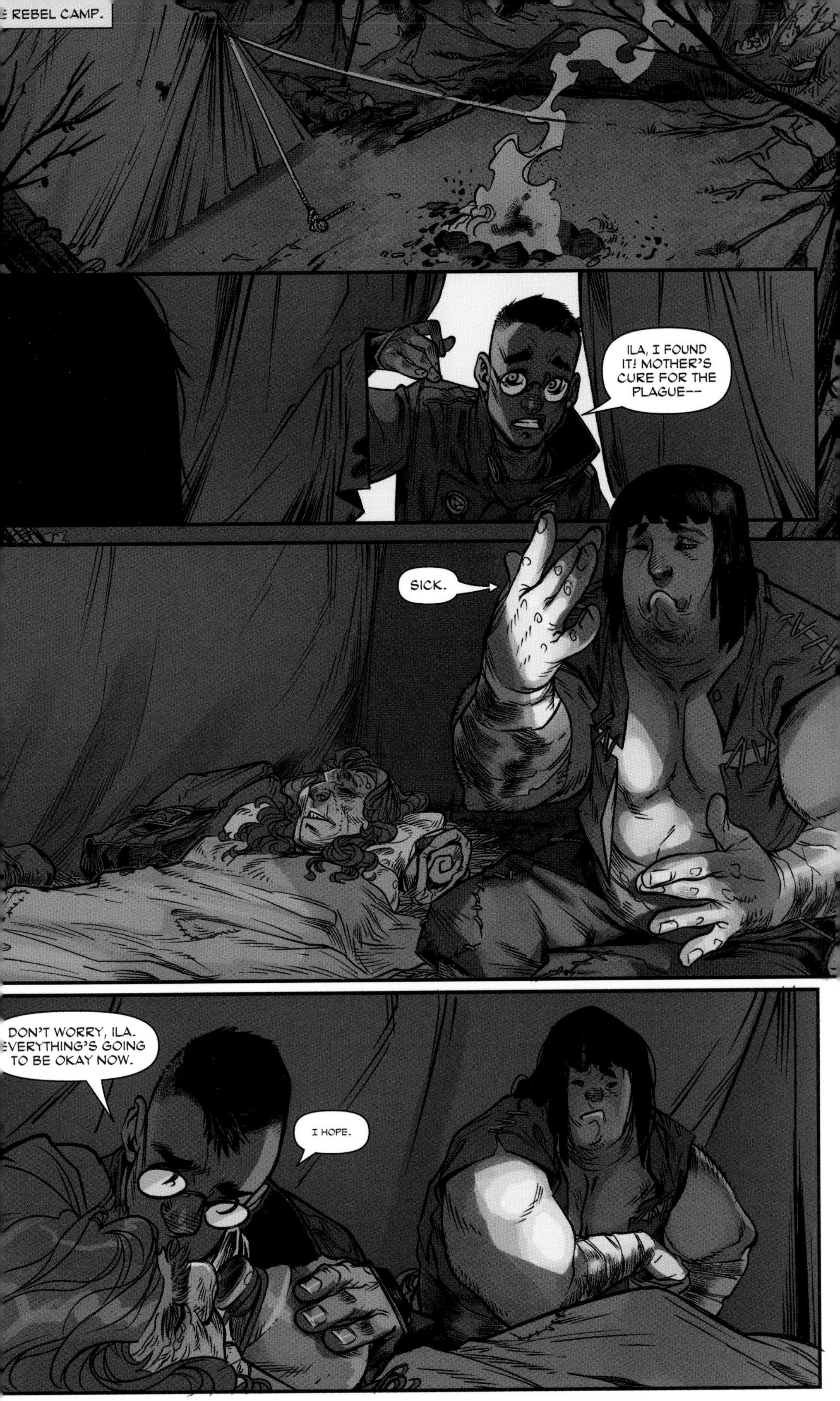
E REBEL CAMP.
ILA, I FOUND IT! MOTHER'S CURE FOR THE PLAGUE--
SICK.
DON'T WORRY, ILA. EVERYTHING'S GOING TO BE OKAY NOW.
I HOPE.

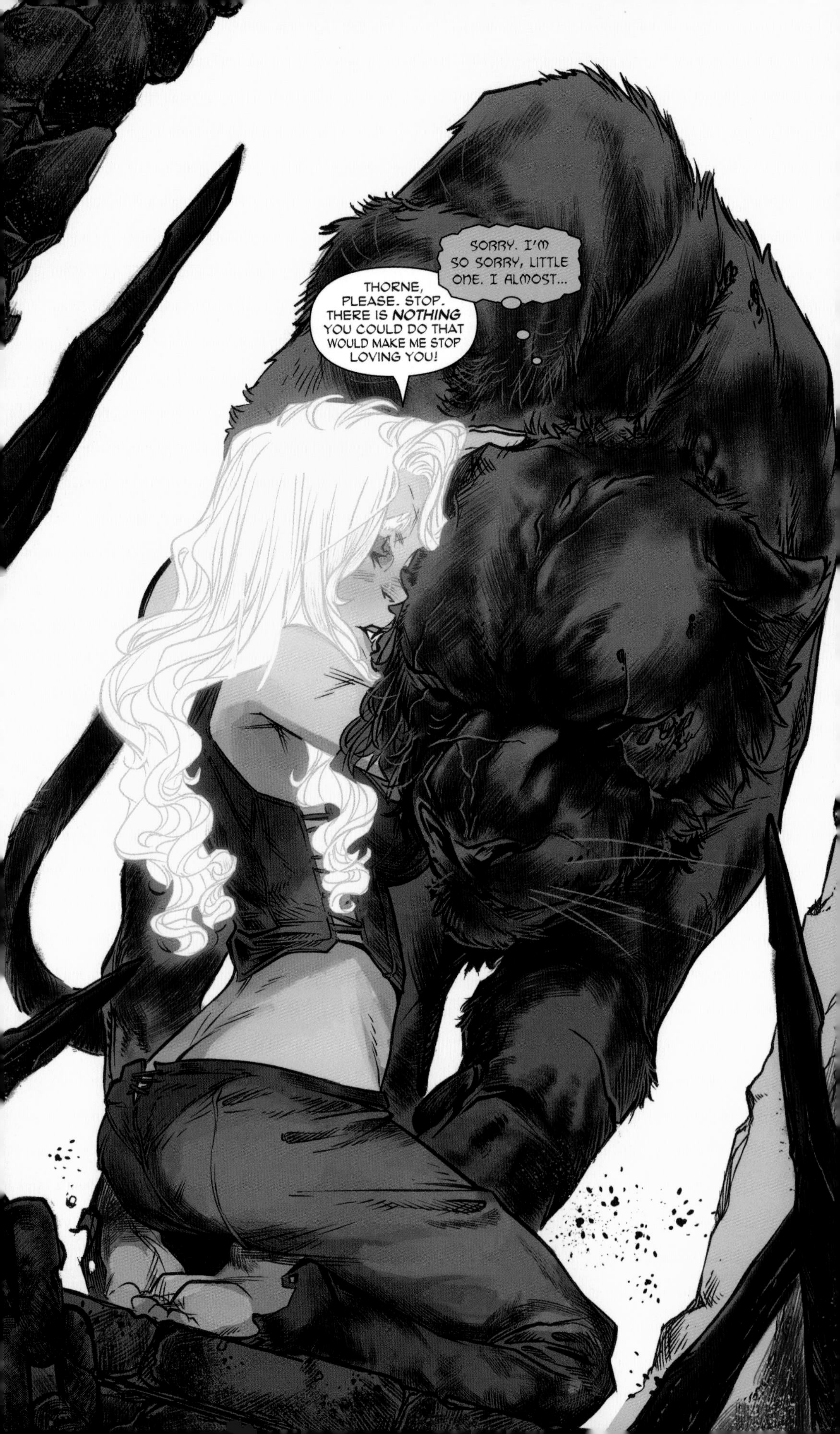
SORRY. I'M SO SORRY, LITTLE ONE. I ALMOST...
THORNE, PLEASE. STOP. THERE IS NOTHING YOU COULD DO THAT WOULD MAKE ME STOP LOVING YOU!

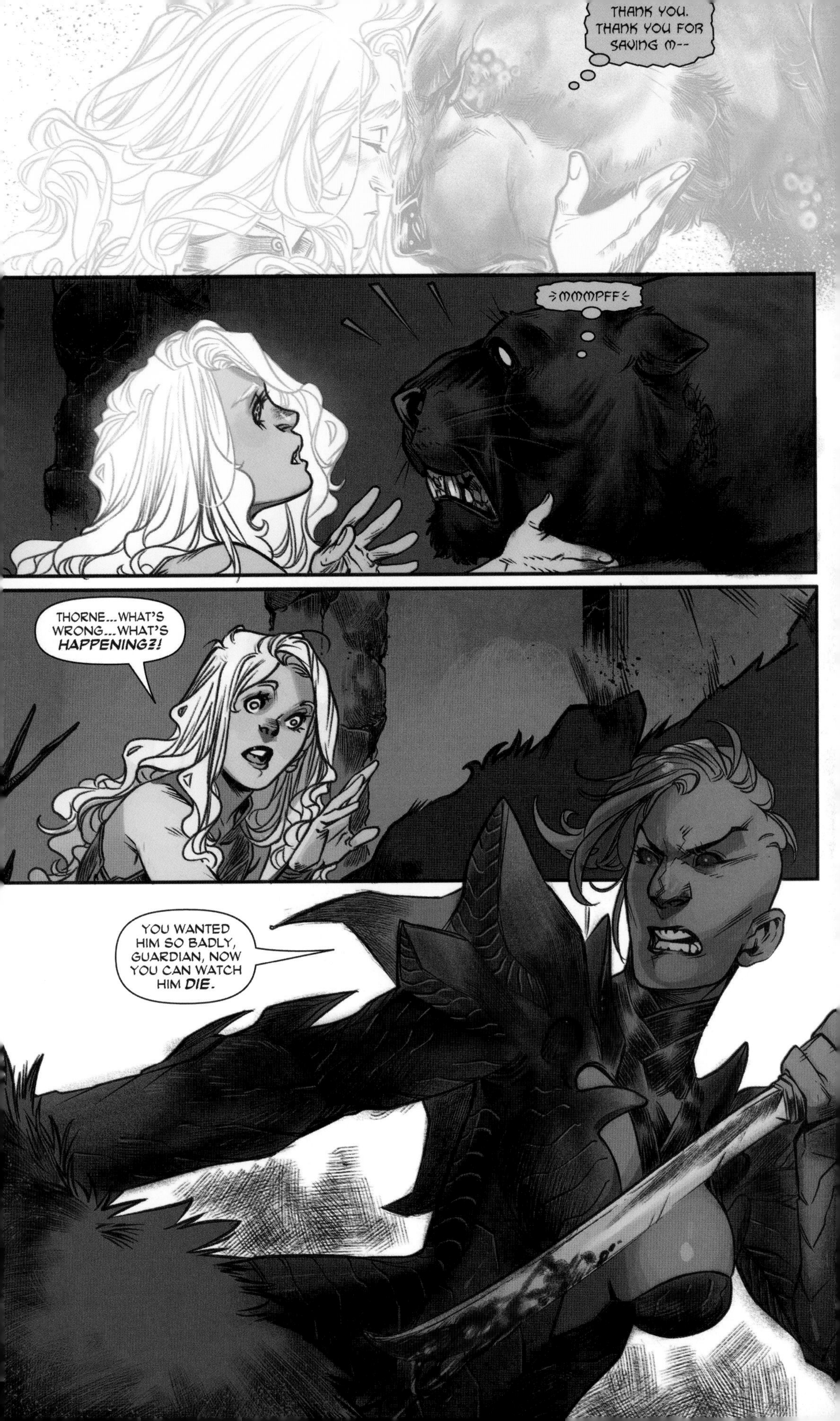
THANK YOU. THANK YOU FOR SAVING M--
MMMPFF
THORNE...WHAT'S WRONG...WHAT'S **HAPPENING?!**
YOU WANTED HIM SO BADLY, GUARDIAN, NOW YOU CAN WATCH HIM ***DIE***.

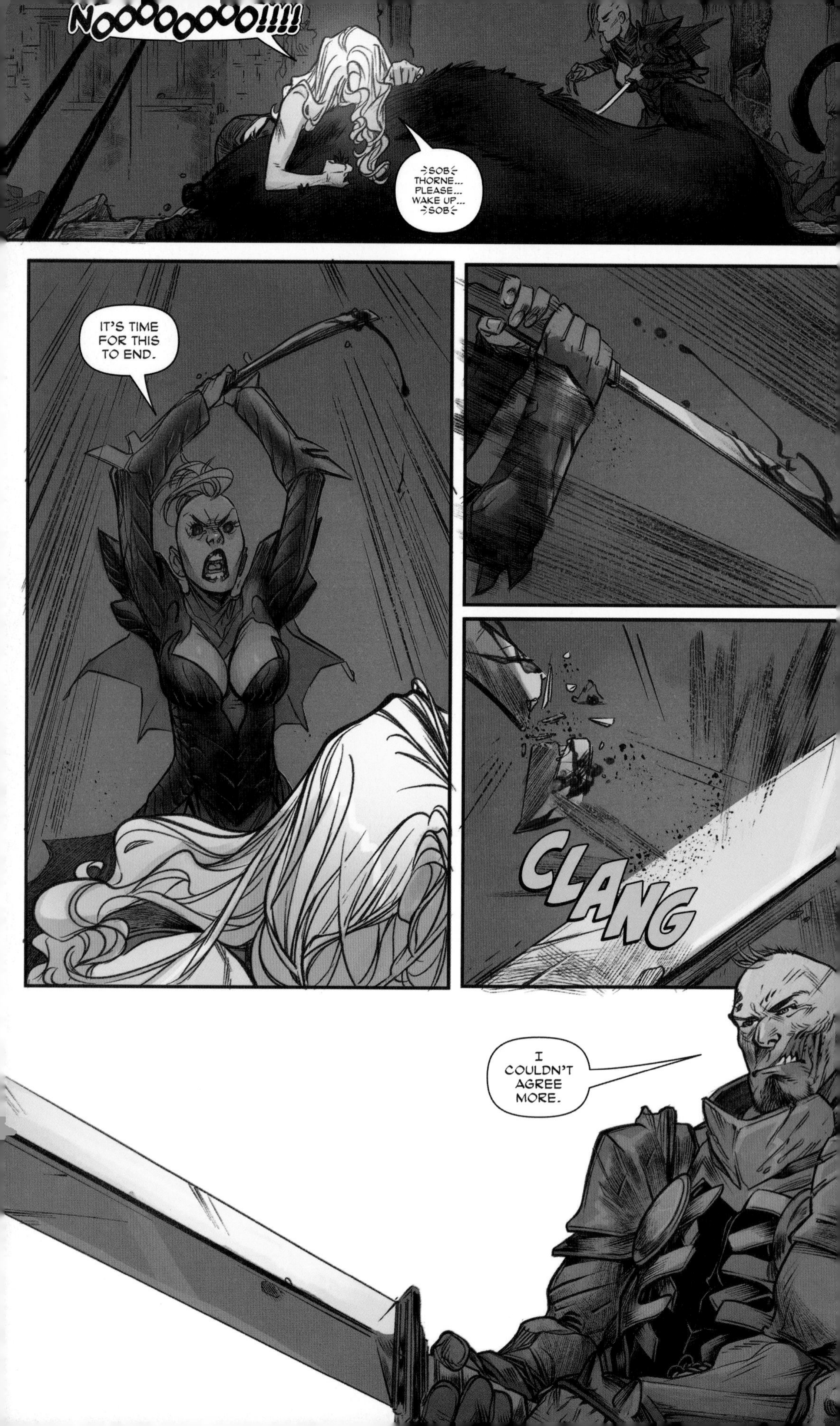
NOOOOOOOO!!!!!
SOB
THORNE... PLEASE... WAKE UP...
SOB
IT'S TIME FOR THIS TO END.
CLANG
I COULDN'T AGREE MORE.

SEVENTEEN

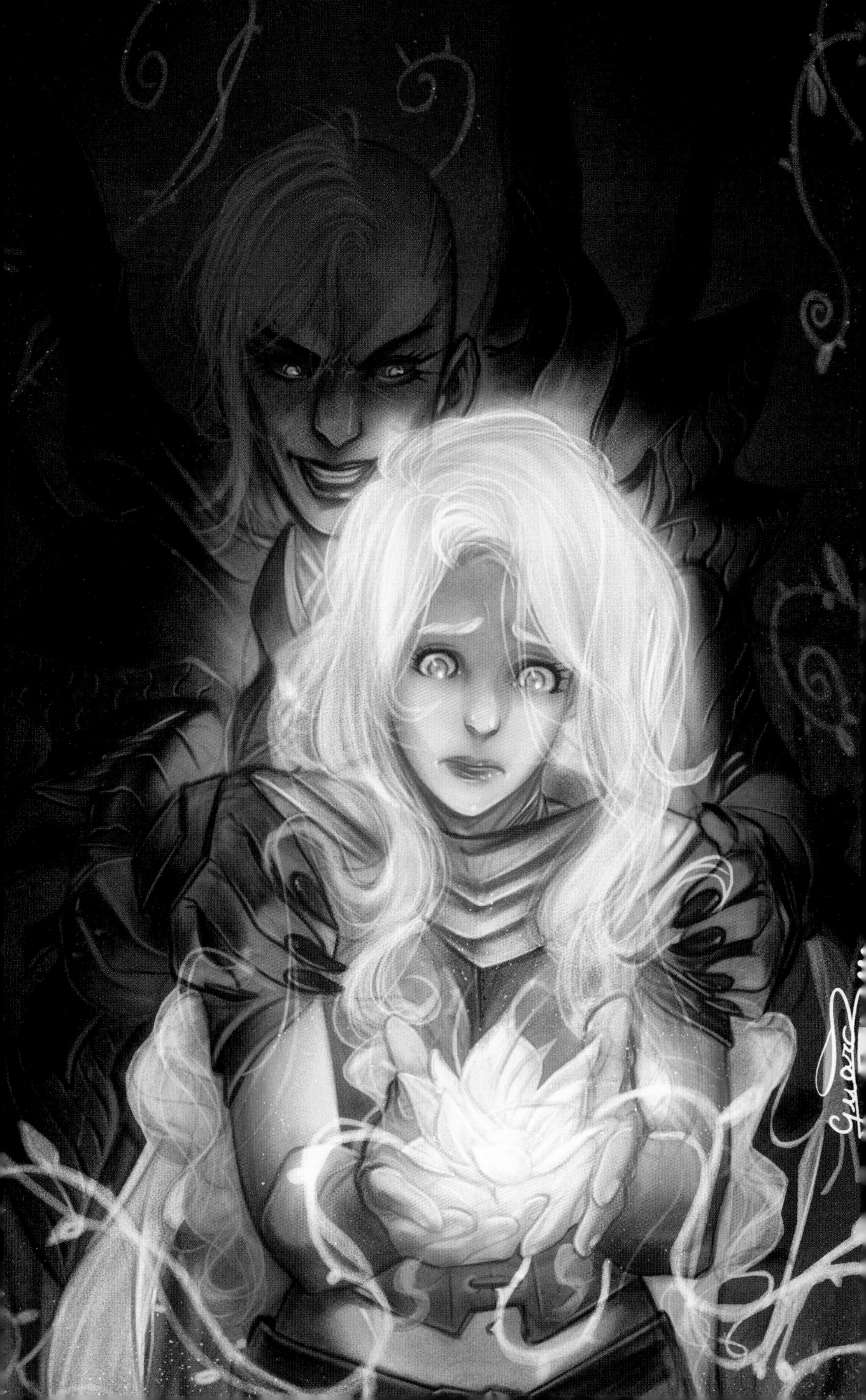

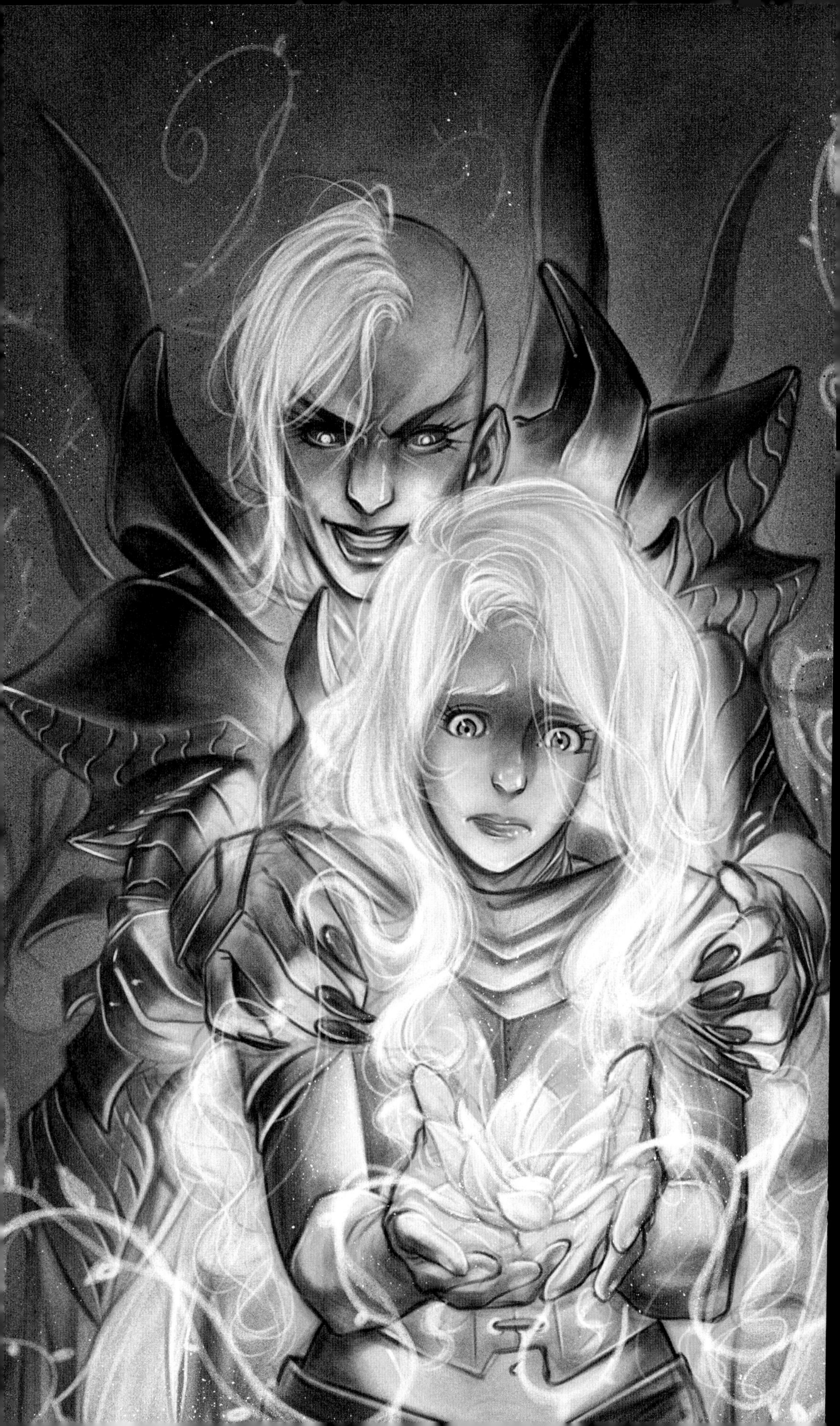

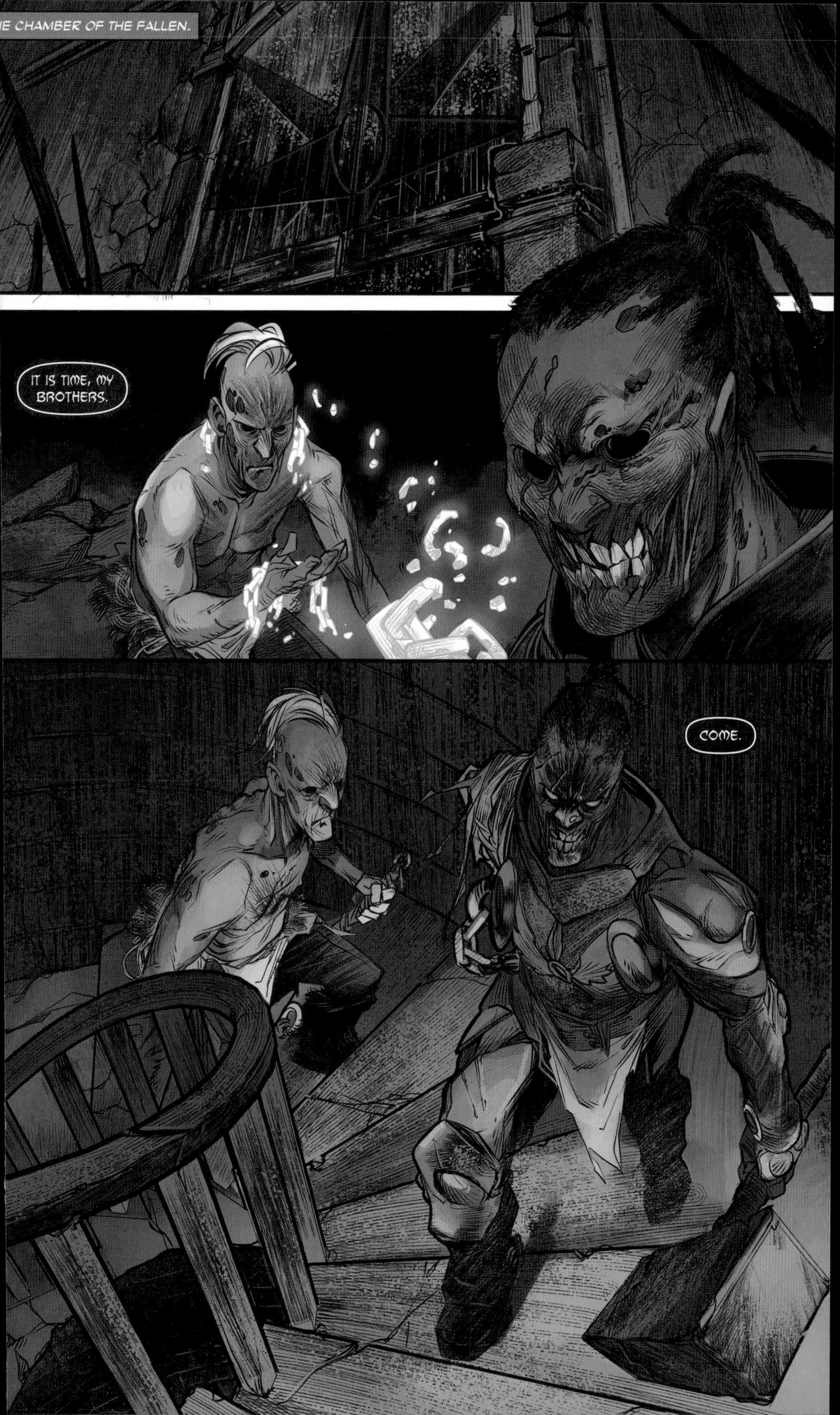
E CHAMBER OF THE FALLEN.
IT IS TIME, MY BROTHERS.
COME.

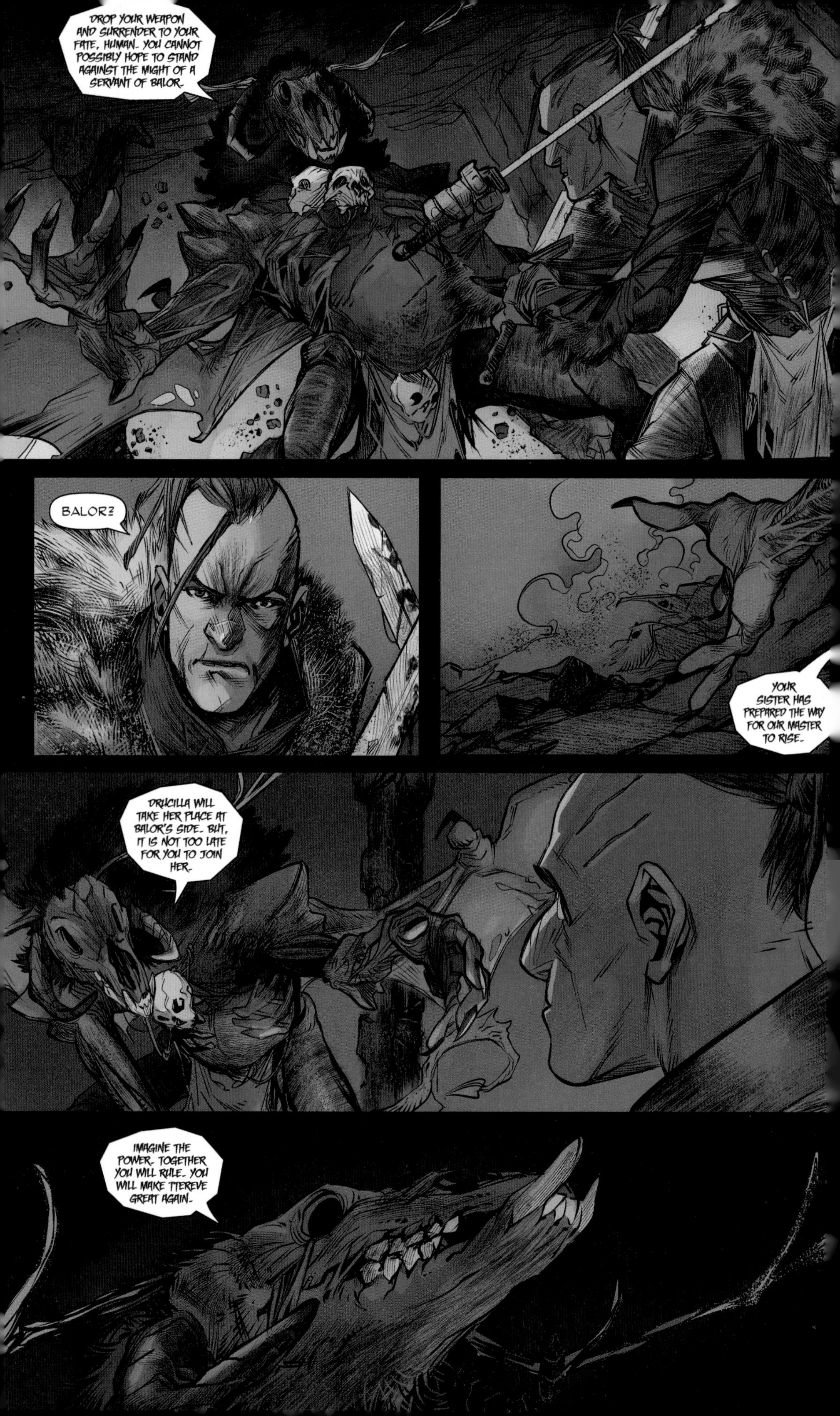
DROP YOUR WEAPON AND SURRENDER TO YOUR FATE, HUMAN. YOU CANNOT POSSIBLY HOPE TO STAND AGAINST THE MIGHT OF A SERVANT OF BALOR.
BALOR?
YOUR SISTER HAS PREPARED THE WAY FOR OUR MASTER TO RISE.
DRUCILLA WILL TAKE HER PLACE AT BALOR'S SIDE. BUT, IT IS NOT TOO LATE FOR YOU TO JOIN HER.
IMAGINE THE POWER. TOGETHER YOU WILL RULE. YOU WILL MAKE TIEREVE GREAT AGAIN.

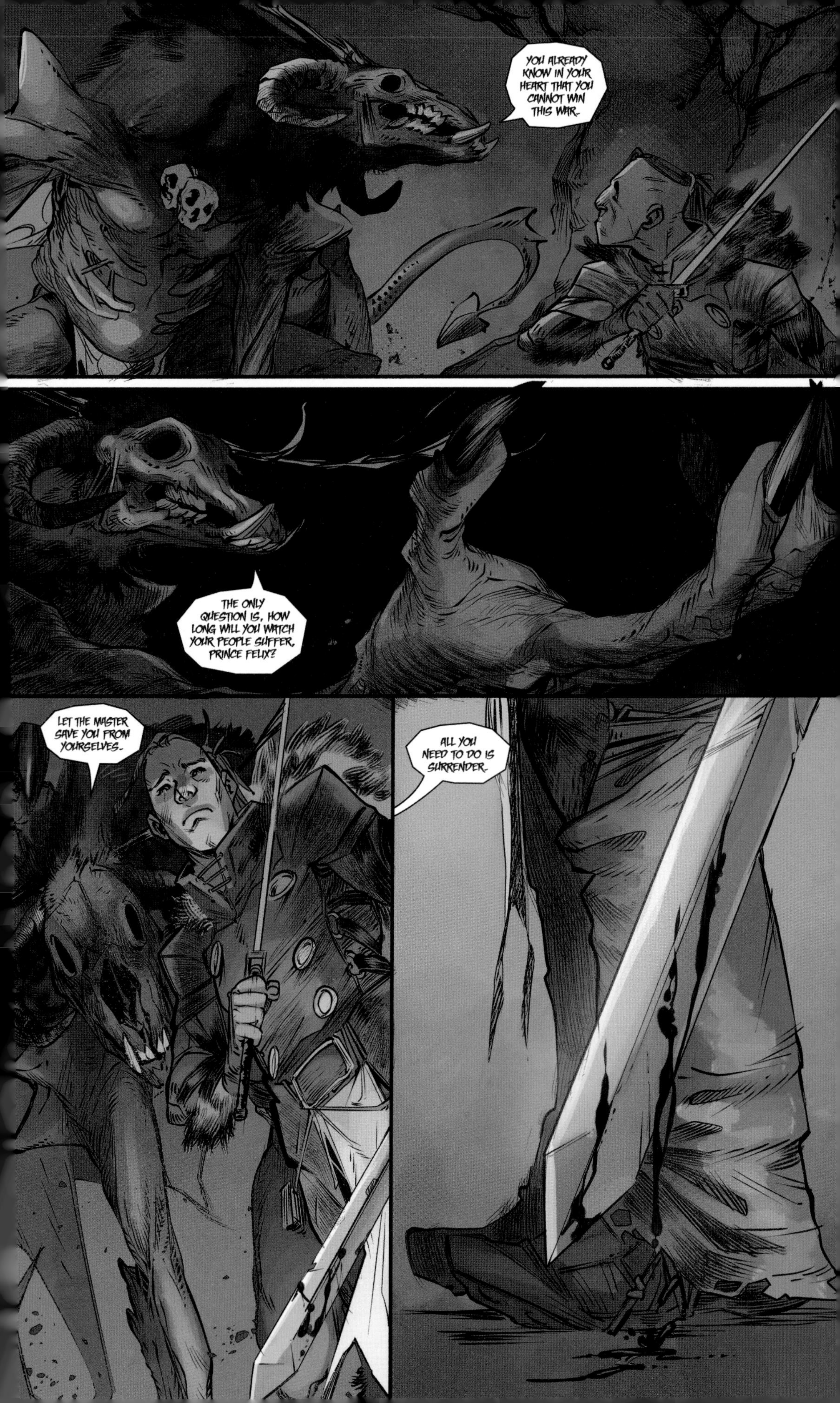

YOU ALREADY KNOW IN YOUR HEART THAT YOU CANNOT WIN THIS WAR.
THE ONLY QUESTION IS, HOW LONG WILL YOU WATCH YOUR PEOPLE SUFFER, PRINCE FELIX?
LET THE MASTER SAVE YOU FROM YOURSELVES.
ALL YOU NEED TO DO IS SURRENDER.

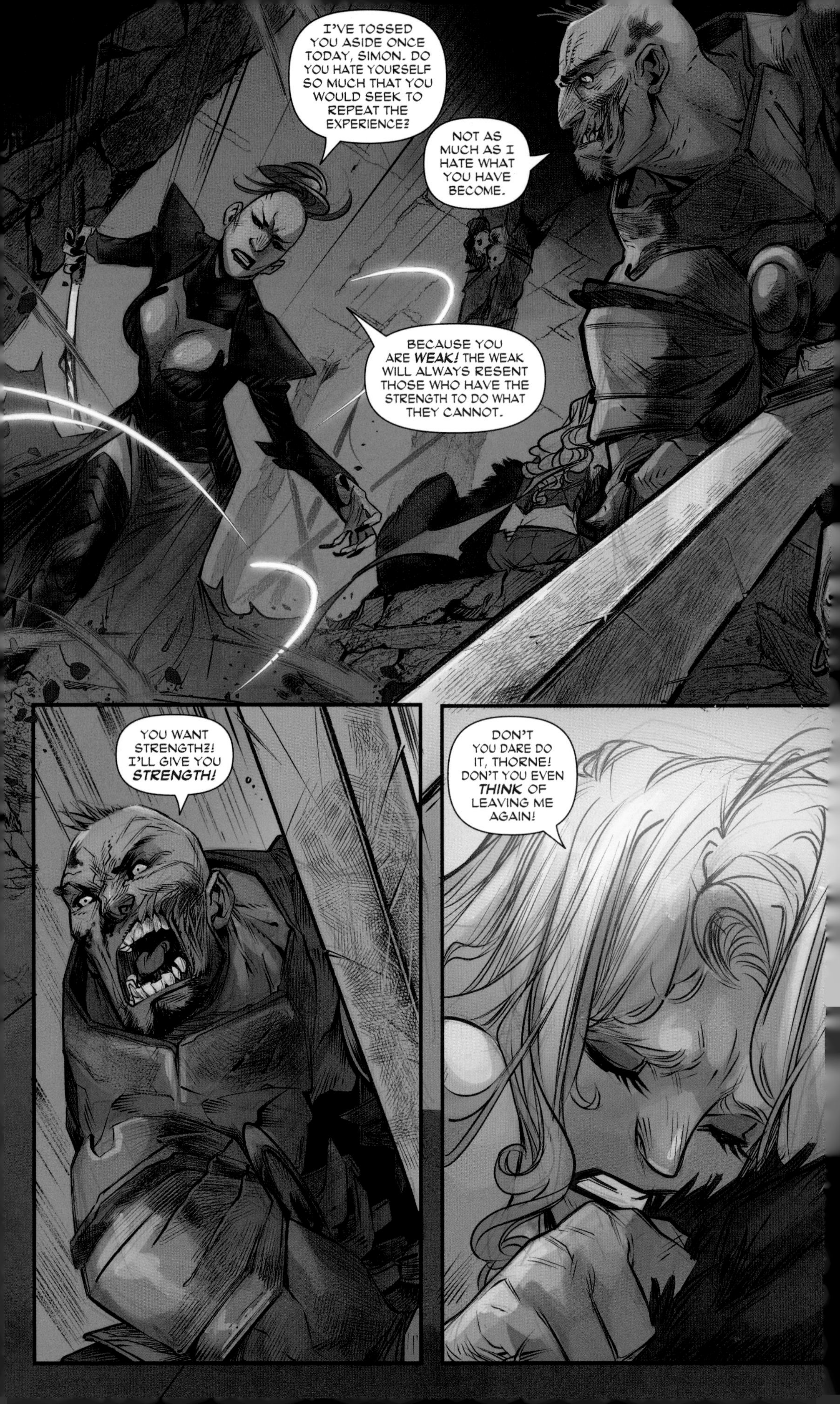
I'VE TOSSED YOU ASIDE ONCE TODAY, SIMON. DO YOU HATE YOURSELF SO MUCH THAT YOU WOULD SEEK TO REPEAT THE EXPERIENCE?
NOT AS MUCH AS I HATE WHAT YOU HAVE BECOME.
BECAUSE YOU ARE **WEAK!** THE WEAK WILL ALWAYS RESENT THOSE WHO HAVE THE STRENGTH TO DO WHAT THEY CANNOT.
YOU WANT STRENGTH?! I'LL GIVE YOU **STRENGTH!**
DON'T YOU DARE DO IT, THORNE! DON'T YOU EVEN **THINK** OF LEAVING ME AGAIN!

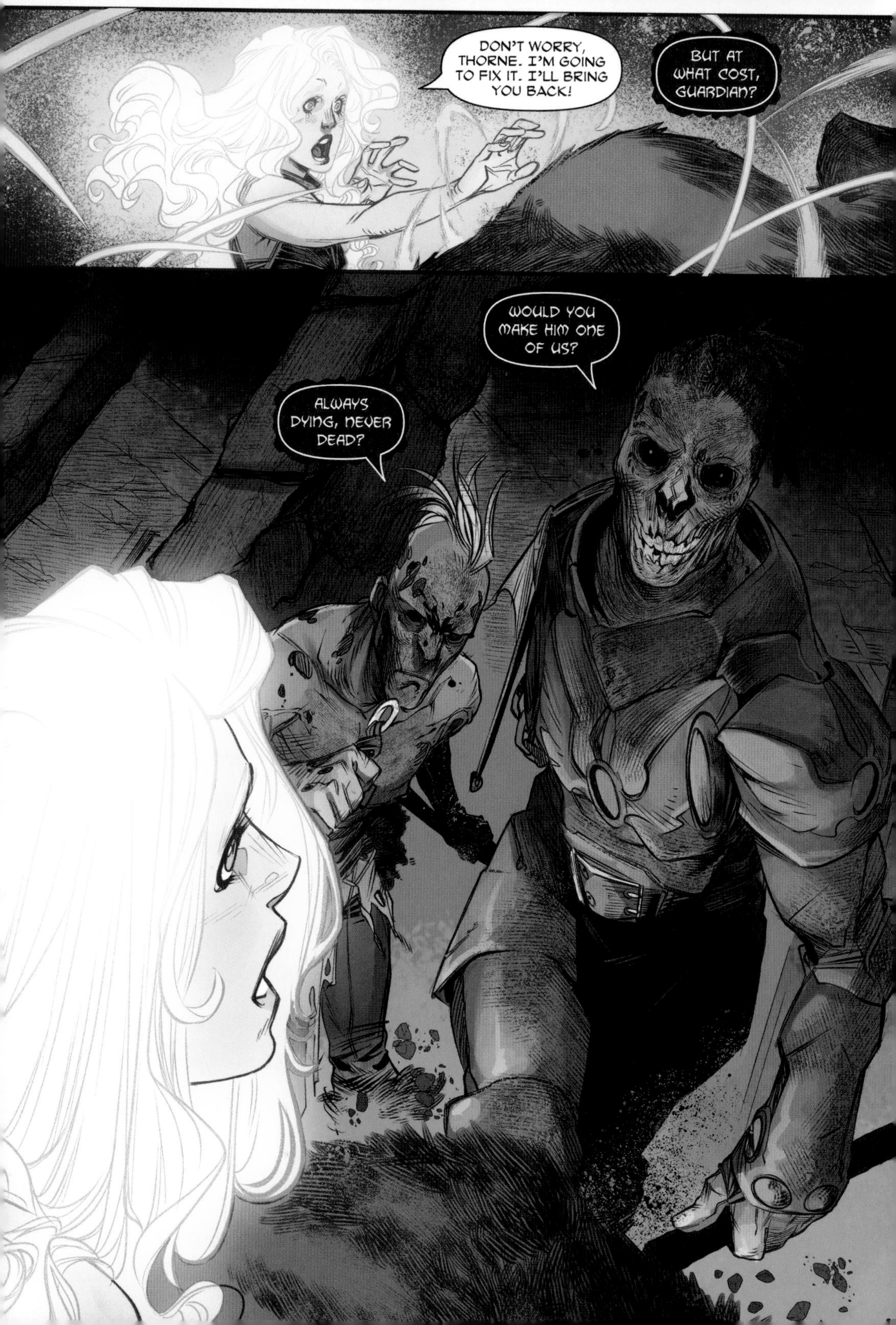
DON'T WORRY, THORNE. I'M GOING TO FIX IT. I'LL BRING YOU BACK!
BUT AT WHAT COST, GUARDIAN?
WOULD YOU MAKE HIM ONE OF US?
ALWAYS DYING, NEVER DEAD?

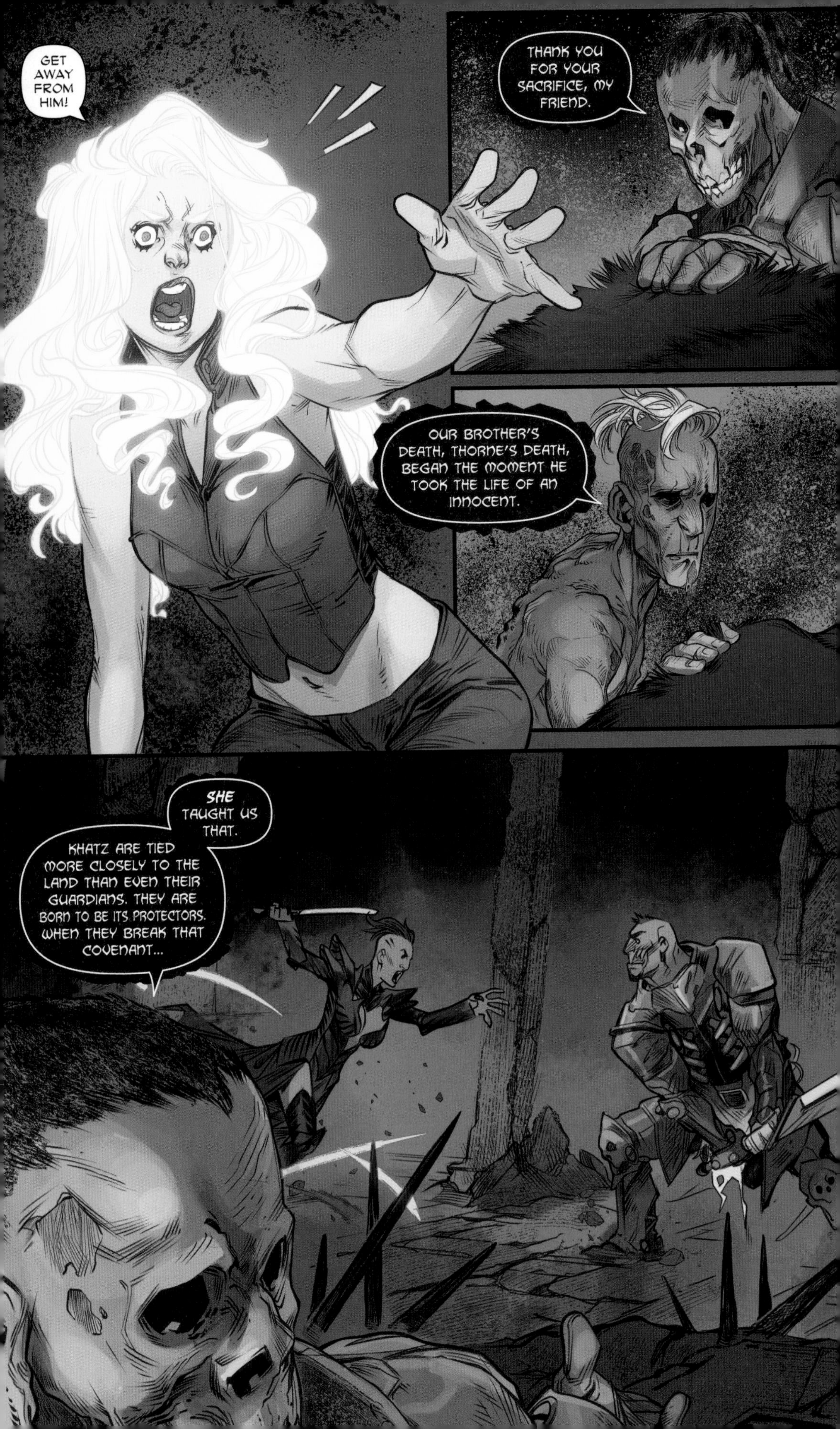
GET AWAY FROM HIM!
THANK YOU FOR YOUR SACRIFICE, MY FRIEND.
OUR BROTHER'S DEATH, THORNE'S DEATH, BEGAN THE MOMENT HE TOOK THE LIFE OF AN INNOCENT.
SHE TAUGHT US THAT.
KHATZ ARE TIED MORE CLOSELY TO THE LAND THAN EVEN THEIR GUARDIANS. THEY ARE BORN TO BE ITS PROTECTORS. WHEN THEY BREAK THAT COVENANT...

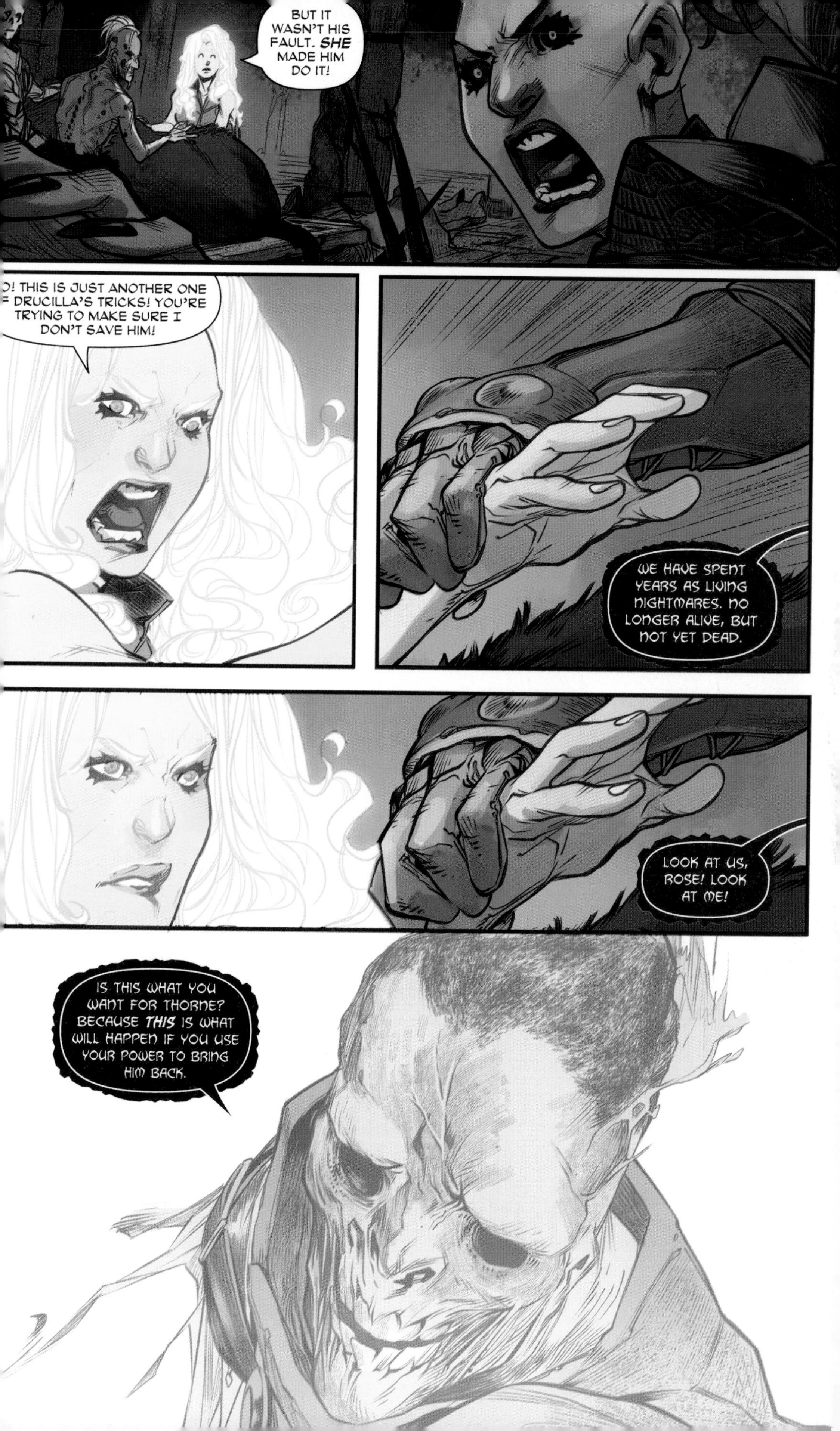
BUT IT WASN'T HIS FAULT. SHE MADE HIM DO IT!
O! THIS IS JUST ANOTHER ONE F DRUCILLA'S TRICKS! YOU'RE TRYING TO MAKE SURE I DON'T SAVE HIM!
WE HAVE SPENT YEARS AS LIVING NIGHTMARES. NO LONGER ALIVE, BUT NOT YET DEAD.
LOOK AT US, ROSE! LOOK AT ME!
IS THIS WHAT YOU WANT FOR THORNE? BECAUSE THIS IS WHAT WILL HAPPEN IF YOU USE YOUR POWER TO BRING HIM BACK.

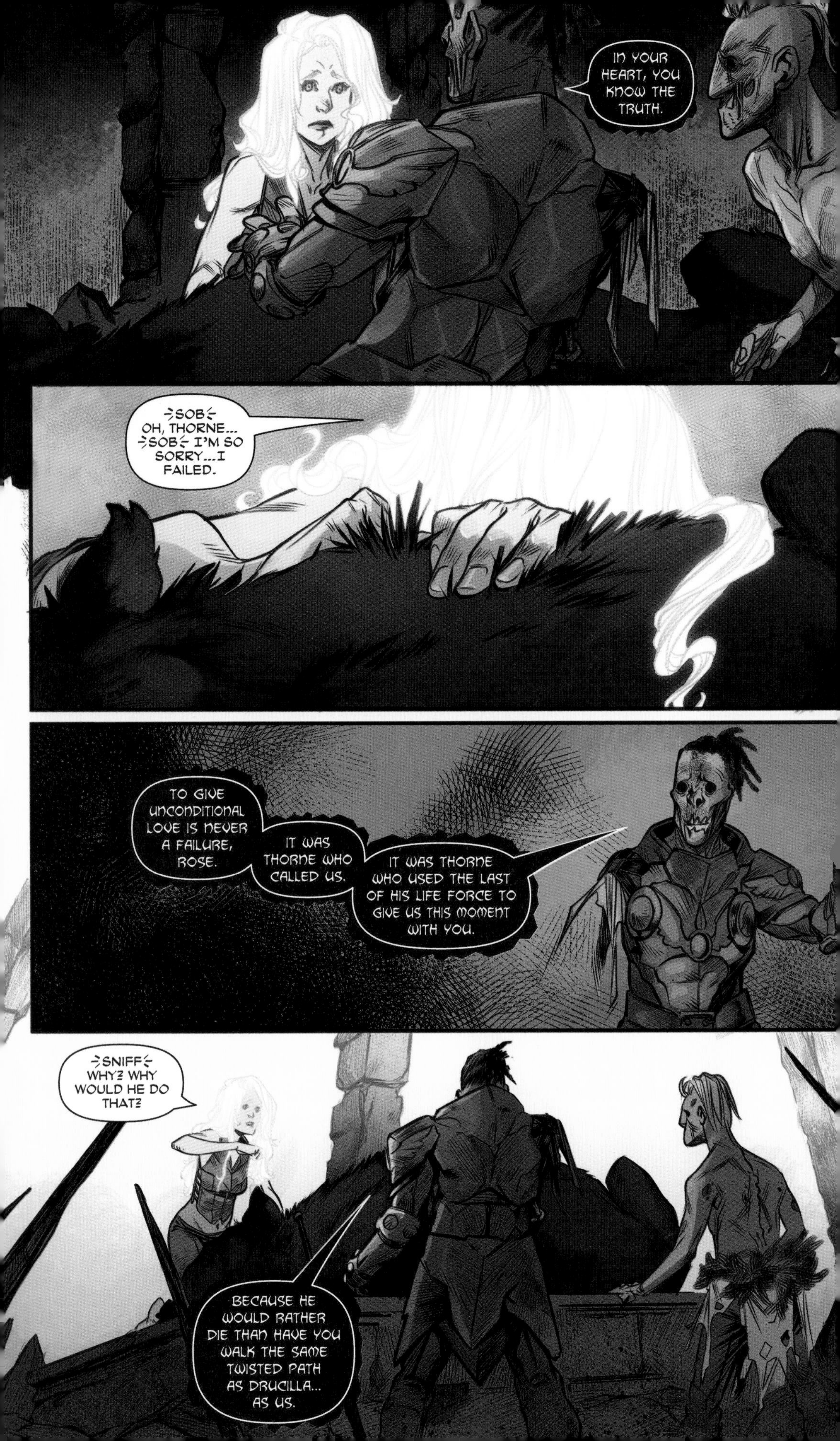
IN YOUR HEART, YOU KNOW THE TRUTH.
≈SOB≈ OH, THORNE... ≈SOB≈ I'M SO SORRY...I FAILED.
TO GIVE UNCONDITIONAL LOVE IS NEVER A FAILURE, ROSE.
IT WAS THORNE WHO CALLED US.
IT WAS THORNE WHO USED THE LAST OF HIS LIFE FORCE TO GIVE US THIS MOMENT WITH YOU.
≈SNIFF≈ WHY? WHY WOULD HE DO THAT?
BECAUSE HE WOULD RATHER DIE THAN HAVE YOU WALK THE SAME TWISTED PATH AS DRUCILLA... AS US.

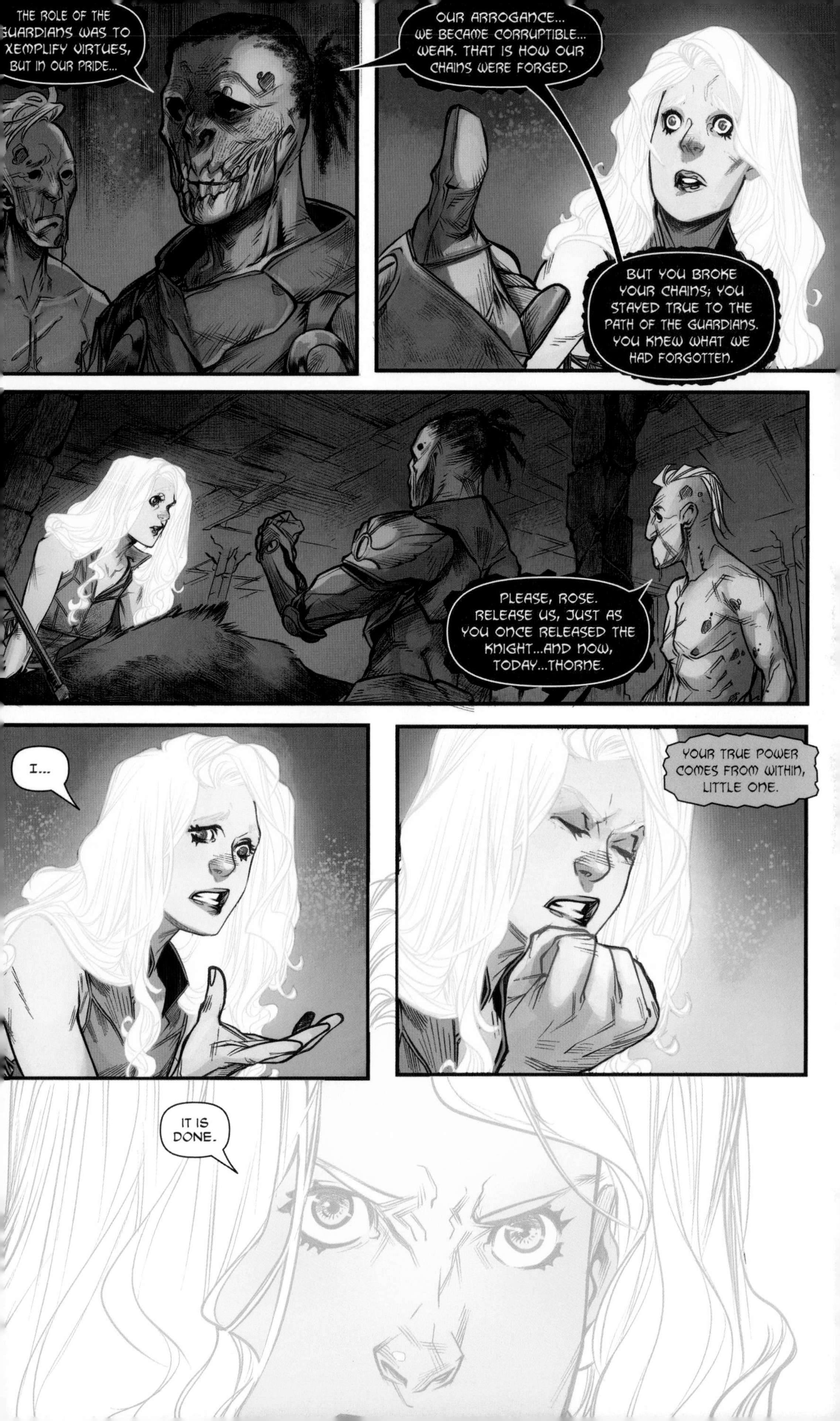
THE ROLE OF THE GUARDIANS WAS TO XEMPLIFY VIRTUES, BUT IN OUR PRIDE...
OUR ARROGANCE... WE BECAME CORRUPTIBLE... WEAK. THAT IS HOW OUR CHAINS WERE FORGED.
BUT YOU BROKE YOUR CHAINS; YOU STAYED TRUE TO THE PATH OF THE GUARDIANS. YOU KNEW WHAT WE HAD FORGOTTEN.
PLEASE, ROSE. RELEASE US, JUST AS YOU ONCE RELEASED THE KNIGHT...AND NOW, TODAY...THORNE.
I...
YOUR TRUE POWER COMES FROM WITHIN, LITTLE ONE.
IT IS DONE.

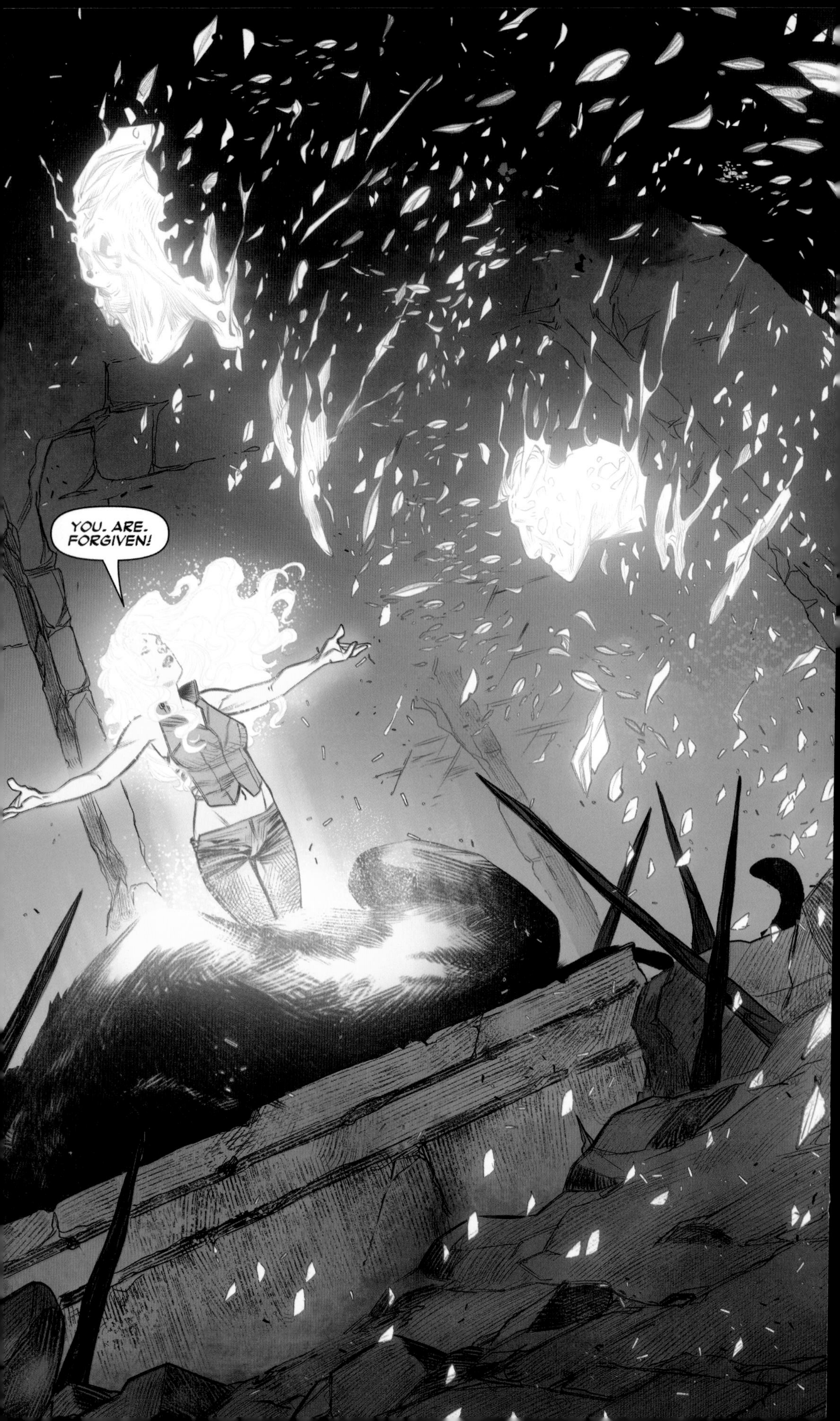
YOU. ARE. FORGIVEN!

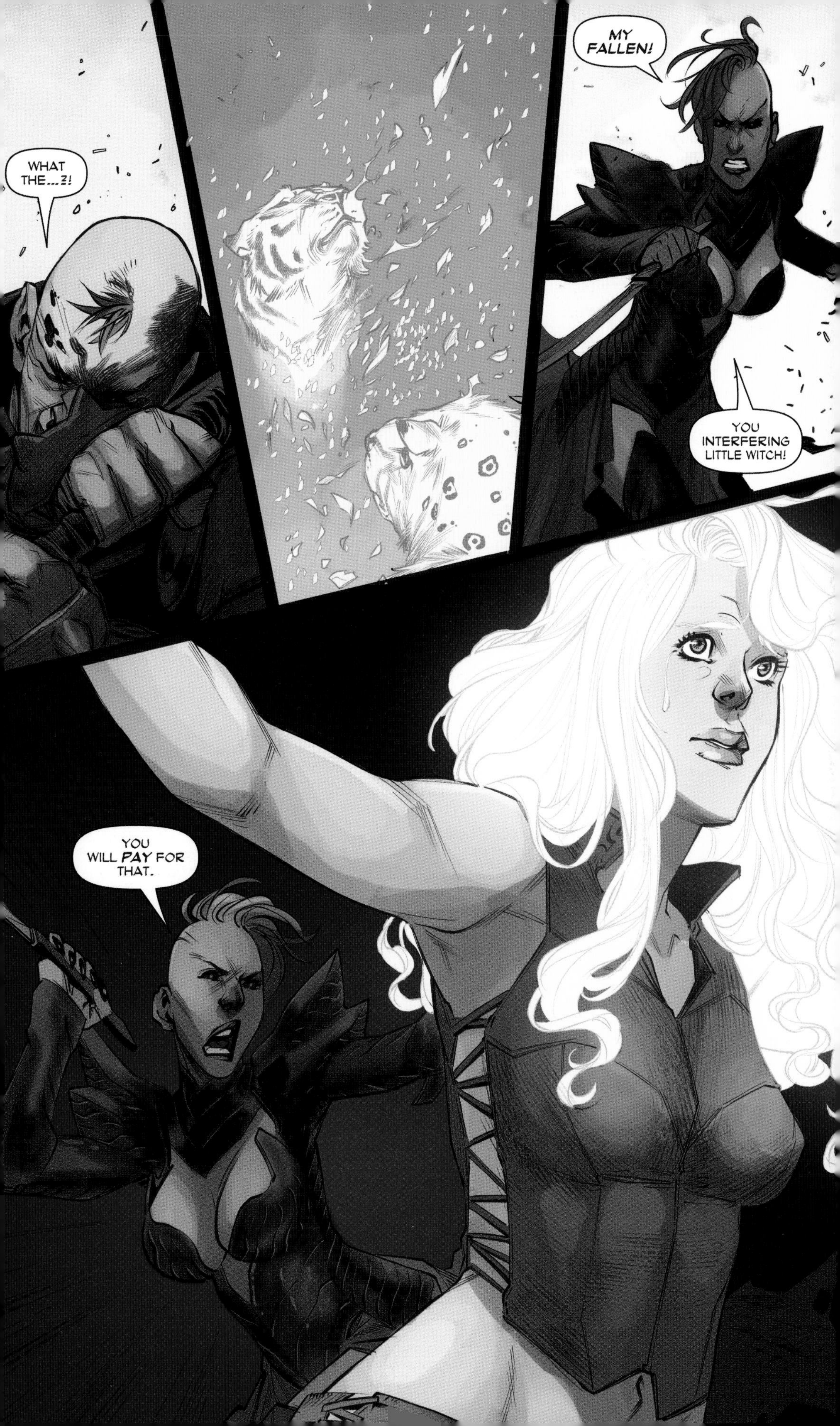
WHAT THE...?!
MY FALLEN!
YOU INTERFERING LITTLE WITCH!
YOU WILL PAY FOR THAT.

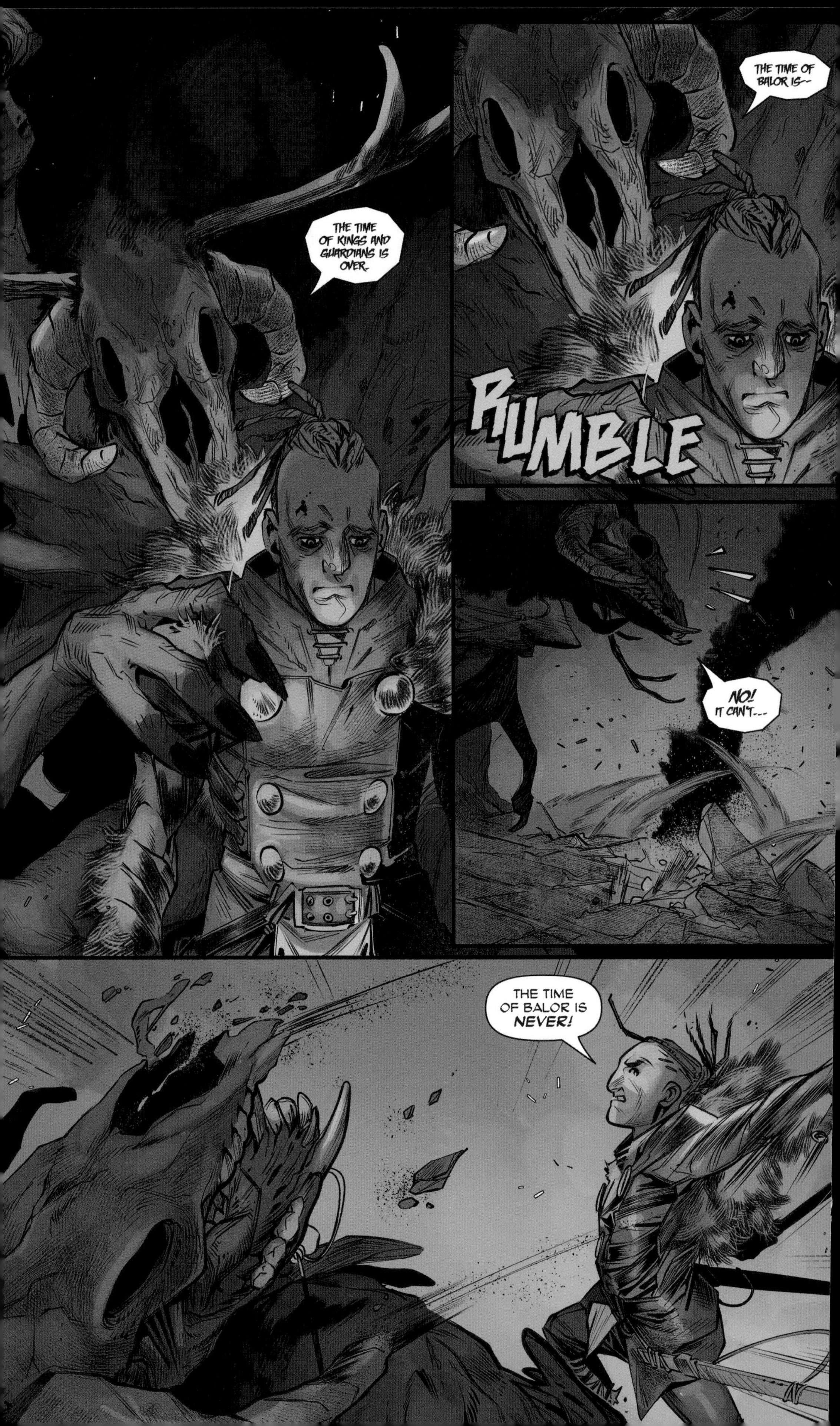
THE TIME OF KINGS AND GUARDIANS IS OVER.
THE TIME OF BALOR IS--
RUMBLE
NO! IT CAN'T--
THE TIME OF BALOR IS NEVER!

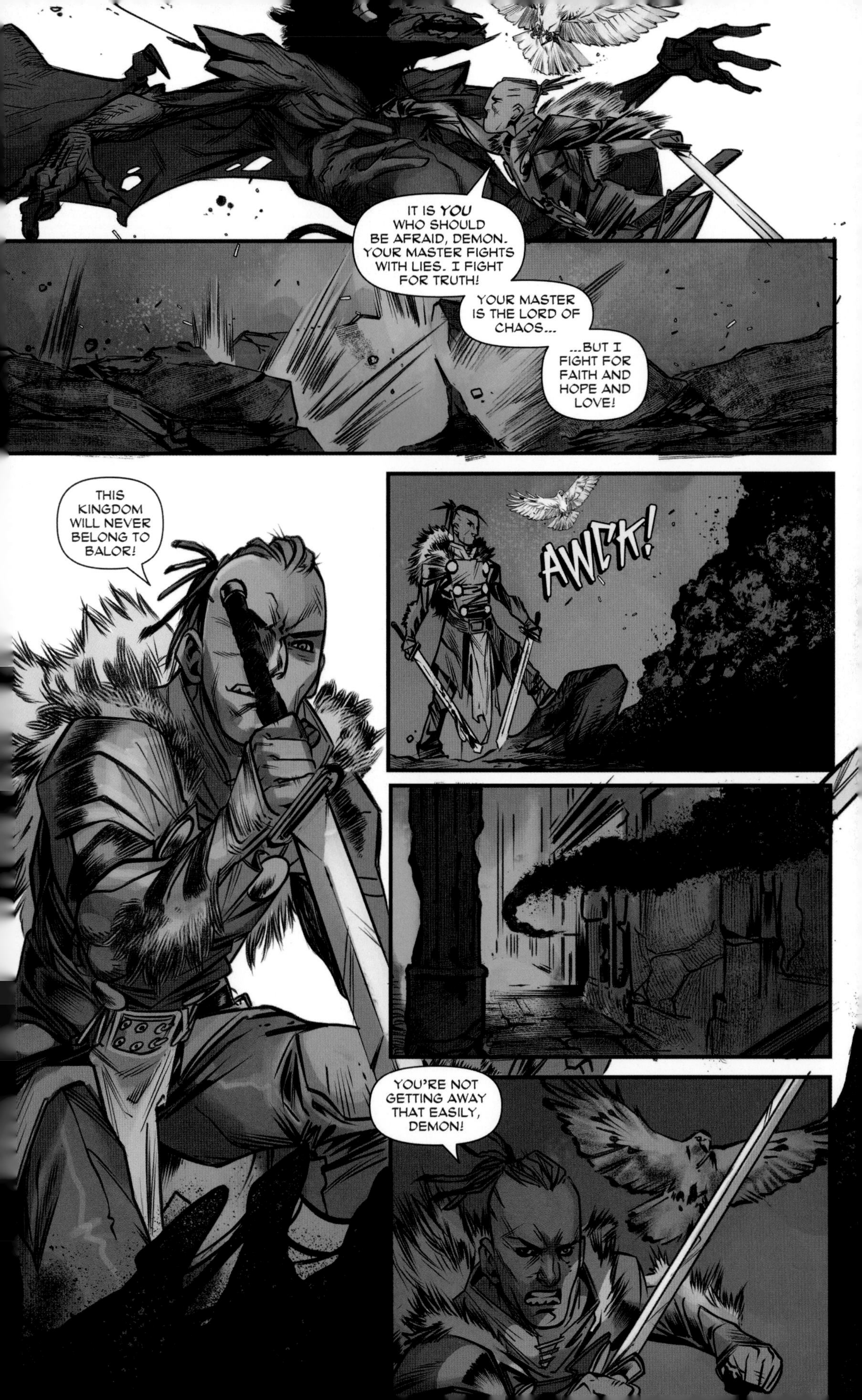
IT IS YOU WHO SHOULD BE AFRAID, DEMON. YOUR MASTER FIGHTS WITH LIES. I FIGHT FOR TRUTH!
YOUR MASTER IS THE LORD OF CHAOS...
...BUT I FIGHT FOR FAITH AND HOPE AND LOVE!
THIS KINGDOM WILL NEVER BELONG TO BALOR!
AWCK!
YOU'RE NOT GETTING AWAY THAT EASILY, DEMON!

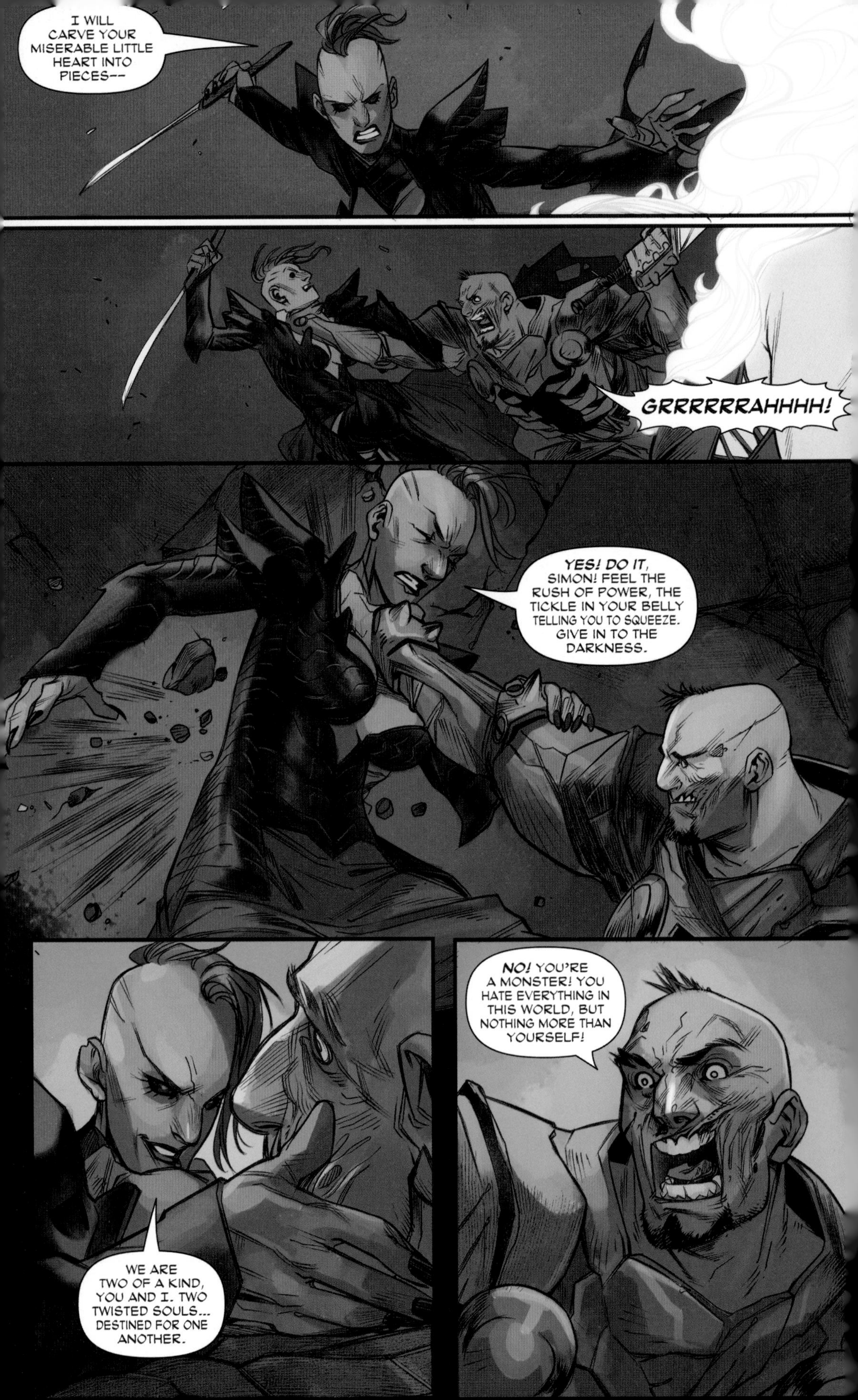
I WILL CARVE YOUR MISERABLE LITTLE HEART INTO PIECES--
GRRRRRRAHHHH!
YES! DO IT, SIMON! FEEL THE RUSH OF POWER, THE TICKLE IN YOUR BELLY TELLING YOU TO SQUEEZE. GIVE IN TO THE DARKNESS.
WE ARE TWO OF A KIND, YOU AND I. TWO TWISTED SOULS... DESTINED FOR ONE ANOTHER.
NO! YOU'RE A MONSTER! YOU HATE EVERYTHING IN THIS WORLD, BUT NOTHING MORE THAN YOURSELF!

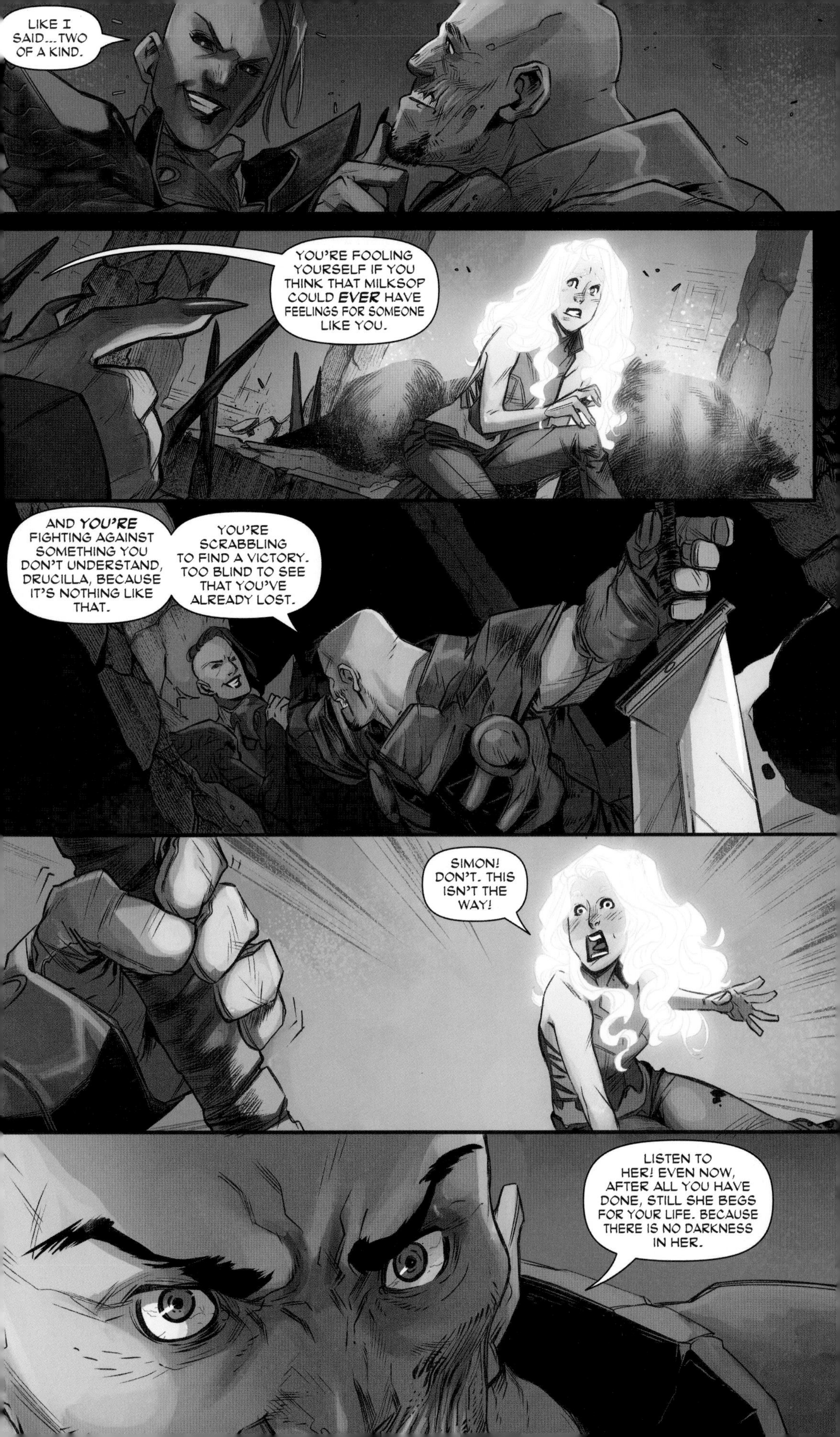
LIKE I SAID...TWO OF A KIND.
YOU'RE FOOLING YOURSELF IF YOU THINK THAT MILKSOP COULD EVER HAVE FEELINGS FOR SOMEONE LIKE YOU.
AND YOU'RE FIGHTING AGAINST SOMETHING YOU DON'T UNDERSTAND, DRUCILLA, BECAUSE IT'S NOTHING LIKE THAT.
YOU'RE SCRABBLING TO FIND A VICTORY. TOO BLIND TO SEE THAT YOU'VE ALREADY LOST.
SIMON! DON'T. THIS ISN'T THE WAY!
LISTEN TO HER! EVEN NOW, AFTER ALL YOU HAVE DONE, STILL SHE BEGS FOR YOUR LIFE. BECAUSE THERE IS NO DARKNESS IN HER.

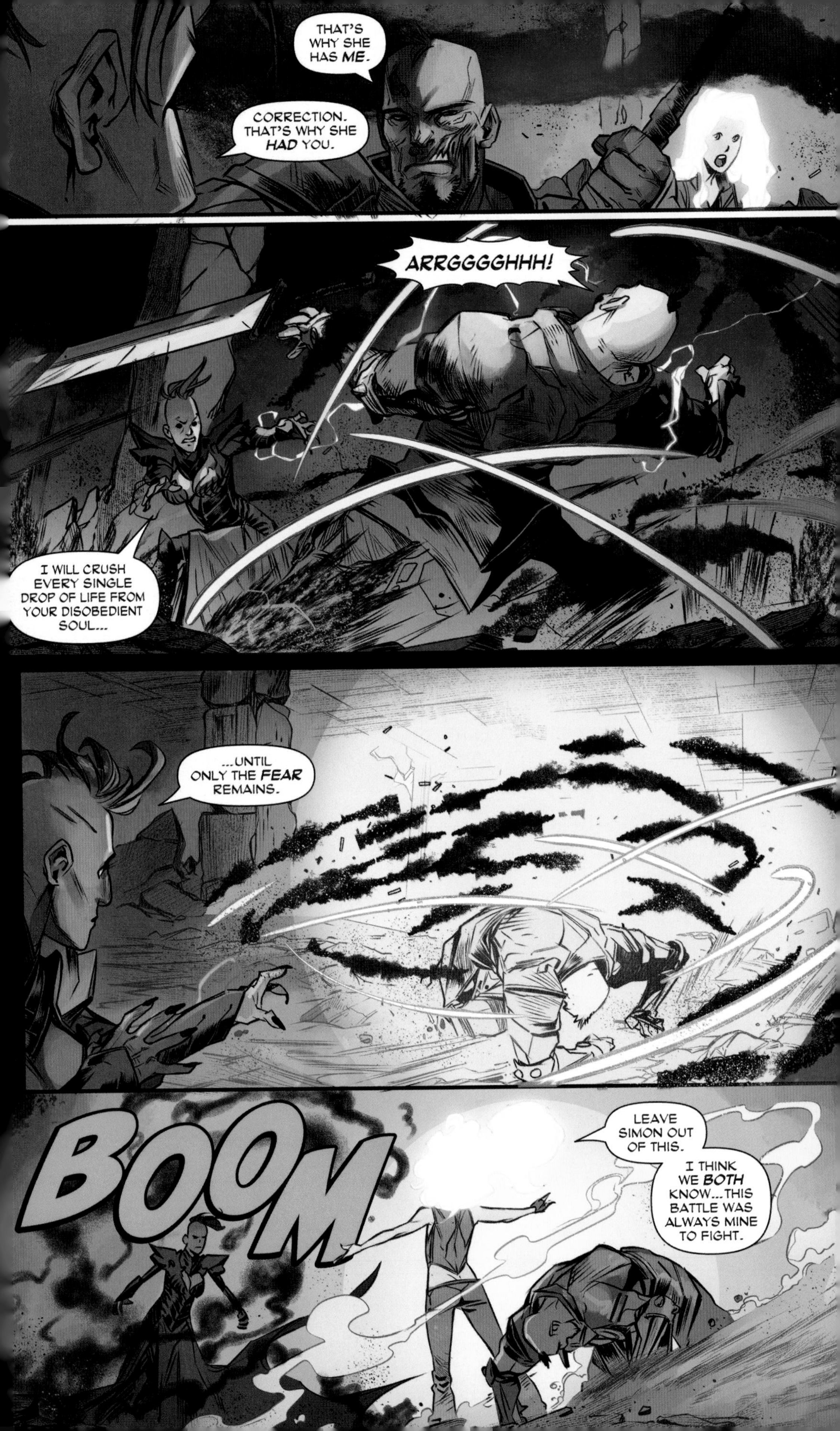
THAT'S WHY SHE HAS ME.
CORRECTION. THAT'S WHY SHE HAD YOU.
ARRGGGGHHH!
I WILL CRUSH EVERY SINGLE DROP OF LIFE FROM YOUR DISOBEDIENT SOUL...
...UNTIL ONLY THE FEAR REMAINS.
BOOM
LEAVE SIMON OUT OF THIS.
I THINK WE BOTH KNOW...THIS BATTLE WAS ALWAYS MINE TO FIGHT.

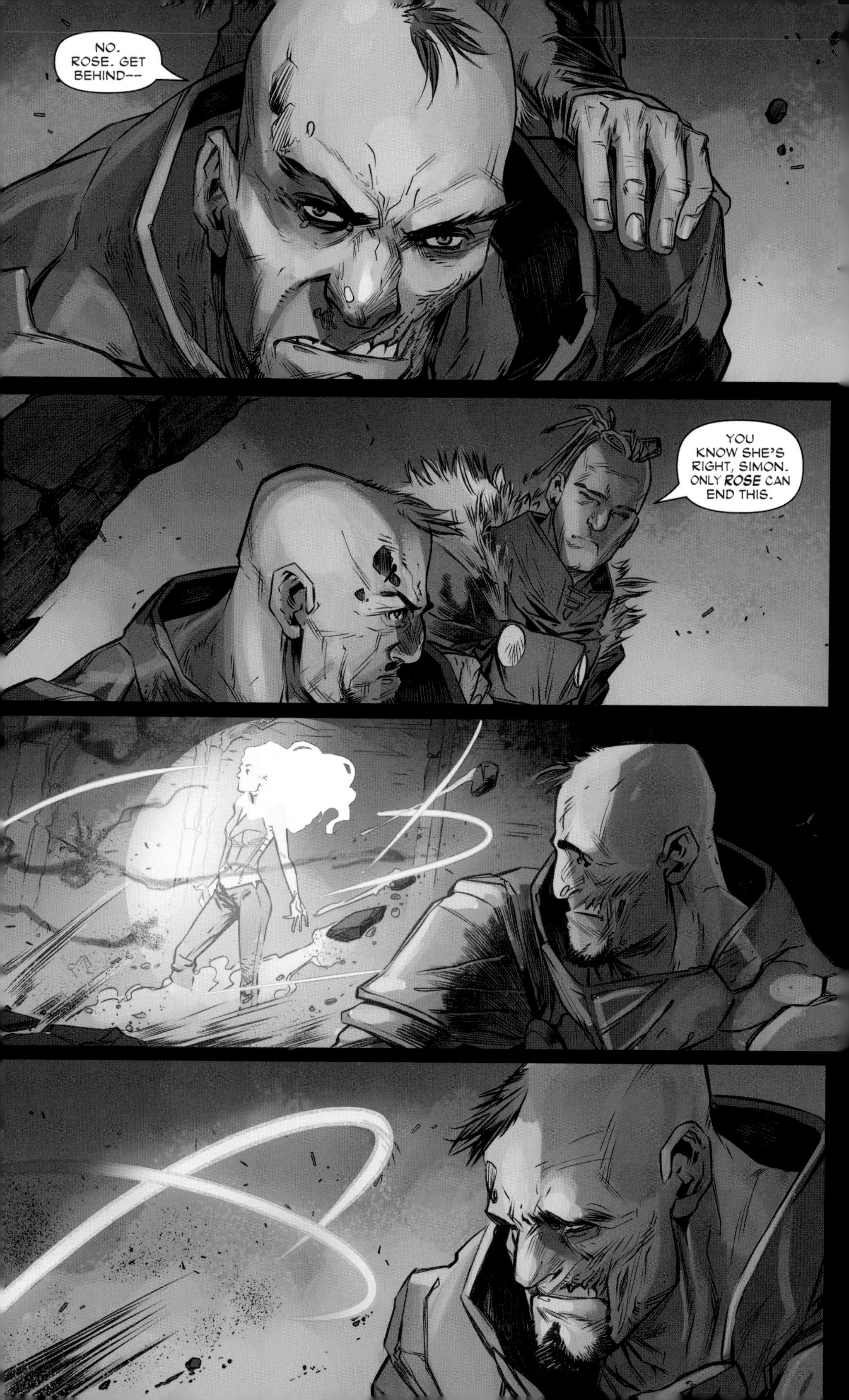
NO. ROSE. GET BEHIND--
YOU KNOW SHE'S RIGHT, SIMON. ONLY ROSE CAN END THIS.

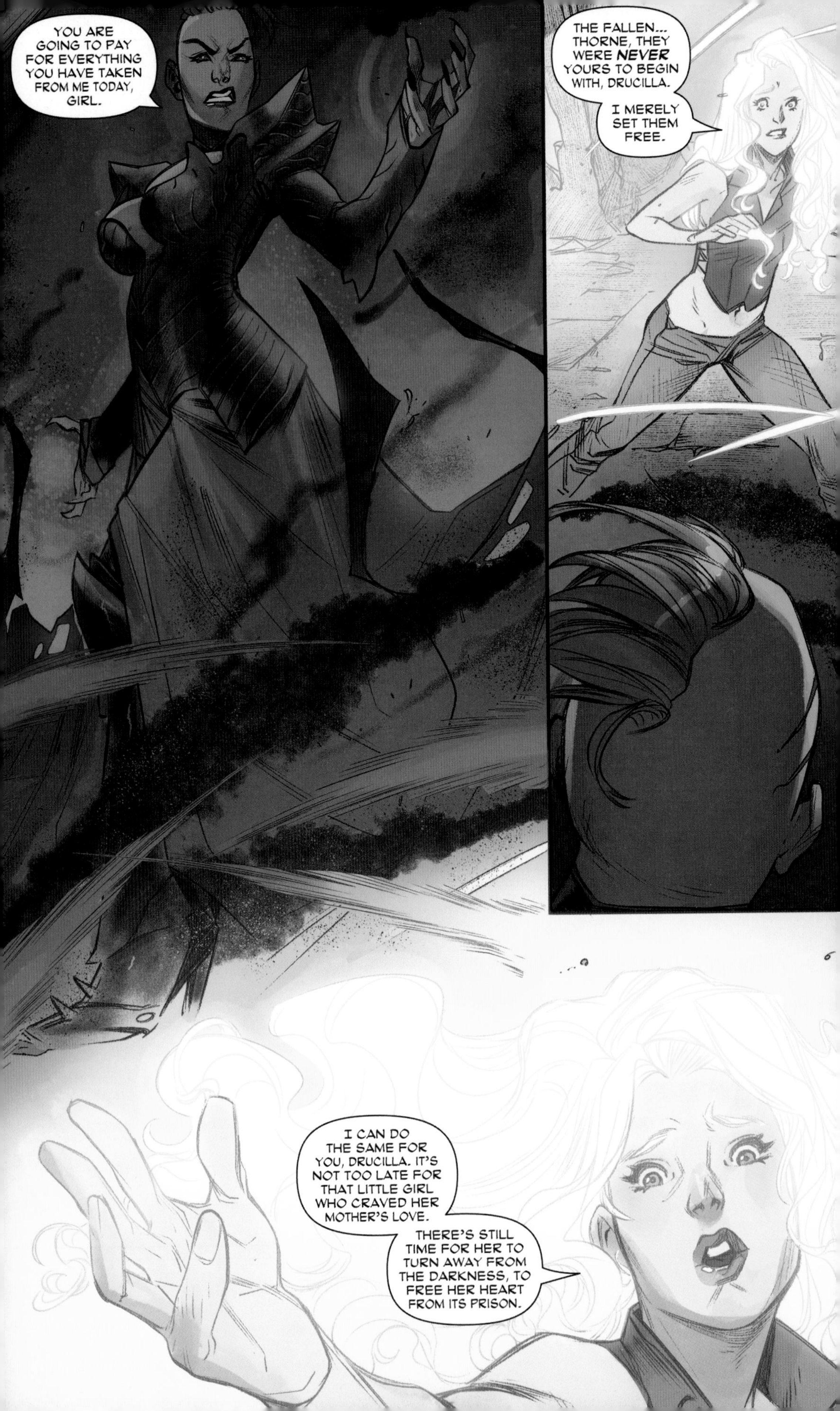
YOU ARE GOING TO PAY FOR EVERYTHING YOU HAVE TAKEN FROM ME TODAY, GIRL.
THE FALLEN... THORNE, THEY WERE **NEVER** YOURS TO BEGIN WITH, DRUCILLA.
I MERELY SET THEM FREE.
I CAN DO THE SAME FOR YOU, DRUCILLA. IT'S NOT TOO LATE FOR THAT LITTLE GIRL WHO CRAVED HER MOTHER'S LOVE.
THERE'S STILL TIME FOR HER TO TURN AWAY FROM THE DARKNESS, TO FREE HER HEART FROM ITS PRISON.

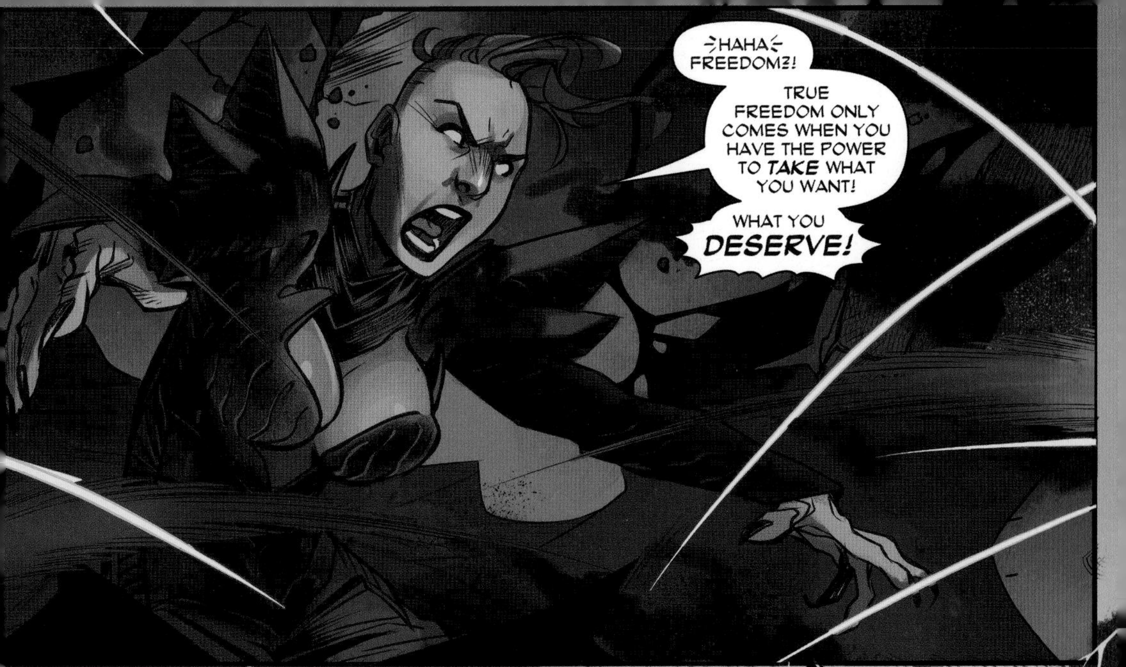
HAHA FREEDOM?!
TRUE FREEDOM ONLY COMES WHEN YOU HAVE THE POWER TO TAKE WHAT YOU WANT!
WHAT YOU DESERVE!

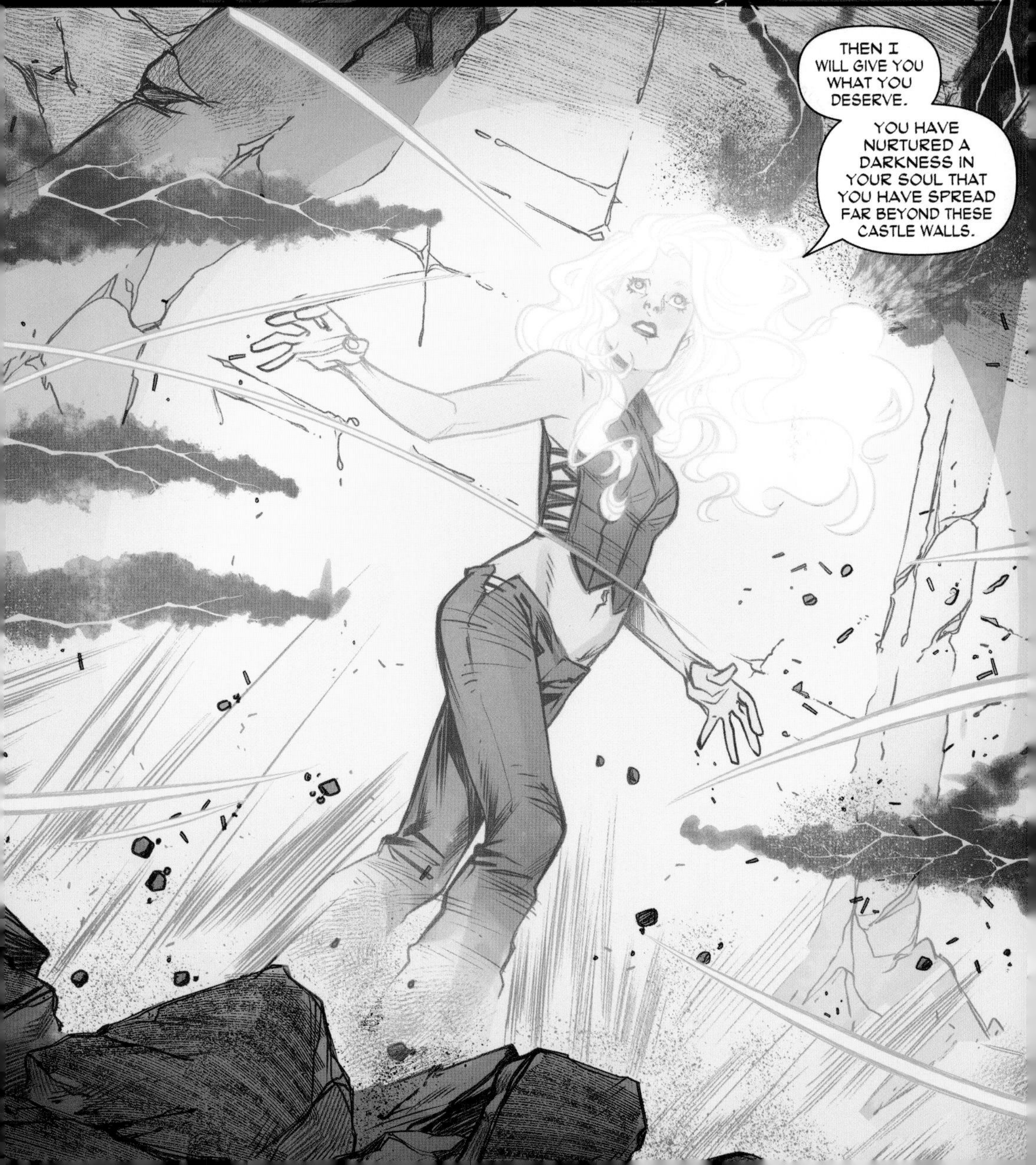
THEN I WILL GIVE YOU WHAT YOU DESERVE.
YOU HAVE NURTURED A DARKNESS IN YOUR SOUL THAT YOU HAVE SPREAD FAR BEYOND THESE CASTLE WALLS.

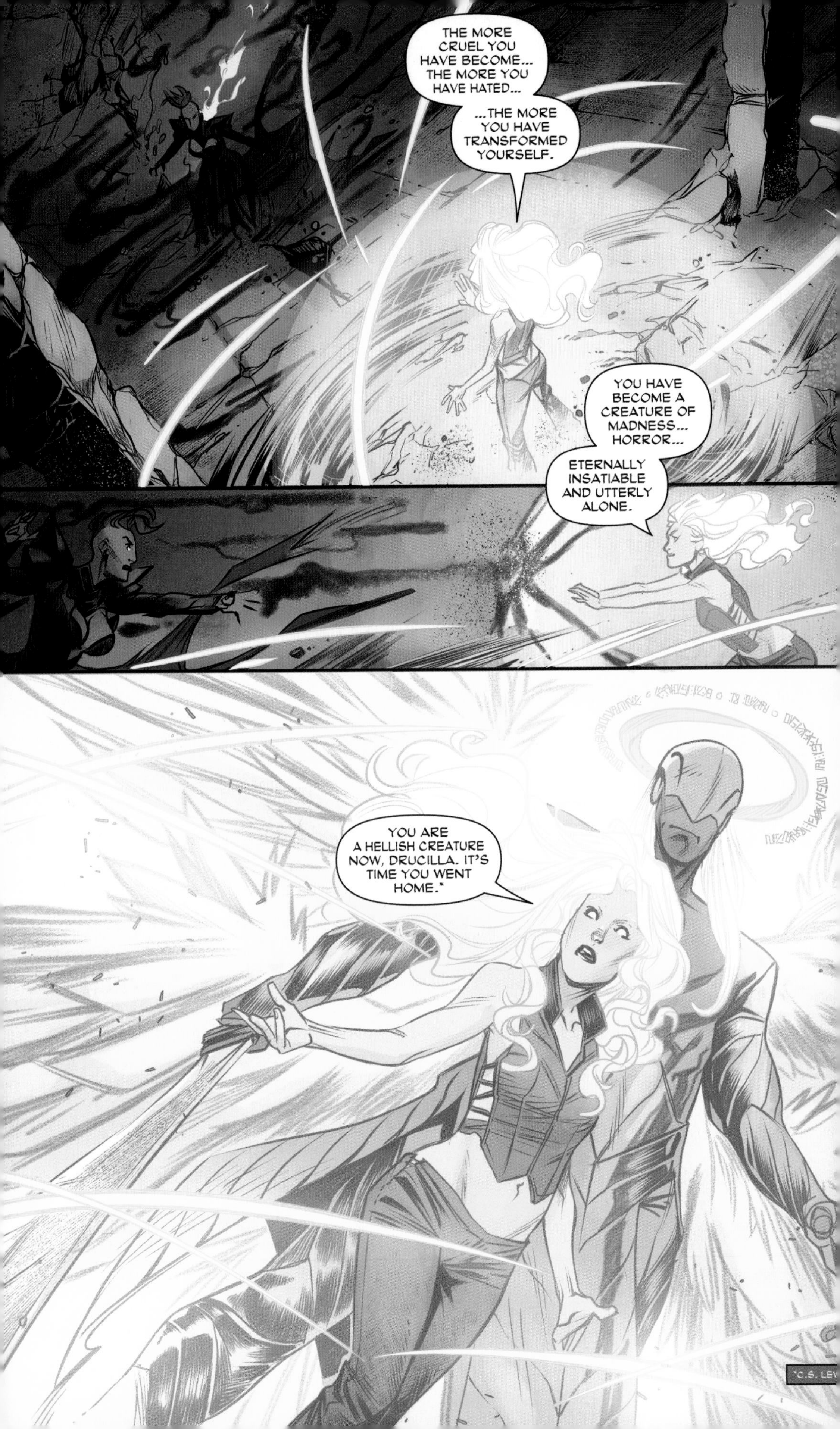
THE MORE CRUEL YOU HAVE BECOME... THE MORE YOU HAVE HATED...
...THE MORE YOU HAVE TRANSFORMED YOURSELF.
YOU HAVE BECOME A CREATURE OF MADNESS... HORROR...
ETERNALLY INSATIABLE AND UTTERLY ALONE.
YOU ARE A HELLISH CREATURE NOW, DRUCILLA. IT'S TIME YOU WENT HOME.*
*C.S. LEV

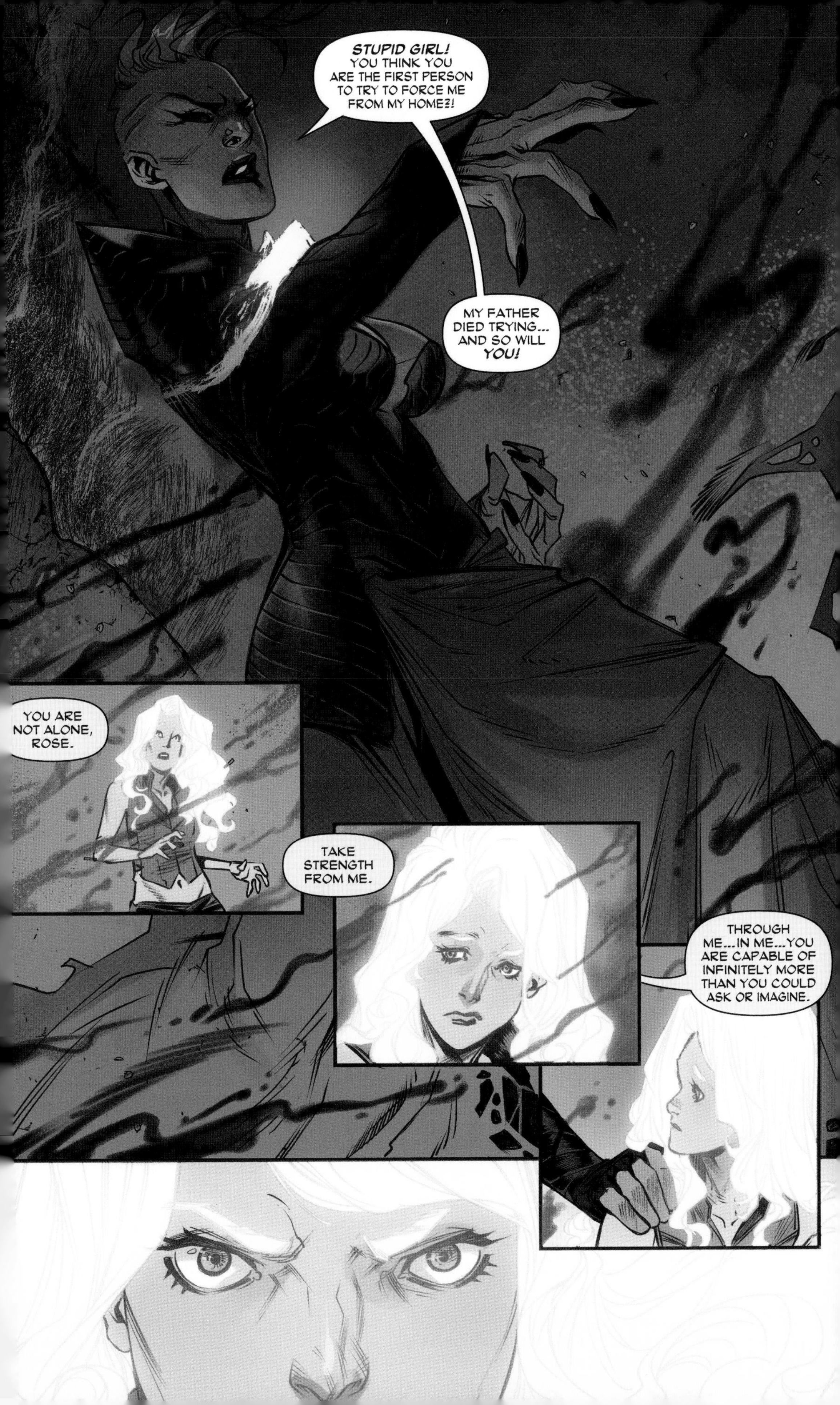
STUPID GIRL! YOU THINK YOU ARE THE FIRST PERSON TO TRY TO FORCE ME FROM MY HOME?!
MY FATHER DIED TRYING... AND SO WILL YOU!
YOU ARE NOT ALONE, ROSE.
TAKE STRENGTH FROM ME.
THROUGH ME...IN ME...YOU ARE CAPABLE OF INFINITELY MORE THAN YOU COULD ASK OR IMAGINE.

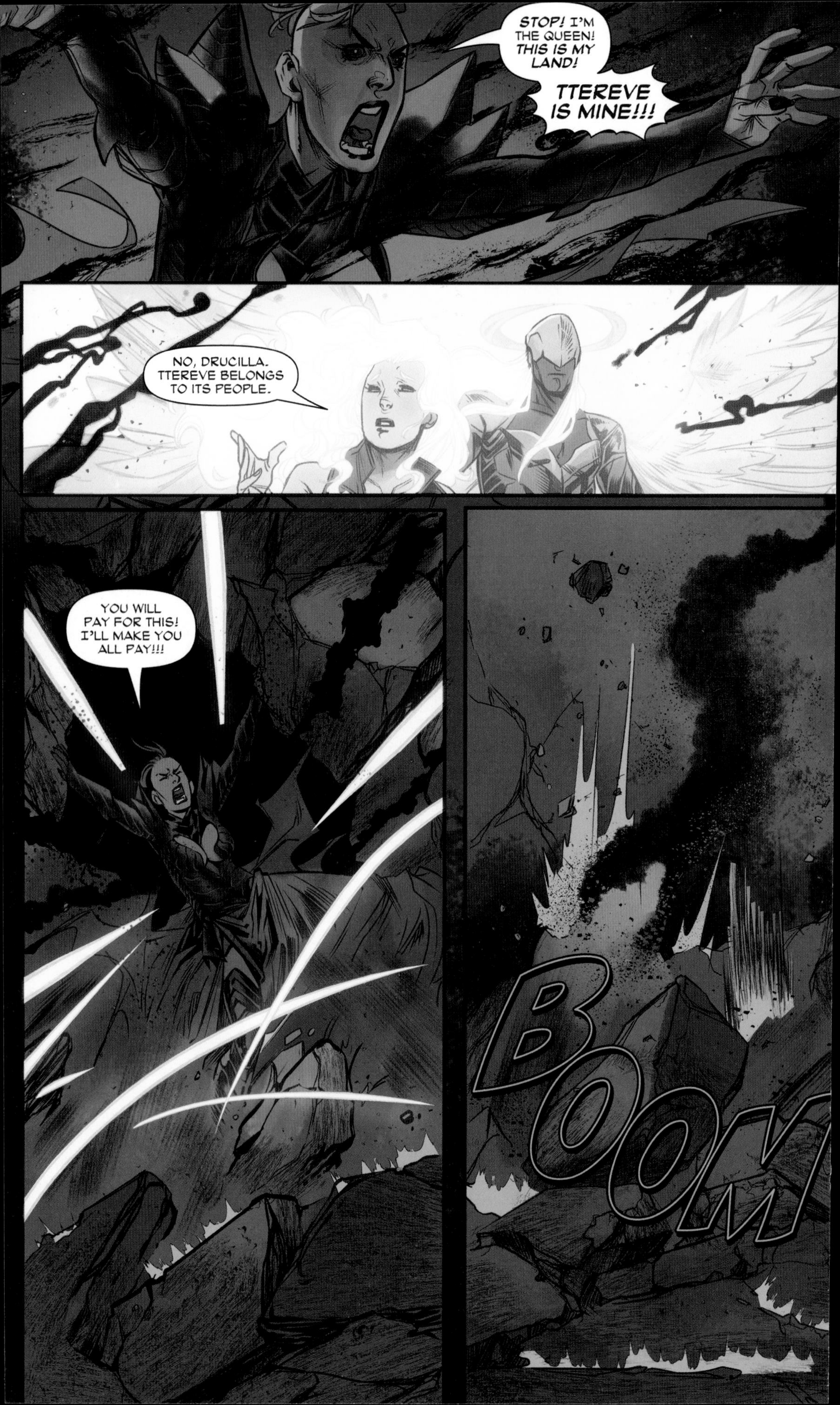
STOP! I'M THE QUEEN! THIS IS MY LAND!
TTEREVE IS MINE!!!
NO, DRUCILLA. TTEREVE BELONGS TO ITS PEOPLE.
YOU WILL PAY FOR THIS! I'LL MAKE YOU ALL PAY!!!
BOOM

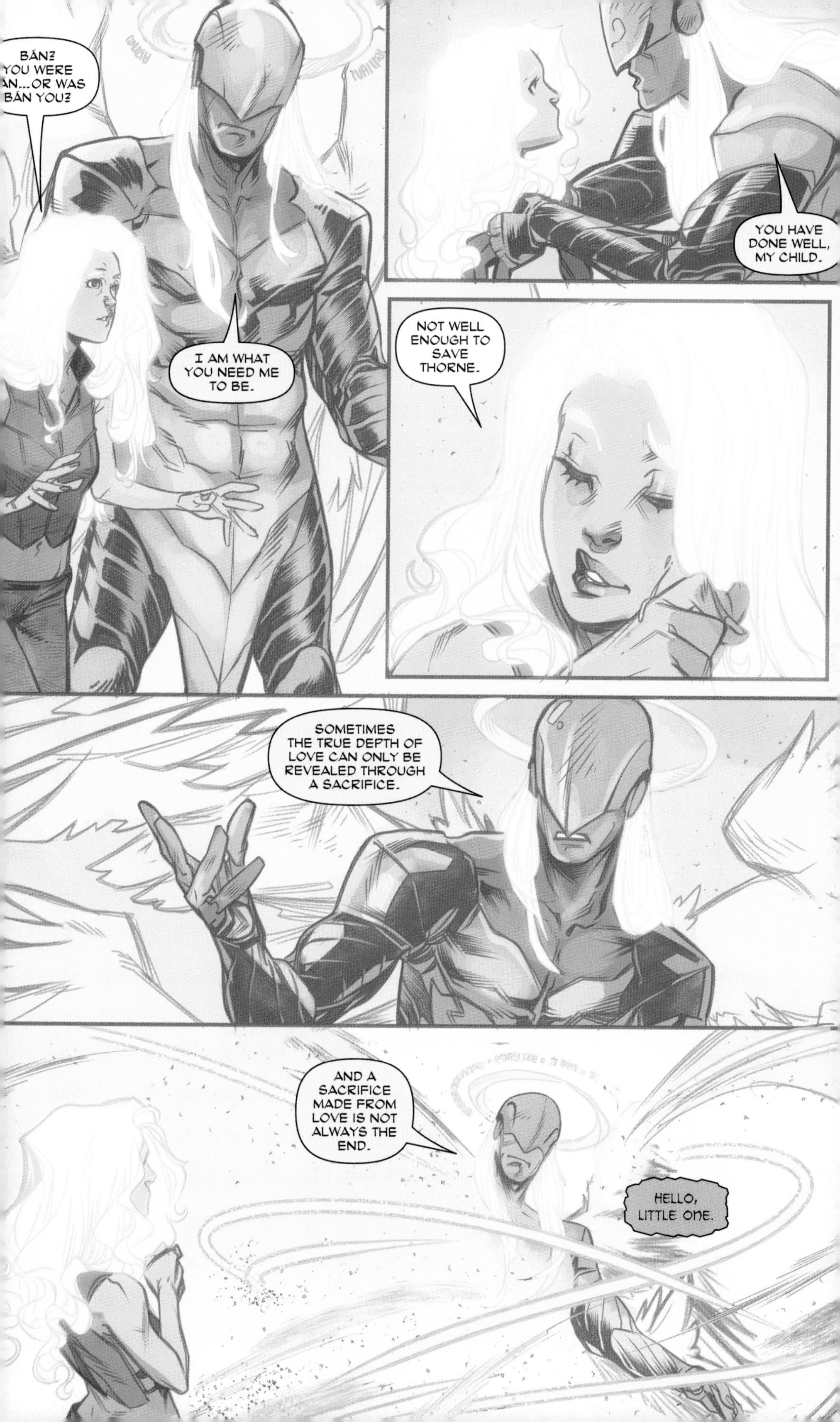

BÁN? YOU WERE ÁN...OR WAS BÁN YOU?
YOU HAVE DONE WELL, MY CHILD.
I AM WHAT YOU NEED ME TO BE.
NOT WELL ENOUGH TO SAVE THORNE.
SOMETIMES THE TRUE DEPTH OF LOVE CAN ONLY BE REVEALED THROUGH A SACRIFICE.
AND A SACRIFICE MADE FROM LOVE IS NOT ALWAYS THE END.
HELLO, LITTLE ONE.

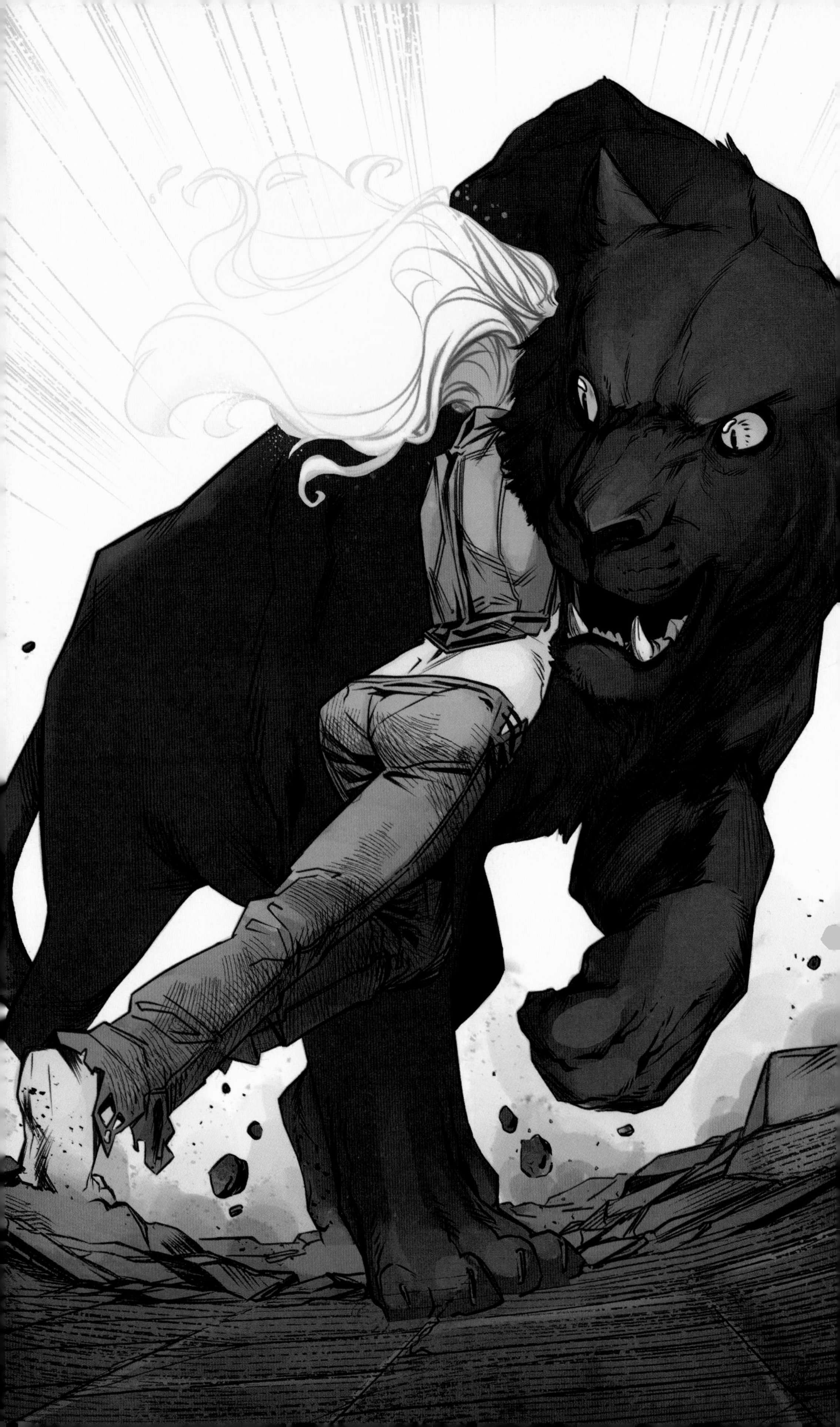

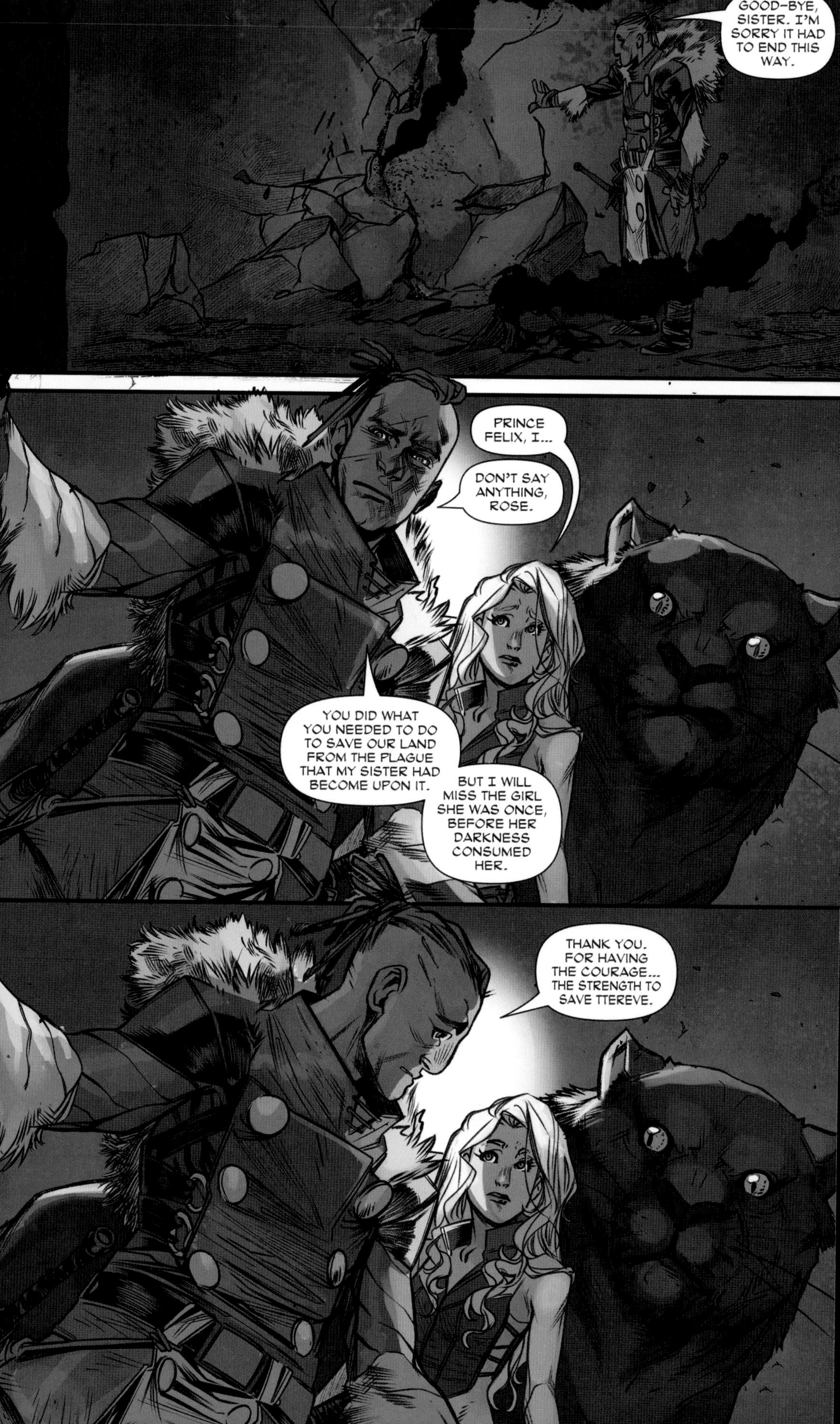
GOOD-BYE, SISTER. I'M SORRY IT HAD TO END THIS WAY.
PRINCE FELIX, I...
DON'T SAY ANYTHING, ROSE.
YOU DID WHAT YOU NEEDED TO DO TO SAVE OUR LAND FROM THE PLAGUE THAT MY SISTER HAD BECOME UPON IT.
BUT I WILL MISS THE GIRL SHE WAS ONCE, BEFORE HER DARKNESS CONSUMED HER.
THANK YOU. FOR HAVING THE COURAGE... THE STRENGTH TO SAVE TTEREVE.

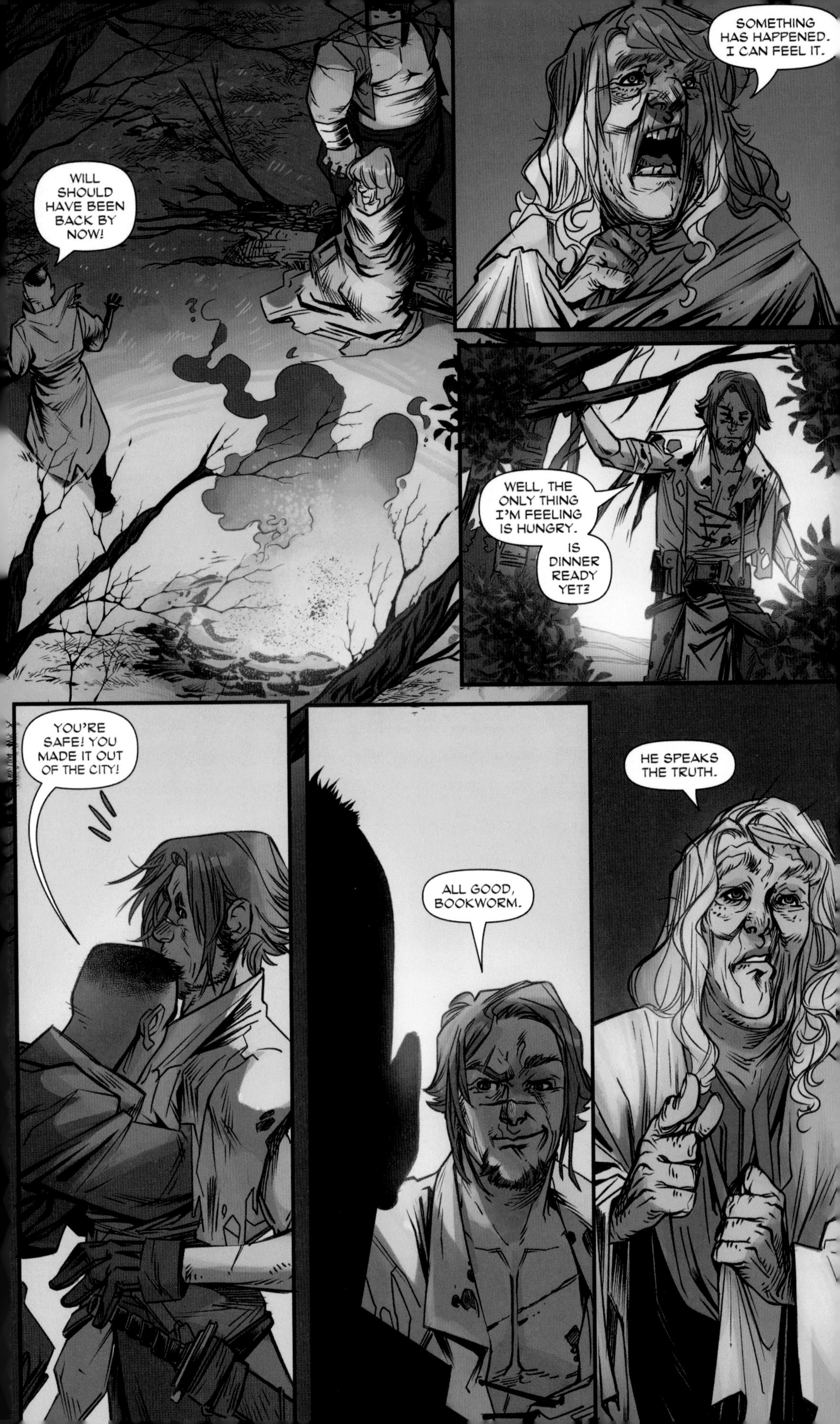
WILL SHOULD HAVE BEEN BACK BY NOW!
SOMETHING HAS HAPPENED. I CAN FEEL IT.
WELL, THE ONLY THING I'M FEELING IS HUNGRY.
IS DINNER READY YET?
YOU'RE SAFE! YOU MADE IT OUT OF THE CITY!
ALL GOOD, BOOKWORM.
HE SPEAKS THE TRUTH.

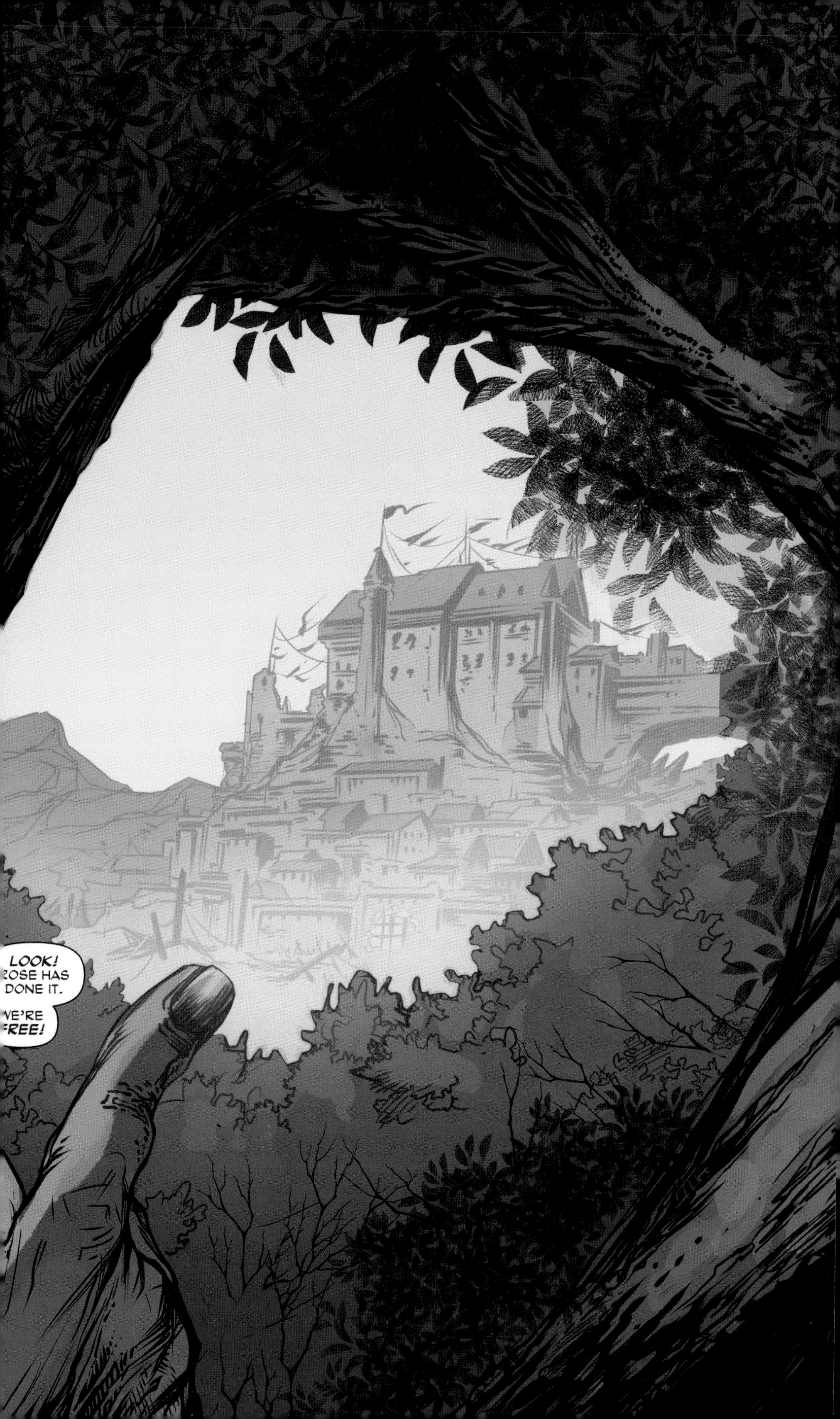
LOOK! ROSE HAS DONE IT.
WE'RE FREE!

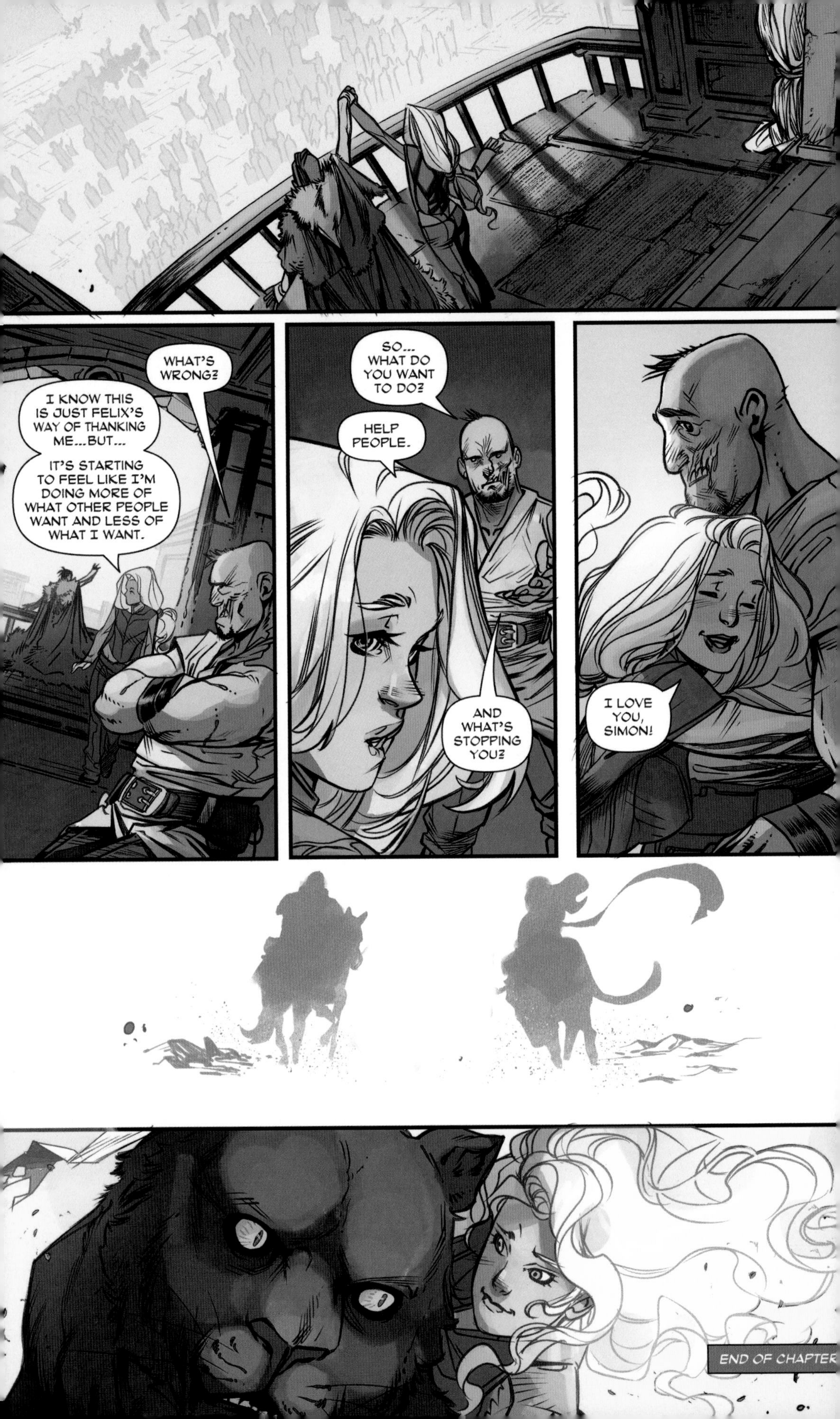
WHAT'S WRONG?
I KNOW THIS IS JUST FELIX'S WAY OF THANKING ME...BUT...
IT'S STARTING TO FEEL LIKE I'M DOING MORE OF WHAT OTHER PEOPLE WANT AND LESS OF WHAT I WANT.
SO... WHAT DO YOU WANT TO DO?
HELP PEOPLE.
AND WHAT'S STOPPING YOU?
I LOVE YOU, SIMON!
END OF CHAPTER

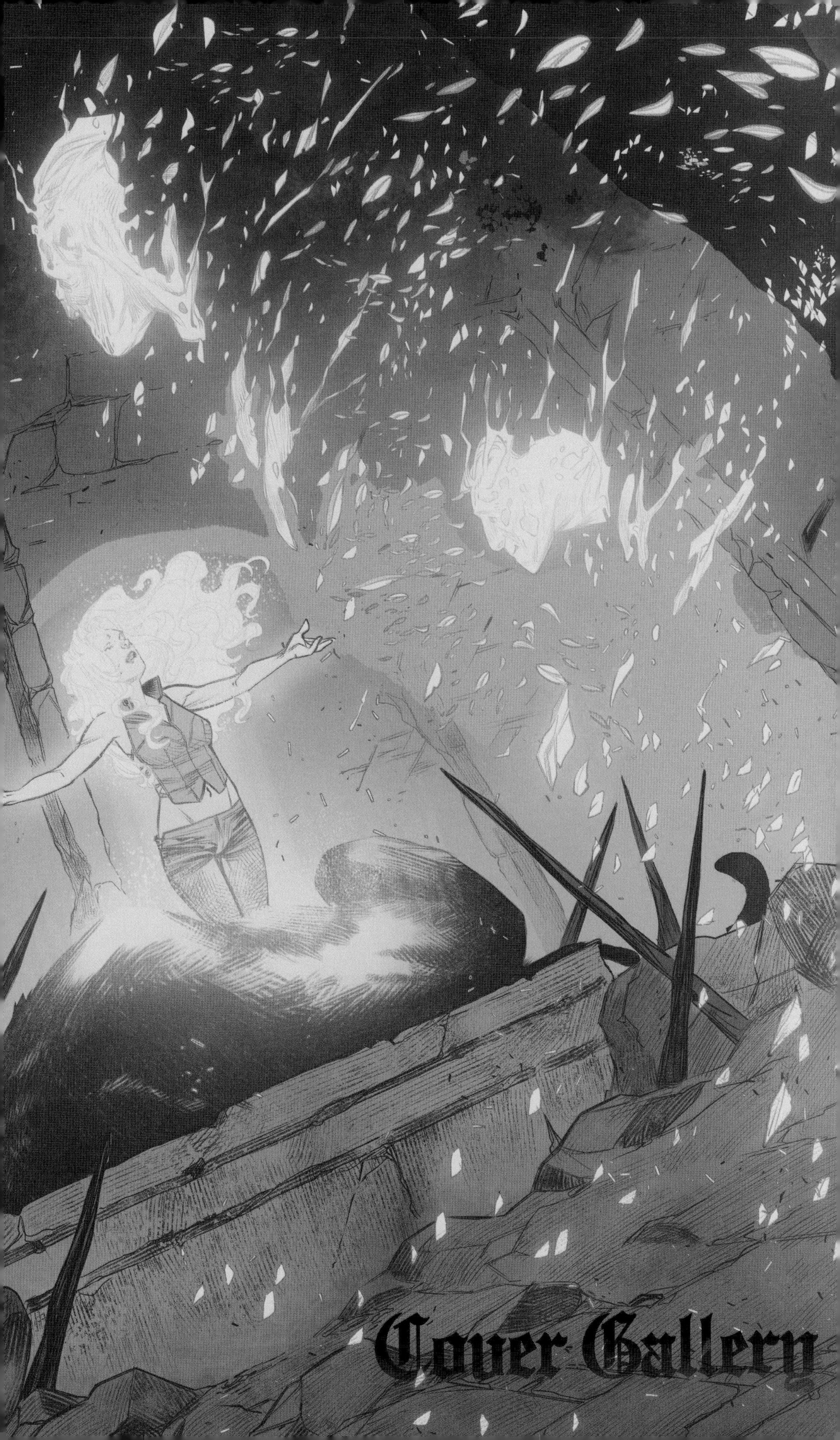

Cover Gallery

ISSUE #13 VARIANT COVER by
JAE LEE & JUNE CHUNG

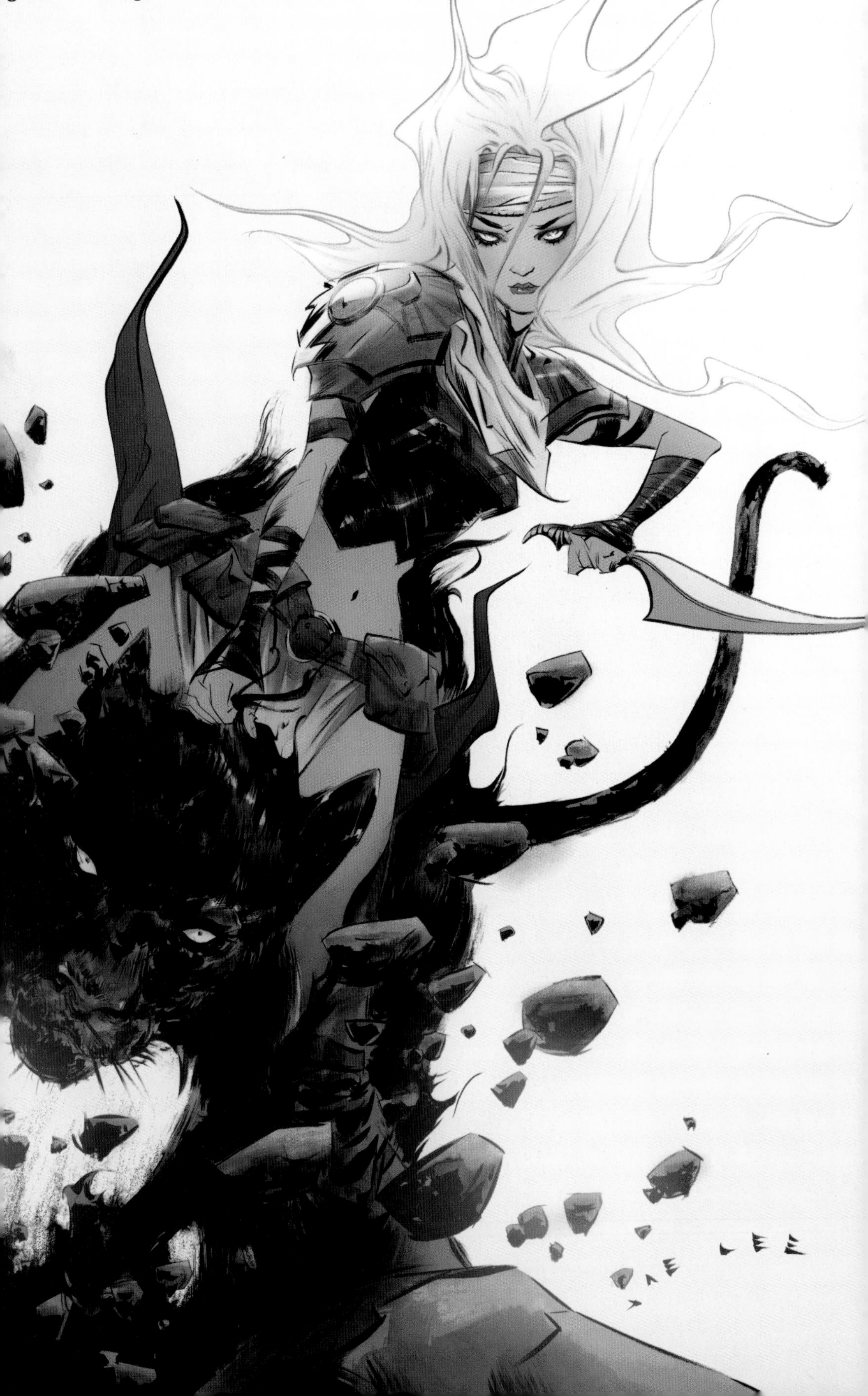
JAE LEE

ISSUE #13 VARIANT COVER by
JON LAM

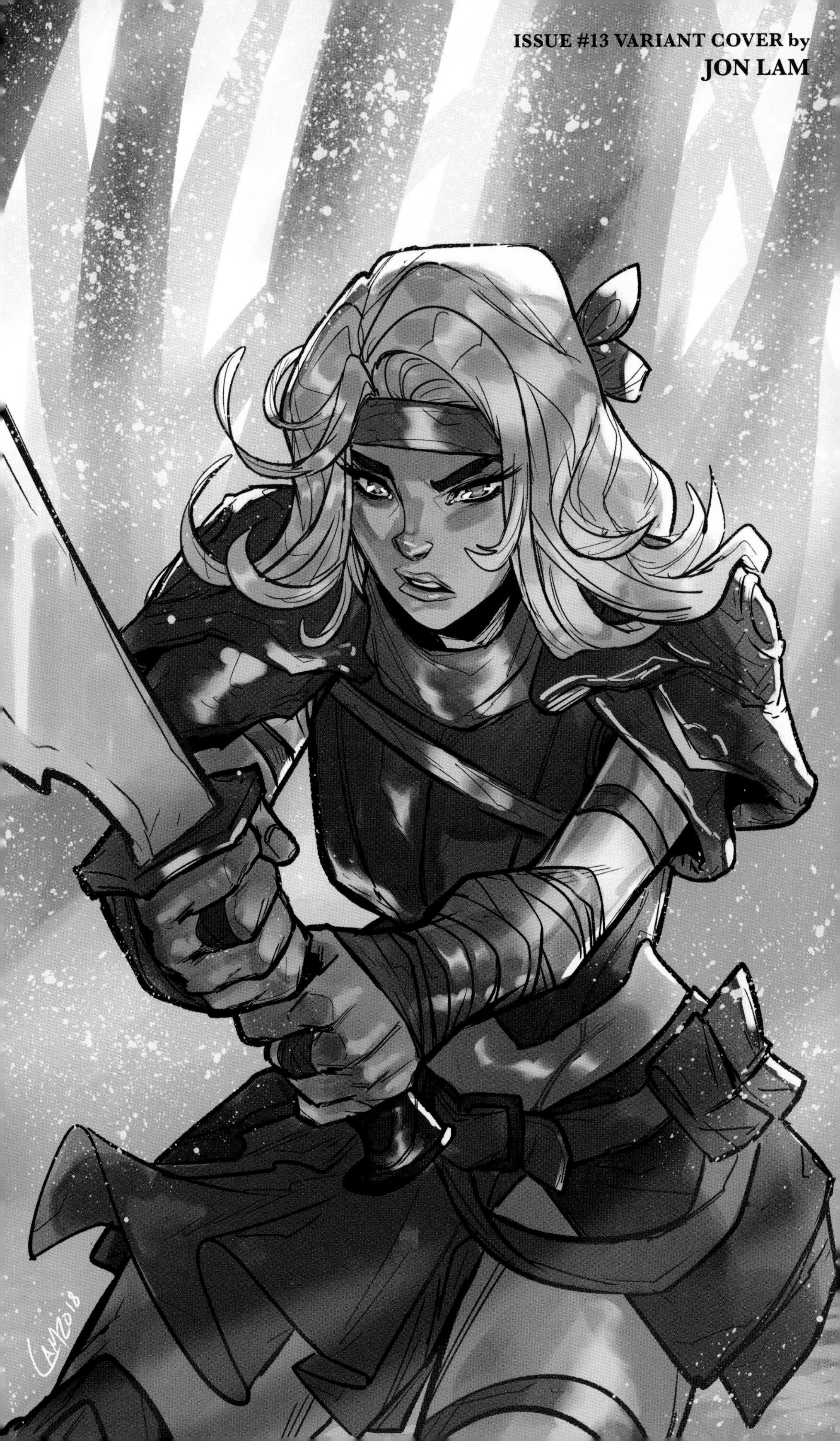
LAM 2018

ISSUE #13 VARIANT COVER by
PATRICK BALLESTEROS

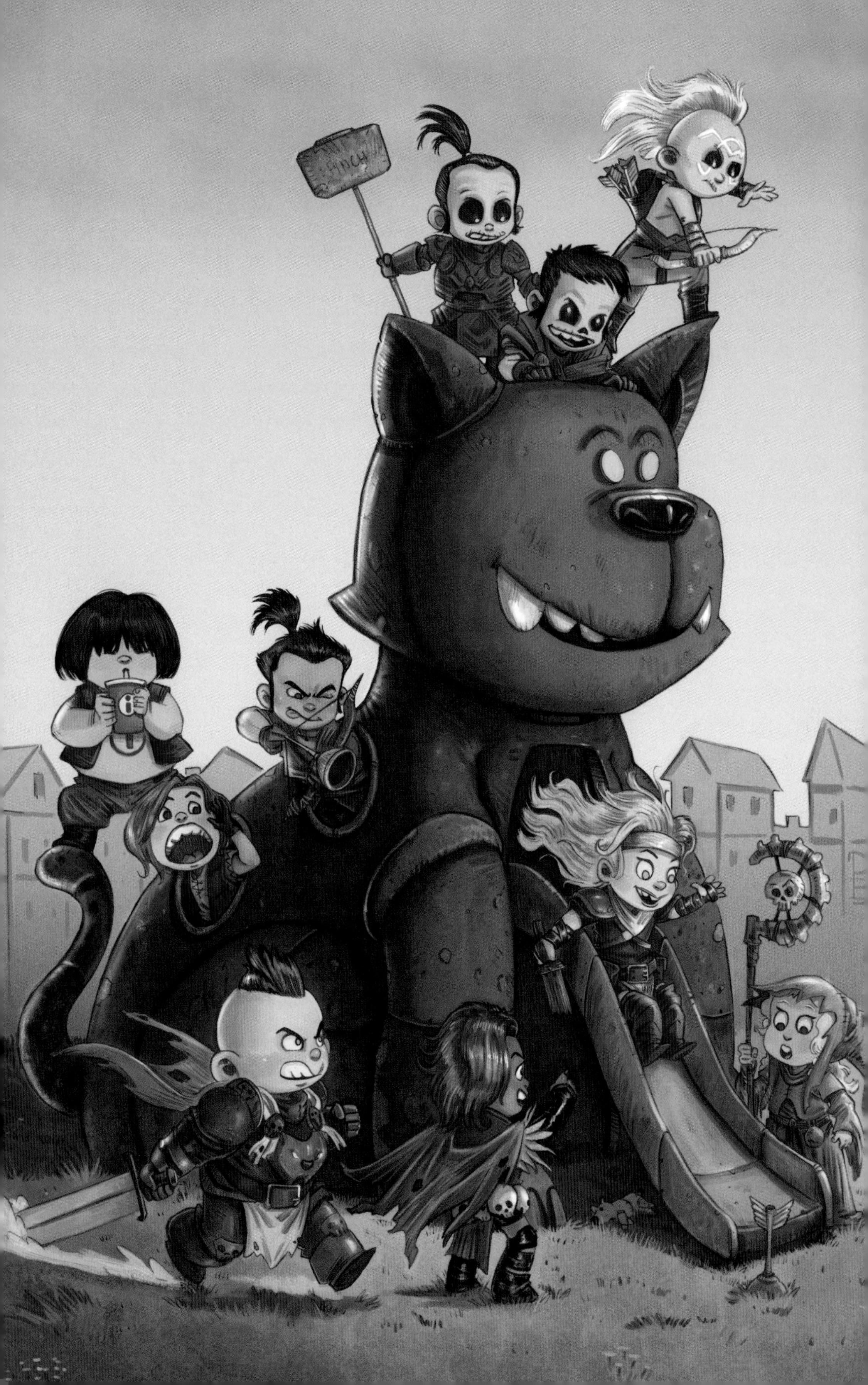

ISSUE #14 VARIANT COVER by
JON LAM

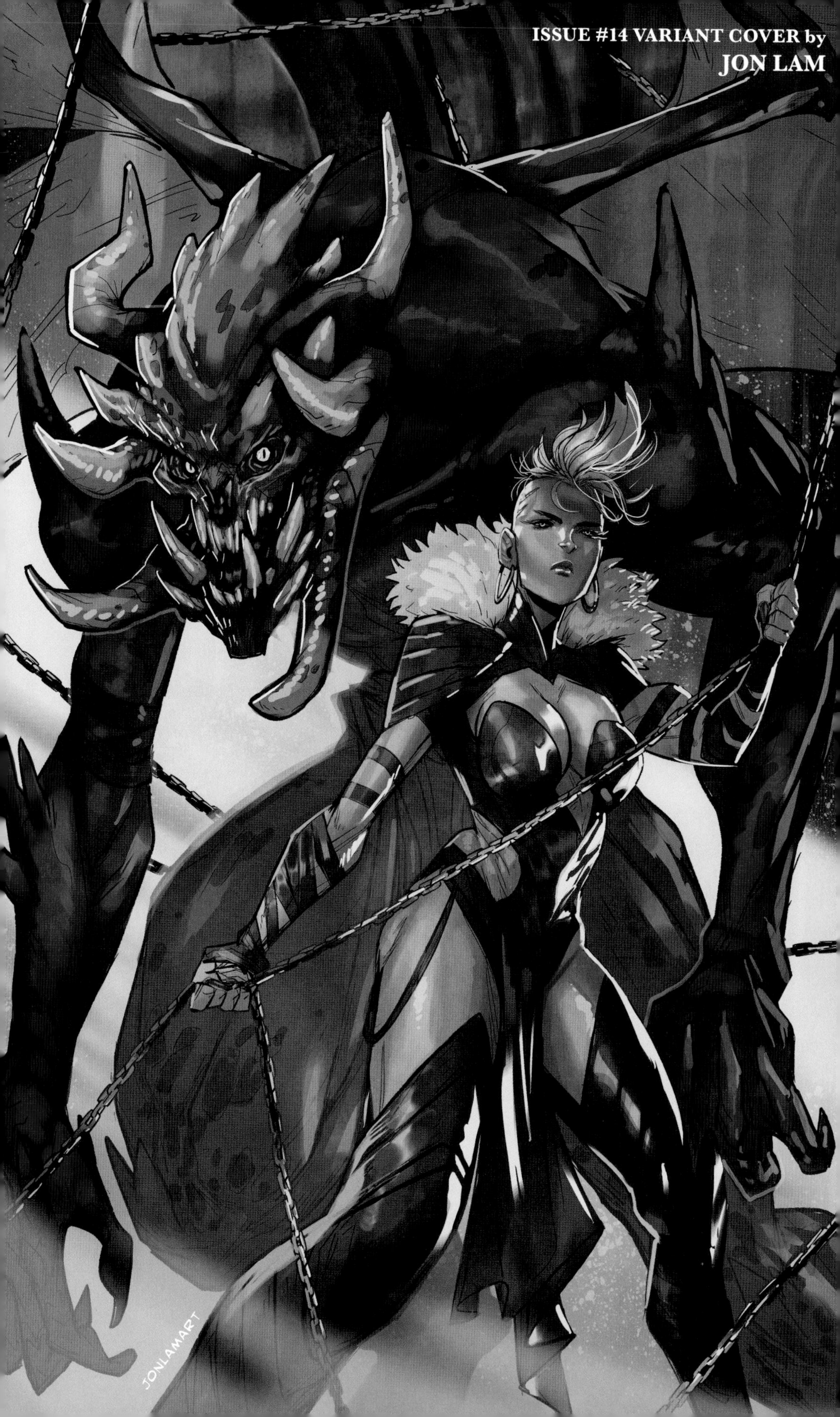
JONLAMART

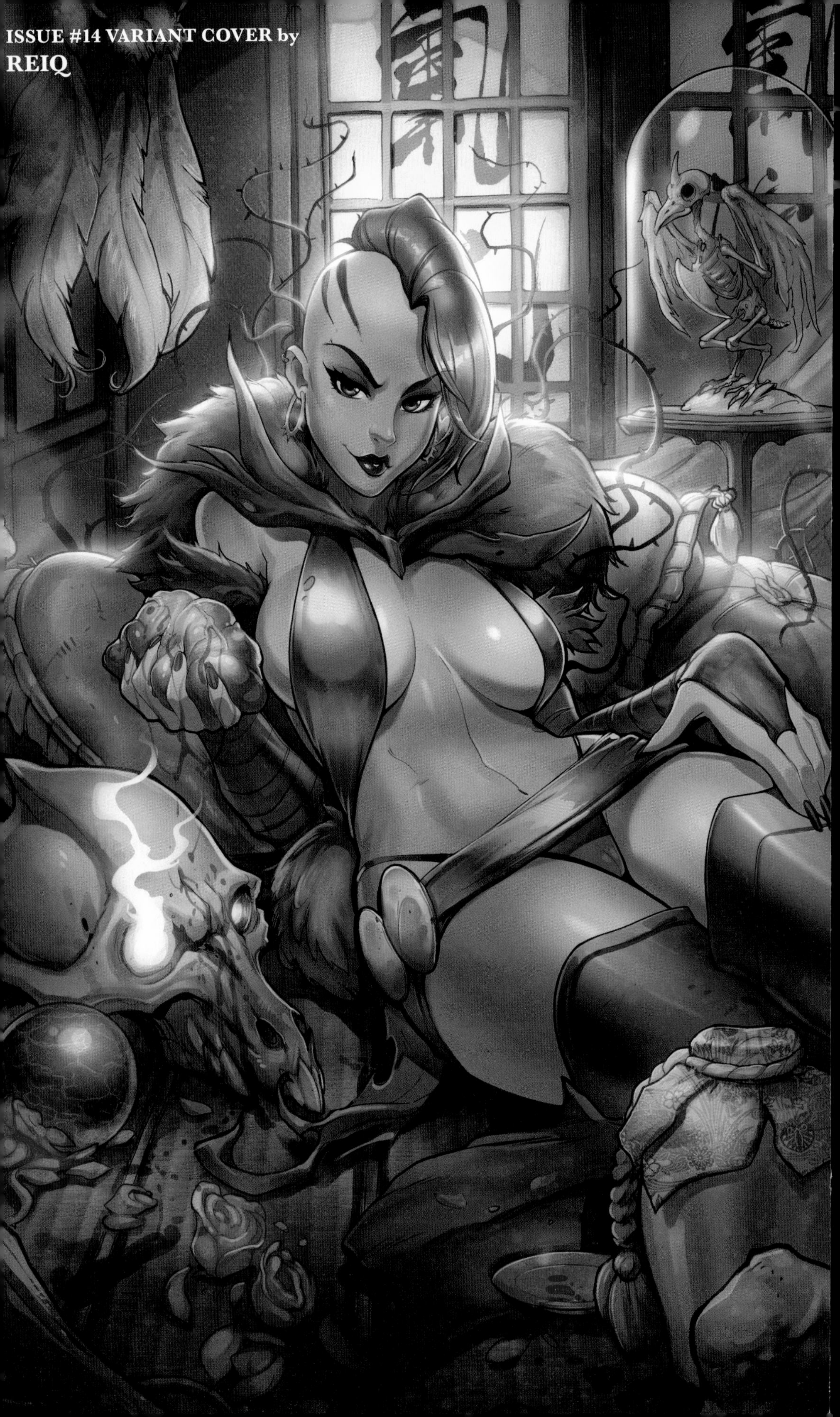

ISSUE #14 VARIANT COVER by
REIQ

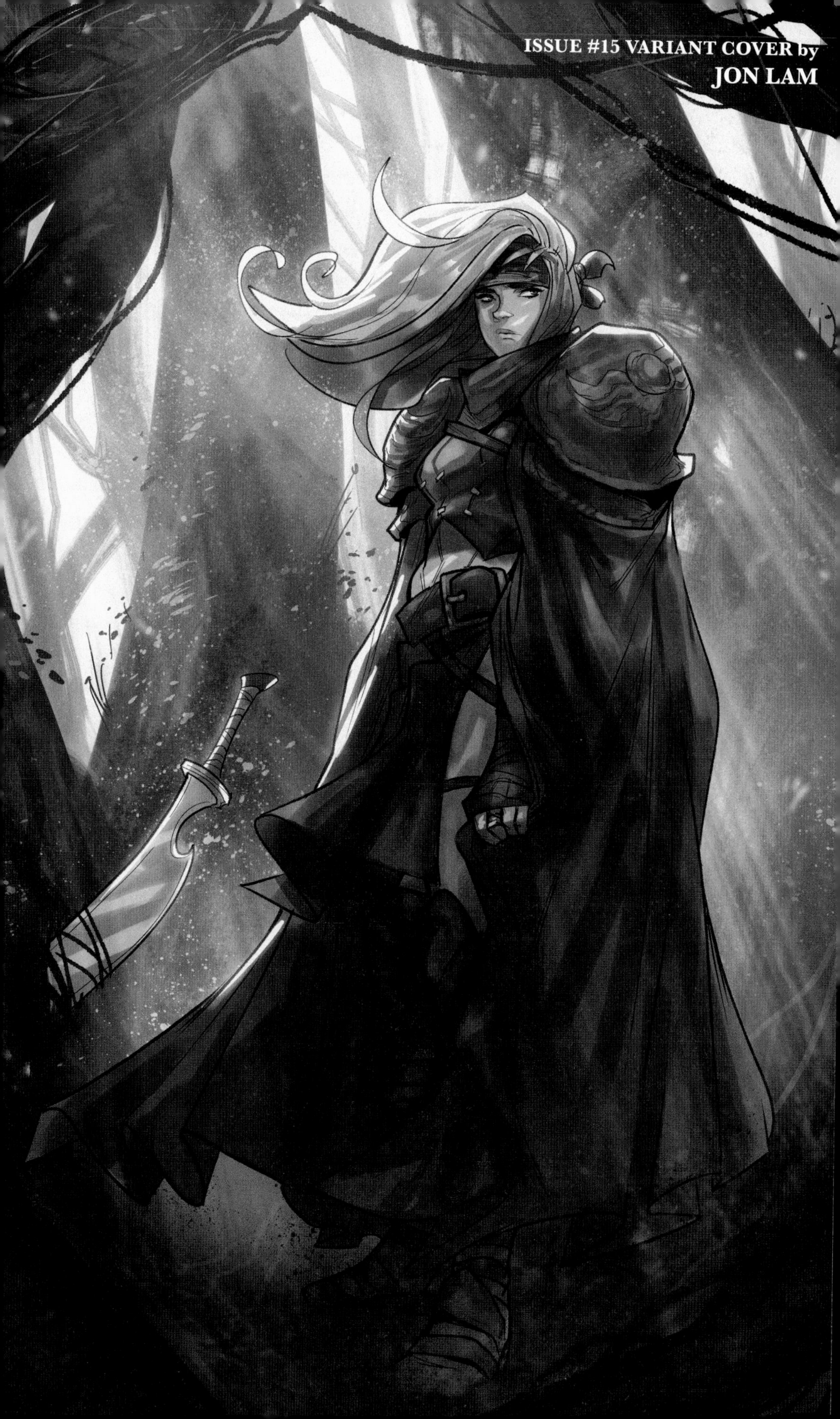
ISSUE #15 VARIANT COVER by
JON LAM

ISSUE #15 VARIANT COVER by
GERALD LANGE

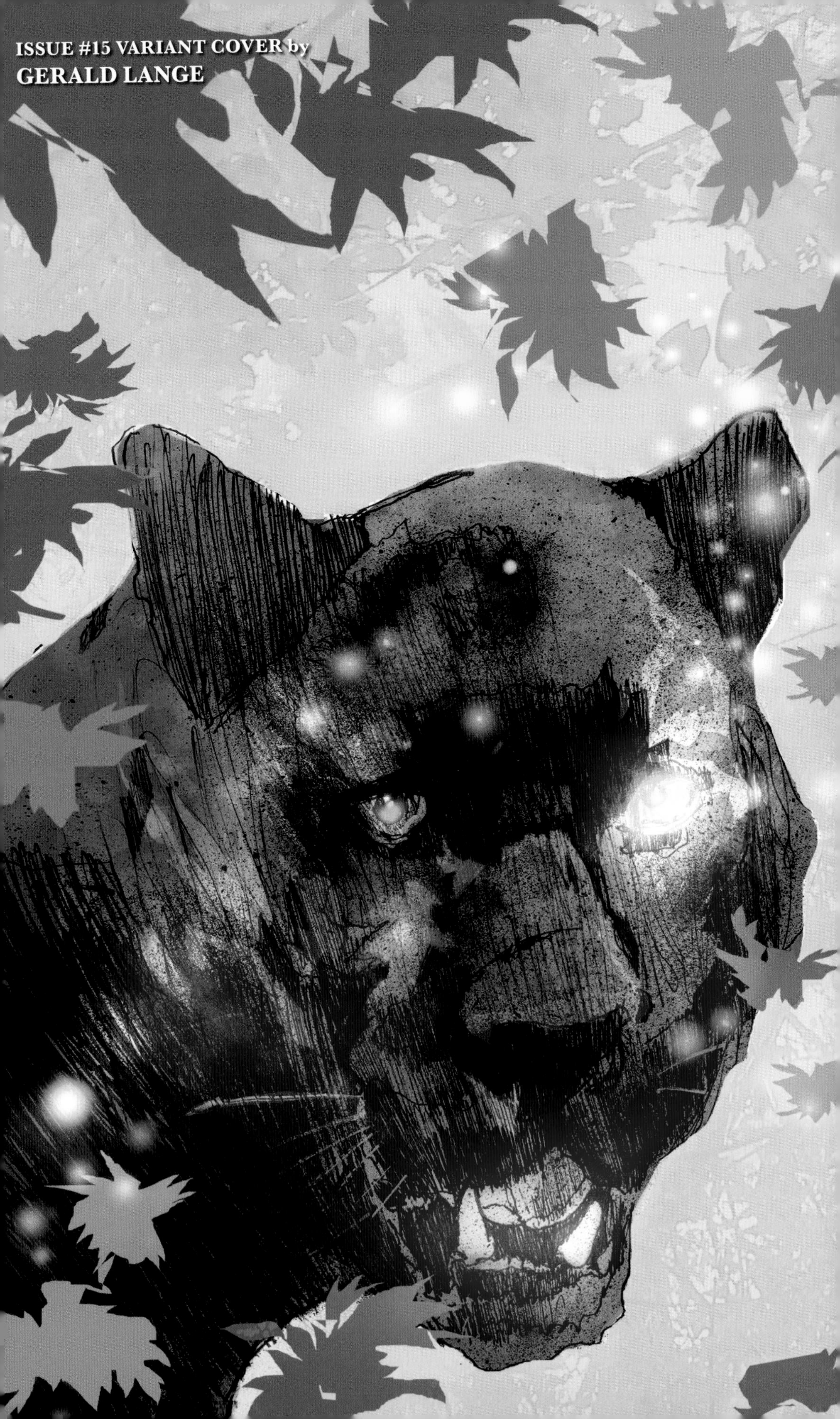

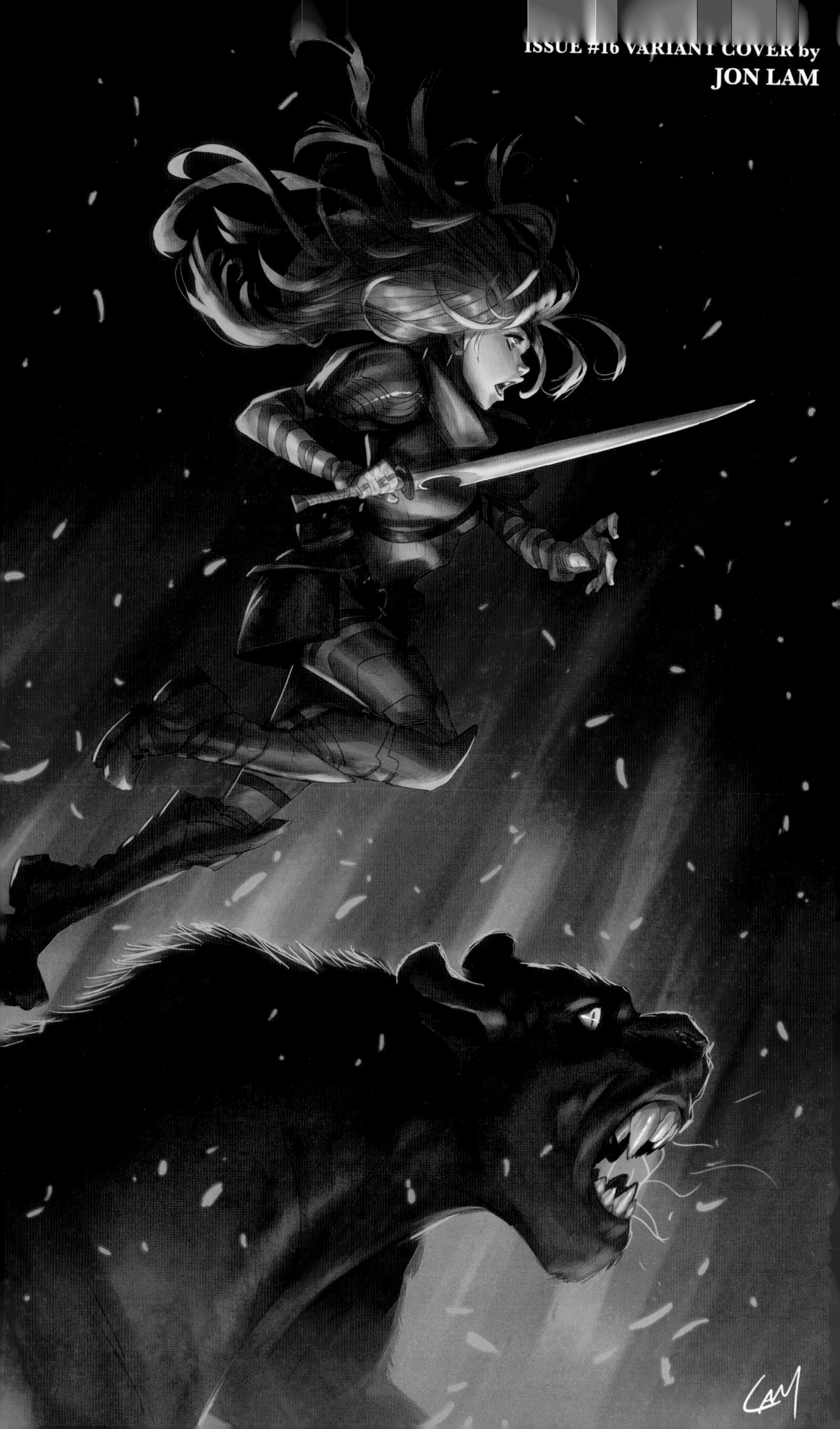
LAM

ISSUE #16 VARIANT COVER by
JON LAM

ISSUE #16 VARIANT COVER by
MIKE KROME

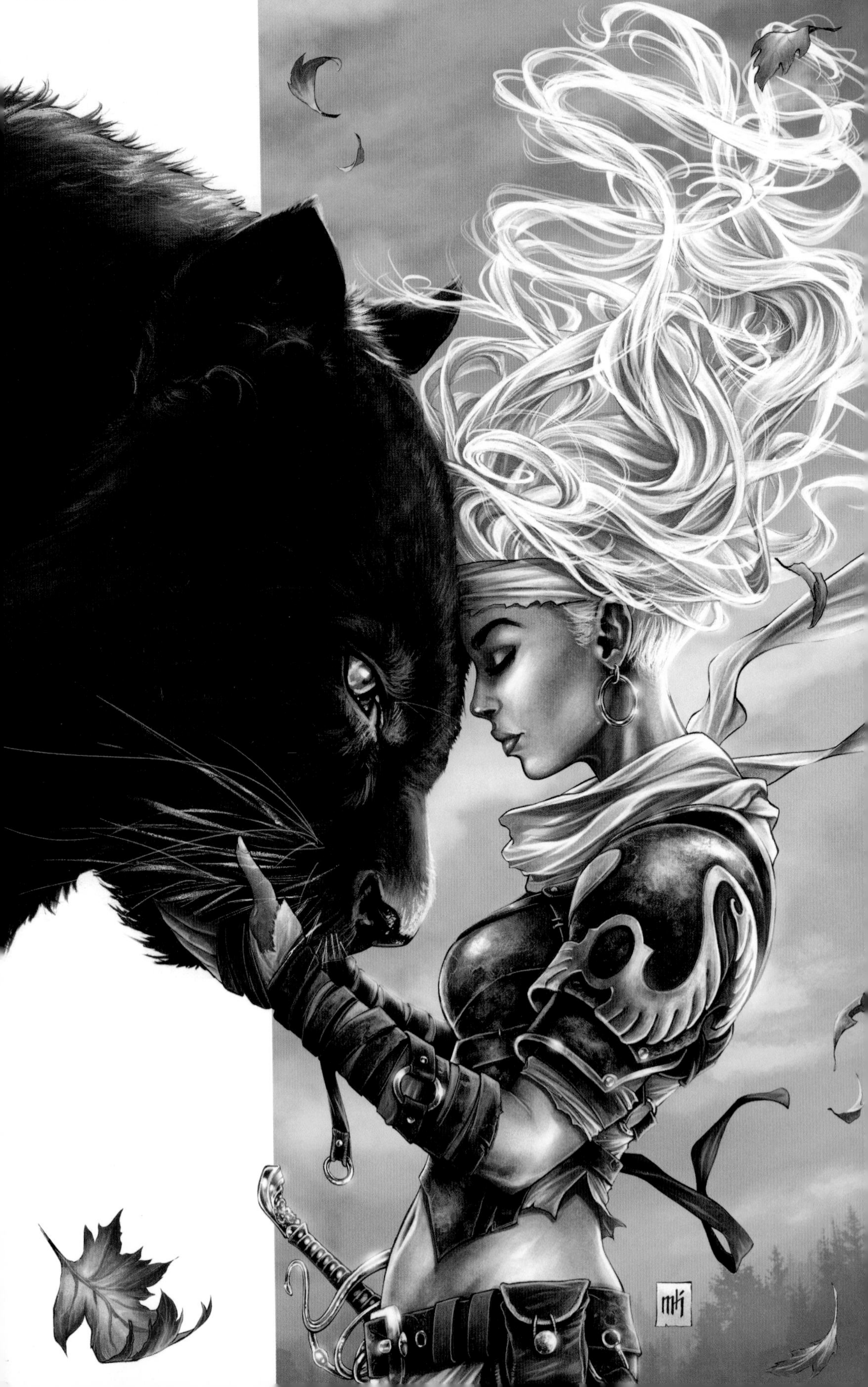

ISSUE #17 VARIANT COVER by
JON LAM

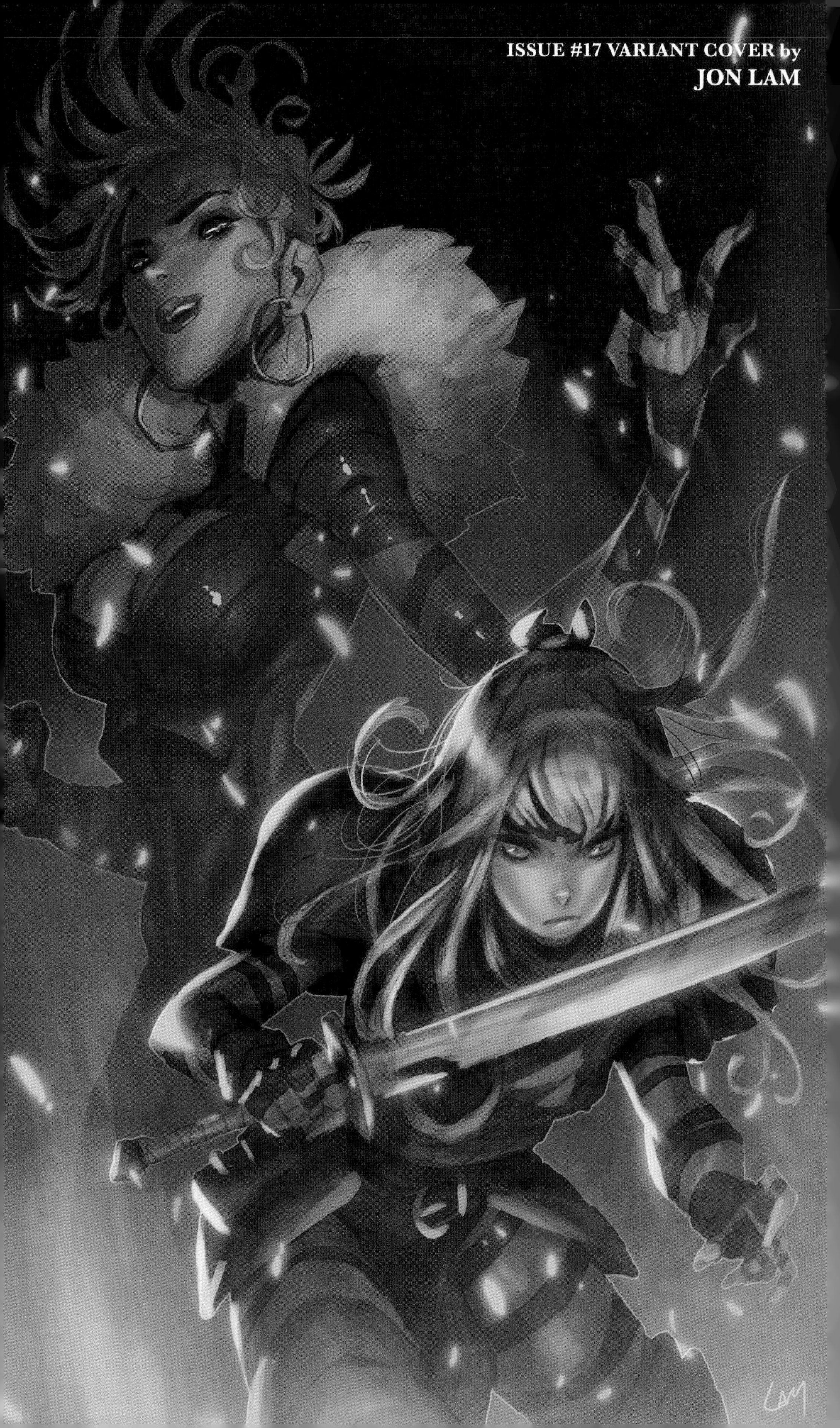
LAM

ISSUE #17 VARIANT COVER by
PETE KATZ

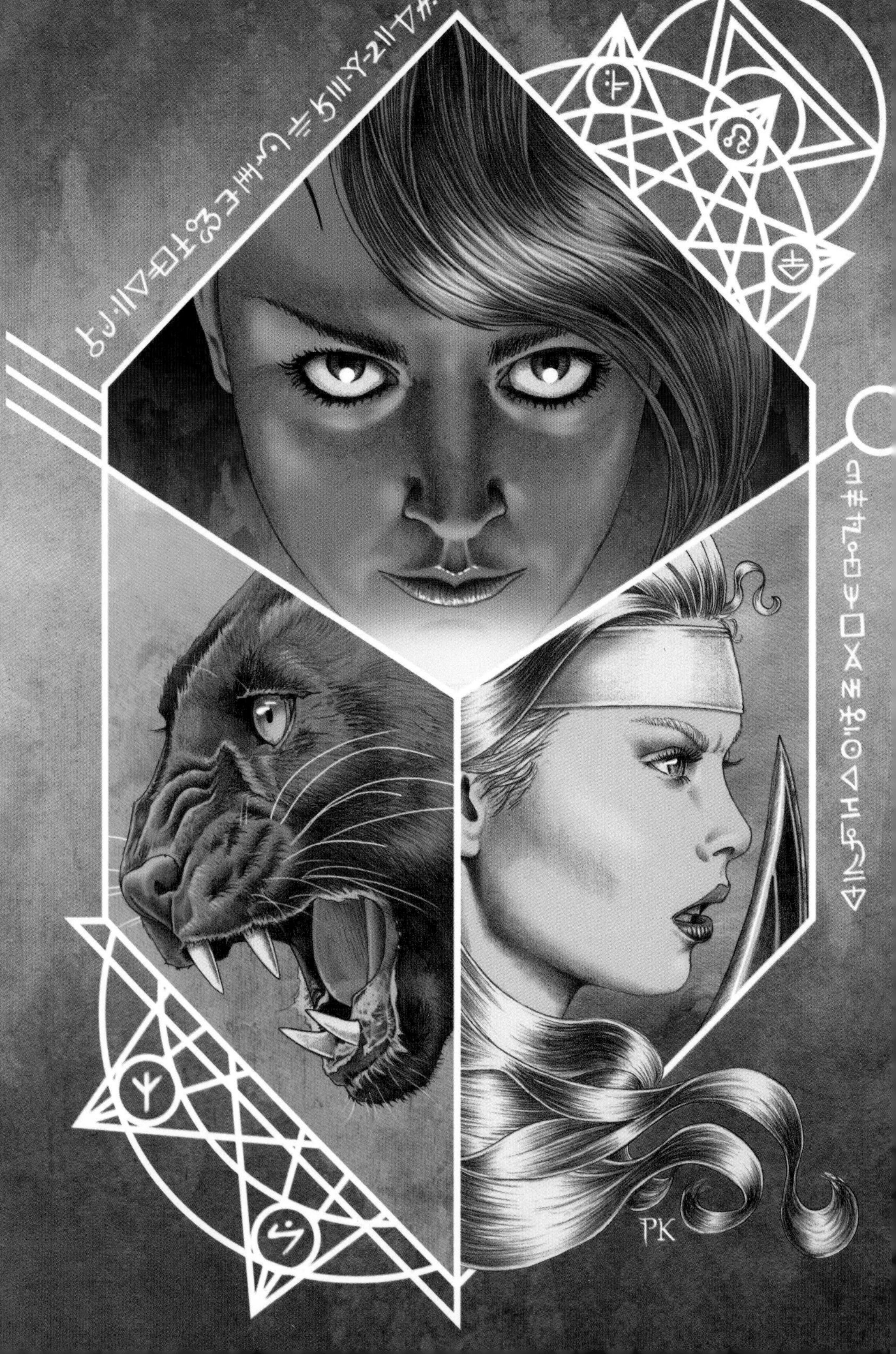
PK

ISSUE #17 VARIANT COVER by
JEFF SHULTZ

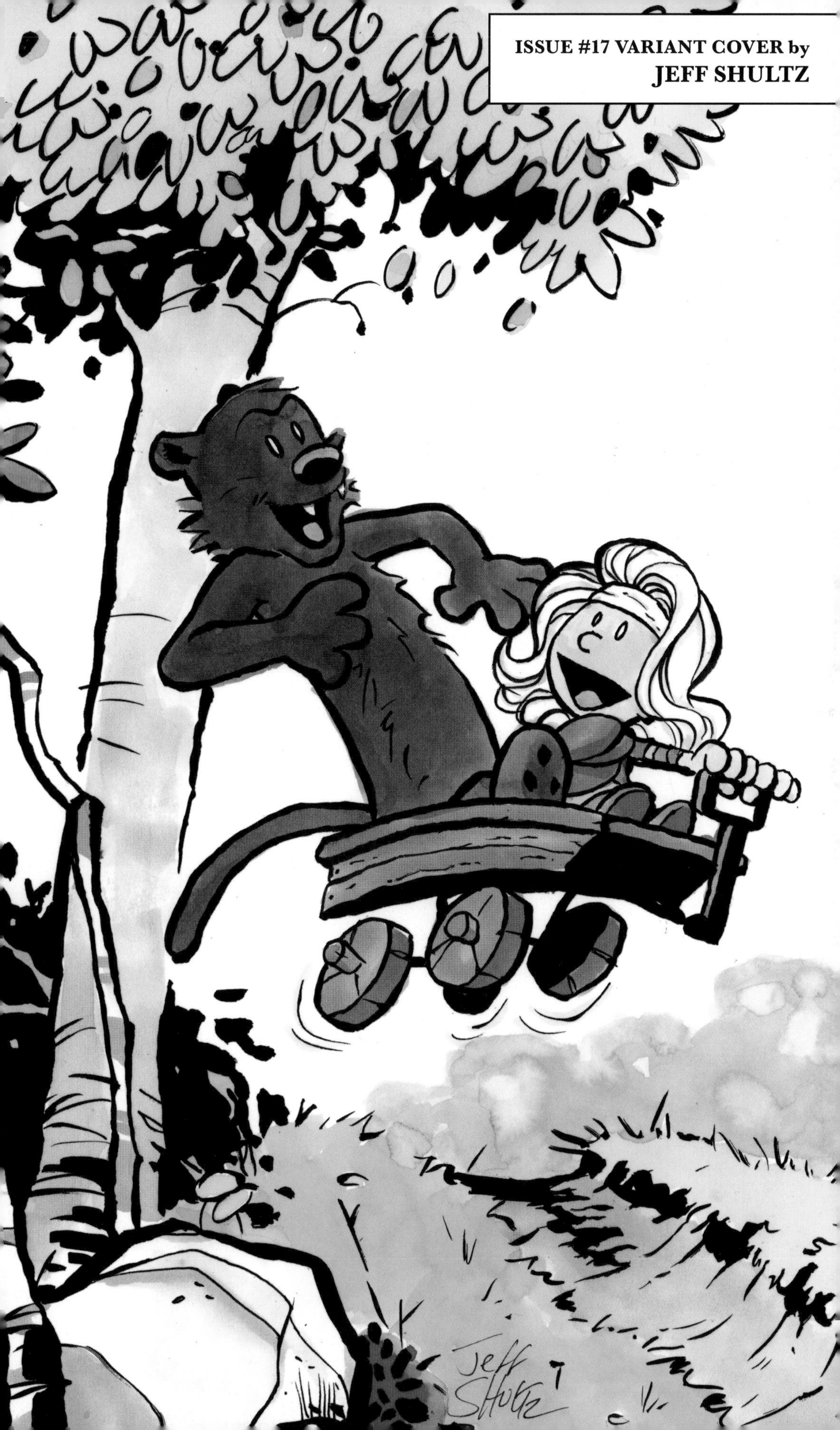
Jeff Shultz

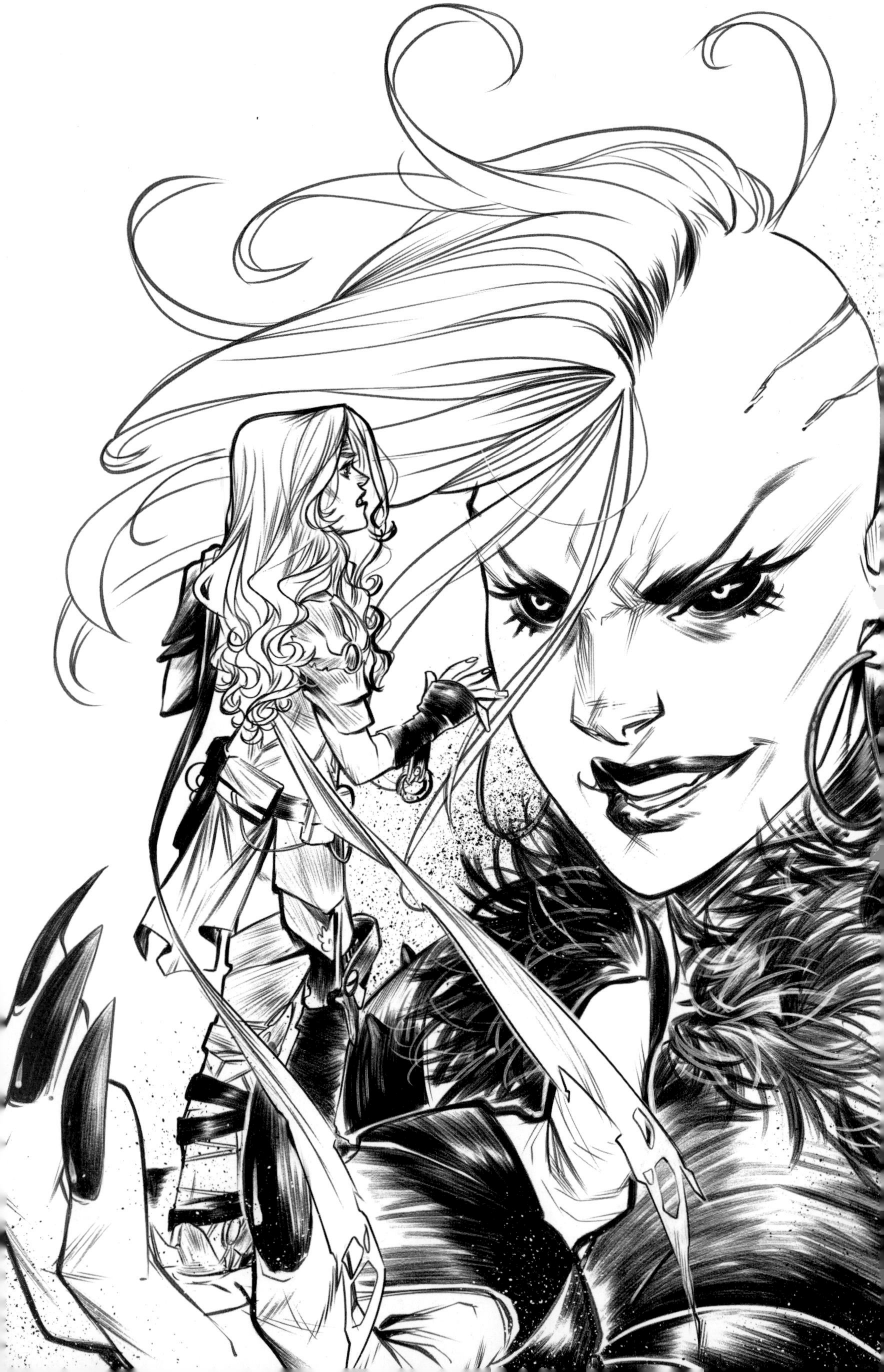